THE WAV

Graham John Parry

For my wonderful wife.

**Thanks to Mr Dave Gunther for his assistance
in naming the 'Hunt' class destroyer.**

Table of Contents

THE WAVES OF WAR

Chapter One . . Sea Command.

Standing on the open, windswept bridge of a small 'Hunt' class destroyer, Lieutenant-Commander Richard Thorburn braced himself against the next plunging twist. With the first, faint light of a midsummer dawn breaking across the English Channel, he made the decision to turn the ship for home. Reluctantly, he straightened up from behind the spray soaked screen, stretched the stiffness from his muscles, and wiped his face to clear the thin residue of salt. Moving warily to the bank of voice-pipes, he leant forward and flicked open a brass cap.

'Port twenty. Steer two-seven-oh.'

From the wheelhouse beneath his feet a metallic acknowledgement echoed up the pipe.

'Port twenty. Steer two-seven-oh. Aye aye, sir.'

Responding sluggishly to the movement of the helm, H.M.S. *Brackendale* leaned to starboard and slid awkwardly into a trough, staggered unevenly in the depths and heaved herself out to the next foaming crest. It took two more long rollers before the warship settled on an even keel.

Other than for two short breaks, Thorburn had retained command of the bridge throughout the hours of darkness.

With that first hint of sunrise he walked forward to the bridge-screen and peered out beyond the destroyer's bow, subconsciously gauging the strength of the oncoming seas. Tired though he was, he proudly recognised the significance of the moment. One hundred and thirty eight members of the ship's company, and his first command, about to return safely from their first patrol of the war.

'Signal, sir.'

He turned to the now familiar voice of the Chief Yeoman and took the offered slip. The message was timed at 05.17 hours, on the 14th July 1940, and ordered him to attend the Captain of Destroyers, 'Captain (D)', at 08.00 hours.

'Acknowledge,' he said, and glanced at his watch. A frown reached the lines at the corner of his eyes and he pursed his lips in thought. The chart indicated he was seventy nautical miles from harbour. Might be possible for the big fleet destroyers, but *Brackendale* was so much smaller, never able to match their speed. But, it was his duty to carry out the order, and he would make the effort. Cursing under his breath he gave the necessary command. 'Full ahead together.'

A lookout called. 'Enemy aircraft, sir. Green two-oh.' It was a measured report, without urgency. Even so, a Lewis machine gunner swung the muzzle in readiness.

Thorburn wiped the spray from his Barr and Stroud binoculars and focused forward to his right, over the starboard corner of the bridge. Above the Kent coast he managed to locate a number of fighter aircraft engaged in a dogfight, but from out here, many miles away on a warship's swaying bridge, it was almost impossible to establish friend from foe. He watched for a while as the tumbling spiral of aircraft swept inland, sunlight glinting off a wing, a distant, crimson flicker of machine guns. For a moment he thought he caught the faint sound of their gunfire. Lowering his glasses, Thorburn placed them carefully on the fore bridge.

'Starboard ten, steady on two-nine-five,' he ordered down the voice-pipe. The warship leaned gently in the opposite direction, to port, punching at the choppy waters, her bow wave drenching the bridge-screen in a salty sheen.

He rubbed his unshaven chin and tucked a strand of dark hair back beneath his battered cap. The premature wrinkles around his eyes were a stark reminder of standing too many watches squinting into the middle distance. An almost black fisherman's roll-neck jumper emerged from a faded uniform jacket, and his trousers, washed out and threadbare, were casually tucked into a stout pair of sea boots. He smiled faintly at his own appearance, a smile directed towards the Admiralty. A captain should always be beyond reproach, but at sea, away from prying eyes, Thorburn preferred comfort.

To his left, over the port bow, he could see down across the channel towards the French port of Calais and the faint, high outline of Cap Gris-Nez. The war was barely ten months old and in that short space of time the Nazis had swept away everything in their path. Thorburn was well aware that it was only the English Channel, those formidable twenty odd miles of water which separated Britain from mainland Europe, that had caused them to stop. Poised on the headlands of northern France, the Germans waited impatiently for Hitler to order the invasion of the British Isles.

He turned his attention back to the sky and caught sight of an enemy fighter, a Messerschmitt, flying erratically above the waves, thick smoke curling from a damaged fuselage. Below the bridge-screen the main armament swung to the same elevation, and although the fighter was out of range, the pair of four-inch barrels followed it round.

Three hundred and thirty miles to the north, in the German port of Bremerhaven, a two thousand ton warship prepared to leave harbour. The ship's commander, recently returned from the Norwegian campaign of Narvik, was now the recipient of an Iron Cross. Once again he was ready for sea, his destination Calais, and only after he arrived would he receive the orders directing him to his new operation. For now, at thirty-five years of age, it was reward enough to be taking his ship back to sea. He leaned on his chart of the French coast and continued to examine the unfamiliar coastline.

Nearby, in a large, luxurious hotel, the German Admiral for Western Operations held court. His name was Mathias Johann Heinrich Krause, Knights Cross, and a senior member of Hitler's Kriegsmarine. Having finished a leisurely lunch, he wiped his mouth and dropped the napkin to the table. He reached for a glass of Cognac and raised it to his fellow diners.

'A toast,' he said. 'To the success of our Seventh Flotilla. May they have many conquests.'

The three Executive Officers of the War Navy's headquarters, touched glasses and drank in salute. Their decision had been unanimous. The man chosen to lead the newly formed flotilla was an experienced commander.

The next phase of operations was about to begin.

In the ancient Cinque Port of Dover, in the cold cellar

of a waterfront hotel, a bearded man in a Post Captain's uniform, Captain (D), stood waiting impassively for an answer to his question. Across the room sitting at an oak desk, the gaunt features of Vice-Admiral Sir Henry McIntyre R.N., K.C.B., D.S.O., looked down on the service record of a young officer. Sir Henry's bony fingers turned a page and he shook his head in concern.

'I'm not sure, James,' the Admiral said, glancing up. ' I'm really not sure he's the man for us.'

Captain James Pendleton continued to stand in silence. Sir Henry had queried, thinking aloud, but not directly questioned.

The final page was turned, impatiently flicked to one side, the sunken eyes pausing to read a last insertion. He compressed his lips into a tight line and with a practised flourish he tapped the papers together and returned them to Pendleton's briefcase. He leaned back in the chair, hands flat on the desk. It wasn't the first time Sir Henry had been called upon to determine a man's fitness for duty.

'I'm almost lost for words,' he grunted. 'On the one hand he's argumentative, to the point of insubordination. On the other hand, he's a bloody brilliant sailor and people seem to worship him.' He coughed, a rasping, laboured bark, followed by a minimal shake of the head. 'And he's very young. I mean, twenty-seven, he's still wet behind the ears.' He shook his head again, more pronounced. 'This is your recommendation. Convince me.'

Pendleton sighed. 'I've met him, sir, about two years ago. Very forthright, speaks his mind. He's intelligent and thoughtful, makes people wary.'

'Me for one,' the Admiral muttered.

'You said you needed someone who could think for himself and wouldn't be afraid to break the rules. Resourceful, you said. For when things get sticky.' Pendleton paused before volunteering the obligatory 'Sir.'

A faint smile softened the Admiral's gaunt features.

'A bit sticky. Yes, you're right, of course.' The chair screeched as he came to his feet. He took a pace to his right, looked at the floor. 'All right, we'll give this rebel of yours a chance, see if he can cut the mustard.' The thin face turned to meet Pendleton's. 'At least he's not one of our experienced commanders, bit more expendable.' He stepped closer. 'Personally, I've got my doubts.'

It was Pendleton's turn to smile. 'Thank you, sir. I'm sure he'll be all right.'

'He'd better be, James. By God, he'd better be.' He coughed again, and then drew a deep breath. 'I'll be on my way. Much to do.'

Pendleton escorted Sir Henry to the door and watched as the chauffeur drove him away.

A lookout on *Brackendale*'s bridge called a warning. 'Enemy Aircraft! Bearing, red two-oh!' He pointed ahead.

Binoculars swung across the port bow and it was Thorburn's First Lieutenant, Robert Armstrong, who caught a glimpse of the dark silhouettes. 'Stukas, sir, twenty plus.'

'Action Stations!' Thorburn could clearly see the dive-bombers heading for Dover, and *Brackendale* was out of range.

'*Vibrant* and *Westeram* ahead, sir,' a lookout called.

Thorburn remembered the two destroyers, moored in harbour the previous day, old 'V&W's from the Great War.

'They're engaging, sir,' called the lookout. The tell-tale signs of anti-aircraft fire began to burst around the gull-winged Stukas, lines of tracer rising in the sky.

Thorburn gripped the bridge handrail, silently urging his ship onwards, even though she had already reached top speed. *Vibrant* and *Westeram* began to zigzag furiously as the dive-bombers attacked, seemingly immune to the streams of tracer and high explosive clouding their passage. With *Brackendale* closing the range *Vibrant* took a hit on her superstructure, a bright flash abaft the bridge, and her shattered mast buckled into the sea.

Thorburn had waited long enough. 'Open Fire!'

The guns opened up in unison, blasting skywards, punching in at the mêlée. Heeling hard under helm the warship raced to close the gap. A pair of Stukas and an escorting Messerschmitt hurtled down, cannon tracer glowing towards *Brackendale*.

'Midships!' ordered Thorburn, a hurried estimate on the angle of attack. Another flight of Stukas dived into the fray, the whistling scream of bombs wailing above the hammering guns. A curtain of steel lifted skywards, the secondary armament of the four-barrelled Pompom and the 20mm Oerlikons thumping rounds into the enemy.

On the starboard Oerlikon, the gunner had his sights set on a Messerschmitt. It swept in low and fast. It dipped a wing and changed direction, coming straight at him. He centred the target, cross hairs aligned, in range. With the two curved rests tight to his shoulders, he pulled the trigger, and the gun shuddered through his body. He saw the shells slamming into the left wing, tearing at the fabric; watched the nose guns flashing a return of fire, and it was gone. The plane banked sharply, climbing to pull

11

out over the searchlight platform, apparently unharmed. He cursed, searching for another target, swinging the gun towards the bow. A dive-bomber flashed through his line of sight and he instinctively fired, desperately following the fleeting shadow, tracer falling behind the target. The Oerlikon clanged to a stop, ammunition spent, and his loader slapped on a fresh magazine of sixty rounds.

Heavier shore guns joined the fray, firing at the upper formation, deep red explosions spitting into black balls of smoke. A Stuka took a direct hit, the wings folded and it hit the sea, bouncing into a pieces.

Thorburn gave the order for a turn to starboard, forcing himself to concentrate, ignoring the confusion. *Vibrant* had turned full circle and looked to be listing to port, smoke pouring from her 'B' gun mounting. Another Messerschmitt hurled itself at *Brackendale*'s forward guns, raking the gun platform and shield, wingtips scything over the open bridge. A column of water engulfed them; Thorburn blinked through a drenching from the portside near miss. Glass fragments splintered into lethal shards, bloody cuts stinging the skin.

And as quickly as it had begun, it was over. The enemy turned away, chased by a scattering of tracer.

'Cease fire,' Thorburn ordered, wiping the taste of salt water from his face.

'Half ahead.' He looked round the bridge. No major casualties, but a bit bedraggled, the sun's warmth steaming their uniforms dry.

Five hundred yards off the port quarter, *Vibrant* limped slowly ahead, the smoke from her fo'c'sle thinning to a grey mist. *Westeram* swept majestically in on her starboard beam and slowed until the two ships idled together on a parallel course. Thorburn could see how vulnerable they were to another aerial bombardment, and he turned *Brackendale* out to sea, bringing her round to give anti-aircraft support if needed. Through his binoculars he watched the two captains talking by loudhailer, and then *Vibrant*, still listing to port, gently increased speed and made for the harbour. *Westeram* lifted her bows and turned south to pass a quarter mile off *Brackendale*'s starboard beam. A lamp flickered from the bridge.

'Signal, sir,' reported the Chief Yeoman. 'From *Westeram*, "Thanks for joining the party." End of message, sir.'

Thorburn started to dictate a comic reply, then thought better of it. *Westeram*'s captain was almost certainly the senior officer, so he sent a respectful, "Glad to be of help" and left it at that.

Damage reports revealed *Brackendale* had come through without serious harm and, thankfully, for the second time that morning, Thorburn ordered her return to port. 'Starboard five, half ahead!' He remained bent to the voice pipe; keen eyes watching the ship swing northeast towards Dover's western entrance to the harbour.

'Midships,' he said. He looked at his watch. The time was 08.35. He was late. Straightening up, he glanced round the crowded bridge; the officers and signalmen, the lookouts and machine gunners, all alert to a possible attack. He waited for the damaged *Vibrant* to limp inside the entrance and swing slowly to port.

'Slow ahead both,' he ordered, and pursed his lips as the destroyer steadied in line with the opening to the harbour. He eased *Brackendale* past the solid grey buttress of the southern breakwater, the relatively placid, oil flecked water lapping quietly round the ship's hull.

'Port twenty, steady.' Thorburn turned her cautiously through the stillness of the inner waters and headed for the quayside on the Western Dock. Conscious of the number of curious eyes focused on his new ship, Thorburn took more than a little extra care in his approach to the dockside, eventually brushing gently up against the old stone pier. With a suppressed sigh of relief he leant to the voice-pipe.

'Stop engines.'

The Special Sea Dutymen, well practised in the skills required to secure the vessel, passed their wires from ship to dockside and the cables were tied off to the old black bollards, the gangway finally clattering into position.

'Finished with main engines,' Thorburn ordered, and heard the faint ring of the telegraph from inside the wheelhouse. Taking a moment to look round the harbour he counted nine warships in various states of provisioning or repair. It was common knowledge within the Navy that the recent losses at the battle of Narvik in Norway, and again during the evacuation of the British Expeditionary Force from Dunkirk, had been heavy. Now more than ever, all available ships were needed. A few minesweepers and assorted gun-armed coastal craft made up the remainder of Dover Command's present disposition.

'Number One!' called Thorburn, remembering why he was here.

Lieutenant Robert Armstrong R.N., just returned from overseeing the tying up to the quayside, stepped from the starboard bridge wing.

'Yes, sir.' Lean and wiry and with an air of quiet confidence, he was content to wait for the captain to acknowledge his presence.

'I'm going ashore, ' Thorburn said and looked up toward the town, dominated by the imposing edifice of Dover Castle. 'You'd better see to repairs and replenish as necessary.'

'Aye aye, sir,' Armstrong nodded, 'another deployment?'

'We'll see,' smiled Thorburn. He turned away for the port ladder and his cabin. 'She's all yours,' he called over his shoulder.

Lieutenant Robert Armstrong sent a request for 'Guns', Lieutenant Howard, to check on the ammunition and asked the Chief Engineer to report to the bridge. Wooden crates and cargo nets congested the quayside, dockyard personnel swarming amongst the boxes. Towards *Brackendale*'s stern, hoses were being passed across, the pungent smell of oil fuel strong in the morning air.

The Chief Engineer, thirty-eight year old Lieutenant (E) Bryn Dawkins R.N.R., was a red haired Welshman who was fond of occasionally slipping back into his customary brogue. 'Hallo, Robert,' he said, hauling himself up to the bridge. 'Captain off to see the Admiral, then?'

'No, Chief, not the Admiral, not yet anyway,' said Armstrong, grinning. 'How much oil do we want?'

'About two hundred should do it,' said the Chief, and scratched the lobe of his right ear. 'But I tell you, Robert, there's a problem on one of the ancillary shafts.' His serious eyes showed the concern. 'Might have happened when we took that near miss.'

Armstrong caught the unease. 'What sort of time to repair it then, Chief?'

Dawkins thought for a moment. 'An hour or so, maybe mid-afternoon at worst,' he replied.

Armstrong hesitated. On the quayside below the captain was stepping into a staff car, so he needed to make a decision. Thorburn had instructed him to carry out repairs. 'Very well, Chief, but let me know as soon as you're done.'

'Right you are,' said Dawkins, acknowledging the order. He was too long a navy man to concern himself with worrying about Armstrong's youth. The First Lieutenant was a competent officer, still learning his trade, but none the less, one to have along if things got tough. He turned away, his thoughts already returning to the problem of that bearing.

Armstrong turned back to the starboard bridge rail, deep brown eyes staring at the town, trying to visualise Thorburn's meeting, wondering again what their assignment might be. They had seen and heard little during their patrol to the northeast of the Thames estuary, although a corvette had apparently tangled with an E-boat north of Sheerness. *Brackendale* was shaping up well, not bad considering a third of the crew were fresh to the Navy.

The evacuation of the army from the beaches at Dunkirk had taken place while the ship was undergoing training on the west coast of Scotland. Two days before her completion, Armstrong had arrived from the fleet destroyer Wassau. His last major assignment on that ship had been to rescue almost four hundred men from Dunkirk; and Robert Armstrong had learned a lot about war at sea.

Taking up his appointment as *Brackendale*'s First Lieutenant, their first deployment was to steam south to

Liverpool, and then escort a solitary freighter down to Falmouth, after which they were ordered to proceed to Dover. At sunset, about to enter harbour, a signal arrived from Dover Command , directing them to patrol northheast of Margate until dawn. So far, they were not specifically allocated an assignment, for the time being guarding the channel against German invasion. Armstrong straightened away from the bridge wing as the ammunition began to be manhandled along the chain of men. There was work to be done.

In the German port of Bremerhaven a warship cast off and eased out to the deep channel. The first leg to Calais was underway.

Chapter Two .. Enemy Coast.

Richard Thorburn strode down a dark corridor towards an oak panelled door on which a varnished wooden plaque proclaimed the office of 'CAPTAIN (D)'. He'd given up wondering about the meeting. His experience of senior officers was not to be recommended, and his own casually off-hand manner did nothing to endear him to those in authority. In this particular case he did know the man's name. They had met before, briefly. Removing his cap, he knocked, heard a muffled acknowledgement and crossed the threshold to stand at attention.

Captain James A. Pendleton, D.S.O., R.N., was a stocky, red faced figure, sporting a handsome beard. He looked up from his paperwork and smiled. 'Morning, Richard,' he beamed, the deep bass voice resonating round the room. 'Have a seat.' He waved towards one of the chairs in front of his ancient desk. Behind him, a large window, half curtained with heavy drapes, allowed for a clear view of the harbour.

'Thank you, sir,' Thorburn said, easing into a well-padded leather chair. He thought back to when they had both served on the China Station, although not in the same ships. Pendleton, a Lieutenant-Commander in one of the large fleet destroyers, and Thorburn, a Sub-Lieutenant on a cruiser. Hong Kong harbour, a fleet regatta, and a sailing yacht. All a long time ago now, a different era.

'How was the patrol?'

'Quiet for the most part, sir,' he replied, matter of fact. 'A bit lively at the end.'

Pendleton nodded. 'Mmm, so I gathered. How's the ship?'

'A few scratches, sir. Nothing a lick of paint won't sort.' Thorburn waited as the Captain stroked his beard.

'Good . . , good. Now listen. It won't have escaped your attention that we're losing a lot of ships. Churchill's a bit worried.' Pendleton leaned back from his desk. 'Everyone's working on the assumption we're about to be invaded. So Winnie wants to establish a channel patrol through the Dover Straights and, initially, up as far as Harwich.' He paused, the grey eyes fixing Thorburn from underneath the bushy eyebrows. 'We're building up a small fleet, anything we can put a gun on with a few naval ratings.'

Thorburn nodded, seeing beyond the bland statement, visualising the fishing vessels being commandeered, larger motor vessels converted to gunboats.

'But that's not what I had in mind for you.' said Pendleton. 'I know this is your first command, but hearing of your appointment, I specifically asked for *Brackendale* to join us down here.' He stroked his beard. 'I have to say I came up against a fair bit of opposition. Apparently you don't instil much confidence in the powers that be.' He tapped the desk with his pen. 'That said, I think I've found you a job, right up your street.' Rising from behind his desk he moved to a chart of the Dover Straits, his Captain's gold insignia glinting on the uniform cuffs. 'The Admiralty is convinced the Navy needs to be a little more pro-active. Patrolling, seeking out the enemy, you know the sort of stuff. Now France is in Nazi hands, the E-boats are a pain in the backside.' Pendleton paced behind Thorburn and returned to his desk. 'As I recall, you were involved with the gunboats on the China Station. Bit of an incident with the Foreign Office?'

'Yes, sir, working out of Chungking, off the Yangtse.' Thorburn had been a Sub-Lieutenant then, one of a shore party escorting a local dignitary on a diplomatic mission. Ambushed by bandits, and with the senior officer wounded, he took command of the situation. His direct assault, using an old motorboat and a machine gun against stiff opposition at the wharf, had earned him a recommendation.

'Helped with your promotion to Lieutenant,' said Pendleton, 'talk of the fleet for a while.' He opened a silver cigarette case on the desk, motioning for Thorburn to take one. Blue smoke drifted as Pendleton watched Thorburn through narrowed eyes. 'Well, here's the job,' he said. 'I want you to proceed independently as close to the hostile shore as you can. We've had some information that a German destroyer is in Calais, en route to Cherbourg, or even Brest.' He took another lungful of smoke. 'See if you can find it.'

Thorburn straightened, the cigarette forgotten, the extent of the assignment becoming clear. He knew his promotion had been surprisingly rapid, more astonishing still that he had been entrusted with a brand new design of destroyer. Not a fleet destroyer, granted, but nevertheless a very capable warship. He thought carefully before replying; this was not the moment for flippancy. 'Thank you, sir. I'm flattered by their Lordships' trust in me.'

'You may not thank me in a while,' chuckled Pendleton. 'The Kriegsmarine might not have much of a navy but those E-boats are a bloody menace, and their mine laying operations are taking out too many ships.' He turned to stare through the window and Thorburn watched as the broad figure jostled with his thoughts. 'We do know there are two operational groups. One of them uses Bolougne, and the other Cherbourg. I think Bolougne would be a good place to start looking.' There was a pause as Pendleton squinted at Thorburn. 'Tonight.'

Thorburn raised an eyebrow.

'No time like the present,' said Pendleton. 'But for God's sake, try and keep *Brackendale* in one piece.' He grimaced. 'This war's only just started. Unlike some, I don't think it'll be short. At the moment I'm not even sure we'll win, but right now we've a chance to hurt them before they settle.' He pushed a sealed, manila envelope across the desk. 'Those are your orders. Any problems, you report to me, whatever happens. All clear?'

'Aye aye, sir,' said Thorburn slowly. 'And if I come up against anything important?'

'Use your initiative,' Pendleton said with a raised eyebrow.

'Right, sir,' said Thorburn, nodding. 'I'll do my best.'

'And I'm sure you will, Richard. I'm sure you will,' grinned Pendleton. The smile vanished, a more sombre note to his voice. 'We're up against it. What little we have is spread bloody thin, and we have to make most of it.' He settled back to the paperwork, but looked at Thorburn to hold him with those piercing grey eyes. Finally, he nodded, 'Good luck, Commander. Let me know when you're ready for sea.' The briefing was over.

Richard Thorburn closed the door behind him and walked thoughtfully along the corridor, mulling over his meeting. 'Seek Out, Engage and Destroy'. Essentially, that was the order he'd been given. How many times had those words echoed through the annals of the Royal

Navy? History, tradition, duty; it was all there and now it seemed more pertinent than ever. There had obviously been doubts raised over his ability to tackle this assignment, but Pendleton must have persuaded the senior staff to accept his nomination for the job. He could almost hear their disapproval.

Bright sunlight greeted his exit from the hotel and with a deep breath he pulled his cap firmly in place. He decided to walk back to *Brackendale*. Unlike the majority of England's towns, Dover was already at the forefront of the war, a large part of the civilian population previously evacuated to live in relatively safer areas. Striding down a side street, he stepped aside for a young mother pushing her pram, who nodded shyly as she passed by.

Around him the fresh green of spring had deepened as the rose buds blossomed into full colour in the borders. Washing flapped in the breeze above a garden fence and an Alsatian barked noisily, straining at the leash. Across the street sandbags protected prominent doorways, and angle-iron pickets supported rusting coils of barbed wire. A multi-layered defence of the coastal roads from beach invasion. Dover's remaining residents went about their business, a young lad on a bike delivering from his basket.

Approaching the Western Pier, the crowded harbour lay before him; armed tugs and Motor Torpedo Boats jostled for a berth amongst the older destroyers, all protected by an assortment of anti-aircraft guns. H.M.S. *Brackendale* was now berthed alongside Admiralty Pier, further out along the quay. Her modern design and strong 'dazzle' pattern paint scheme unique within the port. Thorburn watched the four-barrelled Pompom swing seaward to train upwards as the quarterdeck twin four-inch followed suit. A seagull, calling noisily, hovered over the oily water then settled on a heavy cable attached to the ship's stern. On the quarterdeck, gathered round the depth-charge rails, a team of crewmen inspected the canisters and applied thick grease to the slipways.

To Thorburn's left, against the Prince of Wales Pier, an engine coughed into life followed by the distinctive rumble of a motor launch ticking over. Shouted orders echoed over the water as the boat eased from her mooring. Grumbling and sputtering, machineguns rotating skywards, she moved slowly towards the outer harbour.

Thorburn moved on along the Western Pier until he drew level with *Brackendale*'s forward pair of four-inch guns. He stopped to look down the sleek lines of his command, the latest design in warship technology. There were four of those guns, mounted in pairs, two on the forecastle and two on the quarterdeck. High-angle anti-aircraft or low-angle surface to surface, each one capable of firing up to twenty rounds a minute, with a maximum range of nine miles. Eighty high explosive shells in sixty seconds, formidable firepower. In addition to the main armament was the multi-barrelled Pompom mounted high on the quarterdeck housing. A specialised design in anti-aircraft gunnery capable of delivering a devastating curtain of two pound shells.

Either side of the bridge were his two 20 millimetre Oerlikons and on the bridge itself a pair of Lewis machine guns. He allowed himself a grim smile. H.M.S. *Brackendale* was a formidable weapon, his to command, a lethal destroyer upholding the best traditions of the Royal Navy.

The muster party piped him on board and amidst the sound of heavy hammering from somewhere in the engine room, he ordered a meeting in the wardroom.

The Coxswain, Chief Petty Officer Barry Falconer, a 'Geordie' from Newcastle-upon-Tyne, climbed the ladder to the wheelhouse. He checked the voice-pipes and telegraphs, and made his way to the forward gun mounting. A barrel chested, weather beaten veteran, he had served the Royal Navy for twenty years and had earned the respect of both officers and crew alike. Little if anything escaped his eagle eye. Pausing for a moment to watch the gun crew overhauling their equipment he gave them a gentle reminder. 'We'll have those ready-use lockers re-loaded, lads,' he said, pointing to the quick firing storage bins.

'Aye aye, Cox'n,' a gun layer said, adjusting to the new task.

Falconer lingered to ensure all was as it should be, quietly pleased with their efforts. He dropped to the fo'c'sle deck, leant both hands on the port rail, and watched as a motor launch smoked noisily towards the breakwater and throttling up to clear the harbour entrance.

Down in the wardroom, as Thorburn appeared in the doorway, *Brackendale*'s officers straightened into silence. The majority stood beneath a portrait of His Majesty the King, beside which the Ship's Crest was displayed in an ornate frame. The *Brackendale*, as with all this class of destroyer, was named after a 'fox' hunt. At the launch ceremony local dignitaries from the outskirts of the New Forest had arrived to present the ship with a scroll of dedication. With great formallity they had unveiled the artwork. A pony's head framed by a gold hunting horn.

'Sit down, gentlemen,' Thorburn said, dropping the manila envelope on the table. 'No doubt you're all itching to know why Captain (D) summoned me to a conference.'

A murmur went round the table as they settled down in anticipation.

Thorburn glanced around the room, pausing to check on the assembled group. Standing to the left was Armstrong, his First Lieutenant, a capable officer who had already proved himself, calm and reliable. Next to him was Lieutenant David Howard R.N., the Gunnery Officer, a shock of black hair and never seen without his pipe. At the far end of the table was the Welshman, Lieutenant Bryn Dawkins R.N.R., the 'Chief' Engineer, vastly experienced and with a definite 'hands-on' approach. The two Sub-Lieutenants, Martin, (Navigation) thin and studious, forever pouring over his charts, and Lawrence (Depth-Charges) short and stocky, both beginning to find their feet. Half hidden in the background, the young Midshipman, George Labatt, fresh faced and eager to learn and the general dogsbody, still finding his feet. Finally, the 'Doctor', Surgeon-Lieutenant Peter Waverly R.N., somewhat plump and red faced, but very adaptable and a 'proper gentleman'. So far they had performed well, only a full-blown emergency would tell Thorburn how they might react under pressure.

'The Admiralty,' he said, speaking slowly, 'need someone to look for a German destroyer.' He tapped the envelope in front of him. 'I can tell you that 'someone' is us.' The wardroom was quiet, but every officer watched and waited.

'We're due out tonight, so I want to be sure that all departments are aware of their responsibilities and that any problems are resolved immediately.' He paused to check his orders. 'If there aren't any questions, I need to refresh myself with the charts, and I'm sure all of you have a lot to do.' There was a general movement towards the door, an urgency in their step, a fresh meaning to the day.

'Guns,' called Thorburn, 'a moment, if you please.'

'Sir?' said Howard, hesitating by the door.

'I noticed a couple of Lewis guns on a wrecked M.T.B., I was wondering if we could arrange to, ah, have them installed somewhere more appropriate, possibly amidships?' queried Thorburn, a pronounced cough disguising his underhand suggestion.

'Of course, sir,' said Howard a broad smile lighting his face, 'can't think of anywhere more suitable for their disposal.' Teeth clamped firmly on his pipe, he made off with a jaunty swagger.

Thorburn reached out to the manila envelope and selected another page. His officers were learning, generally fitted in, a good team. Tonight, in the dark, within sight of the enemy coast, they would all be very reliant on each other.

After dark in the northern French port of Calais it began to rain. A German warship, having avoided detection after leaving Bremerhaven, took advantage of the poor visibility to slip away and set a course for the Cotentin peninsula. FlotillaKapitan Werner von Holtzmann, had opened his secret orders which directed him to assume command of the Seventh Schnellboat Groupe operating out of Cherbourg. His mission was to better co-ordinate the torpedo attacks on British shipping moving through the channel.

On clearing the harbour entrance, Holtzmann turned west and as the ship twisted into the first meaningful waves he lit a large fat Havana cigar. A thin smile played over the hard mouth, and the slate grey eyes narrowed in satisfaction. Perfect weather, he thought. An almost fog like drizzle in which to hide. He fingered the Iron Cross hanging from the ribbon around his neck. Admiral Reader's recommendation had culminated in Adolf Hitler presenting it to him at the Chancellery in Berlin. Tomorrow he would begin again. More victories, more medals, perhaps another promotion.

'Coffee, Herr Kapitan.' His steward held out a round tray. Von Holtzmann took the small cup, breathed in the warm aroma, and took a sip. He nodded. 'That is very good.' The steward clicked his heels and withdrew.

Holtzmann relaxed at the back of the bridge, cigar smoke coiling from his nostrils. The drizzle became heavier, sheeting in on a freshening breeze, the two thousand tons of his destroyer a fleeting shadow on the sea.

Back on the quayside in Calais a man stepped out from beneath the skeletal ironwork of a dockside crane. He crossed the wet sheen of railway track and slipped down an alleyway between an office building and a large warehouse. Being very careful, he avoided the glow of a yellow lamp hanging over a side entrance where two German guards sheltered in the doorway, avoiding the constant rain. He turned past a parked lorry into full darkness and reached the perimeter fence. Twice a man's height, the chain link was topped with a double strand of barbed wire. A few cautious paces to his right brought him to a red brick building. At the bottom of the last steel fence post was the small section he'd previously loosened and concealed. He paused, took a last look over his shoulder, then knelt down to squeeze under the jagged wire. Alert for the slightest sound he crawled through a large puddle, came to his feet, and melted into the surrounding trees. Twenty minutes later, in an old stone hut above the French shoreline, the rhythmic pulse of Morse code announced the stealthy departure of a German warship from the port of Calais.

Chapter Three . . Night Patrol.

An hour before midnight, Thorburn called Armstrong to his cabin.

'Number One,' he said, still uncertain as to whether he was doing the right thing. 'I want to speak to the ship's company, everyone.'

'On the quarterdeck, sir?'

'If you would, please.'

Armstrong nodded, a slight hesitation. 'Right, sir,' he muttered and turned to go.

'Everyone, Number One. Clear the decks.'

Armstrong glanced back. 'Aye aye, sir.'

Thorburn waited, heard the piped order, sat uneasily and waited. Making speeches was not what he did, even though it was part of a captain's role. It just wasn't natural, standing in front of a bunch of men and telling them how good it was going to be.

The door opened and Armstrong peered in. 'All ready, sir.'

Thorburn stood and grabbed his cap. 'Very well,' he said. 'Lead on.' He followed Armstrong out to the quarterdeck and climbed up to the Pompom platform. The crew, assembled in the darkness, stood looking up in silence.

Thorburn cleared his throat. 'Gentlemen,' he began, ditching any thought of formality. 'You know me, I'm the one that stands up there at the front and gives the orders.' He gave a vague wave towards the bridge and was relieved to hear a few quiet chuckles. 'I'm not here to give a speech, I just want to put you in the picture. In a few minutes we're going out to look for the enemy, over the other side, Bolougne.' A murmur rippled through the ranks. 'This is as risky as it gets.' He paused to gather his thoughts. 'All I'm asking is that you do your best, for you and your mates. Forget all that rubbish about King and country. The only thing that matters out there is us. Above all else we fight for each other.' He stopped to look at the shadowy faces below him. 'Just thought I'd let you know. That's it then . . . , good luck to you all. Carry on, Number One.' He turned away, dropped to the deck and made his way up to the bridge. He'd told it straight and that was as it should be. Time to make a move.

Thorburn signalled Captain (D) they were ready to leave harbour. Under cover of darkness the ship would move up the coast to Broadstairs and from there, patrol southeast to Bolougne in an effort to intercept the German destroyer. Initially, two Motor Gun Boats (M.G.B.'s) would accompany the destroyer before setting off on their own mission toward the Goodwin Sands.

The tannoy squealed. 'Special Sea Duty men. . . Close up for leaving harbour!' Within moments the ship echoed to the clamour of men moving to their stations.

Thorburn accepted they were ready to proceed, and ordered the ship to cast off.

'Take her out, Pilot,' he said quietly.

'Slow ahead. Port twenty.'

The First Lieutenant stood behind the navigating officer talking softly with 'Guns', and in either bridge wing, the lookouts scanned the horizon. Once clear of the breakwater, the three vessels formed line astern, *Brackendale* turning east in the general direction of Margate. The grey light faded as they drew level with

Broadstairs, and in majestic harmony, the two M.G.B's parted company, forging away at thirty knots.

'Starboard ten,' said Thorburn.

'Starboard ten, aye,' came the reply from the wheelhouse, the Cox'n at the helm.

The destroyer responding by heeling slightly as the helm came on.

'From Captain (D), sir,' said Armstrong, holding out a message slip.

Thorburn took the signal and read, "God speed".

The compass was coming on to bearing and he leaned to the voice pipe, 'Steer one-two-five degrees.'

'One-two-five degrees, aye aye, sir.'

Thorburn handed the message back to the First Lieutenant. 'Make to Captain (D),' he instructed, "Thank you and goodnight".' He thought of Pendleton, remembering the goodwill, the willingness with which he had given his support. It was time to honour the appointment.

Leading Seaman Allun Jones was the portside bridge lookout. In the starlight visibility stretched to a reasonable horizon and through his binoculars, the rising shoreline above Broadstairs was still evident. Sweeping the glasses from stern to stem, only the occasional white breaker showed in his line of sight. His main concern was the French coast. It looked as if the darkness of rain clouds were framing the shore.

The ship settled down on her push across the channel, all hands alert to their situation, everyone straining to be first to spot any danger. An irregular zigzag had been ordered and *Brackendale* now forged on at twenty knots, the normal Asdic underwater search pattern circumvented by the noise of their speed; this could be a long night.

'Signal, sir.'

Thorburn turned to the Chief Yeoman.

'Immediate. From Captain (D), sir.'

Thorburn moved to the poor light of the chart table, leaning over to read. "Report of enemy destroyer departed Calaise at approx 23.00hrs. Moving west."

'Is that all?' The question was as much a thoughtful query as it was to the Yeoman.

'That's all, sir.'

Thorburn nodded, slowly. 'Very well. Acknowledge.' He remained standing over the chart. Pendleton had given him the latest update. It was imperative he found that destroyer. He moved to the bridge-screen and brought his binoculars up to search the darkness. The ship rose gently beneath his feet, riding the long rollers, dipping her stem down the following trough. It was time to commence the first leg of their search .

Two hours into their search pattern Thorburn fretted over the lack of progress and considered closing in to Bolougne. No sign of the enemy destroyer and with dawn approaching he felt the E-boats might yet attempt a pre-dawn strike towards the English coast. If he allowed the Germans a sight of *Brackendale* it would serve as a strong deterrent. Much better to close with the shore and show the flag.

'Ask the First Lieutenant to join me,' he called over his shoulder.

When Armstrong arrived beside the compass binnacle, Thorburn jabbed his binoculars towards the invisible coast. 'I'm taking her in,' he said , 'to Bolougne. Thought we might try stirring things up a bit.'

Armstrong nodded, frowning. 'And the shore battery?'

He left the query open and Thorburn turned and peered at him. There was just enough moonlight to make out the First Lieutenant's indistinct features.

'Nothing ventured, nothing gained,' offered Thorburn, in an effort to deflect the censure.

'Yes sir, but if we end up with E-boats and shore guns splitting our firepower, that might be a bit problematic.'

'True,' said Thorburn rubbing his chin. He could understand Armstrong's concern, duly noting the remainder of the bridge personnel were waiting for his answer. Thorburn made up his mind. 'Right, we'll take her in at half throttle and maintain bow on to the harbour. Should make us a pretty small target. Tell the Chief, if I call for full power, I want everything he's got!' He turned back to the bridge rail, staring in to the gloom ahead. Behind him instructions were issued before the First Lieutenant eventually rejoined him.

'Ready to proceed, sir,' said Armstrong.

'Thank you, Number One,' Thorburn acknowledged, and after a quick look round, he gave the order. 'Half ahead both.'

From the wheelhouse, the telegraph rang to the engine room and the destroyer slowed, her shimmering wake less pronounced. Thorburn became aware of a tension in his body as they edged steadily in towards the enemy coast, his hands aching as he gripped the bridge rail. A dozen pairs of eyes strained for a glimpse of danger, a first sighting of the headland above Bolougne. Only the steady beat of the engines accompanied their progress, the dark sea reflecting their vague presence.

On the portside bridge wing Jones dropped the binoculars away from his eyes. He blinked and rubbed a cool palm across his forehead. Then back in to the rubber

33

sockets of the binoculars, checking the sea astern, turning the centre screw for focus, again commencing his sweep towards the port beam. He hesitated, something solid had slid past his vision and he gently backtracked, waiting for the sighting to re-emerge. There it was; a small, black object, and then it was gone again. Breathing hard, he held the line of sight sure it would reappear, and a moment later he had it.

'Alarm! Bearing Red-Five-Oh, Range, three thousand!'

Thorburn reacted instantly. 'Hard a port. Full ahead together!' he ordered, turning towards the sighting, binoculars swinging in the direction of the bearing. 'What is it, Jones?'

'Looked like a conning tower, sir,' called Jones, who had only ever seen a Royal Navy submarine, and that was in training.

And then Thorburn found it. Every gun on the ship rotated to the bearing. The warship curved round to the target, heeling hard to starboard, the ship's company instinctively leaning to compensate.

'Midships,' called Thorburn and then spotted the deck gun forward of the conning tower. Definitely a U-boat Thorburn confirmed to himself, and realised he could just make out personnel at the front of the bridge.

'Number One, send a sighting report. "Admiralty, repeated to Dover Command. U-boat on surface, course two-eight-oh. Engaging," give our position.' They must see *Brackendale* at any moment; if the lookouts had been awake the boat would already be diving.

'Open Fire!' he shouted, and in the Director Tower, 'Guns' fed in the target information, the destroyer on course to pass well astern of the target.

'Shoot!' ordered Howard. The blinding crash of the forward guns hit them, deafened by the roar, blinded by the flash, the acrid smell of cordite ballooning over the bridge. Beyond the U-boat, two waterspouts, followed by two more from the aft mounting. The figures in the conning tower disappeared. Thorburn saw the midships Pompom punching shells at the target, plumes of water advancing across the sea as the gunners found the range. Diving angle and speed took the U-boat rapidly below the surface at the same time as the four-inch guns fired again, and missed. Even in the poor light they could see a foaming swirl spread over the surface, and the enemy vanished.

'Port twenty. Half ahead,' ordered Thorburn. 'Cease fire.'

'Contact!' called Petty Officer Jennings from the Asdic hut. 'Moving left.'

'Put it on the bridge speakers,' said Thorburn, wanting to hear for himself. 'Stand by, depth charges. Set for fifty feet.' Their course was set to intersect the U-boat's path and Jennings held the contact. The destroyer pushed on at attack speed, ever closer, the ring of the Asdic's pulse quickening on the bridge repeater, until the range closed to zero.

'Instantaneous echo, sir,' he called, and as the depth charge hooter sounded, the canisters rolled over the stern rail in search of their prey. On either side of the quarterdeck the launchers threw out their cylinders, bracketing the U-boat's line of escape. *Brackendale* ran on, and the sea erupted in their wake. Thorburn swung the destroyer in a wide circle to port, waiting for evidence of victory.

'Lost contact,' from the Asdic hut.

Thorburn nodded. That was to be expected; the initial cacophony of exploding depth charges prevented the sound wave from penetrating the noise. On the quarterdeck, with the ship heeling hard to starboard and the deck tilting violently, the 750lb depth charges were reloaded. Seawater swept inboard, battering the legs and feet of those manhandling the canisters. The old hands amongst them led the way, each man helping the other until a full pattern was loaded, the ready to use area re-equipped from below.

Stillness from the sea, a smooth ripple from the disturbed water, but nothing to indicate a damaged submarine. Thorburn looked over to Armstrong and grimaced, receiving a shrug of the shoulders in response.

'Sweep from red-two-oh, to red-one-five-oh,' ordered Armstrong, leaning in to Jennings at the Asdic wheel. The electronic pulse pinged into the depths, probing for an echoing reply. Gun crews cleared away empty shell cases and those in the engine room checked for leaking damage following the underwater explosions.

'No contact, sir,' said Jennings.

Richard Thorburn stood by the bridge rail and leant his chin on his arms in thought. How could they have missed? The U-boat had been right there; they had shot at it, strewn it with depth charges and now they had lost contact. Not a great start to his first real engagement with the enemy. He heard Armstrong redirect the area of search, and Sub-Lieutenant Lawrence reported completion of the depth-charge reload.

'Contact, sir!' called Jennings and the faint echo could just be heard on the bridge repeater. 'Starboard twenty, moving right!'

'Well done,' said Thorburn and to the wheelhouse,

'Starboard ten, steer three-four-five.'

'Target dead ahead, depth one hundred feet,' said Jennings.

'Bridge, Depth charge,' shouted Thorburn to the voice pipe.

'Depth charge!' yelled Lawrence pressing his ear to the pipe.

'Set for a hundred and twenty feet, Sub, but be prepared for a late change.'

'A hundred and twenty feet, yes sir!' shouted Lawrence, and turned to see Able Seaman Thompson altering the depth setting of the first canister. Beneath the stern, their wake spread murky white in a gentle curve and Lawrence blew on his hands, anticipating the next move in the hunt.

Thorburn had a moment of terrible indecision. When he'd finished the briefing in the wardroom the latest charts of the channel had been left for him to familiarise himself with. He quickly turned to the chart table and in the dim light from the bulkhead he checked on the depth of water beneath their keel. Maybe a maximum of a hundred and eighty feet. He rubbed his face, his fingers drumming on the small cleft in his chin. That U-boat commander was either very stupid or extremely brave.

Overseeing operations in the Asdic hut, Armstrong realised he was sweating. Not that it was hot inside the claustrophobic cabin, but more, it was the tension created by the difficulty in holding the plot. They were closing in rapidly and the time delay between the pulses quickly reduced, indicating once again the almost instantaneous echo that placed the U-boat in the perfect spot to release the attack. Again the klaxon sounded and another pattern of deadly canisters bubbled down beneath the waves. This time they knew the wait would be longer, and the warship increased to full power before commencing a turn to starboard.

The black sea burst upwards in a torrent of cascading spray, tons of water collapsing into a seething cauldron, huge ripples heaving from its centre. Aboard the destroyer they waited. The disturbance calmed, ultra smooth as it settled, revealing an empty expanse. Two patterns of depth charges and no evidence of damage, not even a smell of oil.

Annoyed with himself, and frustrated at their lack of achievement, Thorburn considered the situation. Beneath the waves a U-boat, forced under, apparently unharmed. Somewhere not far ahead, a hostile shoreline coinciding with the onset of daylight, the German guns gaining a clear advantage. Pendleton had recommended he keep *Brackendale* in one piece; at this rate the ship might not even exist.

'Number One,' said Thorburn, 'a moment of your time.'

'Sir,' said Armstrong, emerging from the Asdic hut.

Thorburn inclined his head towards the chart table, the First Lieutenant squeezing past to the bridge rail.

He sketched out their predicament and waited for a response.

'With all due respect, sir, I would withdraw *Brackendale* to mid channel and continue the mission,' answered Armstrong, tapping the chart with his fore finger. 'You've driven a U-boat under, maybe damaged, and,' he tipped his head in the direction of Bolougne, ' we must have woken them up.'

Thorburn nodded. Both knew it was more than likely, a quiet smile between them, a recognition of a shared resolve. 'Thank you, Number One,' said Thorburn, 'I'll bear that in mind,'

'Enemy coast visible!' came a call from Jones on the bridge wing.

Thorburn looked up, raising his binoculars to the headland above Bolougne, the harbour nestling in the darkness below.

'Port twenty. Full ahead together!' The destroyer turned out from the shore and came round to the south, away from the danger of the shore guns. Thorburn waited for the ship to run parallel with the coast. 'Steer one-eight-oh.' *Brackendale* settled onto her bearing.

FlotillaKapitan Werner von Holtzmann held the binoculars tight to his eyes, wanting to verify the lookout's call. His report was of a ship manoeuvring at speed, only a glimpse, but he thought it was British. Holtzmann wanted to see for himself. In the darkness there was little to see, just the odd glimmer of light shining off the waves. He changed his search area a little to the east, towards the bows. Was that a ship's bow wave? A phosphorescent wake trailing from a stern rail? He moved the glasses higher and forwards searching for the upperworks, a funnel, something more solid.

For an instant he thought he glimpsed the White Ensign of the Royal Navy. It was enough. He was convinced, the lookout was correct.

'Oberleutnant,' he called. 'You will instruct Bolougne to send a Schnellboat as a decoy. Take the Britisher away from the coast. We will guide him out here with a small lamp on the forward gun. He must stay to the south side. Do you understand?'

'Jawohl, Herr Kapitan!'

'Good, very good. And now we will set course for Bolougne's harbour. See to it.'

The German warship made a turn to the coast away from the danger of being seen, the danger von Holtzmann had so desperately tried to avoid.

A short while later a Schnellboat sped past out to sea and Holtzmann congratulated himself on a timely intervention.

'E-boat off the port bow!' shouted a lookout on *Brackendale*'s flag deck.

Thorburn turned to follow the outstretched arm, catching sight of a white bow-wave curving back from the low silhouette of a German torpedo boat.

'Hard a'port!' snapped Thorburn, bringing the destroyer round to face the enemy. Judging the range to be around three thousand yards, he gave the order. 'Open Fire!'

Brackendale trembled, striving to force her bow towards the adversary, the guns crashing out the initial broadside. Tall fingers of spray bracketed the target as the German gunners replied.

'Starboard ten,' said Thorburn, watching the fall of shot and moving to intercept the course of the E-boat. Vivid streaks of tracer curved between the warships, the destroyer's guns roaring out another deafening salvo. Amidships, the multi-barrelled Pompom hammered shells at the German boat, struggling with the fast closing range. A shout came from the forward guns, a loader falling sideways to the fo'c'sle deck, blood gushing from his left shoulder. Hits on *Brackendale*'s upper works found the bridge, and cursing loudly, Sub-Lieutenant Martin collapsed off the compass platform. Bright sparks flicked across the E-boat, a small fire visible on the quarterdeck.

Needing to get all guns to bear, Thorburn was about to alter course to port when he saw the German vessel turn away, revealing another fire on the bridge portside. As the E-boat twisted towards the coast another of *Brackendale*'s salvoes fell close to target, but the German machine guns continued to sweep the destroyer with bullets. The range opened rapidly, damage to the E-boat obviously not serious. Abaft the funnel the Pompom stopped firing, the shells no longer reaching the target. The first grey of morning gave light to the battle; blackened steelwork leading to a seaman slumped over the starboard Oerlikon, a jagged hole in his helmet. A crimson fluid congealed on his collar.

Thorburn grimaced against the shock of the forward guns, shifting his binoculars to catch the result. In a bright yellow flash, a shell struck the E-boat amidships. The resulting explosion literally blew the craft apart, pieces of smoking debris hurtling into the sea. Clouds of white steam bubbled at the surface, settling slowly before the wreckage slid beneath the waves.

In the momentary silence, Thorburn ordered, 'Cease fire, slow ahead,' and pushed his cap back from his eyes. A ragged cheer broke out along the decks.

'Stand by to pick up survivors,' said Thorburn, 'and get the injured down to the sick berth.' That U-boat was in the area, might be at periscope depth. He knelt down to Martin, concerned for his welfare. Sitting against the compass binnacle, blood oozing from a wound to his temple, he looked up at Thorburn.

'I'll be alright, sir,' he mumbled, 'the Doc'll patch me up. I take it we won?'

'Yes, Sub,' said Thorburn, allowing himself the ghost

of a smile. Shaken up from the hit to his forehead the Lieutenant was beginning to shake off the effects. He rested a hand on Martin's shoulder and straightened to gather his thoughts. Armstrong's voice could be heard on the quarterdeck, apparently directing the rescue operation. A lone German seaman was being helped on board, sodden uniform dripping on the deck. Daylight began to assert itself, the shoreline more prominent, a slight mist greying out the intervening distance.

A thumping explosion off the port beam grabbed their attention, a large plume of water launched skywards. An echoing rumble from the shore signalled they were under fire.

'No more survivors, sir!' Armstrong shouted and helped the prisoner down to the sick berth.

Thorburn took control. 'Starboard thirty, half ahead both!' he yelled to the voice pipe.

'All departments confirm no significant damage, sir,' reported the Coxswain, temporarily fulfilling the role of Number One. 'One dead and three wounded, including Mr Martin, sir.'

'Very well, Cox'n,' acknowledged Thorburn, 'we'll make for mid channel, maximum revs, and then patrol south. I need you on the wheel.'

Falconer, somewhat taken aback saluted. 'Aye aye, sir,' and swung into the wheelhouse. The telegraph rang through to the engine room; a noticeable increase in power, and Falconer personally took the helm to steer them onto a southerly course.

'Yeoman,' called Thorburn, 'Get a message to Dover Command. Send, "U boat active. E-boat destroyed. Under fire by shore battery." And let them know we have a prisoner.'

'Aye aye, sir,' the Yeoman moved to the R/T office leaving Thorburn to his thoughts.

Captain James Pendleton had not slept. In the early dawn his office smelt of stale cigarettes, a dampness by the open window. He was concerned with the battle taking place across the channel. He worried about his choice in appointing young Thorburn to such an important role, and whether a support vessel should be sent to assist. H.M.S. *Veracity*, an old destroyer brought back in to service, was patrolling just off Margate, easily capable of reaching *Brackendale* at short notice. Out there, he thought, a single destroyer had engaged the enemy; Richard Thorburn was either good enough to answer the challenge or he would fail. Maybe Sir Henry was right. Too much of a rebel. He sighed and reached for his cigarettes and the match flared brightly.

Full daylight found *Brackendale* steaming south of Hastings, the morning sun sparkling off the sea, a screeching flock of seagulls wheeling over the stern. In the early hours, a small convoy had made safe passage through to Sheerness, a corvette and an armed tug their only escort. Below decks the crew cleared away after a cold breakfast and Thorburn allowed himself the indulgence of a smoke in his cabin under the wheelhouse. Not that he was relaxed, and the frown deepened because he knew the night's exploits had not gone well. The Oerlikon gunner was dead. A U-boat had escaped unharmed, probably. There'd been no sign of the German destroyer and all he had to show for their efforts was a half-drowned sailor. Not a very good start to his working relationship with Pendleton.

Not far from Thorburn, Able Seaman Dave Stanley, checked the firing mechanism of the starboard bridge-wing Oerlikon. The Coxswain had asked for volunteers with gunnery training to replace Rodgers, killed by shrapnel splinters during the night. Now freshly greased and oiled, the gun felt comfortable under his control; the searchlight now being manned by his 'oppo', Ben Parker. He pushed the oily rag into the storage locker, trailed his fingers down the breech and stood back, contentedly swaying with the ship's motion.

On the anti-aircraft platform amidships, the Pompom gunners basked in the warm sun. The night action had proved to be an exciting initiation for some; an important refresher for others.

'How're we doin' then, Taff?' asked the loader, thumb directed towards the sick berth.

'The Sub ain't so clever. Lost a lot of blood. That hit on the forehead knocked him out,' Taff replied, shielding his cigarette from the wind, 'but he's chattin' alright now..'

There were grimaces and slow shrugs, a genuine sympathy. The young officer was well liked, a major part of the team. They relaxed within the screen, the sun a warming glow on closed eyelids.

Leaving his cabin and returning to the bridge, Thorburn knew the patrol was almost over. The ship's company had been thrown in at the deep end. Some of the hands were showing great promise and the longer this war continued the better they would become. Chief Petty Officer Falconer was a gem. A man in his position played one of the most important roles on the ship, and he was a stalwart. Thorburn knew that Falconer's methods were a little unusual. In general he was patient, gentle with the

44

few youngsters they had on board, but 'try it on' and Thorburn's defaulters table awaited. He was proper Navy, and thank God for it.

'Set course for Dover, Number One,' ordered Thorburn, 'and I want the crew alert for enemy aircraft.'

'Aye aye, sir,' Armstrong replied. 'Gun crews are still at Defence Stations.'

Brackendale, turning hard to starboard, moved north to leave Hastings shrouded in a warm haze on her port quarter. Folkestone drifted by as the turbines powered them up the coast, those on the bridge buffeted by the wind, the ship rising and falling to the undulating waves.

'Smoke rising at Dover, sir,' reported a bridge lookout.

Thorburn spotted the black cloud hanging over the town, wondering how bad the bombing had been. Yesterday, the railway station had suffered a near miss, and the lines entering the tunnel had been damaged, bad enough to prevent trains running until after dark. He decided to remain on the bridge; the written report could wait. Yesterday's return home had become a major engagement. They'd be ready for it this time.

Verner von Holtzmann finished his inspection of the ship's main armament, dismissed his entourage and took a moment to survey Bolougne's dockside facilities. He was pleased with the night's work. He had completed the second leg of his journey without being detected, even though a British destroyer had come close to unveiling their position; and although a Schnellboat had been destroyed, his ship had slipped quietly into the harbour.

Tonight, he thought, and smiled to himself, he would complete the exercise and join forces with his E-boat flotilla. It was said that Cherbourg had many good wines, and the best seafood. And the women could be very friendly; he grinned. . , so it was said.

Chapter Four . . Enemy Contact.

Brackendale had just completed tying up to the Western Pier when a vigilant watch keeper announced the approach of Captain (D). By the time he arrived the Cox'n's side party was neatly assembled and he was duly piped aboard. Brief formalities over, Thorburn ushered him towards the wardroom.

'Your cabin if you please,' said Pendleton, pausing to let Thorburn lead the way.

'Report's not quite ready yet, sir,' offered Thorburn as they settled round the table.

'We'll catch up with that later,' Pendleton said, 'something's come up.' He reached in to his briefcase, pulled out a file and selected a few pages. For a moment he studied Thorburn's passive expression, the casually relaxed posture, but those eyes were keenly alert to every detail of their meeting. 'That German destroyer,' he began. 'Our agents in France reported tracking its movement from Calais last night, possibly started out from Bremerhaven. We understand he made it to Bolougne. You just missed him.'

Thorburn said nothing. He was well aware of his shortcomings.

Pendleton shuffled his papers and dropped a couple onto the table. 'That's a German press release, fairly recent. As you can see, we believe the commander is FlotillaKapitan Werner von Holtzmann. If we're right, he's had a lot of experience with E-boats.'

Thorburn leant forward and swivelled the photograph towards him. The slightly grainy image was of a mature, weather beaten seaman wearing full dress uniform and staring out over the bows of a warship. The Iron Cross hung conspicuously round his neck.

Pendleton leaned back and stroked his beard. 'We think he'll take command of operations down at Cherbourg, call it an educated guess.' He paused, waiting for Thorburn to react, but getting no response, added grimly, 'one of the few commanders to give a good account of himself at Narvik.'

'So, where do we go from here, sir?' asked Thorburn, pushing the paperwork back across the table. The sound of footsteps passed by outside the cabin, shouted orders from overhead receding towards the quarterdeck.

Pendleton followed the sound with his eyes before he continued. 'When our night convoys pass through the channel they have their own close escort. We're going to introduce a different tactic. I want you out as a screening patrol. Your job will be to give additional support to the escort, either to intercept, or to spring a surprise. Whatever the situation dictates.'

'Yes, sir,' Thorburn said politely, sensing there was more to come.

Pendleton rose to his feet, paced round the chair and leant across the back of it. 'The bloody Germans are roaming around as if they own the Channel, and the fleet are tied up in Scapa Flow.' He stood back thrusting his hands deep into the uniform pockets, eyes glittering as he stared belligerently at Thorburn. 'If you can intercept a raid before it reaches the convoy, so well and good. The likelihood is, you'll be patrolling nearby when the alarm goes up. In that case you do everything in your power to upset the apple cart.'

'Right, sir,' Thorburn answered. 'I'm sure we'll be

more than capable.'

'Good.' Pendleton gave an enthusiastic nod in response. 'Now, reference last night.'

Thorburn tensed, waiting for the criticism.

'That was a fine effort out there, even though we didn't find Holtzmann.'

Thorburn breathed out quietly, relaxed a little, relieved at Pendleton's assessment. 'Sorry, sir, I wasn't happy leaving that U-boat, not knowing if we'd scuppered it.'

Pendleton dismissed his concerns with a wave of his hand. 'In your situation, I'd have done the same, it was much more important to find that destroyer.'

So there it was, Thorburn thought, all that anxiety he'd felt over losing the U-boat, and Pendleton had dismissed it out of hand.

Pendleton stood up. 'I think that's what's called using your initiative. Shall we try the wardroom, I think it's time I met your officers.'

'Yes, sir, this way,' and Thorburn stepped into the corridor..

Later that night, in accordance with Pendleton's orders, *Brackendale* set out for the enemy coast. The dark, early hours of the following morning found her cruising ten miles northwest of Cherbourg. A strong wind swept the channel, the rough sea breaking in to white feathers. Low cloud brought occasional bursts of driving rain; visibility reduced to a couple of ships lengths.

For the watch-keepers and lookouts, this was a difficult time. Water found its way inside everything, sodden clothing, clinging and cold, binoculars misted with damp on the lens; worst of all, a constantly changing horizon. A stream of orders issued from the bridge, engine revolutions altered in the expectation of propellers riding out of the waves, and terse reminders to keep the ship's heading on course.

Standing by the chart table, Thorburn reminded himself of the convoy steaming up the channel. Twelve freighters, three oilers, and a best speed of perhaps six to eight knots. The escort consisted of a corvette, H.M.S. *Cornflower*, along with a armed trawler, and a lone tug to assist as required. No lights, trusting in each other's positioning, and tired eyes looking for faint shadows in the rain. Dangerous work.

'Signal, sir,' came a sharp call from behind.

'Read it,' Thorburn ordered.

'From Captain (D) sir. Message reads, "German destroyer reported to have departed Bolougne 23.45 hours, stop, with E-boats." Message ends.'

'Very well, acknowledge,' said Thorburn, sensing the danger behind the predicted threat. Were they out on the hunt or moving down to Cherbourg? He turned to the bridge messenger. 'Ask the First Lieutenant to join me.'

Armstrong arrived as the destroyer lurched unexpectedly and he stumbled forward reaching the chart table with uncontrolled haste.

'Ah, Number One,' Thorburn greeted him, 'a bit lively.'

'Yes, sir,' Armstrong replied, a sheepish grin covering his embarrassment.

Thorburn jabbed at the chart, circling his finger to show their proximity to Bolougne. 'He's out, Number One. Somewhere out here is our German destroyer and a few of his small friends.'

'Right, sir,' Armstrong hesitated. 'So what now?'

Thorburn ran a hand across his jaw, a tight smile

playing round his lips, 'My instinct tells me he'll want to make a good start, make an impression. I think we ought to move north.' He looked up at Armstrong, eyes glinting in the dim light of the chart table. 'He might try to attack up there,' and again he pointed to the chart, indicating the area southeast of the Isle of Wight.

Another rainsquall lashed the bridge and they both ducked from the stinging needles.

'A hunter's night,' mused Thorburn squinting into the darkness. 'But we just might give him more than he bargained for.'

An hour later *Brackendale* made brief contact with *Cornflower* as the convoy passed east below the Isle of Wight. Her commander reported no casualties, although one of the oilers had developed engine problems. The armed tug had remained on standby as the ship lost speed and was about to escort her to the boom-nets off Portsmouth.

Thorburn acknowledged the situation and with a brief, 'Good luck,' increased speed to sheer away southeast.

'Tea, sir?' his steward queried from behind and Thorburn gratefully accepted the hot mug.

'Thank you, Sinclair,' he said, allowing the sweet warmth to linger on his tongue, 'just the job.' His steward nodded, a faint smile brightening the angular face, and he retreated to the captain's quarters.

The storm front moved on up the channel, but the angry sea remained, heavy waves rolling in from astern. Arriving on station a mile to the south off the starboard wing of the convoy, Thorburn reduced speed to eight knots, matching that of the convoy. *Brackendale* responded by mimicking the ride of a roller coaster,

51

quickly followed by a stream of obscenities as the conditions deteriorated below decks.

The warship settled into a period of tense anticipation. Waiting and watching, wishing for something to happen, not knowing how contact would be made. Below the waterline, deep inside their steel walls the engineers and stokers coaxed the machinery in answer to the bridge telegraph, alert to the slightest change in the turbine's revolutions. Steering the set course the helmsman watched his compass, their every move plotted in the chartroom. For many aboard *Brackendale*, this was a time of trying to calm the nerves, almost worse than being in action.

Richard Thorburn suffered with his nerves. Not the full-blown terror type, but the nauseous, pit of the stomach feeling of weakness prior to the beginning of action. Then he would need those extra intakes of air before another cigarette, forcing the anxiety to recede. Not that anyone knew. Outwardly there was never a hint.

'Good morning, Number One!' Thorburn said loudly, as Armstrong arrived on the compass platform.

'Morning, sir,' the First Lieutenant mumbled. The destroyer rolled wickedly and Armstrong steadied himself against the compass housing.

Thorburn sat in the chair staring straight ahead, the tip of a cigarette glowing red in his right hand below the bridge rail. The high-pitched ping of the asdic gave a reassuring background to the windswept bridge, and the yeoman, signallers and messengers swayed with the ship's motion.

'Port fifteen,' ordered Thorburn.

'Port fifteen, aye, sir' from the wheelhouse.

'Midships.'

'Midships, aye, sir. Course oh-eight-oh.'

They zigzagged on, holding station south of the convoy; the routine of ship handling and the quiet words between watch keepers the only interruptions. Very occasionally a lookout reported sighting a ship to the north, a freighter in the starboard column wallowing through the following seas.

A brilliant flash burst into an explosion of white and orange as a deep rumble struck their eardrums. Ahead of the port bow the horizon turned a deep red and then pulsed in intensity. Thorburn's voice cut across the stunned silence.

'Full ahead together!' he snapped at the wheelhouse voice-pipe. 'Action Stations!' he called, mind working overtime, assessing what had happened. Too far ahead to be a hit on the convoy . . , must have been H.M.S. *Swift*, the minesweeper clearing the channel.

'Guns' crews closed up!' Howard reported as he made for the Tower. Thorburn wondered where the German flotilla was. They must have seen the explosion, the night was lit up for miles. Maybe something happened as *Swift* tried to clear a mine. There had been no gunfire.

Armstrong returned a bridge telephone to its hook and turned to the Captain. 'Closed up to Action Stations, sir,' he said. The ship was now a weapon, a destroyer at Thorburn's disposal.

'Very well,' nodded Thorburn. 'We'll see what's happening up ahead.' Already that anxious sensation had left him, replaced by the relief of action.

Flying spray whipped over the bridge-screen as she lifted her bows. Thorburn and Armstrong stood side-by-side watching the ruddy glow diminish, straining to determine the true meaning behind the explosion.

A lookout wiped his glasses and locked his body to the motion of the swaying ship, training his lens on the fiery glow up ahead. The black silhouette of the ship's mast and funnel appeared, shrouded in a haze of red-flecked smoke. The remaining lookouts deliberately avoided the glare of the fires, protecting their eyes from the bright light. Up in the Director Tower, Lieutenant Howard saw it all. The floating remains of a minesweeper, down by the head and leaning to starboard, a whaler swaying free of its davits.

Brackendale ran on, the bow wave surging down her flanks, lifting out astern.

'Starboard ten . . Midships . . , steer one-one-oh,' ordered Thorburn, easing the destroyer on a course to take them about four hundred yards south of the wreck. Less than a mile away, and now they could make out a boat in the water.

'Half ahead together,' said Thorburn, 'make sure Asdic are on the sweep, Number One.' He thought for a moment. ' Yeoman. Make a signal to Portsmouth Command, "H.M.S. *Swift* sinking", give our position and copy that to *Cornflower*.' He paused, and as the Yeoman hurried away Thorburn made plans for the survivors, even if help was on its way. 'Number One,' he said, leaning to look over the port bridge wing. 'Get a boat in the water and tell them to do the best they can.'

'Aye aye, sir,' Armstrong acknowledged, hurrying off and calling for the bosun's mate as he slithered down the ladder. A loud reply echoed from amidships, and with a crew of volunteers, they gathered at the whaler's station.

'Slow ahead,' ordered Thorburn, looking aft down the port side to the small party of seaman hoisting the boat overboard. The bosun's mate stood in the stern directing operations and the four crewmen waited to feel the water under her keel. With the destroyer barely moving ahead the boat dropped the last foot into the waves and made off towards the survivors.

Thorburn saw Armstrong lift his hand to the bridge. 'Full ahead,' he called to the voice-pipe and *Brackendale* surged forward, peeling away to the southeast.

Behind them the minesweeper vented an enormous cloud of steam from her quarterdeck, the stern section lifting skywards before slowly sliding into the depths. Darkness replaced the harsh radiance of the burning ship, just a few pinpricks of life-jacket lights drifting on the sea.

Thorburn tore himself away from the grim spectacle. His ship's company lived with the fear of going down; they didn't need to dwell on the reality. He swung round as Armstrong clambered up to the portside bridge wing.

'Everything under control?' asked Thorburn.

Armstrong nodded. 'Volunteers, sir, they're the most experienced.'

Thorburn moved closer, lowering his voice. 'Right, Number One, I'm going to make a fast sweep in this area.' His thumb jabbed towards the bows. Quieter still he said, 'I'd be grateful if you'd take a quick tour round the crew. Make sure they're on their toes, bit of encouragement wouldn't go amiss.'

'Aye, aye, sir,' he said flatly, 'I'll see to it now.'

'Number One,' Thorburn whispered fiercely. 'A lot of these men won't have seen that sort of thing before. Let's try and settle them down.'

Corkscrewing through the rollers *Brackendale* hunted southwards, her human cargo poised to deal with whatever danger threatened. On the bridge only the

55

occasional correction to the helm broke the windswept silence, a fiercely focused concentration by the remainder of the watch keepers.

Thorburn stood in the middle of it all. On the compass platform he gained a slight height advantage over the rest of the bridge personnel, quietly detached as commander of the ship. It gave him that small space in which to think. Pendleton had tasked him with engaging the enemy free of the necessity to give close support to the convoy. *Brackendale* was not a fleet destroyer. She had been primarily designed as a 'close escort', and the normal practice of mounting offensive torpedo tubes amidships had been waived in favour of greater anti-aircraft weaponry. He knew they had a good rate of firepower, with twin four-inch guns fore and aft, but that might not be enough. The problem was how to counter the threat of the German destroyer. He frowned as he strove to picture a high-speed engagement with the enemy flotilla.

He might be able to attempt a tactical manoeuvre with the aim of drawing the enemy away from the convoy, and hopefully, a first strike to inflict as much damage as possible. The compass showed they were sailing due south, and checking the time he realised the pre-dawn grey would soon be lighting the horizon.

A messenger appeared at his elbow. 'Signal, sir,' he reported, standing rigidly to attention.

Thorburn took the message and bending to the poor light of the chart table digested the news that another minesweeper, H.M.S. *Marksman* had put out from Portsmouth. She would take over minesweeping duties and the armed tug was now to remain with the convoy to assist survivors. The transmission had been for *Cornflower*, his wireless office guessing that Thorburn would be interested.

'There's no reply,' he said, handing the note back to the messenger, and then added, 'Well done, lad. Tell the wireless room to keep me informed of anything useful.'

Armstrong arrived back on the bridge. 'Done the rounds, sir, and managed to get some hot drinks from the galley.'

'Thank you, Number One,' Thorburn said. He patted Armstrong on the arm, 'I would like to have done it myself . . .' and moved over to his chair.

'Light showing, Red, four-oh!' called Jones from the port bridge-wing.

Thorburn raised his binoculars to the direction indicated. White breakers whipping off the waves swam across his vision, the vague movement of heaving water fading in to the darkness. 'Can you still see it, Jones?' he queried sharply.

'No, sir,' said Jones gruffly, 'but it was definitely there, sir.'

Thorburn heard the indignation in Jones' reply and smiled to himself. He leaned to the bank of voice-pipes. 'Guns', sweep the port side,' he ordered.

'Port side, aye, sir.'

For a moment Thorburn paused to watch the range-finder director tower as it swivelled to the port side.

'There it is, sir!' Jones shouted excitedly. 'Red four-five, range four thousand.'

From the voice-pipe, 'Bridge, Guns, I have an E-boat in sight. Looks to be another ahead of it.' After a pause, 'Range, three-eight-oh, course . . , oh-five-oh.'

Thorburn lifted his glasses again focusing over the port beam and scanning steadily round toward the bows. Finally he managed to make out the white wake of an E-boat, intermittent in the heavy seas. Then, he too saw what appeared to be a torchlight flashing briefly. He lowered his binoculars and tried to asses the situation. 'Number One,' he said, moving to the chart table, 'looks like we've found our little friends.'

'Yes, sir,' said Armstrong, leaning over the chart. He traced a line with his forefinger, sweeping along to stop at a point ahead of the convoy. 'Could be that they'll meet the convoy about here, sir.'

'True,' Thorburn began, rubbing his chin, 'but where's the destroyer?'

'Probably leading the way. Looked as if they were line astern.'

Thorburn inclined his head. 'And if they're too busy looking ahead we've a good chance of getting in behind them.' They looked up at each other, weighing up the options.

'Be like a hornet's nest,' grinned Thorburn, but hesitated when he saw the grimace on Armstrong's face. 'Come on, Number One, spit it out.'

The First Lieutenant looked back to the chart table. 'Sorry, I was just wondering how much the odds are in the enemy's favour.'

Thorburn heard the doubts but chose to remain silent.

'Sir, that ship is a sight quicker than we are. I still think we were a bit lucky with that E-boat at Bolougne,' he faltered, but persisted, 'our gunners did a great job but how we didn't get torpedoed, God only knows.'

Thorburn tilted his head to one side, knowing that Armstrong was struggling to be openly critical. He reached out to rest a hand on the Lieutenant's shoulder, 'Sometimes I make decisions that might not be the best,' he said. 'But right now I think the advantage might just be slanted towards us, either way I can't allow the enemy to mix it with the convoy.' He waited for Armstrong's response, seeing the emotions playing across his face.

'Yes, sir,' he said finally, returning Thorburn's fixed gaze, 'I'll buy that.'

'Good man,' said Thorburn. 'Let's see if we can come round on their starboard quarter.' He winked at Armstrong's solemn expression and stepped over to the compass binnacle.

'Port ten,' he ordered.

'Port ten, aye aye, sir,' the Coxswain replied and *Brackendale* began a swing to the enemy's southern flank.

'Guns,' snapped Thorburn, 'what's their speed?'

'Twenty knots, sir,' came the reply, 'range, . . four thousand five hundred.'

'Right, 'Guns' I'm going to try and get us in to fifteen hundred yards,' Thorburn explained, 'if they see us before that, I'll try and draw them south, away from the convoy.'

'Aye aye, sir,' said 'Guns', and Thorburn took a deep breath. They were ready. The decisions he would soon make, calculated or reactionary, right or wrong, was what merited his command. All his years of learning had culminated in the appointment to this destroyer; all he'd ever wanted.

Brackendale hammered on, lifting through the waves, the rigging whining on the mast behind them. Training left, the forward guns probed outboard on the portside. They closed the range, steadily gaining on their quarry.

'Destroyer in sight,' called 'Guns' down the voice-pipe, 'Range, two thousand five hundred.'

Thorburn raised his binoculars, focused beyond the

59

port beam, and spotted the vague outline of the hostile warship. It was a large destroyer, longer than the Royal Navy's 'Tribal' class, and those guns definitely outclassed *Brackendale*'s. 'Someone's asleep,' he said pointedly, picking out the detail of the stern gun mounting. 'Two ducklings and old mother goose,' he offered to those within earshot. 'Lookouts!' he barked, ' stay sharp, there might be another E-boat sneaking about.'

'Target changing course,' from the director tower, 'turning north.

Thorburn frowned to himself, that wasn't supposed to happen. *Brackendale* would now be trailing in their wake, unable to bring all guns to bear. 'Port twenty,' he growled to the wheelhouse. Forced to change tack, he would bring the ship back under their tail, enabling his guns to train to the right, across the starboard side. As she steered slightly west-of-north, he centred the steering.

'Midships!'

'Midships, sir, course three-one-oh.'

'Guns', what's the range now?'

'Two thousand yards, sir.'

'Very well.' Thorburn pondered for a moment. 'Guns', I'll take control of the Pompom and machine guns, you concentrate the main armament on the destroyer.'

'Aye aye, sir,' Howard answered.

'Number One,' Thorburn called to Armstrong. 'Tell the secondary gun crews to take their orders from me.'

Brackendale's bow buried itself into the wall of another wave, seawater foaming down the fo'c'sle deck. Around the ship men braced themselves for the action to come, a few silent with their thoughts, others throwing ribald obscenities at their mates, the laughter a touch too loud.

'They've seen us, sir,' called Jones, and Thorburn turned to see the two E-boats peeling out of formation. The first in line veered to port, the second to starboard, a tactic designed to divide *Brackendale*'s firepower. In the same instant Thorburn saw a brief flash from the quarterdeck of the German destroyer.

'Open fire!' he ordered, and the immediate crash of the four-inch guns thundered out from the ship. He reached for the megaphone and shouted at the midships mounting, 'Pompom! Take the starboard E-boat!' The starboard machine guns joined in and glowing tracer arced out at the powerboat, already bows on to them. A plume of water slammed on the quarterdeck as the enemy destroyer bracketed their stern.

'Yeoman!' Thorburn called above the din. 'Send to Admiralty. "Enemy in sight. Am engaging," and give them our position.'

He watched the other E-boat on the portside bouncing over the waves, two of the gun positions smashing small calibre rounds into *Brackendale*'s upper deck. Bullets ricocheted and whined about the bridge, adding to the difficulty of fighting the ship.

'Jameson!' Thorburn shouted to the bridge machine gunner. 'Give it all you've got!' his outstretched arm pointing to the E-boat. The Lewis gun crackled into action, shell cases rattling on the deck.

'Torpedoes off the starboard beam!' Armstrong called to Thorburn.

'Hard a starboard!' The forward guns crashed another salvo at the enemy destroyer. Listing heavily to port *Brackendale* fought her way to starboard. In the darkness of the rough sea all eyes attempted to track the torpedoes.

'Midships!' Thorburn said, hoping they were pointing

at empty waves, throwing a quick look at the opposing destroyer. *Brackendale* was now beam on to the German's stern, presenting a broad target to hit.

Hidden behind the funnel the Pompom fell silent, unable to get a bearing on the E-boat.

'Torpedoes off the port bow!' someone shouted, and Thorburn leaned over the corner of the bridge as the two lethal cylinders slid menacingly down their port side.

'Port twenty,' he ordered, with the German destroyer still uppermost in his thoughts. The Pompom kicked back into action, the distinctive staccato bark joining the lighter sound of the machine guns.

Thorburn tasted cordite and wiped his lips. He realised he was breathing hard, the intense pressure of danger.

'E-boat withdrawing at speed, sir,' Armstrong said, lowering his glasses. He ducked his head as a stream of orange-white tracer whipped in from the port beam, splintering the bridge-screen as it smashed across the bridge.

Jameson gave a shout and slumped sideways, the Lewis gun pointing skywards.

Thorburn saw an opportunity, knew it was wrong even before he moved to grab the gun and elbowed a seaman out of the way. Sighting on the E-boat as it swung towards them, he pulled the trigger. The machine gun kicked into his shoulders and he clenched his teeth as the bullets tore into the boat, raking over the forward gun and flashing off the bridge.

'Sir!' Armstrong shouted in his ear. 'Sir!' he yelled again, and Thorburn felt him tug his arm. 'The destroyer's pulling away.'

Thorburn cursed and released the trigger, the seaman taking his place. 'Tell 'Guns' I want everything on this E-boat!' He strode to the forebridge as another near miss erupted off the starboard bow.

'Port twenty!' he ordered curtly and looked at the forward twin gun mounting, watched it traverse to port. He wondered if the E-boat had fired its torpedoes, whether they had missed, or maybe failed. Closer now, less than a thousand yards. Smothered in tracer, sparks glinting along the hull, the enemy machine guns still returned an accurate stream of fire.

Brackendale crashed out an explosive broadside and the E-boat erupted in a ball of fire. When the water settled the boat had gone, obliterated.

'Bloody marvellous.' Thorburn grinned through the smoke. 'Nice shooting, 'Guns!'

Fifty yards ahead of their starboard bow more geysers ballooned skywards. A fine drizzle began to fall and the German destroyer's vague shape began to fade from sight.

'Cease fire,' Thorburn ordered reluctantly, standing back as Jameson was carried from the bridge.

'Number One, damage report, please. Yeoman, make a signal to Captain (D), "Enemy destroyer undamaged, course oh-four-oh, speed thirty knots," and repeat our position. Copy that to *Cornflower*.'

The signal pad closed and the Chief Yeoman made his way to the wireless room. The damage reports came in slowly. Thorburn acknowledged that most were superficial although a depth charge hoist had been destroyed; reloading would be less consistent.

Armstrong returned from 'Doc' Waverly and reported five casualties. Jameson was the worst with a hit in the chest, the others suffering minor injuries.

Thorburn slumped in to the bridge chair. Behind a cupped hand he lit a cigarette and tried to sum up the situation. Shadowing on the same course as the destroyer, but lacking the speed to catch it. One E-boat destroyed and the other last seen fleeing for home. His biggest concern was his failure to divert the enemy away from the convoy. Rain splashed through the broken bridge-screen and he pushed his cap back, enjoying the cool freshness.

He frowned, knowing that he'd been outmanoeuvred, and he was worried about the whaler's crew.

'Signal, sir,' he heard from the back of the bridge and Armstrong offered him the message.

'No, you read it,' he said, pushing it back.

The First Lieutenant cleared his throat and said loudly, "Rendezvous with convoy. Take station with H.M.S. *Marksman*. Air cover with you soon." That's all, sir.'

Thorburn banged his hand on to the arm of the chair. 'Sometimes,' he said sharply, 'I wonder who's side they're on!' He looked up at Armstrong seeing the surprise in his face. 'Sorry, Number One,' he laughed self-consciously. 'Set course for the convoy. Best possible speed, if you please.' Hopefully the boat's crew had been picked up. To the east he noticed the first grey of dawn and in that moment, the rain stopped. The exhilaration of engaging the enemy faded and he sought the comfort of his chair. He wondered how Pendleton would view the recent events; in his own mind they had given a good account of themselves. Unfortunately, what the commanders did at sea sometimes looked a whole lot different to those on shore.

Swivelling in his chair he found himself drawn to Able Seaman Jones. His was the first sighting of the enemy flotilla, just a momentary glimpse of an unguarded light. He called him over.

'Yes, sir,' said Jones, standing a little uneasily in such

personal contact with the skipper.

'Well done, Jones,' Thorburn said warmly, 'first class job of yours. That wasn't an easy sighting, sorry for doubting you.'

'That's alright, sir,' said Jones. 'Doubted it too as I reported.'

'Well, it was a good shout and I won't forget it.'

'Thank you, sir,' Jones mumbled, obviously embarrassed by the praise.

'Very well,' Thorburn said, seeing how uncomfortable he'd become. 'Carry on.'

Jones saluted smartly and returned to the port bridge wing. Thorburn watched the swagger in his stride. Be all over the ship soon.

Heading northeast *Brackendale* hurried through the calmer seas, finally bathed in the weak sunlight of early morning.

'Signal, sir,' the Chief Yeoman reported.

Thorburn took the hand written note and after a moments pause he looked up smiling at those on the bridge.

'That was from *Marksman*. Her Captain stopped to recover survivors from the *Swift* and all our people are on board.'

A general murmur of thanks to the *Marksman* buzzed around and Armstrong sent a messenger to pass the word to the ship's company.

'Starboard watch to defence stations, I think, Number One,' said Thorburn, 'and let's get some breakfast in the crew.' He looked up at the people filling the bridge space and added, 'Some hot drinks up here wouldn't go amiss.'

Aye, sir,' said Armstrong. He stretched and noticed the

clouds were clearing from the west. He loosened the lightweight towel that stopped the rain running down his neck and shrugged the tenseness from his shoulders. With the sun on their backs and with hot drinks inside them, the tension of the last few hours slipped away.

Grabbing a bite to eat, the Cox'n left the galley to check on the crew. He poked his head into the sick berth, the disinfected smell of cleanliness strikingly pungent. Jameson was on the main operating table, his chest heavily bandaged, but his eyes were open and he managed a half smile in Falconer's direction. Able Seaman Patterson, loader on the forward guns, peered out from a bloodied bandage. He sat next to a table with 'Doc' in attendance, surgical tweezers to hand. Falconer nodded and squeezed back to the corridor, closed the door with a gentle click. He never spent longer than necessary in the sick berth area. On a mission during the Spanish civil war he'd been hit in the thigh by a piece of bomb shrapnel. It had been removed without anaesthetic. He sighed, rubbed his leg, and straightening to his full height, continued his rounds.

Thorburn stood with his hands resting on the back of his bridge chair. Either side of him the lookouts were focused over the front screen, and with the bow wave rising higher than the fo'c'sle, braced themselves with elbows and knees. His own glasses had been in constant use but now hung on his chest, a small doubt niggling at the back of his mind.

The plot showed that *Brackendale* should be within sighting distance of the convoy. For the last ten minutes, with clear skies and fair visibility they had scoured the horizon. Not even the slightest sign of smoke, just an empty sea. He paced back to the chart table staring

66

blankly at the line of intersection. A change of course? Already in danger? A multitude of questions and no answer.

Werner von Holtzmann fretted while he headed south for Cherbourg. Daylight, it had come so quickly. So close to England he had to break away. The Royal Air Force were too much of a threat and Admiral Krause had warned him of senseless bravado. Reluctantly, Holtzmann swallowed his pride and withdrew. There would be other chances to take on the Royal Navy.

Chapter Five .. An Old Friend.

'Ship! Bearing, red-one-hundred,' a lookout called, and Thorburn hurried to the port wing. Sure enough his glasses revealed the ungainly silhouette of a freighter purposefully pushing her way east. Striding back to the voice-pipes he leaned down and said, 'Port ten,' watching as the bows swung round towards the merchantman.

'Midships,' he ordered as *Brackendale* came on to the new course. 'Steady as you go,' Thorburn said, and after a few minutes, straightened in satisfaction as his earlier doubts evaporated.

'*Cornflower* signalling, sir,' said Wilson on the port signal lamp. "Glad . to . see . you," he read out, and clattered a short acknowledgement.

'Make, "sorry we're late, uninvited guests," and check our position with the Chief,' Thorburn said. As the corvette emerged from round the freighter, the entire convoy emerged, spread out to the north.

Lieutenant Robert Armstrong, having cajoled the galley into organising breakfast, reported back to the bridge just as *Brackendale* turned east along the convoy's southern flank. Out on the port beam he watched *Cornflower* riding the swell remembering his six weeks aboard one of her sister ships. Lively in anything but a flat calm, they were cramped and uncomfortable, but were now proving to be extremely useful as convoy escorts. Unusually the mast had been positioned directly in front of the bridge, aesthetically hopeless, but it did make for easy identification.

He noticed the captain was back in his chair on the forebridge and wondered how he was coping. Constantly on call, with no real respite from the demands on his time, and the responsibility of fighting the ship. He deliberately stepped forward and stood at the front bridge-screen, swaying to the motion of the ship.

Thorburn looked up. 'Hello Number One, everything in order?'

Armstrong nodded. 'Yes, sir, the galley's doing a roaring trade,' he hesitated, 'I can take the bridge if you want, sir,' he offered.

'I think I just might take you up on that,' Thorburn said, rising to his feet. 'We're making for the *Marksman*. I think I'll have a wash and shave, and a bite to eat. Call me when we're on station.' Armstrong again felt the pat on his shoulder as Thorburn walked behind him. 'You have the bridge, Number One.'

He heard the captain's steps leave the bridge and propped his elbows on the bridge rail, enjoying the moment. The destroyer rose and fell rhythmically, humming through the waves, the sun shimmering off the sea. He smiled to himself and moved round to check their bearing against the compass. Thirty minutes later, with the convoy receding into the distance, the starboard lookout gave a call.

'Ship, bearing, green-one-oh, seven thousand yards. It's the *Marksman*, sir.'

Armstrong raised his glasses to confirm the sighting and saw her 'minesweeping' pennant flying at the mast. That warning was very clear and he had no hesitation in guiding *Brackendale* to the south.

'Starboard ten,' he ordered.

'Starboard ten, aye, sir.'

Armstrong waited for the bows to come round. 'Steady,' he said.

'Steady as she goes, aye, sir. Steering oh-three-five degrees.'

'Very well,' Armstrong said, and waited a moment longer to check their course. As they closed in to what he judged as 'on station' he rang down to reduce engine revolutions, matching the speed of *Marksman*. Satisfied that all was well, he called the Captain.

Thorburn bounced on to the bridge and noted the minesweeper about half a mile off the port beam. 'Thank you, Number One,' he said brightly. 'I have the bridge.'

Armstrong responded with a brief handover of their course, speed and position before making his excuses to go below.

It was a beautiful day and Thorburn relaxed into his chair. The doubts of the previous hours ebbed away and he accepted the imperative of reinforcing the convoy screen. Pendleton was obviously aware of the situation and whatever the outcome, he had done his best.

'Aircraft! Bearing red-one-oh!'

Thorburn raised the binoculars and found a pair of Hurricanes approaching from the northeast, possibly out of Manston.

'Friendlies!' he announced quickly, calming the sudden activity round the guns. The fighters were coming in at about fifteen hundred feet. As Thorburn watched them flying in, it struck him that the enemy destroyer must have withdrawn during the last of the bad weather before dawn. Daylight and the threat of air cover had put paid to the German's exploits and he'd scampered for home.

About half a mile away, the leader of the two

Hurricanes dropped a wing and swept down to almost sea level, leaving his wingman to fly on at the same altitude. Roaring between the two warships, only a fraction higher than *Brackendale*'s bridge, the pilot raised a gloved hand in salute. A loud cheer and shouts of 'Up the Air Force!' rippled round the ship, arms waving in reply. A waggle of the wings, a glint of sun reflecting off the cockpit, and the pilot swept the fighter skywards to rejoin his wing-man. Banking gracefully to the south both planes momentarily showed their camouflaged fuselage and clearly identified roundels.

Thorburn turned away with a broad grin wrinkling his tanned features. After only a few days on patrol the ship had already lost her pristine newness. The crew had fought the boat well, the long hours of training overcoming their sense of awe. For some of them, thrown into a life of naval discipline far removed from their civilian occupations, it must have been a shock. At the forefront of their newfound aptitude was the Coxswain, and the Captain knew that in Falconer he had been gifted a wonderfully capable seaman.

Quietly, tirelessly he had supported his executive officers without question. Thorburn knew that on more than one occasion Falconer had surreptitiously changed a naïve order to ensure it complied more thoroughly with shipboard routine. Even now he was in the paint locker detailing a small party to a clean and paint job. Normally the off-duty hands would tend to these minor repairs in harbour but they had quickly come to the conclusion that Dover was never off duty. Everything from Harwich to Portsmouth was in the front line and Dover was particularly hard pressed.

By 08.00 hours, about fifteen miles due north of their

position, the convoy sighted Beachy Head, the high cliffs just visible through a slight haze.

'*Marksman* signalling, sir,' said a Yeoman from the port side. His lamp clattered a brief response before *Marksman*'s lamp flashed a message.

'Reads, "Channel swept, returning to Portsmouth. Dover minesweeper ahead. Do you want your waifs and strays?" End of message.'

Thorburn smiled at the choice of words, warming to whoever captained the *Marksman*. To the Yeoman, he said, 'Reply, "forever in your debt. Bosun's chair?" '

Within a surprisingly short time the two ships had closed to within twenty feet. Heaving lines were tossed between the decks and in typical seaman like fashion, a bosun's chair was quickly rigged. As the warships settled to a matching speed, and with the sea squeezing angrily between the steel hulls, a first unfortunate was hauled over to *Brackendale*. Ironically, the last to be swung precariously over the white turmoil was the Bosun's mate, greeted to a standing ovation by both crews.

Loudhailer to his lips Thorburn's voice boomed across to the *Marksman*'s bridge. 'Hope they behaved themselves?' he called.

'Worked like Trojans,' came the reply, 'glad to have had 'em on board.'

Thorburn heard the faint ring of the telegraph within the minesweeper and she began to widen the gap. He saw the Captain raise his hailer.

'Good hunting!' echoed over the water and a cap waved in farewell.

'Thank you and God speed!' shouted Thorburn, and lifted his cap in reply. The minesweeper sheered away to the north, her White Ensign standing out from the signal mast. Dangerous work, thought Thorburn, not for the faint hearted.

The pair of Hurricanes that had been circling in the distance flew in from the southwest. Reaching the centre of the convoy they banked east to head out over *Brackendale* and on towards Hastings.

'*Westeram* approaching at Red one-oh, sir.' Jones emphasised the sighting with a pointed finger.

Thorburn gazed into the distant haze, squinting against the easterly sun. With the naked eye only a misty horizon marked the boundary between sea and sky. He stared hard at an area of darker grey and then saw the challenge of a bright signal lamp. *Brackendale*'s pendant number flashed back in recognition and they waited while the distance shortened. *Westeram* may have been a relic of the last war but Thorburn watched her bows cleaving the water at what he estimated to be thirty knots. It was a powerful display of seamanship, charging headlong between the rows of ships, dashing about like a newborn foal. Her signal lamp, almost obscured from view, flickered across the water and Thorburn realised that *Cornflower* was the recipient. Closing to the corvette's portside *Westeram*'s bow wave fell away and Thorburn guessed the two captains were in conversation.

'Ships off the port bow!' called Jones, 'looks like *Veracity*, sir, can't make out the other two.'

The Yeoman, working the lever on his signal lamp, filled in the details. 'The minesweeper *Hengis*, sir, and an armed trawler . . . the *Pebble Spratt*, sir.'

Thorburn nodded in conformation, the distant haze beginning to burn off. So, he figured to himself, this must be Dover Command's escort taking over the next leg of the convoy. The south coast was clearly visible and the last remnants of sea mist had dissolved. He glanced up at the cloudless blue sky. Not the best weather for moving through bomb alley, he thought, remembering their previous encounter with Stukas.

'*Veracity* coming along side, sir,' the Yeoman reported.

Thorburn turned to see the warship coming up from astern, her starboard side showing rust streaked anchor ports. The destroyer eased along the port beam until her bridge was level with *Brackendale*'s. Thorburn contemplated the destroyer's approach with a certain amount of disbelief. This was the second ship alongside today and it all looked a bit close. He leaned to the wheelhouse voice-pipe. 'Who's on the wheel?' he asked.

'Leading Seaman Broad, sir.'

'Right, now listen, Broad. *Veracity* is coming along our port side and it'll be fairly close. Watch your heading.'

'Aye aye, sir,' Broad called up the pipe. 'Holding her steady, sir.'

Thorburn turned back to watch *Veracity* edging closer and he felt his body tense as the gap reduced. Now it was less than fifteen feet and he became conscious of his nails digging into his right palm. Did all of these V&W captains throw their ships around in such a cavalier fashion; this one certainly didn't lack confidence. A loudhailer was raised and balanced over the old destroyer's bridge-screen.

'Hello, Richard,' came a deep voice, 'Peter Willoughby here. I hear you've been a bit busy?'

For a moment Thorburn was speechless. There had been little time to find out who captained the other ships of Dover Command but this was entirely unexpected. He

74

and Peter had been shipmates in Hong Kong. Almost inseparable off duty, they were long time friends, matching one another's exploits amongst the genteel society of the colonial territory.

'Good God, Peter, what brings you here?' Thorburn called across. 'Come to join the party?'

'Not likely,' said Willoughby, 'I'm trying to keep out of mischief these days.'

Thorburn laughed at the reference to staying out of trouble. Swimming pools and best uniforms didn't mix well. 'So you say,' he shouted, 'but if you bring that ship any closer we'll all be paddling about!' As if to emphasize the point a jet of seawater shot skywards from between the hulls showering Thorburn and his staff in a torrent of foaming green. *Veracity*'s bridge personnel almost collapsed with laughter.

'If you can hear me, Richard,' Willoughby called, trying to stop laughing, 'Pendleton wants you to stay with us until we're relieved by the escort from Sheerness.' There was a pause as he turned aside and conferred with his people on the bridge. The loud hailer returned.

'I'd like to have you take over from *Cornflower*. Might do more damage from there.'

Thorburn detected the hint of escort command in Willoughby's voice and quickly assured him of his co-operation. 'Right oh, Peter,' he shouted, 'southern flank, anti-aircraft cover.'

'Thanks. *Pebble Spratt* will be astern, *Hengis* sweeping ahead and *Westeram* covering the starboard bow. I'll just put my feet up.' His white teeth grinned across the void, the loudhailer disappeared and Willoughby raised a hand as the old destroyer sheered away to port.

'Starboard twenty, full ahead,' Thorburn ordered, and *Brackendale* lifted her bows to sweep back towards *Cornflower*, the little corvette still cruising south of the convoy. As the distance shortened she turned away, her signal lamp twinkling a message.

'Message reads, "Your turn now, good luck," that's all, sir' said the Yeoman, and Thorburn sent a "God speed" in return.

Throughout this time the merchant ships had maintained their eight knot progress, holding course and ignoring the agile warships showing off in their midst. Eventually the Royal Navy settled into place and under a cloudless blue sky the convoy and its valuable cargo pushed on along the southern coast. Now and then *Veracity* took off to shepherd a straggler back into line, signal flags flying importantly from her mast. Occasionally her lamp flashed a routine change of course and the convoy would make a gentle turn to the new heading. The early afternoon sun bathed the sea in sparkling reflections, glinting off the breaking waves.

Thorburn, one foot braced up on the bridge rail, wondered how long Willoughby had held his command. He was the only son of Sir Leighton Willoughby, a Rear-Admiral currently serving with the Home Fleet at Scapa Flow. Born into a life of relative luxury Peter had been a winning yachtsman before entering the Royal Navy academy at Portsmouth.

'Enemy aircraft!' shouted the starboard lookout, 'Bearing, Green four-five.' He stood with glasses raised aloft and Thorburn, following his direction, saw a formation of enemy aircraft.

'Bombers, sir, look like Heinkels.'

As Thorburn watched he could just make out a group

of escorting Mescherschmitts hovering above the formation; the R.A.F. would have a lot of defending to do, but at least they weren't after the convoy.

Sub-Lieutenant Lawrence, as Officer-of-the-Watch, stood on the slightly elevated compass platform, and young Labatt, having returned from the chartroom waited patiently for any instructions. The Captain, flanked by the First Lieutenant and a lookout, stood at the front bridge-screen. It was hot. Perspiration trickled down their faces, uniforms with dark, damp patches sticking to their skin. Although accustomed to the brightness they all squinted at the blue sky awaiting the inevitable appearance of an aerial attack.

Thorburn was reluctantly beginning to understand that putting to sea in daylight anywhere in the vicinity of Dover, with its narrow strip of sea, almost guaranteed a skirmish with the Luftwaffe.

'Watch your course, Helmsman!' Lawrence barked at the voice-pipe, 'you're wandering!'

'Aye aye, sir,' echoed back from the pipe, 'steering oh-nine-oh degrees, sir.'

'That's better,' said Lawrence, 'hold it on that!' and snapped down the voice-pipe cover. A moment of annoyed disapproval and a small error had been corrected early, and Thorburn took note of the reprimand.

'Enemy aircraft! Bearing, green three-oh!'

Thorburn grabbed for his glasses and picked out a flight of Stuka dive-bombers. 'Bring the ship to Action Stations if you please, Number One,' he said quietly, and once again the crew raced to their posts. No longer the chaotic scenes of those early days, but more, a smooth, well-rehearsed response to the frequent alarms.

Situated above the quarterdeck housing the Pompom's

gunners swung their four-gun mounting towards the aircraft. The planes were out of range, but the team of loaders and layers readied themselves for action.

'Sod this bloody helmet,' said Kendrick, loosening the chinstrap. 'Hurts my bloody neck.'

'I'll hurt your bloody neck if you don't get it on properly.' Leading Seaman Jack Barton's voice clearly allowing no room for argument.

The chinstrap was about to be grudgingly tightened when a hand reached out and slapped the helmet sideways. It resulted in the tin hat slanting down over Kendrick's right eye and his embarrassment raised a chorus of light-hearted jeers from the others. Jack Barton smiled to himself. As a regular he'd seen it all before, but behind the comic result he felt it would now be remembered. He had joined *Brackendale* just before her working up exercises and informed rumour said he'd been aboard a cruiser during the Battle of the River Platte. The entire navy knew the Graff Spee had been damaged and eventually forced to scuttle at the delta mouth outside Montevideo. Not that Barton said much about it, brushing aside any queries with a short, 'got what they deserved', and few pushed it further. Only the Captain knew he'd been recommended for a medal and was awaiting the award.

Thorburn took command of the bridge. He stood at the bank of voice-pipes, the heart of *Brackendale*'s control, and with that familiar flutter in the pit of his stomach, he waited for the enemy's first move. It wasn't long in coming. There were twelve Stukas escorted by six Messershmitt 109s. Arriving at a position above the leading freighter in the starboard column they launched their attack.

'Full ahead both!' Thorburn ordered to the wheelhouse, and the first Stuka dived out of formation. *Westeram* was the first to open fire but her main armament was limited to a low angle of defence, restricting her ability to defend against a high strike. *Hengis* joined in with her Pompoms and the tracer from both ships arced outwards, miniature fireballs chasing the fleeting shadow. The Stuka dived through the anti-aircraft shells beyond *Westeram* as a second dive-bomber plummeted down with a yellow-nosed 109 as escort. A plume of water leapt up close to an oil tanker as *Veracity* raced up from astern the convoy, every gun brought to bear.

Thorburn flinched as *Brackendale*'s guns let fly, the fused shells bursting ahead of the next screaming Stuka. It was obvious that the target was the same tanker. A bomb wobbled downwards and he held his breath, certain it would hit the forward tanks. A large waterspout on the far side of the ship showed where it missed, and Thorburn breathed again. The front of the convoy was almost obliterated by smoke. Ears were deafened by the harsh crackle of gunfire, the screaming whine of aircraft engines. There were shouts of command and warnings too, almost lost in the chaotic din. A Stuka, flying away after dropping its bomb, took a direct hit and disintegrated, blown apart by the explosion. Somehow the tanker sailed on, steadfastly maintaining her speed and position.

Traversing left, the forward four-inch guns swung hard to port, and Thorburn found himself looking down the gun barrels. When they fired again he had to swallow hard to clear the ringing in his ears. The Pompom poured a continuous stream of shells at the attackers, the four barrels recoiling in harmony. The crews worked tirelessly; fetching, carrying and loading; feeding the hungry guns.

Another pair of Stukas dropped in to the assault heading down at a freighter close on *Brackendale*'s port quarter.

'Port ten!' shouted Thorburn, turning the ship to intercept the enemy's line of attack. The starboard Oerlikon latched on to the leading dive-bomber, the main guns swinging to find the target.

'Steady!' Thorburn called to the wheelhouse.

'Steady, aye, sir,' the Coxswain answered, spinning the wheel to cancel the ship's swing.

'As she goes, Cox'n,' ordered Thorburn. He watched as a Messershmitt machine-gunned *Veracity*'s depth charge rails.

Every gun on *Brackendale* opened up at the German planes. Shells and bullets, tracer and shrapnel, everything the ship could use. A Stuka fought its way through and dropped a bomb. A red flash exploded abaft the freighter's bridge, and Thorburn saw thick smoke blowing out over the stern rail.

'Aircraft, Green-eight-oh!' yelled a lookout and Thorburn jumped to the starboard bridge-wing. He ducked under the Lewis gun and shouted to Stanley on the Oerlikon. 'Messershmitt!' he pointed, and the gun swivelled out to sea.

The fighter was flying straight at the bridge. Machine guns flamed from its yellow nose, slamming into the steel panels level with the wheelhouse.

Stanley fired the Oerlikon. Shells and tracer smashed into the engine cowling. White smoke blew out over the cockpit and the propeller splintered and flew apart. Staggering down it crashed onto the fo'c'sle deck and tore off its right wing. The rest of the fuselage bounced hard and careered over the port side, leaving the jagged ruin of the wing lodged in the guardrail.

'Good man!' yelled Thorburn, lifting his thumb and grinning down at Stanley. 'Bloody marvellous!'

There was a final flurry of attacks by the remaining Stukas, beaten off before inflicting any more damage to the convoy and *Veracity* began to gather the ships back into their columns. Willoughby signalled Thorburn to assist the bombed freighter, which had wandered out of line smoking badly.

'Number One!' Thorburn shouted to Armstrong on the fo'c'sle. He had a damage control party pushing the wing over the side. 'Get some water on the freighter, see if we can stop those fires.'

Armstrong waved in acknowledgement and set about rigging up some canvas hoses.

Beneath the starboard Oerlikon, caught in the gantry cross bracing, a body hung unnoticed. Blood pooled on the deck under the suspended knees, and the right arm swung aimlessly with the ship's motion. Eventually a passing Steward made the sad discovery and his dead shipmate was gently prised from the metalwork and taken below.

By now, Thorburn was receiving damage reports and casualty figures. The news of the sailor's death brought a sombre quietness to the noisy bridge, and Thorburn felt a twinge of sadness on discovering he had died alone. It was a reminder of how quickly death could come. Voices from amidships drew him over to the starboard bridge ladder as a solid jet of water leapt across to the freighter. The bomb had exploded in the freighter's coalbunker, cushioning the blast and limiting peripheral damage. The helmsman had been knocked unconscious by the blast and the ship had rapidly lost direction but she now began to recover her position. Steam replaced the smoke as a face appeared at the bridge and signalled the fires were under control. Within a short time the freighter had rejoined the column and was pressing on at her best speed.

Thorburn studied the remainder of the wounded convoy. Confused and damaged, the ships steadied and found their bearings, hauling themselves back into line, discipline overcoming the turmoil. Ahead of them all was the narrowest strip of water; Dover to the north, and Calais to the south. Mid-afternoon would see them passing beneath Dover Castle, the apparent security of its defences unable to ensure a safe passage.

It was to the chair that Thorburn went; to recover his thoughts and consider their recent actions. Willoughby's deployment of his meagre escort had proved to be effective. An airborne attack of that magnitude should have had serious consequences, but the convoy had escaped without a sinking and that felt like a victory.

Brackendale had again escaped serious damage, superficial was the official description, although there would be another letter to write, to a man's next of kin. The crew had fought well; he couldn't have asked for more.

'Signal, sir,' said the Chief Yeoman.

Thorburn read the message. Once relieved by the Sheerness escort, *Brackendale* was ordered to proceed to Chatham Dockyard and he was to present himself at the Admiral's Office.

'Thanks, Chief, you can acknowledge, and ask the First Lieutenant if he could join me on the bridge.'

Chapter Six . . Plans Afoot.

'Lieutenant-Commander Thorburn?' asked a female voice from an oak panelled door at the far end of the foyer. Thorburn stood up and adjusted his uniform, tucking the Naval cap under his arm.

'The Admiral will see you now,' she said.

Thorburn pushed his way purposefully through the assembled officers. The woman waved her hand towards the inner office and Thorburn stepped over the threshold onto a plush blue carpet, standing silently to attention.

A huddle of senior officers had gathered at a large window, their animated conversation reaching Thorburn's ears as a jumbled murmur. Sunlight slanted through a haze of smoke drifting from an ashtray. Above the large fireplace was a painting of the battleship Hood, flags at the masthead and bow waves swirling out from the proud stem. Two framed photographs balanced the mantelpiece. On the right, a Cruiser in the livery of the China Station, and to the left, a destroyer of the V&W class, moving past the Liver building at Liverpool.

Rear-Admiral, Sir Henry McIntyre, with a strikingly thin face, and a heavy thatch of grey hair, turned away from the window. Thorburn found himself on the receiving end of a thorough appraisal from the eagle-eyed gaze.

'So,' said Sir Henry, the strong, rich sound of Scottish ancestry within his voice, 'we finally get to meet.' He brushed a miniscule speck from his left breast pocket.

To his right stood a tall army Staff Officer, the brown uniform adorned with scarlet flashes on each collar. The face of tanned leather had the most piercing blue eyes, a vivid scar running back across the right cheekbone. Behind them was a nondescript soldier, a young Lieutenant, standing with his hands behind his back and looking at the floor.

By way of introduction Sir Henry gestured towards the man with the scar. 'This is General Bainbridge,' he said, and then clasping the man's shoulder, ' may I present Lieutenant-Commander Richard Thorburn. Apparently he makes an ideal candidate for your bird brained scheme.'

General Scott Bainbridge gave a tight lipped grin. 'Good man.' It was a voice of authority, of confidence. He walked slowly over to Thorburn, the narrowed eyes making a thorough assessment of the young naval officer who had been so highly recommended.

Thorburn met his inquisitive stare without blinking; patiently waiting for whatever came next.

'Your Admiral has been kind enough to allow us the use of a destroyer,' said the General, nodding his appreciation. 'My planners have come up with a bit of an expedition, thought you might like to join us.' It was more of a statement than a question and Thorburn remained silent, sneaking a glance beyond the General to the anonymous Lieutenant hovering in the background. 'Captain Pendleton suggested that the *Brackendale*'s Commander might enjoy the diversion.'

Thorburn wasn't surprised by Pendleton's involvement and inclined his head without answering. The General clapped his hands with enthusiasm.

Sir Henry stepped forward and beckoned Thorburn to a heavy oak table. Amongst the empty coffee cups and numerous pieces of paper, a milk jug balanced precariously on a thick notepad.

'Where's that briefing?' he asked, rifling through the various forms.

The anonymous Lieutenant reached out and selected a half hidden sheaf marked 'SECRET' in large red letters.

'Well done, laddie, that's the one,' said Sir Henry, glancing quickly over the first few pages. 'By the way Thorburn,' he said without looking up, 'this is Lieutenant Wingham, of the Sherwood Foresters. He'll be working with us.'

Thorburn shook the Lieutenant's hand, and was met by a pair of inquisitive dark brown eyes.

'Morning, sir.' Wingham said, a subtle hint of the West Country in the warm voice.

'Good morning,' Thorburn replied, aware of an immediate affinity with this quiet character.

'Right, gentlemen,' said the Admiral, 'sit yourselves down and we'll let the General explain.' He settled himself into a well-padded, red leather chair, cupping his bony chin in the palm of one hand.

Bainbridge sat down, fingered a folder on the table and then stood up. 'I have to tell you Commander,' he began, looking down at Thorburn, 'we recently received a message from one of our sources in Normandy. What I'm about to tell you must not, as yet, pass outside these walls.' He emphasised the point by holding his gaze. 'After the evacuation of Dunkirk a lot of our people remained in the occupied countries. There were diplomats, embassy staff, businessmen and their families; people who had been far enough away from the threatened borders that no one expected them to be in any immediate danger. Unfortunately the speed of the German advance took everyone by surprise and a number of important people were cut off.' He glanced down at a large map of France. The fingers of his left hand touched the scarred cheek. Picking up a brass tipped pointer he moved over to stare down at the layout. The pointer slid over the map and stopped on the town marked Bricquebec. Bainbridge cleared his throat. 'Shortly after Dunkirk the German army captured the Cherbourg Peninsula. On the outskirts of this town,' he tapped the map, 'which is about twelve miles south of Cherbourg, there is a small chateau, a large farmhouse really. Bainbridge looked about him to see he had their full attention.

'On the First of June, Lord Bernard Moncrieff arrived at this Chateau to visit his uncle, the Viscount Jules Dubois. Moncrieff extended his stay in the hope of persuading his uncle to return with him to England; he was still there when the first German patrol arrived.' Bainbridge moved round the desk and faced them with his hands on his hips.

'He managed to avoid discovery but when the Viscount was warned of an impending takeover, Moncrieff escaped to friends. The Chateau de Montbarre was occupied by Colonel Wolfgang Manheim of the 22nd Light Panzer Regiment.'

He was interrupted by a knock on a side door and a dark haired young woman in a Navy uniform entered with a tray of coffee. She placed it carefully in front of the Admiral and quickly gathered the used crockery.

'Thank you, Miss Farbrace,' he said, reaching for the pot.

'Biscuits, sir?' she asked over her shoulder.

'No, that's fine for now.' As the young lady closed the door behind her the strong smell of coffee wafted round the table.

Thorburn noticed Lieutenant Wingham had followed her with his eyes, and on seeing Thorburn watching him, he pursed his lips in a silent whistle.

The General cleared his throat. 'If we're all done,' he said pointedly, 'I'll continue. Moncrieff has to be rescued, but first we have to find him. At the moment we think he's going to Auderville, close to Goury.'

Sir Henry McIntyre carefully returned his cup to the saucer and then, standing to his full height, thrust his hands deep into his jacket pockets. 'We got the backroom boys involved straight away,' he said, 'and they managed to come up with Lieutenant Wingham. Quite useful really,' he explained, 'he used to live in the Channel Islands, on Alderney. Speaks French, and regularly sailed to Goury with his father.'

Thorburn began to get an inkling of why he was at the meeting.

McIntyre scratched his nose. 'In case you're not aware, Goury is situated on the north-west tip of La Manche, closest point to Alderney.'

Thorburn was aware and had navigated the area as a Midshipman. 'From what I remember' he said, 'it's all coves and rip tides.'

Lieutenant Wingham nodded. 'Yes, sir, you're right.'

Thorburn breathed deeply, exhaling with an audible hiss and addressed the General. 'Well, sir, if you don't mind my asking, where do I fit in to all this?'

Bainbridge suddenly found his folder needed organising, and the Admiral made a point of pouring another coffee.

It was Wingham who broke the silence. 'I need you to take me there.'

'What, to Goury?' Thorburn asked in surprise. 'I think

87

you'll find that's inside German waters now,' he added, clarifying his response.

'We realise that,' the Admiral broke in, 'but with a night approach in the right conditions the Lieutenant would be ashore in no time.'

Thorburn stood up and walked to the window. This was Pendleton's idea; he just knew it. What was it he'd said? Chosen for the job, right up your street. Well, if the Admiral ordered him to go, then that was his duty and he wouldn't hesitate. But the old boy was doing his best to persuade him, as if he wanted some sort of reassurance as to the course of action. Agreeing would be the easy thing to do, but he found it hard to accept endangering the entire ship's company in return for retrieving one foolhardy member of the aristocracy. He turned and paced slowly back to the table, pondering the alternatives.

'How about a submarine, sir?' he asked softly.

'None available,' came the sharp reply, an obvious irritation in McIntyre's voice.

Thorburn ignored the show of annoyance. His priority was the safety of the ship and to that extent he needed to make himself understood.

'Sir, a short time ago, I was promoted to Lieutenant-Commander and awarded the Captaincy of H.M.S. *Brackendale*. My duty to ship and crew were reinforced by Captain Pendleton's personal instructions to try and keep *Brackendale* in one piece.' He stopped, beginning to wish he hadn't started on this tack, but determined to put his point. 'Now you want *Brackendale* to put one man ashore, in some fairly dangerous seas, in enemy controlled waters. Not really the best way to ensure that one of the channel's few destroyers is kept in one piece, is it, sir?' He knew he'd been a bit too blunt.

General Bainbridge pushed himself up from the table scratching the back of his head. 'Now look, Commander,' he began, bypassing the provocation, 'we wouldn't be setting this up unless we thought we had good reason. We have a contact living in the area and Wingham here knows her.'

Thorburn caught the young officer's eyes, trying to establish what determination he had to accomplish his part in the plan.

Sir Henry eased himself from the chair and stepped to the side of the table. 'Believe me, Commander, we're struggling at the moment.' He held his forehead between thumb and fingers, peering at Thorburn as he gathered his thoughts. 'I have been tasked by the Prime Minister with the job of accumulating any and all information that may prevent, or help to prevent, an invasion. Any and every piece of intelligence is vital in achieving that aim.' He turned away, head bowed, reaching out for the back of the chair. 'The recovery of Moncrieff is central to that aim.'

Thorburn nodded slowly, showing he understood the implications. He moved to stand in front of Wingham. 'Reckon you can do it?' he asked abruptly, probing for a hesitation, a weakness. 'You really think the risk will be worth the end result?'

Wingham looked back with a steady gaze and in that quiet but determined voice, said, 'Yes, sir, with your help I can make contact. Just get me ashore.'

Thorburn pursed his lips, nodded slowly. He wondered about this 'contact' and whether Wingham was all he appeared. Churchill was rumoured to have instigated a movement of resistance in France, underground organisations and agents. This 'contact' might well be involved, but there seemed to be a hell of a lot of guesswork going on. But Thorburn tended to trust his own instincts and Wingham seemed strong. Maybe he'd argued enough. The ship's company would jump at the chance; clear of the shore and out from under the Admiralty's gaze.

Thorburn lowered his eyes and turned to face his superiors, his mind made up. 'When do we go?'

The General raised an eyebrow at the Admiral. 'In the next couple of days I would imagine,'

'Yes, I'm sure that'll be about the mark,' McIntyre agreed, 'just need to set a few things in motion. I suggest we meet again tomorrow.' He looked up at the large mantle clock. 'Two in the afternoon, I think,' and he sat down with a look of satisfaction spreading over his gaunt features.

Thorburn picked up his cap and straightened to attention. Wingham stepped round to join him.

'Right, gentlemen, tomorrow it is,' Bainbridge said, and Thorburn heard the door open for them to leave.

A momentary hush greeted their appearance in the foyer. As the assembled personnel saw who it was, the general hubbub resumed, and they were swallowed up in the crowd. Thorburn picked his way through the array of officers and Wingham matched his efforts to exit the building. They departed by descending the steps from the small lobby and walked off in the direction of the dockyard gate.

'Fancy a bite?' Thorburn asked. He wanted to know more about the man.

'Thank you, sir, missed breakfast this morning.'

'Call me Richard,' said Thorburn as they walked past the Commissioner's House. Returning the guard's salute, they passed under the main gate and then strode down the hill toward Chatham's town hall. In the warmth of the summer sun they walked together, the River Medway shimmering off to their right.

He found a small hotel, situated just off the high street, and Thorburn led them up the steps. Inside they were greeted by a matronly woman dressed in white cap and a pinafore worn over a plain black dress. By chance they had walked into a well run hotel which had become an informal naval officers' retreat.

'Good morning, gentlemen,' she said, as they chose a table in a secluded corner. She took their order and Thorburn offered a cigarette to his companion.

'So why you, Paul?' he asked, dropping the match into an ashtray.

'Two reasons,' Wingham said promptly. 'One, I've already had my fill of training and exercises.' He paused, studying the fine tendril of blue smoke rising from his cigarette.

'And the second?'

'This girl I happen to know. I might be able to get her away when I leave,' Wingham added, as if the thought had only just occurred to him.

'This girl got a name?'

Wingham looked at him for a long moment. 'Marianne. Her name is Marianne.'

Thorburn inhaled deeply giving himself some time to let that revelation sink in. The waitress interrupted. 'Here you are, gentlemen.'

They settled down to their meal, the conversation turning to the war in general. Behind a small counter, near the rack of mail pigeonholes, a small wireless played quietly in the background. As one o'clock approached the waitress came back and turned up the volume. An announcer began his introduction.

'This is the BBC, . . Home news,' said the cultured voice. 'Yesterday, a large formation of enemy aircraft attacked a convoy in the English Channel. The Royal Air Force drove them off. Our casualties were light and none of the ships were lost.' The newsreader cleared his throat. 'The enemy lost fourteen aircraft and the RAF lost three, but all the pilots are reported safe.' There was a pause and then he continued, 'The Prime Minister is today meeting with the war cabinet for urgent . . .'

'I wonder if we're doing as well as it sounds,' Wingham offered. 'Propaganda can be a wonderful thing.' He took another mouthful and chewed thoughtfully.

'Well let's hope our little escapade helps,' said Thorburn, 'I don't want to lose the *Brackendale* on a wild goose chase.'

Wingham stopped eating and squinted at Thorburn, tilting his head slightly to one side. 'I can assure you,' he said, the brown eyes fixing Thorburn's gaze, 'once I'm ashore it certainly won't be any kind of a wild goose chase!'

Thorburn grimaced and narrowed his eyes. 'Sorry, guess I chose the wrong phrase.'

Wingham held his gaze for a moment longer and then smiled lazily. 'You've every right to be concerned, and I only have myself to think about. The responsibility of your ship and the crew; like I said, it's just me.'

Thorburn nodded and they fell into a relaxed silence until the meal was finished.

'All done?' asked Thorburn, delving inside his jacket for his wallet.

Wingham nodded, wiped his mouth with a napkin and rose from the table, standing back as Thorburn walked over to the small counter and settled the bill.

They stepped out to the warmth of the alleyway and found themselves weaving through the crowded pavements, slowly making their way back to the town hall.

The ugly wail of an air raid siren jarred the senses, a mournful howl, rising and falling, echoing over the rooftops. People began to run for shelter, shouting and pointing. Thorburn saw the familiar burst of flack above the river, the noise of the guns moving closer as each battery came in range. It was obviously a raid on the dockyard and he quickened his pace fearing for *Brackendale*'s safety

Hurrying up the hill the first bombs made their presence felt, thumping explosions throwing up plumes of smoke. The two men broke into a run, their breath coming in great gasps as they desperately strove to shorten the distance to the main gate. Thorburn found himself trailing behind, the Sherwood Forester stretching the gap between them. With only a few yards to run, Wingham suddenly threw himself sideways shouting for Thorburn to stop, pointing left towards the river.

A Messerschmitt 109 screamed in from over the Medway, smoke and flames billowing from the nose. A wing tip clipped the upper arch of the dockyard gate and the fighter slewed sideways. Out of control, the right wing dipped over their heads and hit the road. Sparks flashed as the wreckage somersaulted, snapping the fuselage behind the cockpit, the crumpled propeller buried in the cowling.

Thorburn and Wingham scrambled to their feet, hesitating for a moment, inching towards the carnage.

93

Wingham held up a hand. 'He's finished,' he said, pointing to the crushed cockpit. The pilot's head was distorted, squashed to a pulp. A muffled explosion blasted a ball of flames into the air, the fiery heat robbing their lungs. When the smoke died, a mass of smouldering debris littered the road.

'We're no use here,' shouted Thorburn above the din of detonating bombs. 'Come on,' he yelled, and they sprinted through the gate. Deep explosions shook the buildings, the road trembling beneath their feet, and they weaved on through the flying shrapnel.

'This way!' shouted Thorburn, darting swiftly behind a sandbagged machine-gun emplacement. A flurry of arms and legs, and Wingham collapsed beside him. Crouching behind the faded bags Thorburn peered out at the Medway and saw *Brackendale* still in one piece. He felt some of the tension ease, relieved to see the guns swinging after their targets. Near the far bank an armed trawler was down by the head, smoke lifting from the stern rail. He looked around as the sound of aircraft engines moved away and a stillness rolled over the dockyard. The guns had stopped, a momentary hush before the ears acclimatised to normal sounds; the crackling flames glowing in the darkness of thick smoke, flickering in the haze. There was a rattle of spent shells being cleared away by the machine gunners, men coughing dust from choked lungs. A voice of authority called and in the distance men appeared from doorways and passages. Stretcher-bearers hurried towards a covered slipway and a naval ambulance pulled up outside, the rear door thrown open.

Wingham levered himself up from the sandbags and slapped the dust from his uniform. He stopped, looked out at the Medway and pointed. 'Is that yours?'

'It is. H.M.S. *Brackendale* at your service,' Thorburn said with a touch of pride.

Wingham seemed to make an assessment. 'She has nice lines.'

'Yes, I like to think so. Where are you staying?' asked Thorburn, straightening his jacket.

'Officers Mess, Brompton Barracks, for now. As long as they don't draft in any more sailors. It's getting a bit crowded up there.'

'In that case,' said Thorburn, 'I'll see you with Sir Henry tomorrow.'

'I'll be there,' said Wingham, and held out his hand. 'Can't thank you enough for going along with this.'

Thorburn nodded and once again caught sight of that twinkle in the soldier's eyes, the soft smile creasing his cheeks. He let go of the handshake and Wingham stepped back with a smart salute.

'Sir,' he said, turned on his heel and marched away.

Thorburn stared after the departing figure and hoped the people in charge had everything under control. He coughed in a drift of oily smoke, ducked through the smell, and made his way down to the dockside. Somebody on *Brackendale* noticed his approach and he detected movement around the motorboat's davits.

Thirty minutes later he was back in the familiar surroundings of the ship's wardroom listening to a description of their gun action at anchor. Unfortunately there were no reported 'kills' and Howard had nothing to show for his efforts except a broken pipe, which had snapped in a pocket. And then of course, as the excitement waned Thorburn caught a furtive glance between officers, a raised eyebrow about his meeting. A shrug of the shoulders in return, curiosity deflected. His tumbler of gin was almost empty when Armstrong took another from the steward, using the replacement of Thorburn's empty glass to offer the question.

'How'd the meeting go, sir?' he asked, all eyes swivelling to the Captain's face.

'Very interesting,' Thorburn said, but not yet willing to divulge everything that had taken place in Sir Henry's office. He stepped over to the ship's badge, looked up at the intricate design. 'Usual stuff about the war.' His fingers traced the outline of the pony's head before he turned to find himself confronted by Armstrong's close scrutiny. 'I can tell you that we are to welcome a visitor aboard, probably tomorrow afternoon. Show him to my cabin when he arrives, I'm sure you'll make him feel at home.'

Leaving Armstrong with that small detail he withdrew from the wardroom as the others crowded round the First Lieutenant. In the cabin he dropped his jacket onto the back of a chair and stretched out on his bunk. No need to elaborate yet, he thought, wait for the official go ahead.

The day after Thorburn's first meeting in Chatham's dockyard, at the allotted time of 14.00 hours, he stood waiting for the new conference to begin. Rear-Admiral Sir Henry McIntyre, hands behind his back, stood surveying the assembled officers. Thorburn felt he was more than satisfied with proceedings, a lot of uniforms were in attendance. As arranged, General Scott Bainbridge had also arrived, standing by the window talking quietly to Wingham. Pendleton's bearded face listened in to their conversation. Jennifer Farbrace, the Wren officer who had served the coffee yesterday, was seated with a notepad at the ready. Two Flag Lieutenants leaned over a chart on the big table and the blue uniform of a Royal Air Force pilot pointed out a detail between them.

At the far end of the large fireplace stood an army Sergeant. Something in his bearing made Thorburn stop to take note. Average height with a slight build there was nothing to indicate anything out of the ordinary. Only when Thorburn took in the face did he realise the mesmerising power in the bony features. The eyes, which momentarily caught his own, were strikingly dark, neatly framed with black brows. Difficult to gauge his age, but Thorburn settled for early thirties. He wondered where he fitted in to all this.

Leaning on the near end of the ornate mantelpiece, he was surprised to see his old friend, Lieutenant-Commander Peter Willoughby. As he caught Thorburn looking at him, he winked casually, that familiar grin spreading to a dimpled jaw line. A cough brought Thorburn back to the focal point.

'Gentlemen,' the Admiral began, 'as some of you are aware, we're here to thrash out the detail of a forthcoming action.'

Thorburn noticed a slight glance at Bainbridge, and an almost imperceptible nod in return, before the Admiral continued.

'Lieutenant Wingham is to be put ashore at the port of Goury, in German occupied France, at the earliest opportunity.' A small gesture indicated Paul's presence. 'I have decided that Lieutenant-Commander Thorburn in *Brackendale* will facilitate that landing.' He cleared his throat and checked on Second Officer Farbrace's ability to keep pace with her notes. 'Lieutenant-Commander

Willoughby in *Veracity* will mount a diversionary raid near an old French fort. Its over on the eastern side of the headland, and that will commence twenty minutes before Lieutenant Wingham goes ashore.' He moved away to a tall, covered easel. A quick flick of his right hand and he revealed a map of the French peninsula known colloquially as La Manche. He pointed to a curved bay on the west coast. 'Goury, gentlemen, a small fishing port. When the tide's out, there's no water.'

Bainbridge moved to join Sir Henry and Thorburn watched the old warhorse take control.

'Sergeant Mason,' the deep voice began, his right hand pointing out the dark eyed warrior, 'will put ashore with twenty volunteers. Their main objective is to create a diversion, inflict as much damage to the enemy as they can.' He grinned widely as he caught the Sergeant's eye and continued enthusiastically. 'By the time they're finished the bloody Germans will think an entire battalion has hit them.' He clapped his hands with relish. 'Sir Henry has agreed that *Veracity* will stand off and give support with her main armament. We estimate a forty minute engagement which should be enough for Lieutenant Wingham to get ashore.'

Thorburn again felt a strange reluctance to accept their eagerness. His superiors had initially formulated a simple plan to land Wingham and leave. Now the mission had escalated. Consideration of the population seemed to be non-existent. He wondered what pressures were being applied from Whitehall. None the less, he was delighted to have Willoughby taking part.

Sir Henry beckoned to the young flying officer. 'Tell them what you saw.'

'I made a reconnaissance of the area this morning,' he

said, immediately securing a respectful silence. 'There was a small amount of troop activity to the south of Goury.' He pulled a small pad from a breast pocket. 'I counted two 88 millimetre flack guns and three field guns being positioned along the northern coast.' He paused to read again. 'There was a destroyer and three to four E-boats in Cherbourg harbour, and a couple of E-boats were patrolling about a mile to the north west.' He looked up and added, 'I caught sight of a freighter on passage to Cherbourg so I gave it the once over.' He had the undivided attention of everyone in the room. 'I was a bit surprised by the reception but I'd seen some guns and armoured cars on deck.' He returned the pad to his pocket. 'I swung round and attacked from the bow, gave it a long burst as I flew down the deck. I don't think I caused much damage, but it got a bit too hot to hang about.' He gave them all a shy grin and turned to the Admiral.

Thorburn knew there was an understated nonchalance in this pilot's report. He would have flown through heavy anti aircraft fire, a lot more than a 'bit hot'. His priority had been to gather intelligence, but he'd been unable to resist a quick squirt at the freighter.

'Thank you,' said Sir Henry. 'Are there any questions before we move on?'

'Yes, sir,' said Wingham, closing in from the window and addressing the pilot. 'Did you notice any troops between Goury and the east coast?'

Looking down at his feet, the pilot thought for a moment before giving his reply. 'South on the west coast, yes,' he said, 'and up at that old fort, yes there were troops up there, too, but in between on those cliffs and coves,' he shook his head, 'no, I can't say I saw much of anything.'

Wingham persevered. 'And the village of Auderville?'

'Not that I could see.'

Wingham grudgingly nodded his thanks, and stepped back next to Pendleton.

Thorburn felt the report on the warship lacked clarity and stepped towards the pilot. 'Can you be a bit clearer on the type of destroyer?'

'Five main guns, two up front, and two funnels. Not one of those older Torpedo boats. A proper destroyer.' The pilot was adamant.

'Zerstorer by the sound of it,' Sir Henry decided. 'Probably 1936 design.'

Thorburn caught Pendleton's eye as he gave an almost imperceptible nod. It was more than likely von Holtzmann's ship.

A knock on the door was followed by the appearance of an elderly naval Captain, who paused to peer over his spectacles before passing a note to the Admiral. He read the message in silence, passed the paper to the chart table and muttered something to the General. The two flag officers busied themselves with plotting the new information. Jennifer Farbrace took a moment to rest her note pad and smooth her skirt.

'Gentlemen,' Sir Henry resumed, 'our met-office have forecast a rain front approaching from the southwest, probably reaching the coast by tomorrow evening.' His eyes drifted over the assembled personnel. 'The rain is predicted to last for the following twelve hours on a strengthening wind.'

'Poor visibility, sir,' said a flag officer from the table.

'And that is precisely what we wanted,' the Admiral said looking at his watch. 'This operation is planned for the early hours of tomorrow morning, the landing of Lieutenant Wingham to be in conjunction with the high tide at 02.30 hours.' He turned away and picked up his cap and briefcase. 'Unfortunately, business calls. I have an appointment in Whitehall so I have to leave you in the General's good hands.' He and Bainbridge turned away together and Jennifer Farbrace led them to the door. Sir Henry paused to look back, the assembled personnel maintaining a respectful silence. 'I would like you all to remember that dear old England is struggling to survive. We've recently suffered defeats and losses on an unprecedented scale and any small thing we can do to address that is invaluable.' Again he paused, allowing the silence to add emphasis to his point. 'We might seem somewhat insignificant,' he said, 'two small ships and a handful of raiders. But Lord Moncrieff is a very important asset. Don't underestimate the importance of this little operation. We have to get the Lieutenant ashore to find our man. That's the first stage, we'll worry about his recovery when we have more to go on.' He raised a weary hand in salute. 'Good luck to you all.' The door closed behind him and for a moment the room was hushed, the Admiral's words lingering in his absence.

Converging on the big table the officers began thrashing out the detail of the operation. General Bainbridge took charge, his obvious expertise in the complexities of planning, easily adapted to the current situation.

Thorburn found Willoughby at his elbow and the handshake was as firm as ever.

Willoughby locked his dark eyes on Thorburn's face. 'Well Richard, seems a bit frantic, don't you think?'

'I think the whole thing's been rushed, Peter, and I

hope to God they've got this right.' They still shared that old understanding, an instinctive recognition of good tactics. Thorburn tried to lighten the mood. 'I've managed to spend a bit of time with Wingham. I think we're lucky he fell in with this.'

Willoughby raised an eyebrow, tilting his head slightly. 'Fell in with this?' he queried sarcastically.

'Well, however he got involved. He really does knows that peninsula, and there's a girl too,' Thorburn explained. 'I'm sure that's enough motivation for anyone.'

'Mmmm. . Let's hope you're right. That aside, we might be able to turn this whole episode to our advantage,' Willoughby announced, a secretive smile slowly creasing his cheeks.

'Meaning?'

'Be a pity to leave that German destroyer all alone in Cherbourg, free to come and go as he pleases.'

Thorburn frowned his disapproval. 'I think we should just stick to the plan and get Paul ashore.' He hoped Willoughby wouldn't get too excited at the prospect of exchanging blows with the enemy.

'Perhaps,' Willoughby said without much conviction. 'I wonder if it's the same blighter you met the other day?'

'That one was operating out of Bolougne,' Thorburn assured him, trying to deflect his guesswork.

'Might have relocated, we haven't shown as much interest in Cherbourg.'

'Even so,' Thorburn said forcefully, 'I really feel we should leave well alone.'

'I'm sure you're right, Richard,' Willoughby conceded. 'We'll just deliver our cargoes at the appropriate time and sneak away as ordered.' There was a heavy irony in his friend's voice but Thorburn let it go.

Willoughby changed the subject. 'That Jennifer's a bit of alright, you know. About time I introduced myself.'

Thorburn allowed himself a smile. Still the same old Peter, he thought, always looking for a pretty face. He glanced over to where she stood and found himself caught by her gaze. For a moment she held his look, confident, assured. The faintest of smiles before she looked away. He was probably mistaken, she must have been staring at Willoughby. The two friends walked toward the table to join the others.

Situated to the north of the Cotentin Peninsula, Cherbourg's harbour basked in the afternoon sunshine. Inside the ancient breakwater, Verner von Holtzmann had secured his destroyer to the granite quayside. Three of his Schnellboats were tied up and swaying gently on the still waters, the remainder he had ordered on patrol to the north. In the middle of the harbour a damaged freighter was undergoing emergency repairs. According to her captain a Spitfire had attacked with machine gun fire, killing two of the crew and inflicting minor damage to an anti-aircraft gun. The hidden cargo of torpedoes for the Schnellboats had already been hoisted ashore unharmed. Suitable locations on the heights overlooking the anchorage had been found for the extra guns.

Holtzmann stood in his cabin studying the strategy he had planned for patrolling the surrounding seas. The fast torpedo boats had been tasked to cruise off shore intercepting any suspicious vessels. They would patrol until dark and return to harbour for a nights rest. In the morning they must prepare for another strike against the channel convoys. His last attempt to attack a convoy had met with failure, a Royal Navy destroyer taking them by surprise. Two Schnellboats were lost during the action and even though he had shaken off the pursuit, daylight and air patrols had forced him to disengage. Next time he would be better prepared.

Chapter Seven . . Goury.

Lieutenant-Commander Peter Willoughby stood in the darkness of *Veracity*'s bridge with his face turned away from the driving rain. Shielding the voice-pipe with both hands he called down to the wheelhouse. 'Slow ahead, both,' he ordered, with a sideways look at the bridge-screen. By his reckoning they were less than two miles from the ancient walls of Fort Sainte Martin, and according to the pre-arranged schedule, time to get the army moving.

'Warn Sergeant Foster,' he called to his Officer-of-the-Watch. 'Assemble on the quarterdeck in five minutes.' He looked out over the starboard bridge wing to where an extra cutter had been secured amidships. Two boats in all, twenty-one men and their equipment, not a very imposing force. He peered at his watch. Somewhere off the west coast on the other side of the peninsular Richard Thorburn would be guiding *Brackendale* on a slow approach to the rugged shoreline. A single codeword had arrived ten minutes previously. 'Mole' was the pre-arranged signal that verified Thorburn's ability to accomplish his landing, and that Willoughby should execute the plan.

Shadowy figures began to appear on deck as *Veracity*'s motorboat was lowered from the davits. A large party of seamen emerged from between the torpedo tubes and quickly manhandled the other boat over the low waist. An outboard motor was passed to the sailors in the stern of the cutter and secured to the housing. Heavy machine guns and mortars were stowed swiftly between the soldiers, Bren guns, rifles and grenades glistening in the damp.

Sergeant Foster arrived on the bridge and saluted. 'Ready when you are, sir,' he reported, sharp eyes shining from the darkened face.

For the first time Willoughby became aware of Foster's battle dress. Even within the gloomy confines of the bridge the Sergeant's appearance had a formidable look. There was no helmet, just a khaki woollen hat, and a short-barrelled sub machine gun hung from a strap on his right shoulder. A lethally long knife hung from a scabbard at his waist and a handful of grenades were clipped on between the ammunition pouches.

'Right, Sergeant. Once the party starts we'll close in and give you fire support. Now if you'd like to join your men, my Number One will get you under way.'

Foster snapped open the cover of his wristwatch. 'Beach in about twenty minutes from now, sir,' he growled. 'See you in an hour.'

Willoughby watched him leave the bridge remembering the rumour about Churchill's new 'Commando'. If this was an example, God help the enemy. Another glance at the time, and with the rain noticeably harder he saw the First Lieutenant give the order to cast off. The boats moved out in line astern, lifting and falling on the waves, undulating into a simple chain. Within minutes their faint outline merged with the rain and spray, a final glint of steel easing them out of sight.

'Slow ahead, both,' Willoughby ordered. 'Starboard twenty.' The warship swung slowly to the right of the raiding party and followed them into the gloom.

H.M.S. *Brackendale* wallowed uneasily in the heavy

sea, her forward momentum reduced to the minimum required for sea keeping. Richard Thorburn waited at the compass platform, his eyes stinging with the constant effort of peering through the rain. Until he was certain that Foster's raiding party had made contact with the enemy, *Brackendale* would remain almost hove to off the west coast, an invisible presence on the sea.

An inflated three-man rubber dinghy lay ready near the quarterdeck housing. Two of the crew had volunteered to assist Wingham in paddling ashore, and one would help in landing his equipment. Thorburn was concerned with the rising wind. If the landing was to be successful, they might have to release the dinghy from as little as five hundred yards.

Armstrong addressed him. 'Captain, sir.'

Thorburn found Wingham standing in the darkness, almost unrecognisable in his battle tunic.

'Hello, Paul,' Thorburn smiled. 'All ready for the off?'

'Yes, sir,' came the terse reply, 'should see the balloon go up shortly.'

Thorburn detected an edge to his voice. Anxious to get under way, he thought, uneasy about getting to shore. 'I'll take you in as close as I can,' he offered. 'A few hundred yards.'

The Lieutenant's shoulders visibly relaxed. 'That's all I need,' he said, the tension melting away. He pointed towards the coast. 'Those currents are pretty strong . . . turbulent.'

'Depends on the visibility,' Thorburn elaborated, not wanting to sound too optimistic. There was no reply, only the rain lashing on the bridge-screen as they continued to wait.

A faint rattle of machine gun fire arrived in the wind.

A sharp explosion followed by the sound of other small arms fire. Flashes of orange glowed through the rain, more explosions thumping in the distance.

'Time to go,' said Thorburn, 'half ahead both, starboard twenty.' He felt a tap on his arm.

'Thanks for your help,' said Wingham, 'hope to see you in a while.'

Thorburn reached out with both hands, responding to the warm handshake. 'Good luck, Paul,' he said, 'let me know when you need a ride back, we'll do the rest.' He sounded more confident than he felt.

More explosions and a sudden increase of gunfire broke the moment. Thorburn turned back to the business of command.

'Slow ahead,' he ordered, a brighter glow from the battle highlighting a headland through the rain.

'The cove is ten degrees on the starboard bow, sir,' a lookout reported.

Thorburn checked the compass bearing. 'Report your depth Mr Lawrence,' he ordered.

'Eight fathoms, sir.'

Enough for now, Thorburn figured, the ship idling forward in the rain. He peered through the gloom, blinking water from his eyes. The cove was just visible through the murk, a crescent-shaped curve framed by the black headland. He needed to decide on his approach, how to present the ship for Wingham's best chance of getting ashore. Get this wrong and the mission might be over before it started. He made up his mind and leant to the wheelhouse voice-pipe. 'Cox'n!'

'Cox'n, sir,' came the reply.

'I'm going to turn to port, get her nose into the wind. I want you to hold her steady when I give you the course, should be enough to get our guest over the side.'

'Aye aye, sir,' the Cox'n called up the pipe. 'Turn to port and hold her head to the wind.'

'That's it,' said Thorburn, and straightened up to watch for the moment. He tried to blot out the sound of gunfire pulsing in on the wind, to ignore the spray almost blinding his view of the shoreline.

Thorburn briefly considered the keel's clearance as he squinted at the cove. 'Depth?' he barked.

'Seven fathoms, sir,' Lawrence called sharply.

Enough he thought, and as near as he dared.

'Port thirty!' he ordered.

'Port thirty, aye, sir,' the Cox'n yelled up the pipe.

Brackendale turned slowly into the blustery weather, rocking over the swell. Thorburn hoped that anyone on shore was now fully distracted by the raiding party's efforts. After a minute of ungainly lurching the bows met the oncoming sea, perfectly aligned with the wind.

'Midships!' ordered Thorburn, a quick glance at the compass. 'Steer two-oh-oh degrees.'

'Two-oh-oh degrees, aye, sir,' and the Cox'n span the wheel to catch *Brackendale*'s turn to port.

Thorburn held himself still for a moment longer, then nodded to Lawrence, pointing astern. 'Tell Number One to get them under way.'

A dozen hands launched the black dinghy over the side to the bottom of a scrambling net, two of the crew clinging on at wave height in an attempt to steady the glistening rubber. A wave lifted the dinghy and Jack Barton jumped in. He settled himself and beckoned Wingham to join him. A pause as the dinghy lurched down a trough. When the next wave rose up, Wingham made a total mess of his jump and landed on Barton, almost tipping them both into the water. Recovering, they spread themselves fore and aft; the remaining space adroitly filled by Able Seaman Chris Owen, one of the Special Sea Duty men.

Pushing away from the ship the dinghy bobbed precariously across the foaming water, the three men paddling hard for the cove.

Thorburn watched through his binoculars as the waves threatened to swamp the tiny craft. It slid down out of view only to reappear as if thrown out with the foam, paddles flailing in the air. *Brackendale* corkscrewed violently the quarterdeck taking a surge of seawater, the crew scrambling for a hold. Thorburn almost dropped the glasses, losing sight of the dinghy. A hurried scan of the shoreline and he had them, paddling hard, spinning in the surf. They hit the beach in a rush, almost overturned by their impetus.

The destroyer wallowed sideways towards the shore and Thorburn reacted. 'Watch her head, Cox'n!'

The ship steadied into the wind, holding the heading, and Thorburn raised the glasses again. To the sound of distant gunfire across the headland, a figure could be seen running up the beach with the suitcase, obviously Wingham on familiar terrain. Barton followed with his hands full, leaving Owen with the dinghy. Darkness at the rocks swallowed the running men from view while the lookouts watched the high ground for any sign of movement.

From across the peninsula Thorburn heard heavy gunfire, possibly *Veracity*'s main armament, a faint red glow reflecting through the rain.

'Come on, come on,' he muttered to himself, the ship riding unevenly beneath his feet, the Cox'n fighting hard

110

to keep her head into the wind. A slight movement from the shadows and Barton ran down the beach, grabbed Owen by the arm and pointed frantically up the beach. A brief hesitation and they pushed the dinghy into the surf, wading out until the water was chest high. With a final lunge they threw themselves on board and fought their way over the breaking surf.

'Stop engines!' Thorburn snapped to the voice-pipe. He had to give them a chance against the wind, the same wind which began to push *Brackendale* back toward the small rubber boat. The waves appeared to swamp the dinghy and for a moment she seemed lost, then rose from a deep trough to pitch uncontrollably down the next wave. Thorburn eyed the distance between ship and dinghy fully aware of the depth decreasing beneath his keel. Another minute and the destroyer might be aground. He gripped the bridge rail harder, biting his bottom lip. *Brackendale* was losing direction her bows swinging in to the shore, rolling with the sea. Fifty feet, maybe forty feet from the stern rail to the dinghy. He must regain control of the steering, get some forward momentum.

Reluctantly he gave the order. 'Half ahead, together.'

Another wait. Ten seconds. . , Fifteen seconds, then *Brackendale* responded, the propellers gaining purchase, the Cox'n fighting to bring her back on bearing.

At the starboard depth charge thrower, Armstrong waited, legs braced to counter the ship's motion. As the propellers found thrust he saw the men in the dinghy look up in despair. He held up his hand to a seaman on the quarterdeck.

'Now!' Armstrong shouted.

Reaching back, the seaman checked his coil of heaving line and with a mighty effort hurled the rope out beyond the guardrail. Just short of the dinghy the loose end splashed into the sea. With a last desperate attempt, Barton and Owen found the strength to paddle the remaining six feet and gratefully dragged the line aboard.

On the destroyer a dozen pairs of hands hauled them through the foaming sea until they drew level with the small scrambling net hanging over the side. Those same friendly hands quickly brought the bedraggled pair to safety, laying them gently on the deck.

Armstrong stepped into the crowd of men surrounding the exhausted pair. 'Give them some room, lads,' he called, bending to kneel at Barton's side. He saw the keen eyes looking up at him. 'What happened back there?' he asked, grabbing for support as the ship heeled over.

Barton wiped water from his face, pushed himself to one elbow and took a deep breath. 'The Lieutenant took us up the rocks in a bit of a gulley, sir. There was a small cave and he stashed all the equipment inside.' Barton's breathing calmed as he recovered from his exertions and using the guardrail he climbed to his feet. A row of expectant faces waited for him to continue.

'As I came out we heard a noise, right close, it was.' He glanced round at the crew. 'It was a Jerry, sir, with his rifle ready, and the Lieutenant jumped him.' He looked down at the deck remembering.

'And?' Armstrong prompted.

'He killed him, sir. He grabbed him by the head, jerked it over and snapped his neck. Told me to get going and not to worry.'

The sound of gunfire from the far side of the island became stronger and Armstrong felt he should return to the bridge.

'Well done the pair of you,' he said, and to the rest of

the crew, 'get them below and stand by your action stations.' He turned to make his way forward, dodging the wet dinghy as two of the crew squeezed it through a hatchway.

On the bridge Thorburn stared through his glasses at what could be seen of the red glow radiating from the battle. A check on the time convinced him of the battle's conclusion. Foster's commando were being recovered from the beach.

Armstrong arrived at his side. 'The men are back aboard, sir,' he reported.

'Very well,' Thorburn acknowledged calmly. He turned towards the signal deck. 'Chief Yeoman!' he called.

'Sir.'

'Make to *Veracity*, in clear. "Hill." Just that,' he ordered.

'Aye aye, sir.'

Thorburn knew how dangerous the waters were to his west. Rocky islands half submerged, it would be better to turn southwest and have a clear run. Leaning to the wheelhouse voice-pipe he issued his next order. 'Cox'n?'

'Wheelhouse, sir,' came the reply.

'Port ten. Steer two-one-oh degrees.'

A slight pause and then the Cox'n came back up the pipe. 'Port ten of the wheel on, sir. Steering, two-one-oh degrees.'

As *Brackendale* settled on her new course, Thorburn stepped down to the forebridge, blinking the rain from his eyes, peering ahead through the dark night. Hold this for a while longer he mused to himself, then turn north for home. He wondered if Willoughby had managed to extricate all the commando; that battle had sounded a lot more ferocious than he'd expected. *Veracity*'s guns had been in constant action.

Armstrong sought his attention. 'Sir.'

'Yes, Number One.'

' I spoke to Barton, they ran into trouble.'

Thorburn listened to Armstrong's report with growing apprehension. How long before the Germans discovered the guard was missing? And what would Wingham do with the body?

'Starboard ten,' he ordered. 'Steer three-one-oh degrees.'

The ship heeled slightly, then pitched awkwardly down a deep trough burying her stem into the oncoming wave. Thorburn steadied himself on the bridge rail. 'Well let's hope Wingham's still in one piece,' he said. *Brackendale* clawed her way back to an even keel, seawater sluicing aft along the deck. 'We're lucky not to have grounded back there.'

The faint sound of heavy gunfire reached them and they both turned to look back at the French headland.

'I thought *Veracity* would have withdrawn by now,' Thorburn said with a frown. 'They must pull out soon.'

He checked his watch. Fifty minutes since the first gunfire. Seemed longer. That gnawing sensation returned to the pit of his stomach and he shivered. Something was wrong, exactly what, he wasn't sure.

'Number One, I have a feeling all's not well.' He held up a hand at Armstrong's expression. 'Make sure the lookouts are on their toes. I don't want to be caught unawares.'

Armstrong nodded. 'Aye aye, sir,' he said and swung away to the rear of the bridge. 'You lookouts keep a sharp watch there,' he snapped. 'And that applies to you two as

114

well,' he added to the pair on the port side. They straightened in response, busily rearranging their telescopes. Armstrong walked on with a tight face, knowing he'd made his point.

Heavy rain drove in from the northwest, stinging the faces of the unwary few. *Brackendale* pushed on, her small vague outline shrouded from view, blending with the sea.

Werner von Holtzmann was not in a good mood. Far too much time had been wasted in getting steam to the turbines, the drive shafts barely turning after the prolonged effort in raising pressure. He passed the order for his destroyer to turn on a southwesterly course as he eventually managed to clear Cherbourg's harbour. From the moment he had received the report detailing the battle at Fort St Martin, more than forty minutes had elapsed. Precious wasted minutes. He cursed the absence of the Schnellboats which he had ordered to patrol Plymouth, hoping to catch an unwary convoy.

His binoculars picked out glowing evidence of a battle on the northern tip of La Manche.

'We must have more speed!' he shouted, slamming his fist on the steel bridge-rail.

'We have twelve knots, Kapitan, and the speed is building,' said the First Officer, tight lipped with the embarrassment of being shouted at.

Holtzmann snorted his disgust without reply, tightening his grip on the handrail. Heavy gunfire echoed through the rain and for the first time, silence followed. Too late, he thought. We are going to be too late.

Chapter Eight . . The Bowchaser.

In the blacked out heart of London, deep under the Admiralty buildings, a telephone rang in the outer office of Rear-Admiral Sir Henry McIntyre. The duty officer for the night reached to remove the handset from its cradle. He listened for a moment, thanked the caller for the message and carefully replaced the receiver. Glancing at the door to the Admiral's office, he pursed his lips before rising to tug his jacket straight. The old man was not in the best of moods but none the less he had to disturb him. Tapping on the door he poked his head round to see McIntyre immersed in paperwork.

'Message, sir,' he reported to the bowed head.

'What is it?' came the growl.

'The code words 'Mole' and 'Hill' have been received within the last half hour, sir,' he said.

The Admiral looked up, and then checked the time. 03.15 hours, still dark outside. He allowed himself a small grin. 'Get me General Bainbridge on the blower,' he said, pleased with the thought of disturbing Scotty from his sleep. 'And some coffee.'

When the buzzer sounded from the switchboard he was quick to respond.

'General Bainbridge for you, sir,' said the girl, and McIntyre settled back into his chair.

'Hello Scotty,' he said brightly, needlessly loud and cheerful. 'Sorry to wake you, but we've just received confirmation of the landings.'

'Casualties?' asked an obviously sluggish General.

McIntyre kept the smile out of his voice. 'Nothing to

116

that effect yet, just the code words.'

'Good . . , good,' the General mused, 'shouldn't be long before Wingham starts transmitting. Seems like Thorburn did all right,' he offered.

McIntyre allowed a pause before he spoke again. 'Yes, possibly,' he said evenly, 'but if the lad wants to get on he might be well advised to be a little more enthusiastic.'

His coffee arrived, carefully placed within reach.

Bainbridge cleared his throat. 'Just an opinion,. Your jurisdiction, Henry. I'll reserve judgement. Are you coming down for the debrief?'

'No, can't make it today. I'm in with the Joint-Chiefs-of-Staff later.'

' Right,' the General said emphatically. 'Thanks for the information.'

McIntyre thought for a moment. 'Can you make sure Pendleton's in on that debrief? I don't want any old jumped up Flag officer thinking he's the bee's knees on this one. Pendleton's seen it all before, proper sailor.'

'Will do, Henry. Talk to you later.'

The connection went dead and the Admiral replaced the handset. Returning to the paperwork his thoughts drifted back to their conversation. He was certain of one thing. Lieutenant-Commander Thorburn had already demonstrated a natural flair for leadership, just needed a little more on the diplomatic front when confronted with senior officers. The third sheet of foolscap required two paragraphs to be reworked and he roughly underscored the offending article.

Still, he thought, the lad was learning. Not quite the rebel of the rumour mill. Plenty of time to acquire the art of diplomacy.

Later, when daylight came, the early morning sun glistened off the damp quayside of Chatham dockyard, tendrils of mist rising in drifts of grey. As *Brackendale* moored up to her allocated buoy, Thorburn could see *Veracity* in the process of unloading casualties.

'I'll be going ashore, Number One. Ship's boat if you please.'

Armstrong had foreseen the order and moved slightly to portside of the bridge, lifting his hand to the boat's crew. The davits squealed in release as the motorboat splashed down.

'Boat's ready, sir.'

Thorburn gave him a tight smile. 'Smartly done.' He looked around him, and then looked at the dockside. 'Don't quite know when I'll be back on board, have to play this one by ear.'

'Yes, sir,' Armstrong grinned. 'We'll try and cope the best we can.'

Thorburn laughed and backhanded him as he moved to the bridge ladder. 'And probably not very well!'

Inside ten minutes Thorburn's motorboat reversed engines as the helmsman expertly eased the small craft alongside an ancient set of steps. Thorburn dropped lightly onto a worn slab and climbed swiftly to the top. Walking the short distance along the damp quayside he was in time to see *Veracity*'s last casualties being stretchered off. He spotted Sergeant Foster with his right leg bandaged up to the thigh.

'How'd it go, sir?' asked the tough commando, propping himself on one elbow.

'Mission accomplished,' Thorburn said. 'What about your end?'

'Jerry won't forget us for a while.' He grimaced as

pain flooded up from his leg. 'S'all right, sir. Just a scratch.'

Thorburn pursed his lips and nodded, taking in the amount of blood on show, then swung lithely up the brow to be greeted by *Veracity*'s First Lieutenant.

'Captain's waiting for you in his cabin, sir,' he said, and led Thorburn aft. Striding beneath the flag deck and past the main funnel there was plenty of evidence of small arms damage. Shrapnel damaged bulkheads and an irregular line of bullet holes. They ducked inside the quarterdeck housing and a moment later the Lieutenant knocked on a door marked 'CAPTAIN'. 'Lieutenant-Commander Thorburn's here, sir.'

'Richard!' called Willoughby with all his usual enthusiasm. 'Come in; how did it go? Have you had breakfast?'

Thorburn shook his head in answer to the last, and Willoughby gathered some papers together to clear the table. 'In the middle of writing my report,' he said, pushing the captain's log to one corner.

'Cooper!' he called to an adjacent room. 'Leave all that for now. We'll have two coffees and whatever the wardroom are having for breakfast.'

A small man appeared holding up a uniform jacket. 'Yes, sir,' he said. 'Coffee and breakfast for two.' The clothes brush gave a final flick along a cuff. 'You'll be needing this later, sir,' he said, and hooked the coat hanger into a louvered locker door.

Thorburn sat at the far end of the table while Willoughby spread a chart of the French peninsula in front of them. Pointing to the plot he explained *Veracity*'s action during the engagement, emphasising the enemy's advantage and the commando's disciplined withdrawal.

119

Finally with an exasperated slap on the table he looked straight at Thorburn. 'Bainbridge set this up,' he hissed. 'Even though you managed to put Wingham ashore, this diversionary raid was suicidal. If *Veracity*'s firepower hadn't been available they would have been slaughtered.'

'Trouble is,' said Thorburn quietly, 'getting Wingham ashore didn't go undetected. They had to kill a guard.'

Willoughby frowned. 'And the body?'

'We're not sure. Apparently it was a broken neck, and on those rocks in that weather, might be viewed as an accident.'

A tap on the door brought the aroma of freshly brewed coffee. Two plates of sausages and eggs on toast were served to the table. The conversation waned as they began to eat and Thorburn saw Willoughby's annoyance begin to subside. Hunger superseded the need to talk, only the clatter of knives and forks disturbing the quiet of the cabin.

Barked commands from amidships were followed by a loud knock on the door and *Veracity*'s First Lieutenant appeared. 'Prisoner going ashore, sir.'

'Thank you, Number One. Any problems?'

'Only the damage to his head, sir. Doc checked him over ten minutes ago. Seems okay.'

Willoughby nodded. 'Very well.'

The Lieutenant withdrew.

'Prisoner?' asked Thorburn between mouthfuls.

'Mmm . . ,' Willoughby mouthed, pushing his empty plate away. 'Sergeant Foster's lot picked him up on the beach.' A shaft of sunlight beamed into the cabin and for a moment they relaxed with their coffee and cigarettes, Thorburn's pack of Senior Service left open on the table.

Willoughby smiled, and then laughed. It was a loud

120

throaty laugh and with that he banged the palm of his hand onto the table. 'At least we saw some proper bloody action instead of all that swaning around on escort duty!' He chuckled to himself, merriment in his eyes. 'What's your official deployment, Richard, Dover Patrol?'

Thorburn rubbed his chin. 'Well, yes, strictly speaking. Pendleton asked for me but we're not exactly on convoy escort. Proceeding independently, right up your street, really.'

A full minute of silence followed while they eyed each other, then Willoughby stubbed out his cigarette and stood up.

'My street maybe,' he said, 'but I think you've been singled out. I think you've fallen foul of something underhand.' He walked to a scuttle looking out over the Medway. 'They're using you. Something's in the pipeline and McIntyre's got you in his sights.'

Thorburn snorted his disbelief. 'No chance,' he said vehemently. 'Pendleton just wanted an extra ship to use on this assignment. We'll be on escort duty tomorrow, no doubts.'

'You don't get recommended for Special Operations at the drop of a hat,' Willoughby protested, vigorously shaking his head.

Thorburn watched his friend's reaction with a faint amusement. It was unlike Peter to get so animated over anything, let alone the devious workings of their Lordships. 'Well, I'll bear it in mind, but I don't think the Admiral would take me as first choice for anything at the moment.'

A sharp rap on the door and Thorburn looked up to see a Petty Officer Yeoman with a message slip in his hand.

'Signal to Officers Commanding *Brackendale* and

Veracity, sir.'

'You can read it,' said Willoughby.

'Report to Admiralty House at 11.00 hours.'

Willoughby glanced at Thorburn, the twinkle back in his eyes.

'Acknowledge,' he ordered, and turned to reach for his report on the table.

'Finished it?' asked Thorburn.

'No!' Willoughby said forcefully. 'I'd best get it seen to before I'm relieved of my command and sent to languish in some Godforsaken clerks office.'

'Fair enough,' Thorburn grinned. He grabbed his cap and pushed it firmly into place. '11.00 hours, and be sharp about it.'

'Sod off!' was the shouted reply, and Thorburn chuckled as he found his way out onto *Veracity*'s quarterdeck.

At a quarter to eleven Second Officer Jennifer Farbrace, responding to a knock on the office door, looked up from her typewriter. 'Come in,' she said, sliding the carriage along for the next paragraph. The door inched open and revealed the smiling face of Richard Thorburn. She glanced at the clock, surprised at how early he was. 'It'll be another fifteen minutes yet, sir, but you're welcome to wait.'

'Thank you,' he said, placing his briefcase on a chair, 'but I actually wanted a quick word with you.'

Jennifer pouted. She was taken by the open smile and his friendly way, the blue eyes warm and inviting. Even so, she had to be on her guard. Her position in this office was all about 'in confidence' and careless talk was not in her remit.

122

'By all means,' she said with a smile, 'how can I help?'

'I wondered if we'd heard from Lieutenant Wingham yet?'

Jennifer saw the subtle change in Thorburn's face, heard the sombre note in his voice. The Lieutenant-Commander was clearly concerned for Wingham's well being, but left her with the dilemma of being in breach of trust.

Thorburn shuffled slightly, obviously embarrassed by her silence. 'I'm sorry,' he said, turning to sit down, 'I shouldn't have asked. Didn't mean to be awkward.'

She thought he looked very much like a guilty schoolboy, and then lowered her voice to speak. 'A signal came through an hour ago. It was incomplete but his call sign was clearly deciphered.' Her eyes caught his brief frown of concern. 'I really can't say anymore,' she added, 'I've already told you more than I should.'

'Yes . . , yes, you're right, of course,' Thorburn said quickly. 'I shouldn't have imposed.'

'I'm sure he'll be fine,' she offered. 'We often receive partial transmissions from our agents.'

Thorburn raised an eyebrow. 'Agent? I thought he was just a lucky find, but he's not the only one you're in touch with?' he asked sharply.

She felt those blue eyes studying her carefully, feeling the colour rise in her cheeks, knowing she had said too much. 'He happened to be unusually suitable and available. And we do occasionally receive signals from other contacts,' she said, very deliberately closing the subject to any further discussion.

He laughed, a broad smile lighting up his features. 'I've obviously asked far too many questions. I'll sit quietly now and let you get on.'

She found Thorburn's company a pleasant distraction. Conversation amongst the staff officers had quickly established Thorburn in a favourable light; honourable, strong willed, warm-hearted, and filled with a sense of duty.

'You've been having a busy time of it with Captain Pendleton,' she said carefully. 'He does tend to make life hectic.'

Thorburn fixed her with his blue eyes. 'You work for him?'

'At times,' she replied, smiling. 'He answers to Sir Henry rather than Dover Command. Special operations, that sort of thing.'

Thorburn frowned, said nothing.

Jennifer giggled. 'Surely you knew Pendleton answers directly to Sir Henry?'

'No . . , I wasn't aware, suppose I never thought one way or another. Willoughby thought there was something in the wind, I didn't believe him.'

She stopped smiling. 'I think he might be right. Sir Henry, Bainbridge and Pendleton work under the direction of the Joint Chiefs of Staff. It's their job to facilitate any unusual operations dreamed up by the top brass.'

The ringing of the telephone interrupted. She lifted the receiver. 'Yes?'

Listening intently, she scribbled a few notes, interspersed with a few acknowledgements. Finally she said, 'Thank you, I'll let him know,' and dropped the handset onto it's cradle.

'You'll have to excuse me. I have to speak to the General.'

124

Gathering a notepad and pen she straightened her jacket and smoothed her skirt, then slipped silently into the General's office. Inside the room a red leather topped desk sat diagonally across the far corner. Bainbridge was perched on one end with a large map skewed to one side and he looked up as she entered.

'Sir, I've just taken a message from the intelligence people.'

'Then I suggest you share it with me young lady.'

Inwardly, Jennifer smiled. Prickly today, she thought.

'Lieutenant Wingham intends to carry out first reconnaissance tonight. He also reports more troops than expected.'

'Damn it!' Bainbridge hissed. 'I counted on him having a fairly easy time of it. Still, if he thinks he can go for a wander, it can't be too bad. Anything else?'

'No, sir,' she answered briskly, but on turning to leave added, 'Lieutenant-Commander Thorburn is outside.'

He stared into space for a moment, lost in his thoughts. Then he caught her eye. 'Mmm . . , Pendleton'll be along shortly. We'll wait.' He looked back to the map already pondering his next move.

Jennifer walked through to her office and saw that Willoughby had joined Thorburn. She gave them a brief nod, she sat down in silence and began to type. The clatter of the typewriter reinforced her frown of concentration, and she hoped that would be enough to stop Thorburn asking any more questions.

Outside the front entrance in the warm morning sunshine, Pendleton climbed from his staff car and told the driver to wait. Moored out in the Medway he could see *Brackendale* swinging to her buoy, just one of the many ships harbouring up river. Approaching the steps to Admiralty House, the Captain returned the Royal Marine's salute and strode inside the familiar building. His footsteps echoed in the large foyer and his eye caught the clock as it chimed eleven. He made his way up to the first floor, breezed into his outer office and with only a nod to Thorburn and Willoughby he allowed Jennifer to lead him in to where Bainbridge had made himself at home.

'Are we ready?' Pendleton asked.

Bainbridge nodded and glanced at Jennifer. 'Yes, call 'em in.'

Thorburn entered the office cautiously, allowing Willoughby to take a seat opposite the desk before he plumped for one slightly angled to the side. Jennifer took her seat to the right, straight backed and attentive, poised with her pad to shorthand the proceedings. Bainbridge muttered a final quiet word to Pendleton, straightened in his chair and fixed Thorburn with a frowning gaze.

'I'm sure you'll be pleased to hear that the mission was a success.'

Thorburn watched his face. He didn't look very pleased.

Bainbridge rubbed his chin. 'Unfortunately, the diversionary raid by Sergeant Foster did not quite live up to expectations. I think there could have been better co-ordination between the two forces and I regret that *Veracity* was unable to give closer support on the commando's withdrawal.'

Thorburn felt the blood rising in his cheeks and a brief glance at Willoughby showed his usual relaxed cheeriness had gone. He sat rigidly motionless hands clenched on his knees. But neither spoke to argue; Pendleton had their reports, he would understand.

'On the plus side Lieutenant Wingham has made contact and will shortly carry out an initial reconnaissance.' Bainbridge glanced at Pendleton. 'Sir Henry has been informed of the situation.'

Thorburn swallowed hard. The General had imparted his information with little enthusiasm, in contrast to his bombastic attitude of previous days. Subdued, Thorburn thought, not much of the gung-ho leader of special operations that he liked to portray. He looked across to Pendleton who still remained silent, peering at some notes he held, oblivious to the proceedings.

Enough was enough. He felt compelled to speak. 'If *Veracity* had gone any closer she would have grounded. As it was, she stopped your men being decimated!' Thorburn was surprised by his own vehemence. 'If all you wanted was a diversion, a shore bombardment would have done. As it is they took a lot of casualties, and for what? To satisfy your ego.' He took a deep breath. 'Even if the diversion hadn't taken place, the weather was bad enough for us to have succeeded anyway.'

Bainbridge reacted. 'And you were in *Veracity* were you?' he snapped. 'How the hell do you know what happened?'

Thorburn let rip. 'Because I've read the bloody reports. I was Officer-in-Command at sea and its my job to find out what happened.'

Bainbridge was silent, the pale scar vivid against the colour of his cheek.

Pendleton moved to stroke his beard. 'Gentlemen,' he said quietly, 'I have the reports of your actions and I understand how you feel. None the less, its no good shouting the odds, doesn't help anyone. My reading of the situation is that you both demonstrated a good degree of leadership under trying circumstances and that no blame can be attached to the navy's part in this operation.' The last was directed towards Bainbridge, and after a moments pause, he continued, 'I have to say, sir, that any criticisms of their actions is totally unwarranted.'

Bainbridge held up a hand. 'Yes, yes, with hindsight, I suppose you're right,' he said reluctantly, 'but I really didn't expect so many casualties. Even Sergeant Foster got hit.' He cleared his throat, 'That pilot should have used his eyes more, might have come up with a better idea of how many Germans there were.'

Thorburn wasn't about to accept that. 'He only reported what he saw on passing, sir. If the troops were hidden from view . . ,' he stopped short, transfixed by the General's withering stare.

After an ominous pause Bainbridge spoke. 'Thank you, Commander. Your opinions have been duly noted.'

Richard Thorburn, as angry as he was, sat back in his chair. From the corner of his eye he had seen Pendleton's almost imperceptible shake of the head. The signal was clear; back off.

An awkward silence lingered before Pendleton noisily pulled a sheaf of papers from his briefcase. 'I should like to remind everyone that although we had our difficulties, Lieutenant Wingham is ashore.' He looked round the room. 'That was our main objective.'

Jennifer Farbrace scribbled rapidly, finished with an exaggerated flourish, and then waited expectantly, her pen poised over the page.

Pendleton continued. '*Veracity* sustained some superficial damage and I suggest she completes her repairs today, after which she will await new orders. As for *Brackendale*, she'll remain here to have an additional gun fitted.'

Thorburn straightened in surprise. 'Another gun, sir?'

'Yes, Commander,' Pendleton said. 'A bow-chaser no less. With all these E-boats about it should give you a good frontal advantage.'

Thorburn felt a dig in the ribs.

'Bow-chaser, eh,' Willoughby laughed. 'Raise the battle ensign! Signal the fleet, enemy in sight!' He slapped a knee in delight. 'What's your name, Nelson?' He stopped, almost crying with laughter.

Thorburn grinned with embarrassment and realised Pendleton was also chuckling. Even Bainbridge smiled, unable to hold a straight face against Willoughby's infectious laughter.

'No, seriously Richard,' Pendleton managed, 'we've fitted a number of the coastal patrol vessels with bow-chasers and they've proved very effective. First Sea Lord wants a lot more issued.'

Thorburn came back quickly. 'Will that mean additional gun crew, sir? I'm already down on numbers and Lieutenant Martin is still out of action.'

'Mister Martin will rejoin ship this weekend. His recovery is such that the doctors could no longer refuse his request to rejoin and is passed fit for duty. Otherwise, no. There will be no increase in the ship's compliment.'

Thorburn stood up. 'In that case, sir, we have much to get on with.'

Pendleton raised an eyebrow to the General and waited.

Above the scarred cheek his eyes carefully scrutinised both of the young officers before he decided to speak.

'The original idea of landing Lieutenant Wingham at

Goury has been achieved. As for the diversion,' he paused to look at Pendleton. 'I'm not in the habit of explaining my reasons but in this case I will make an exception. Suffice it to say that the commando raid was an attempt by the Joint Chiefs of Staff to implement a suggestion which may have come from Churchill himself.' He rubbed the back of his neck then placed both hands on the desk. 'With a little more forethought it's possible we could have done a better job.' A knowing look from Pendleton made Thorburn hold his silence.

Bainbridge stood up. 'So, gentlemen, I think that wraps it up for now.'

'Indeed,' said Pendleton, 'that about covers it. All done, Miss Farbrace?'

'Yes, sir,' she replied quickly, and closed her notepad.

Pendleton reached for his briefcase. 'I'll want a summary of the action, these officers' reports, and a copy sent to Sir Henry. My own recommendations will need to be enclosed.'

'I'll make a start now, sir,' she said, and opened the door.

Thorburn saw the turn of her head, momentarily met her gaze, and she gave an almost imperceptible smile. She dropped her eyes and twirled out through the door.

Pendleton led the two captains through Jennifer's office and out to the corridor. He stopped and replaced his cap and then turned to Thorburn.

'In future, Richard, you would be well advised to put your brain in gear before you open your mouth.'

'I thought I had a valid point, sir. And he needed telling.'

Pendleton sighed. 'Believe me, gentlemen, General Bainbridge is an extremely capable staff officer, highly regarded in Whitehall. He might be a bit unorthodox in how he operates but that's what he's all about.' He gave a small grimace as they walked towards the stairs. 'He knows this one didn't go according to plan and blames himself. Especially with the injury to Sergeant Foster. They go back a long way.'

Outside the building Pendleton bade them farewell, acknowledging their salute as he climbed into the staff car. A cloud of blue smoke signalled the engine starting and the car moved away.

Thorburn watched it go in silence, wondering whether Bainbridge would complain to Sir Henry. Probably, he thought, but was certain he'd been right in speaking out.

'Richard!' Willoughby said loudly, and Thorburn looked up from his pondering.

'No good worrying about all that now, our ships await . . , M'lord.'

Thorburn grinned at another reference to Nelson and responded by slapping Willoughby on the shoulder. They laughed together and walked down to the covered slipways, the hot sun reflecting off the rippling Medway.

As they approached *Veracity*'s stern, Lieutenant Robert Armstrong, along with Chief Petty Officer Falconer could be seen leaving the ship. Deep in conversation the appearance of the two captains took them by surprise.

'What's up, Number One?' asked Thorburn, returning their salute.

'Er, well, sir. We were just discussing the new directive for Dover's flotilla,' said Armstrong.

Thorburn glanced at Willoughby who shrugged his shoulders.

'Explain,' he said.

Armstrong took the lead. 'Dover is to be patrolled from either Portland or Sheerness, sir. *Westeram*, and Bulwark who came up from Portsmouth yesterday, have both been lost. Thirty plus Stukas and Messerschmitt. The RAF couldn't hold them. *Westeram* had her back broken and sank, Bulwark caught fire and couldn't be saved.' He paused for breath.

Falconer took over. 'They'd already jumped an outbound convoy at Dungeness, sir. E-boats hit 'em first and by the time the Stukas had finished, only six out of fourteen ships made it to safety.'

'Then they hit Dover harbour,' Armstrong continued. 'The oiler's gone, the depot ship was hit and flooded, and three MTB's were written off.'

Willoughby spoke first. 'How did you find out?'

'Signalman called in for the latest codes, sir. Had a word with his opposite number.'

Thorburn frowned. 'So how're the convoys going to operate?'

'Apparently it's going to be night runs only for the time being,' Armstrong answered.

Willoughby gave a cynical laugh. 'I can't see Churchill letting that happen for long.'

Thorburn pursed his lips. 'Unless he gets some more destroyers down here I don't think he'll have much choice.'

Willoughby nodded. 'You're probably right,' he said reluctantly. 'I'd better get back on board and see how the repairs are going.'

They separated to follow their own needs and Thorburn allowed the Cox'n to lead them to the old stone stairway from which they stepped easily into the motor boat.

'Cast off.' Armstrong gave the order, and the Cox'n throttled up for the short journey to *Brackendale*.

A few minutes later a boathook engaged with a cleat on the quarterdeck and Thorburn swung onto the ladder to be piped aboard by the side party. He waited for Armstrong.

'We'll be called to one of the covered slips shortly,' he said as they walked forward past the searchlight housing. 'Believe it or not but they're fitting us with a bow-chaser.'

Armstrong wasn't sure that he'd heard correctly. 'A what, sir?'

'I think you heard me, Number One. They're fitting us with a bow-chaser, you know, a gun up at the pointy end.'

Armstrong was grinning. 'In that case, sir, we'd better get 'Guns' to brush up on his 'ball and shot'.'

Thorburn couldn't help himself. 'I have a feeling we'll all be ribbed over this one.'

Somewhere down river an air raid siren began to wail accompanied by the faint thump of anti aircraft guns.

'Action stations, Number One,' Thorburn ordered and ran for the bridge.

As the ship came to life the gunfire increased along the river, the black balls of ack-ack marking the path of a probable intruder. On the bridge Armstrong acknowledged the reports of the individual stations manned and ready. A few barrage balloons were belatedly rising over the dockyard as the noise of heavier guns joined in.

A lookout called sharply, 'Enemy aircraft at Green five-oh!'

Thorburn swung his glasses over towards St Mary's Island twisting the knurled spindle for focus. He located the Heinkels at about twelve thousand feet, mere specks glinting silver. He held them as they flew through the visible flak, holding their formation.

Armstrong voiced an opinion, 'Only two or three, sir.'

'Hmmm,' Thorburn agreed. 'As long as they stay up there and let us get into the covered slipway.'

They watched the enemy until they disappeared behind high cloud and the guns stopped firing.

'Defence stations for now,' Thorburn said, 'but let me know when we're called in.'

He left the bridge as the 'all clear' sounded over the dockyard, making his way to the cabin below the wheelhouse. Sunlight streamed in through the scuttles and slipping out of his jacket he lit a cigarette and settled down to a pile correspondence that always seemed to be awaiting his attention.

It was late afternoon before *Brackendale* inched slowly into Number Three covered slipway. Most of her crew had appeared on deck to assist in the distribution of fenders and cables, quayside bollards and cleats tied up to, wires and hawsers given the appropriate tension.

Midshipman George Labatt stood abreast the anchor chains watching carefully as the First Lieutenant took personal charge of the docking. Overhead on the bridge, Labatt knew that Thorburn was overseeing it all with a keen interest.

'Tighten that line, Harvey!' Armstrong snapped to the quayside, and enough slack was taken out of the heavy rope to enable another turn to be whipped round the bollard.

Labatt spotted a number of dockyard workers as they appeared from a wooden hut, a tall figure in a bowler hat and briefcase leading the way. They were met by Howard and Dawkins as they came aboard, handshakes and introductions quickly dispensed with, and ushered forward to the bow. Gathering together at the jack staff the briefcase was opened and a blueprint was spread out on the deck. Three of the men wearing dirty blue boiler suits backed off to the guardrail where they began to talk amongst themselves.

Labatt heard the 'bowler hat' talking. 'A reinforcing job with beams under the deck plates,' he said, and 'Guns' gave a nod pointing to something on the drawing.

Dawkins grunted, the Welsh baritone loud in the slipway. 'And how long is all this supposed to take then?'

'By the morning,' said the man. 'We'll be working round the clock. It'll be finished,' he added in response to the Chief's raised eyebrow.

Labatt heard footsteps behind him and snapped to attention as the captain strode past towards the gathering.

'I've a job for you, Mid,' he said over his shoulder. 'Report to my cabin an hour from now.'

'Aye aye, sir,' Labatt said, and quickly checked his wristwatch. He felt a touch of apprehension about what the skipper wanted him for. Stepping cautiously over the port anchor chain he moved a few feet closer to the huddle on the bow. Unfortunately, unless he joined the perimeter of the party, their voices were inaudible, and as he hadn't been specifically invited, he chose to remain at a distance.

A movement caught his attention down at the entrance to the slipway. A large brown tarpaulin was being removed from a wooden framework and as the canvas slumped to the floor Labatt had his first glimpse of the new gun. He squinted in the gloom and recognised the outline of a Quick firing two pounder, a single Pompom.

He was astute enough to appreciate how that type of armament could focus down across the bow and fill the blind spot in the ship's defence.

He turned his attention back to the men in charge, just in time to see the blueprint being folded and returned to the briefcase. Thorburn had moved to one side with Howard, and as the meeting broke up, the Chief led the party aft. Labatt walked away to the port side and dropped easily to the main deck. He glanced at his watch, forty-five minutes to go.

The rich smell of coffee filled the wardroom and Thorburn, with his back to the fireplace, surveyed his officers over the lip of his cup.

'We'll need a good supply of ammo for that Pompom. Any thoughts?'

Howard breathed a stream of blue smoke from his pipe. 'The dockyard are saying there'll be plenty of 'ready use' lockers and they'll let us have the last word on exact location.'

Thorburn nodded slowly. 'Fair enough.' He placed the coffee cup on the mantelpiece. 'I intend to have Mister Labatt assume responsibility for it's operation. Give him a first chance at proper leadership. That just leaves the problem of gunners. Anybody in mind?'

'I'd like to use Barton and Jones, sir.'

The Captain thought about that. Barton had a proven record in gunnery and was actually recommended for a gong, should be through any time now. And Jones was about to be promoted in recognition of his expertise.

'Yes, I think we'll try that and see how it goes.'

Armstrong motioned with his cup. 'Sorry, sir, but that removes two of our best men from the Pompom.' He

136

looked at Howard. 'Is that wise? I mean, if we have to defend against E-boats and aircraft at the same time.'

Thorburn answered. 'Unlikely, Number One. If there are E-boats we're unlikely to have a simultaneous attack by enemy aircraft. Might hit their own.' He looked at Howard. 'Having said that, I'm sure the other gunners are more than capable.'

'Good crew, sir. They'll cope,' Howard said through his pipe.

Armstrong inclined his head to show his acceptance of the decision.

Thorburn spotted the reluctance in Armstrong's nod.

'Don't worry, Number One. If things get too bad we'll have a go ourselves.' He laughed with them, but hoped Howard was right. 'Just so you know, I want to say how much I appreciate your efforts in getting this ship up to scratch.' He reached for his cap and hushed their protests with a raised hand. 'I know everyone plays their part but I just wanted to personally say thank you.' He left the wardroom before they could say anything, remembering his appointment with Labatt.

Ten minutes later there was a knock on the Captain's door.

'Come,' he called.

Midshipman George Labatt entered, closed the door, and marched quickly to Thorburn's desk, his headgear tucked smartly under his left arm.

'Well done, Mid, a timely arrival, have a seat.'

'Thank you, sir,' Labatt said brightly, settling himself comfortably into the chair.

'So how're things going, still learning?'

'Yes, sir, a lot more than I ever thought possible.'

Thorburn nodded. 'Good, you keep it up. Everyone

137

tells me you're doing fine. The Cox'n thinks you'll make a fine sailor.'

Labatt grinned. 'That's not quite how he puts it to me, sir.'

Thorburn smiled in return, visualising the Cox'n's barked instructions to the young officer.

'Right, young man, as I said, I've a job for you. I hope you hadn't pinned your hopes on a run ashore. I'm afraid you'll have to remain on board.'

Labatt said nothing, leaning forward in the chair, waiting.

'I'll be allowing the ship's company a limited run ashore tonight. But for you I have a different itinery. Midnight is when the tradesmen will make a real start. That's when I want you to join them. From then on in you'll remain in their presence until you understand everything there is to know about that gun.'

Labatt nodded, a small frown appearing. 'Aye aye, sir,' he said quietly.

Thorburn watched him for a moment as the quizzical expression returned to the usual boyish smile.

'When we next put to sea you'll be in charge of that gun. I want you to be able to load and fire it yourself if necessary, understand?'

'You want me to be the gunner, sir?'

'No, Mister. We've decided to use Barton and Jones, but I want you to be just as useful if the occasion arises. Think you can do that?'

'Yes, sir, of course I can,' and for a moment the boy was a man, convincing them both of his growing abilities.

'Very well,' Thorburn said. 'If there's anything you're unsure of, any questions you might have from a naval perspective, both the First Lieutenant and Mister Howard

138

will be on board. The Cox'n will be on deck when you get there so I suggest you tie up with him and then get some rest.'

Labatt nodded his understanding as he stood up. 'Aye aye, sir.'

'Right then, carry on.'

The young man walked proudly from the Captain's cabin. First things first, find the Cox'n.

FlotillaKapitan Werner von Holtzmann, following a fruitless search for the British destroyer, had returned to Cherbourg harbour. He had immediately ordered the engine room to ensure the ship could move at a moments notice. He would not be caught so flat-footed in future. However long the Kriegsmarine required him to remain in this area, power for his ship must always be available. Standing on the bridge and looking out over the sunlit houses that bordered the harbour, it was hard to appreciate the events of last night's stormy weather.

When he had reached the area on which the enemy had landed there had been no sign of their soldiers or the ship. Taking himself quickly to the north, and then northwest had achieved absolutely nothing; no sighting, nothing. All he had to go on was a confused description from the idiots in the Wehrmacht as to what they thought the ship looked like. Walking slowly round the bridge the only conclusion he had come to was that the British warship may have been one of their old V and W class.

Another problem causing him some concern was a further report from a guard at Fort Quesnard in the northeast of Alderney. The man had notified his Unterofficier of a destroyer steaming north. Only a short sighting but the description and timing indicated there had to be two British warships involved. Thirty minutes ago Holtzmann had decided the second sighting was a similar destroyer to the one he had recently engaged near the Isle of Wight. All these things he thought about, but how did they benefit the Royal Navy?

'Herr Kapitan.'

Von Holtzmann turned to acknowledge Oberleutnant-zur-See Max Bauer.

'Ja, what is it?'

'Sir, I have just spoken with Major Gerhard Brandt of the 83rd Grenadier Battalion, They guard the west coast near Goury. One of them did not report back from patrol. He sent men to find him.'

Holtzmann nodded. 'Go on.'

'They found him at the bottom of some rocks. His neck was kaput.'

'So he fell. Probably slipped in the storm.'

'But they could not find his rifle, sir. They are not sure what happened.'

Holtzmann pursed his lips. 'So,' he said slowly. He turned to look at the harbour. 'See if you can find out anything more. And drive over to Goury with some of our men to search for the rifle. Down at the water's edge.'

There was a click of heels. 'Jawohl, Mien Kapitan,' and his footsteps receded from the bridge.

Chapter Nine . . Wingham Alone.

Lieutenant Paul Wingham squeezed cautiously out of his cave. There was enough moonlight available for him to negotiate the dangerous rocks with a reasonable amount of certainty. Noiselessly he pulled himself to within a few feet of the top and paused to listen, forcing his breathing to steady. Crouching below a rocky outcrop, his wiry frame merged with the darkness of the black granite, and he waited for his heart to quieten. Raising only his eyes above the edge he peered intently over the dim terrain. Away to his left the faint outline of rooftops were just visible. He thought he detected a movement to his right and slowly swivelled his head to check, but nothing materialized.

The weight of his Webley pistol gave a comforting reassurance so with a final look round he levered himself over the top and lay prone. Bellying forward he slithered into a low gorse bush and raised his shoulders just enough to sweep a glance along the headland.

Something attracted his attention; indefinable, a vague shape intermittently seen against the shadowy background. He hesitated trying to decipher the image. Concealment was his first priority. If the Germans became aware of his presence and went on the alert his job would be nigh on impossible. Wet soil soaked through to his elbows and knees as he crawled forward. After ten yards he was sodden, damp and cold. The moonlight dimmed, hidden by a cloud. He jumped to his feet and sprinted forward to a small gulley. Dropping to one knee he took a moment to catch his breath and estimate the distance to the nearest dwelling. Four hundred yards? Possibly . . , more like three. The moon reappeared casting a pale grey light over the landscape. There were a few scattered dwellings around him, the houses of farm labourers, or fishermen down by the harbour to his left. His destination was the outskirts of Auderville, maybe three quarters of a mile. Her house lay south of the village, a four bed roomed cottage standing in a quarter of an acre. By memory, her bedroom overlooked the back garden which contained a large shed, a long greenhouse, and a smaller shed at the hedge near the back gate.

Another cloud began to obscure the moon and he gathered himself for the next move, about two hundred yards to an old broken gate with a stack of fence posts heaped nearby. He set off on a crouching run under the starlight, hoping the cloud cover would last. Fighting for balance on the uneven ground he passed the half way mark. Then his foot slipped and he crashed to the ground. Struggling to a sitting position he felt a sharp pain in his left shoulder blade and very slowly stretched his arm above his head. Painful, made him grimace, but probably just bruised. Nothing broken. Peering ahead he thought there was about another sixty yards to the gate. He winced against the pain as he stood and glanced at the clouds. Time enough to reach cover and then have a go at reaching the house. Wary now of the ground beneath him he strode out at a fast walk, a twinge in his ankle making him feel the need to protect it. The last few yards were covered and as the moon's light returned he sank down in the shelter of the fence posts. A smell of damp wood filled the air as he checked the village for movement. His wristwatch showed it was one thirty. Satisfied all was still he turned his back to the woodpile and surveyed the ground just covered. No signs of anything stirring. He studied the area for a full minute while the pain in his shoulder eased to a dull ache. From what he could remember Marianne's house was down an old leafy road to his right. He rose to his knees with his chest leaning against the wooden staves and took a last look toward the village. Something made him freeze. The sound of male voices carried clearly on the night air and he searched again for any sign of movement. Then he saw them. Two German soldiers were walking slowly from between the houses, rifles slung over their shoulders, distinctive rear swaged helmets reflecting the moonlight.

Wingham cursed under his breath, easing himself silently to the ground. Instinctively he reached for his pistol. Along the left side of this heap of fence posts two or three staves had been stacked to lean on end, slanting outwards at the base. The gap at ground level looked big enough for Wingham to crawl into and possibly camouflage the entrance with some strategically positioned pieces.

He sneaked another look over the broken gate. They were closer now, the glare of a match flaring yellow on their faces. They walked on and turned in Wingham's direction. He bent silently to the opening. Preying that he wouldn't dislodge anything he squeezed feet first into the gap. Once inside he moved a few posts to block the entrance and, propped on one elbow, he cradled the gun and waited.

The voices moved closer, their boots crunching on gritty shale. Laughter between them as they neared the pile of wood, and the footsteps stopped. Wingham tensed, curling his finger round the trigger. Silence . . , what had they seen? A sound of scraping, a metallic clink, and one of the German's sighed, followed by the distinct aroma of coarse tobacco smoke. He realised they had sat down on the far side of the stack. With the painful throb back in his shoulder he cursed again and prepared to wait them out.

Chapter Ten . . Devon Star.

At ten minutes to midnight Midshipman George Labatt reported to the Cox'n on the port side anchor chain. Amongst the paraphernalia of welding gear and toolboxes, the craftsmen of the dockyard were assembling a base on which the new gun would be installed. The Cox'n was in conversation with a man wearing a heavy leather apron, but he acknowledged the young man's presence with a nod. 'Mister Labatt,' he said, and carried on talking.

Beyond them there was a board propped up on the starboard bow rail. A large blueprint was pinned to it and Labatt made his way over the various hoses and equipment to give himself a better look. For a full minute he studied the meaningless lines and annotations, and then began to slowly decipher the drawing's detail.

'All right, son? Know what you're looking at?'

Labatt turned to find an old man at his elbow. The whiskered face had a kindliness and he nursed a dirty white enamelled mug of tea.

'I think so,' Labatt said, haltingly. 'I was just wondering what these bits mean.' He pointed to a complex mass of lines and numerals.

The old man answered quietly. 'That's the engineer's theory for angle of deck in relationship to true horizontal. We use that calculation to make sure the whole thing's level.'

'I see,' said Labatt slowly, not really sure that he did. 'Looks a bit complicated.'

The man stroked his whiskers and chuckled. 'I'll let you into a secret, sonny.' He finished his tea and tipped the dregs over the side. 'It don't matter how complicated something looks. Take this whole ship for example. To the landlubber it's a boat floating on the water, even though it's made of steel, and steel sinks. The engineering that goes in there to make it happen remains a mystery to them.' He rubbed his nose and winked at Labatt. 'What you need to remember is that after the engineers have done their bit, us lot put it together. Just lots and lots of little bits.' He waved his hand at the drawing. 'Lots and lots of steel parts held together by lots and lots of nuts, bolts and rivets.' He smiled, and the smile was warm and generous. 'Don't ever be afraid of engineering, son. Just use your noddle and think it through.' He nodded to himself and turned away, leaving Labatt to ponder his words.

The Cox'n's voice penetrated the noise in the slip yard.

'I think that's enough for me, lads, but if you need the Royal Navy, Mister Labatt here, is your man.' The Cox'n deliberately caught Labatt's eye and motioned for him to move away

'There are only seven of them here tonight,' Falconer elaborated. 'At the moment three of 'em are in the paint locker working on the deck head. There's a young apprentice brewing up in the hut down there, and the rest you can see.' For a moment he stood, legs braced apart and hands on his hips, watching the work being done. 'I don't think there's much of a worry. I've managed a chat with most of 'em, been in the dockyard for years. Even the youngster's one of the family.'

'Thanks, Cox'n, I'll be okay,' Labatt said, hoping the Cox'n was right.

'Right then, sir.' Falconer allowed the subtle distinction of their relationship to come to the fore. 'I've just seen the First Lieutenant on the bridge. Don't s'pose we'll sleep much tonight, not with the bloody noise their making.'

Labatt stole a sideways glance at the Coxswain and tried to analyse the man's assessment of the situation. If the Cox'n judged these civilians to be sound, that was good enough for a young apprentice officer. The blueprint still fascinated him, so, remembering Thorburn's instructions, he walked over to the drawing.

Across the Channel near the French port of Goury, two German soldiers were in no hurry to resume their patrol. Only when they'd finished another cigarette did they finally sling their rifles and trudge off towards the nearest house.

Wingham wasn't about to take any chances. Inside the stack of wooden stakes, he waited while the footsteps receded. He strained to catch the last words, and even when he heard no more he remained motionless, forcing himself to be still.

After another few minutes he reached out to touch the stakes covering the entrance. Holding his breath he gently eased the first one to the ground. It was another seven pieces before he managed to wriggle free. He hugged the damp earth, listening. Rising to one knee he peered out in the direction the Germans had taken. There was no sign. In the faint light of the moon he carefully checked his immediate surroundings. He paused to double check the shadows.

Mind made up he stepped tentatively on the gravel track and crossed over to the quiet softness of the grass verge. He aimed for the nearest house, from where the Germans had first appeared, and moved off the cobbled street to skirt the rear garden. A vague silhouette of a line of trees marked the edge of the road he was looking for. The shortest route would take him across the corner of the meadow and he pushed on through knee high grasses. A dry ditch ran alongside the road and he stepped down out of sight.

Somewhere behind him a dog barked, and he froze. It was a distant bark but he felt compelled to wait. When all was quiet he moved on, carefully negotiating the bottom of the ditch. A familiar dark roof and chimney appeared from between the trees, just visible against the paler sky. Wingham climbed out of the ditch, wary of his aching ankle. Three hundred yards ahead was the small white picket fence along the front of the property. A tree trunk offered a chance to take the weight off his foot and he took the time to consider his options. Front door was too exposed; it was the back garden with the sheds which offered the best concealment. He tested the ankle and set off to find the rear entrance, feeling his way down the old perimeter wall.

The wrought iron gate squealed slightly but he slipped inside and found cover in the tool shed at the back of the vegetable patch. He was sweating freely as he watched the back of the house. Her bedroom window curtains were drawn, raising his hopes of finding her at home. He wondered if she was alone. Reluctantly he pulled out the pistol and cautiously walked down the little pathway to the back door. He tried the catch but the door wouldn't move. Cursing under his breath he stepped back and looked up at her closed window. He decided to knock on the door. Using the knuckle of his forefinger he tapped lightly, three times, and stepped away to watch her window. She failed to appear.

Taking a deep breath he stepped over to the door and knocked again, persistently loud. Away from the door he looked up and saw movement at the corner of the curtain. He whipped off his beret and turned his face to the moon. The curtain dropped back and a minute later he heard the bolt being withdrawn.

'Paul,' she whispered. 'I didn't recognise you in uniform. Inside, quickly! What are you doing here?'

Wingham stepped into the darkness of the large kitchen, the sweet smell of wood smoke permeating the room. 'Sorry to wake you,' he said. In the blackness he felt her close presence.

'This way,' she said, and he felt her hand guide him across the flagstone floor. A door was unlatched.

'There are steps down. Mind your head.'

He crouched, feeling a wall to his right, and walked down a short stone staircase.

'Wait,' she ordered, forcing him to stand still. A match flared, bright in the dark cellar, and a small candle glowed on a bench.

'Why are you here?' she hissed.

Wingham took in the beautiful face, the dark hair falling to her shoulders, the liquid eyes glinting with anger. 'I have orders to help get a man out of France and he's in this area.'

She pushed the hair from the side of her face. 'I think you are very lucky, there are many Nazis here.'

He nodded. 'I guessed as much. How many do you think?'

'Four hundred, maybe more. There were Gestapo, but they are gone. Just some SS in the village hall.' She

149

tightened the cord of her robe and folded her arms. 'Who is this man?'

Wingham ignored the question and slipped the pistol back in its holster. 'Have you heard from anyone in Bricquebec?'

Marianne narrowed her eyes. 'Of course not, why would I?'

He chose not to answer immediately, holding her petulant gaze with his own. When he finally answered it was with studied care. 'Marianne, I know you are with the local resistance. Another group is trying to bring an Englishman to Auderville so I wondered if they'd made contact yet.'

'How do you know this?' she asked defiantly. 'Who are you working for?'

He sucked in air and breathed out slowly. 'Churchill,' he said. It was a lie, but not too far removed from the truth. Indirectly it was the Prime Minister who had ordered the operation.

'I can not help you,' she said. 'The messenger is dead.' The liquid eyes blinked in sadness.

'Oh, sorry,' he said. 'What happened?'

She turned away and lowered her head. 'A group of men were caught by the SS and taken for questioning. When one of them tried to escape so the officer shot him.' She came back to him and he saw the tears. 'It was Pierre.' Her shoulders shook and he folded her into his arms, her head buried against his chest.

Wingham ran a hand slowly up and down her back in sympathy. Pierre was her brother and he remembered they'd met once or twice last summer. 'I am really sorry,' he whispered.

She shrugged in his arms. 'We all knew it could

150

happen; you just hope it won't.'

Wingham held her for a moment longer then pushed her back to look into her eyes. 'Is there no other way to get a message to the others?'

She stared at him, thinking. 'It might be possible. Three days in the week a farmer comes with milk, his horse and cart. I think he knows more than he tells. He will be here tomorrow.'

Wingham didn't like the sound of it. 'So,' he said thoughtfully. 'You will try to ask him if he knows of these men. If you are right and he agrees, where do we meet?'

'There is an old shepherd hut, not used now. We could meet them there, try for tomorrow night, or the night after.'

Wingham hesitated studying her face in the candle's glow. 'Marianne, this is very dangerous. If you are wrong, he might inform on you, to the SS.'

'What have I to lose?' She asked defiantly. 'Pierre is dead. I have no one else.' She shook her hair back from her face. 'At least I might help to avenge his death.'

Wingham straightened, reached for her hands. 'I'll come again tomorrow, same time. You decide when to have them at the hut. All I ask is that you make it at night, in the darkness.'

She raised a hand to touch his cheek. 'For you, Paul, whatever you ask. There will be no problems.' She stretched up and kissed him on the cheek. 'Now you must go.' The candle light disappeared and they climbed up the steps to the kitchen. At the back door she held him back while she checked the outside. 'All clear,' she whispered.

'Until tomorrow,' he said, and making his way up to the back gate, slipped away to find the ditch.

At Chatham, when dawn broke the following morning, the fitting of the bow-chaser was complete. The majority of battle damage patched up and repaired, and most of the work repainted. It was still early when Thorburn received a message to report to Pendleton's office. When he arrived the Captain wasted no time on formalities. There was a damaged freighter in need of assistance and the nearest available help was *Brackendale*. Pendleton had already instructed the dockyard to release the ship and even as they talked the small destroyer floated free of her berth. Thirty minutes later and the boilers were raising steam; within the hour she was running past the outer defences of Sheerness. Rounding Margate's headland *Brackendale* was making twenty-two knots and Thorburn had his first chance to review the situation.

Overnight, a northbound convoy had been attacked by E-boats. Two of the escort vessels had put up a spirited defence and finally succeeded in driving them off. Unfortunately the SS *Devon Star*, a four thousand ton coal freighter, had sustained damage to her steering gear. The skipper had managed to affect a partial repair, but because of her continually erratic behaviour, was forced to reduce speed. An Admiralty built trawler was keeping her company, standing by 'just in case'. Shore staff had made the decision to give the *Devon Star* more help, believing the trawler to be better employed on her minesweeping duties. It was *Brackendale* that was ordered to 'Proceed with all Despatch', and was now pushing on as she turned on a southerly course.

A glimmer of crimson sunrise lifted from the east as

Thorburn arrived on the compass platform. He made a quick check on the lookouts and swept the channel with his own binoculars. Not much of interest at this level.

'Evans,' he called to one of the lookouts.

The man turned his head. 'Sir.'

'I could do with your eyes up top,' he said, lifting his chin to the mast. The ship lurched and yawed sideways, meeting the larger waves of the channel.

Evans grinned. 'Aye aye, sir,' he answered and scrambled for the main mast.

Thorburn glanced at the compass.

Martin was quick to notice. 'Steering one-seven-oh, sir.'

Thorburn nodded. 'Very good.' There was cool spray on his face as *Brackendale* rose and fell, riding the oncoming seas. He settled onto the seat, one foot braced against the screen. Daylight came swiftly, spreading the glow of warm visibility, every minute extending the visible horizon. The old harbour of Broadstairs slipped by on the starboard beam, familiar landmarks to give 'Pilot' an accurate plot. Next up was Ramsgate around to their right.

'Starboard five. Steer, one-eight-four,' he ordered.

The ship swung gently to her new course allowing the destroyer to run parallel with the coast. This time of day there was no obvious movement to be seen. Ramsgate's harbour and houses disappeared astern as *Brackendale* crossed the outer reaches of Pegwell Bay.

'Ship on the starboard bow!' came a call from overhead.

Thorburn came to his feet and looked up at the mast. Evans was clinging to the crosstree, his telescope scanning the way ahead.

153

'It's a freighter, sir,' he shouted, 'standing out from Deal. In trouble, sir.'

Thorburn raised his glasses and found the target. She was broadside to the waves and rolling uncontrollably, the fo'c'sle getting swamped. He thought for a moment, considering his options. Not that he had much choice. They would have to try and tow her into deeper waters.

'Mister Martin,' he called sharply. 'Ask the First Lieutenant to join me.'

Thick smoke billowed from the freighter's funnel and Thorburn guessed the engine room were striving to give the skipper full power. She was dangerously close to shore, time was short.

Armstrong arrived. 'You wanted me, sir?'

'Yes, Number One. We'll have a go at getting a tow on her. Won't be easy this close in but it's worth a try.'

'I'll get a party on the quarterdeck,' Armstrong said, nodding. 'Special sea duty men, sir?

'Yes, they'll probably be the most familiar with this sort of thing.'

Armstrong hurried off the bridge, immediately calling out a string of names.

Thorburn turned his attention to the freighter. Studying her closely through the glasses he could see she was making very little headway. Wallowing heavily in the troughs and broadside on to the waves the ship was struggling to survive. If only they could get near enough.

'Wheelhouse!' Thorburn called down the pipe.

'Cox'n on the wheel, sir,' came the expected reply.

'We have the *Devon Star* in sight now. We're going to try and get a tow on her. Not far from shore so I need to get this right first time.'

Falconer's voice came back strongly. 'Aye aye, sir.

154

Understood.'

The morning sun had risen clear of the horizon and *Brackendale*'s passage was marked by her shadow rippling over the dancing waves. The two ships were three thousand yards apart with the destroyer closing in at twenty-two knots. The freighter had her bows pointing towards the southwest and it was Thorburn's intention to bring his ship along her port side while he explained to her captain.

'Half ahead, both,' he ordered.

'Half ahead, both, aye aye, sir.'

Thorburn heard the ring of the telegraph and moments later the ship's twin screws slowed and *Brackendale* assumed a more comfortable advance. At a distance of fifteen hundred yards he began the manoeuvre.

'Starboard ten.'

The destroyer swung towards the shoreline. Thorburn waited as the ship turned, feeling the corkscrew motion from under her port quarter.

'Steady.'

'Wheel's amidships, sir,' from the Cox'n.

A salt-water rainbow spirited across the bow and was gone. Thorburn glanced at *Devon Star*, squinted at the shoreline, forced himself to wait before attempting to turn under the freighter's lee. 'Port thirty!'

'Port thirty, aye, sir.'

'Slow ahead port,' Thorburn ordered. His eyes narrowed, gauging the distance to the rusting side plates, watching *Brackendale*'s bows sweep round, aware of the uncomfortable ride. He glanced at the compass and back at the freighter. They were almost parallel.

'Midships, slow ahead both,' he said into the bell shaped end of the pipe.

155

'Midships, slow ahead both, aye, sir.'

Thorburn could see the violent wash of foaming water between the two ships.

'Steady now, Cox'n. Steer, one-three-five degrees.'

'One- three-five, degrees, aye aye, sir.'

A tall figure emerged from the freighter's enclosed bridge. As he stepped on to the bridge wing a battered cap was pushed firmly over the eyes, the distinctive insignia of a captain, glinting gold on the peak. Thorburn reached for the megaphone and hailed the skipper.

'Would you like us to give you a tow?' He knew the answer would be yes. No captain worth his salt would allow his ship to remain in such jeopardy.

The man nodded and jabbed two thumbs upwards in agreement.

The decision was made. 'I'll put a line on your bows. You'll need to make secure.'

Again a thumb came up followed by a brief wave, and the skipper turned to the bridge and disappeared.

'Half ahead,' Thorburn ordered. Moving to the starboard wing he looked aft to the quarterdeck. A party of men stood clustered about the depth charge rails with Armstrong looking forward awaiting his signal. A check on the *Devon Star* showed four crewmen weaving their way past the cargo hatches and stopping near the anchor windlass. *Brackendale*'s stern had drawn level with the freighter's bow plates, less than twenty feet between them.

'Stop engines!'

A raised hand to Armstrong and a line whipped across between the ships. Practised hands made it secure before the heavy towing cable was gradually pulled from the destroyer.

'Slow ahead,' Thorburn barked, juggling with *Brackendale*'s engines, trying to maintain an even distance between vessels. Minutes seemed to stretch forever but Thorburn bit his tongue and waited. It wouldn't do any good to start shouting at anyone, they were all doing the best they could. Eventually an older member of *Devon Star*'s crew signalled that they had the cable fastened off and Thorburn reached for his megaphone.

'I'll move ahead and take the strain. If all's well, we'll begin the tow.'

The older crewman waved a hand and shouted an acknowledgement, almost lost in the wind.

Thorburn turned to see Armstrong looking at the freighter's bow as *Brackendale* eased slowly ahead.

'Starboard fifteen,' Thorburn ordered. He had to bring the destroyer in line ahead of the freighter. The heavy cable lunged clear of the waves and dropped down in a gentle curve, just clear of the water. *Brackendale* was now angled half way across the bow of *Devon Star* and that was the moment he ordered a turn to port. An undignified corkscrew marked her swing, the oncoming waves lashing at the port bow, seemingly determined to prevent any progress. Moments passed as Thorburn waited, looking over his shoulder until the two ships finally converged into line astern.

'Midships.'

'Midships, aye aye, sir,' Falconer called in reply.

On the quarterdeck, Armstrong raised his clenched fist to indicate the freighter's weight being taken up and Thorburn felt *Brackendale*'s momentum slow. Between the ships the cable snapped tight, an aura of spray whipping around the hawser.

Thorburn ordered an increase in revolutions and the warship responded, digging in her stern as the twin screws boiled the sea astern. *Brackendale* started to yaw, from side to side, straining to pull the heavy load.

'Full ahead both!' he called sharply, knowing as he gave the order the danger of parting the line. But within moments the ship came under control. 'Half ahead both,' he adjusted, willing *Brackendale* to maintain her heading.

'Watch her, Cox'n!' he snapped at the voice-pipe, instantly regretting the outburst, knowing that Falconer was doing his utmost. But that short burst of speed had done the job. The destroyer settled, the tow was still intact and they had managed to increase the distance to the shore. Thorburn wiped the film of salt spray from his face, working out his options. Next priority was to bring both ships head on to the waves, at which time they would be able to ride the waters in a more seamanlike fashion.

'Starboard five,' to the wheelhouse.

'Starboard five, aye aye, sir,' Falconer replied.

Now the waiting game, waiting for the destroyer to come into the wind, to meet the waves. At the same time that towline must not be put under too much or too little strain. It mustn't get snagged in his own propellers and it wouldn't do to tighten so much that the line broke. His fears were well founded. Twice Thorburn thought the cable had snapped as the ships closed the gap and the line slackened beneath the waves. On the second occasion the freighter rose from a trough as *Brackendale* slid bow first down a wave, the resulting crack of the cable scattering men who feared the whiplash of a loose end. But the line held and both vessels ended up riding more comfortably into the wind. Their speed was manageable and Thorburn felt it was a major achievement to be moving ahead at six knots.

'Enemy aircraft! Red four-oh, angle of sight, three-oh.'

Thorburn cursed loudly and reached for his binoculars. A moment to focus, then a sighting. A single Mescherschmitt, cloud hopping, probably sending his report right now, he thought; two ships, sitting ducks. The Mescherschmitt flew into a cloud and as Thorburn was unable to control events in the sky, he returned to the more immediate problem of nursing the freighter to safety. Holding themselves to the oncoming waves put them on a southwesterly course. Ideally he wanted to track northeast towards the sanctuary of Chatham's dockyard.

'Yeoman!' he called to the bridge signaller. 'See if anybody can read semaphore in that ship.'

The man gave him a look which well expressed his doubts, but to which his professionalism would not be compromised. 'Aye aye, sir,' he acknowledged, and moved quickly to the flag locker and delved inside. Having found what he needed, he moved over to the starboard deck. With unusual formality his arms began to move through the customary pattern. When nothing appeared to happen in response Thorburn grimaced and returned to the forebridge bracing himself against the incoming waves. A long gentle turn to port, he thought, frowning at yet another complex bit of seamanship.

'Sir, the freighter's signalling!'

Thorburn swung round in surprise. Sure enough a member of the crew was standing on a forward hatch cover waving what looked like a large pair of handkerchiefs.

'Can you read it?'

'Yes, sir. No mistakes.'

'Right. Tell them we will make a slow turn to port and make for the Medway.'

The Yeoman began the lengthy process of relaying the message and Thorburn picked up the handset which linked the bridge to the depth charge station.

A voice rattled his eardrum, 'Depth Charges!'

'Captain speaking. Tell the First Lieutenant I'd like a word.'

A moment passed before Armstrong's distant metallic voice came on. 'Yes, sir?'

'How's it going back there, Number One?'

'Everything seems to be holding at the moment. Not that I'm very practised at this sort of thing.'

Thorburn smiled to himself; little did Armstrong know his captain wasn't all that experienced either, but it wouldn't do to let him know. The handset crackled in his ear.

'Well done, Number One.' He pitched his voice higher trying to ensure clarity. 'Thought I ought to warn you, I'm going to make a turn to port. Might get a bit tricky.'

There was a prolonged silence before Armstrong replied. 'Right, sir . . , we're protecting the line with a lot of padding, same on the freighter. Trying not to fray it on the steelwork.'

Thorburn digested the warning. If the cable slipped away from the protection. . , a broken tow might not be repairable.

'Right,' he said slowly. 'I'll make a wide circle to port. Keep me informed. By the way, we have a Mescherschmitt for company. Keeping out of range.'

Armstrong gave a sharp chuckle. 'I've not invited him to the party, sir.'

Thorburn smiled. 'Well if he gets too close we'll try

and keep him occupied,' he said, and replaced the handset. He looked up over the screen.

'Where's that Mescherschmitt now?' he asked staring at the sky.

'Lost him, sir. Dived behind that big one,' said the lookout, pointing to a bank of cloud.

'Very well.' Thorburn squinted at the white mass, taking in the broken edges, willing the enemy to make an appearance.

'Mr Martin,' he said over his shoulder. 'Let the hands know we'll be turning to port. Could get a bit lively.' And with hardly a pause, ' have you got that message across yet. Yeoman?'

'Just getting an answer now, sir.'

Thorburn waited. No point in rushing this, better to have the freighter's Master informed.

'Reply, sir. Reads . . .' Thank you. Will try to assist'. That's all, sir.'

Thorburn nodded. Four to six knots, tethered to the coaler, and unable to manoeuvre if they were attacked.

Martin returned to report that all hands were prepared.

'Very well,' said Thorburn. 'Here we go.' The voice pipe waited. 'Port ten!'

Falconer acknowledged.

Brackendale crested a rolling wave, twisted down the trough and then responded to the rudder. The destroyer turned in a corkscrew coming round too quickly, much tighter than Thorburn expected.

'Midships!' he ordered sharply.

The Cox'n's reply was unflustered. 'Midships, aye aye, sir.'

'Hold her steady on that, Cox'n.' Thorburn looked aft. Over the starboard bridge wing he could see Armstrong and his crew fighting with the padding. It was obvious the drag of the freighter had caused the steering to over react and Thorburn had to take it more gently.

'Cox'n!' he called, bent to the voice pipe.

'Wheelhouse, sir.'

Thorburn raised his voice. 'The weight of the freighter is acting like a pendulum. Give the wheel a five degree turn to port but bring it round slowly, point at a time.'

'Five degrees point at a time. Aye aye, sir.'

Thorburn straightened with one eye on the compass, half turning to glance astern, having to absorb everything at once. Cable stretched taut with the freighter wallowing to starboard, Armstrong balancing precariously on a depth charge rail, and the boiling sea foaming out from the stern. He saw the First Lieutenant turn to look at the bridge, a waved 'thumbs up' held until he gave an acknowledgement.

'Hold her on that, Cox'n, we're coming round.'

'Not quite on five degrees, sir.'

Slowly, gradually, the two ships made a protracted turn. Riding unevenly through the worst of the waves as they passed due south, continuing to pull round until both vessels eventually rode a parallel course to the coast. From ship to shore the gap had opened up to three thousand yards and Thorburn nodded in satisfaction.

'Steady on oh-nine-five degrees,' he ordered and allowed himself a moment to gather his thoughts. The damaged freighter was down on power but had managed to centralise her steering. *Brackendale*'s twin screws were producing most of the effort but now had a better grip on the direction of travel. So far Armstrong had somehow, miraculously, kept the tow in place and intact, to the extent of allowing the pair of ships to achieve almost nine knots. The Mescherschmitt had not reappeared and, he smiled to himself, the sun was shining.

'Signal, sir!'

Thorburn turned to his Chief Yeoman and read the message "What is your situation?" It was Pendleton's inquiry and Thorburn conjured up an image of his concerned boss.

'Take this down. "I have the *Devon Star* in tow. Making nine knots. Recovering to Chatham," and give our position.'

The Yeoman finished writing and gave a quick salute. 'Aye aye, sir.'

Thorburn nodded. 'Carry on.' He looked round at the men manning the bridge, the lookouts ever watchful, the signallers at their lamps, machine guns manned and ready. He moved over to join Martin on the compass platform. 'I think a hot drink wouldn't go amiss, Sub.'

The young man bobbed his head in agreement. 'I'll see to it, sir,'

Brackendale dipped her head into a big roller, staggered, and slowly lifted clear of the water, a cascade of foaming sea swilling back along her decks. Thorburn tasted the salt laden spray, squinting over the misted bridge-screen. Ahead of the port beam lay the small Cinque port of Sandwhich and beyond that, Pegwell Bay. He wished they could go faster.

'Enemy aircraft! Green, eight-oh'

Thorburn grabbed his binoculars but spotted the 109's without their aid. Low down off the starboard beam they were flying at the two ships with intent.

'Stukas! Red, nine-oh.'

Thorburn spun round towards the coast where an outstretched arm showed four more aircraft diving in from the opposite side. He grabbed a handset. Howard answered. 'Concentrate on the Stukas, 'Guns'. I'll put secondary on the 109's.' He slammed the handset back in it's cradle and leaned on the bridge-screen. 'Barton!' he shouted.

The gunner's face turned to answer.

Thorburn pointed at the two 109s. 'Open fire!' he yelled, and the bow-chaser cracked into action. He moved quickly to the starboard bridge wing and the Oerlikon. That was enough; the gun shuddered, hammering shells at the targets. Beside Thorburn the two Lewis guns joined in. The four-barrelled Pompom burst into life just as both forward guns crashed out a salvo. Thorburn winced, instinctively hunching his shoulders. A multi-coloured stream of tracer converged on the Mescherschmitts and Thorburn clenched his fists, anticipating a strike. Instead, he saw a ripple of canon fire from the nose of the lead aircraft as it pressed home the attack.

A loud cheer from the quarterdeck housing dragged his attention back to the dive-bombers. One of the Stukas was trailing black smoke and peeling away from the attack. The whistle of a bomb reached a crescendo and exploded off their port quarter, a mountain of seawater erupting higher than the bridge. Canon shells smashed through the steel screens of the bridge, fiery sparks and splinters ricocheting dangerously in the confined space. Thorburn ducked as another rattle of shells bounced around him. He peered out at the Stukas and watched another bomb drop.

A dreadful pain lanced through his left shoulder. He fell against the compass binnacle, grabbing it to hold himself from falling. He sucked air through clenched teeth, eyes closed against the burning pain. He was stunned, shocked by the hurt to his body, fighting to

164

recover his balance. His legs felt weak and he couldn't make them operate.

'Sir!' Martin called, and reached out in support.

Thorburn felt an arm come under his good shoulder and he forced his legs upright. 'Thanks, Sub,' he managed.

'Your chair, sir,' Martin raised his voice above the din, and Thorburn found the stable security of the seat beneath him. A burning agony surged through his left arm and when he looked down, there was a lot of blood.

'They're coming in again!'

Forcing himself to concentrate through the pain Thorburn realised the gunfire had slackened, but almost instantly the noise level increased. He coughed from a waft of gun smoke, the spasm jolting his wound.

'Steady, sir, hold still.' The reassuring voice of 'Doc' Waverly penetrated his being and he felt fingers probing around his arm and shoulder. More pain coursed through his chest, a sickening, white hot agony.

'Got it,' Waverly pronounced in triumph.

Thorburn managed to raise his eyes as the pain diminished. Waverly's bloodied fingers held an ugly shard of steel.

'Shrapnel,' came the explanation. 'Lodged at the top of your shoulder blade. No real damage, we'll have you patched up in a minute.'

The level of gunfire had reached a peak and Thorburn struggled to make himself heard. 'Thank you, Doc,' he managed through gritted teeth. 'You'd better see to the others.'

'Spitfires! Red, one hundred. Three of 'em, sir.'

Thorburn forced himself to glance up over the port beam and even managed a brief smile. The Royal Air

Force, diving straight at the enemy.

'Cease fire!' he ordered as the Stukas took evasive action, scattering under a hail of machine gun fire. One of the Spitfires latched on to the back of a dive-bomber and gave it a long burst. The Stuka tried to turn away but was too late. An explosion ripped through the fuselage and it fell away burning fiercely.

The port Oerlikon rattled off a short burst and Thorburn turned to shout a reprimand. The gunner jabbed a finger in alarm. 'They haven't seen the 109's!'

Both Mescherschmitts had survived unscathed and everyone on *Brackendale* watched as they climbed below the tail of the last Spitfire. They looked on helplessly, unable to intervene as the enemy closed the distance. The nose cannon smoked from the leading 109 and tracer rounds hit the Spitfire's tailplane. The R.A.F. pilot instantly reacted and threw his aircraft into a spiral, a momentary escape from death. The second Mescherschmitt had anticipated the move, and cutting down across the angle, let off a quick burst in his path.

Unable to avoid this ultimate line of fire the Spitfire's engine coughed, spluttered and stopped. It banked round towards *Brackendale* with the pilot fighting to hold the aircraft in a nose heavy glide, and just managed to avoid the ship's funnel before hitting the waves. As the watery impact subsided the fuselage dipped beneath the surface, the tail rose up, and the Spitfire slid from sight. Thorburn turned away, saddened by the loss of the pilot.

When he looked back above the mast he saw the attack was over. Fleeing from their victory the Germans were making for the nearest clouds. One of the Spitfires gave chase but the other swept in low over the crash site banking hard to get a better look. It straightened sharply, waggled its wings and turned to fly over the destroyer's bridge, swaying from side to side.

'Pilot on the surface!' Jones called from the Lewis gun.

Thorburn peered out beyond the starboard bow, squinting at the shining water. A head and shoulders slid out from a trough, an arm waving for help. Thorburn smiled grimly. He was lucky to have survived, but how to save him; and save him we must, tethered to the freighter or not. Pain stabbed him in the shoulder and lanced down his arm. He cursed and breathed in with a hiss. They had to get that pilot out.

'Sub, . . get the Cox'n up here.'

Moments passed as the pilot was swept remorselessly past the ship's beam.

Falconer climbed into the bridge. 'You're 'urt, sir?'

Thorburn dismissed the concern. 'Flesh wound. Doc'll see to it.' He motioned for Falconer to come closer. 'What do you feel about launching the motorboat while we're moving like this?'

Falconer gave him an old fashioned look and edged over to the starboard bridge wing. He looked at the waves and then at the boat hanging in it's davits. Turning back to Thorburn, he grinned. 'Done it once off Portsmouth, sir. Not sure we was goin' this quick, but I'll give it a go.' He looked around him. 'I'll need the bosun and . . , Leading Seaman Talbot in the boat.'

Thorburn nodded thoughtfully, head tilted to one side.

'Piece of cake, sir. Really.'

Thorburn allowed himself to be convinced. 'Right then,' he said, with a lot more conviction than he felt. 'Let's get it done. That pilot will be out of sight soon.'

Waverly intervened. 'That wound needs cleaning up

167

properly. I'll make a better job of it in the sick berth.'

Thorburn shook his head as Falconer ran from the bridge.

'A few more minutes, Doc. At least until that pilot is on board. Then you can have all the time you want.'

'If you insist,' Waverly snorted, and reluctantly walked away muttering under his breath.

At the boat station the securing straps and sea-going covers had been whisked away and Thorburn turned to look for the pilot.

'Off the starboard quarter, sir,' Jones pointed.

Thorburn searched through his binoculars.

'Yep, I've found him, Jones.' His wound throbbed again and he dropped the glasses to his chest.

'Boat's almost ready, sir.'

Rubbing his left arm to relieve the pain, Thorburn moved to the back of the bridge. Hovering above the waves the boat swayed with the ship's motion. The three men were crouched ready for the drop. Falconer signalled for the stern to be lowered again and as the propeller found water the Cox'n hit the starter. Bow up and bouncing with the waves he whipped a hand across his throat in a cutting motion and the bosun made the release. The small boat skittered wildly and thumped *Brackendale*'s side plates, almost turning broadside to the waves. Somehow Falconer regained control and a moment later the three men swept away in pursuit of the pilot.

Thorburn swallowed hard, relieved that no one was hurt and surprised that Falconer had managed to pull it off. Ignoring the pain from his shoulder he raised the glasses and held the motorboat in focus as she careered towards the small figure of the pilot.

'Enemy ships! Green one-seven-five. Ten thousand yards'

Thorburn spun to face the stern. 'Now what?' he uttered in disbelief, and dialled in his binoculars off the starboard quarter. The freighter filled his vision pitching and rolling along in their wake. 'I can't see a bloody thing,' he grunted. Then a distant topmast appeared briefly a dark red and black flag of the German navy catching his eye. 'I have them,' he muttered, and relaxed his grip on the glasses. Above him the control tower turned onto the target's bearing.

'Yeoman!' Thorburn called, and the Petty Officer stepped forward.

'Send a signal to Dover Command. "Enemy in sight. Request priority air cover." Send it in clear.' Being as the enemy could see them, coding up the message would be a waste of time. 'Get our position off pilot. Quick as you can,' he added, constructing a plan of action for his next move.

'Bridge-Director.'

'Go ahead, 'Guns.'

'That German destroyer, sir. Looks like our friend from the other night.'

'Right,' said Thorburn. 'If it gets in range, open fire.'

Howard acknowledged.

'Motorboat returning, sir,' Jones called.

Thorburn looked round for Armstrong, then caught sight of him down at the boat station. He preyed Armstrong would be his usual efficient self. No mistakes. He suddenly felt tired, drained of strength. The bridge chair took his weight and he took a deep breath to clear his head. He tried to consider how best to minimise the enemy threat. The Germans were coming in from the freighter's stern. That had limited their chance of being seen and he felt lucky to have located them so early. Without air cover his options were extremely limited. In fact, the only sensible course of action was to slip the tow and position *Brackendale* off the freighter's starboard quarter. That would give him a degree of flexibility for manoeuvre.

'Jacket off please.'

Thorburn looked round to find Doc Waverley at his side.

'I'm obviously not going to get you below, so the best I can do is dress the wound and make you more comfortable.' While he spoke the torn jacket and blood soaked shirt were removed. Thorburn realised his steward was standing by with a fresh shirt and jumper. The blood was sponged away, an antiseptic ointment applied, and Waverley made short work of placing a fresh dressing to the wound. 'Right, let's get this shirt on,' and between them Thorburn managed to slip into the sleeves without too much discomfort. Luckily his preference in knitwear was always on the baggy side, allowing him to ease painlessly into the chunky wool. A white sling followed and Thorburn found he felt a lot more comfortable.

'Thanks, Doc, much better,' he admitted. 'Think I'll live?' he grinned.

Waverley ignored the flippant remark. 'You've lost a lot of blood,' he warned. 'Might make you dizzy.'

'Well I'll just have to live with it. I'm a bit busy right now,' he said brusquely, and reached for a handset.

The First Lieutenant answered. 'Sir?'

'Sorry, Number one, but we'll have to slip the tow. There's a German destroyer off the starboard quarter.'

'Now, sir?'

'Yes. I'll try and inform the freighter's captain. And let me know when you're done,' Thorburn ordered.

'Aye aye, sir,' Armstrong acknowledged, and hung up.

Thorburn stepped over to the starboard wing. The ship's motorboat was being secured and he just caught a glimpse of the bosun carrying the pilot below.

Clambering on to the bridge, the Cox'n made his report. 'Pilot's on his way to sick berth, sir. Taken a few knocks.'

Thorburn nodded his satisfaction. 'Well done, Cox'n, bloody marvellous! All looked a bit dodgy there for a moment.'

'Piece of cake, sir.' Falconer half closed one eye in a slow wink.

Thorburn gave another single nod. 'Yes, Cox'n, I'm sure it was,' he said dryly. 'I suggest you dry off and grab a hot drink. There's a German . .'

'Destroyer coming up on the starboard quarter,' Falconer interrupted.

'We'll slip the tow,' Thorburn explained. 'Going to get busy.'

'I'll just check the wheelhouse first, sir.'

Thorburn played along. If he went to the wheelhouse he'd take the wheel.

'Very well, carry on.'

The Cox'n turned away to the ladder, stepping smartly to one side as Armstrong arrived.

'Tow's gone, sir,' he said quietly.

'Thank you, Number One.'

Brackendale was steaming north-north-east, up the coast, but now it was time for Thorburn to bring her round to face the enemy. He checked their bearing from the compass, gave a moments thought for the safety of his people and gave the order. 'Starboard thirty. Full ahead both. Steer one-seven-oh.'

Free at last from any restraint the ship surged forward and leaned hard to port as she swept away from the shore. Managing to get a clear line of sight down the coast Thorburn freed his arm from the sling and trained his glasses on the enemy destroyer. There was something familiar about that ship. Not obvious, more a subconscious feeling, and it was a big destroyer, similar in size to the other night. Holding the enemy in vision Thorburn called out an order. 'Number One, hoist the battle flag.' When he lowered the binoculars everyone was grinning.

With bow wave flying *Brackendale* powered down *Devon Star*'s side. Thorburn felt a twinge of guilt in cutting the tow, leaving those men to take their chances. A faint cheer reached him on the bridge and he looked in surprise at her crew waving them on, with headgear held aloft. At maximum speed they powered on towards the enemy flotilla.

'Range?' he queried.

'Five thousand yards, sir.'

A cloud of spray washed the bridge and Thorburn tasted the salt. Cold and wet, refreshing. He glanced over his shoulder at the freighter. Experience told him it was far enough. 'Port twenty, half ahead both.' A voice echoed up from the wheelhouse and Thorburn half smiled to himself. As he expected the Cox'n had returned to his action station.

Obeying the rudder *Brackendale* turned away from the coast and swung around to run about eight hundred yards from the freighter's stern rail. Thorburn could see the damaged ship was drifting towards the shore again. At least that gave her some protection from an attack on her port side. The German's would be reluctant to tempt fate in the shallows.

'Number One,' Thorburn said, 'you might check with W/T on that air cover.'

'Director-bridge!'

'Go ahead, 'Guns.''

'Almost in range, but I only have our rear turret at the moment.'

Thorburn took the point. 'When they open fire I'll turn out into the channel. That way you'll have both turrets and I'll have more sea room.'

'And the E-boats, sir?'

'Secondary armament under my control.'

'Guns' gave a sharp acknowledgement. 'Aye aye, sir.'

Armstrong appeared at his side. 'No cover for at least thirty minutes, sir.'

Thorburn nodded, not surprised, must be an air raid somewhere he concluded. A stabbing pain flared in his shoulder, subsided to an ache and he breathed out slowly. He turned and leant on the front bridge-screen and watched the freighter with Armstrong. She struggled on, pitching heavily in the long rollers.

The twin four-inch guns of the rear turret exploded into life. Thorburn turned to look for the fall of shot. The guns ripped out another salvo as the first pair of shells plunged short, but it was enough for the enemy to change course. Then a ripple of flame from the German guns.

'E-boats fanning out, sir!' Jones called.

A waterspout shot up off the starboard bow, another followed.

Thorburn gave the order. 'Hard-a-starboard. Steer one-nine-oh.'

173

Brackendale responded, heeled hard over to port and swung away at right angles to the shore. Below the bridge 'A' gun traversed rapidly to starboard the twin barrels rising to target elevation. A moment's pause before they fired. The crash of cordite, two flashes of orange flame and the billowing coils of white smoke.

Thorburn caught a glimpse of the E-boats veering out to deeper waters away from the German destroyer. Bouncing and skittering over the sea, angling ever nearer at high speed. The three boats closed in rapidly and he called for the Pompom and Oerlikons to open fire. *Brackendale* erupted into a roaring cacophony of gunfire. The four-inch guns bellowed out another salvo and Thorburn watched for the result. Missed left and right. But now all four guns were firing and a steady stream of shells were hurtling towards the enemy.

He ducked as a shell hissed over the bridge.

'Things are warming up,' Armstrong grinned tightly.

Thorburn nodded with a grim smile. Thick cordite whipped over the bridge-screen

'A hit!' yelled Jones. 'We hit their 'B' gun, sir.'

Thorburn raised his binoculars. 'Bloody marvellous.'

'Torpedoes! Green three-oh.'

Thorburn reacted automatically. 'Hard-a-port!' He had to turn at the torpedoes, make the ship smaller, limit their target area. He found the twin tracks of white bubbles and gritted his teeth. The bow tightened in, she was heeling well over to starboard, thumping round in the waves, too slowly. And then the phosphorescent lines fizzed down the port side a few feet away.

On the bow chaser, Jack Barton had seen those tracks coming straight for him. Live or die, there was nothing he could do about it so he just kept on firing. He felt certain some of his shells had hit the target. All he could do was carry on punching rounds across the sea. He might get lucky.

'Starboard twenty,' Thorburn ordered, turning *Brackendale* in the opposite direction. He must zigzag, unsettle the enemy guns.

'Sir.' Armstrong called sharply, and as Thorburn looked round, the First Lieutenant's outstretched finger led to an E-boat circling close inshore. The starboard Oerlikon hammered out a stream of shells, plucking a line of miniature spouts on the sea.

'He's trying to get to the other side of the freighter, sir.'

Thorburn shouted at the Pompom crew. 'E-boat on the starboard quarter. Engage!' The gun platform turned after the target. On the port beam the remaining E-boats were vanishing into the distance.

'Port ten,' he said to the voice pipe. A quick glance at the enemy destroyer; closing rapidly, soon to be firing over open sights.

A shuddering detonation staggered *Brackendale*. Dirty smoke flashed orange and up on the bridge Thorburn almost lost his footing as she leaned heavily to port. A jagged hole appeared by the portside windlass exposing the fo'c's'le flats to the elements.

'Damage control, Number One!'

Armstrong was already on his way down the ladder.

Thorburn could see the smoking edges of the crater but no flames. No tell tale signs of fire, they might be lucky. He coughed on the acrid gun smoke from the four-inch. His shoulder hurt and he eased his arm in the sling. Deep red blood was spreading over the white support. Through the smoke and noise of battle Thorburn managed to focus

175

his attention back on the German destroyer. Broadside on to *Brackendale*'s port bow at about twelve hundred yards he caught the moment of torpedo launch.

'Hard-a-port!' he shouted above the din. At a maximum speed of twenty-six knots *Brackendale* leaned dangerously to starboard swamping the starboard rail in a foaming sea. Four torpedoes arrowed toward towards *Brackendale*'s port beam and Thorburn preyed she would turn quick enough. Gunfire echoed from all round the ship, spent brass casings clanging to the deck, the taste of cordite thick on the tongue. He lifted the binoculars to the enemy and found the aftermost bank of tubes still deployed outboard. Four out of eight so far. The first incoming torpedo was on line for *Brackendale*'s port quarter the remainder had been fired too late. If he straightened course now . ? 'Midships,' he ordered and waited for the turn to stop. It was all a matter of judgement. 'Steady as you go.'

The Cox'n moved the wheel a little to port and watched the compass settle. The warship powered across the sea as those on the upper decks desperately tried to follow the torpedoes, willing the ship to fly. A collective sigh of relief as the nearest line of bubbles skimmed past the stern, and when Thorburn looked again at the enemy destroyer, he smiled in grim determination. The enemy had held her course presenting Thorburn with a wonderful opportunity to rake her port quarter.

'All guns. Engage!' he shouted above the din.

At less than eight hundred yards, and with *Brackendale* crossing the enemy's stern, every weapon obeyed his command. A violent maelstrom of explosive shellfire swept the enemy quarterdeck. Steel fragments ripped skywards; lethal shards of shrapnel tore a way through

176

human flesh. The bow-chaser sprayed the aft deckhouse punching ragged holes in the thin plate. An armour piercing shell exploded on the after gun mounting, a blast of black smoke billowing in the wind.

The German ship twisted abruptly, to port, and cut inside *Brackendale*'s arc of travel. Their main armament fired a broadside but with the ship heeled hard over the hurried shots passed overhead.

'Hard-a-port!' Thorburn ordered, willing the ship to come round after the enemy. A German shell hit the Pompom and blood sprayed the screen. Men were blown away, wounded, dying. Somehow more people filled the void and the guns began firing again.

Armstrong heaved himself into the bridge to make his report. 'Fire's out. There's a hole in the portside below the fo'c'sle deck, being patched up. No casualties down there, sir.'

Thorburn felt a small sense of relief. 'Well done, Number One. Check the Pompom will you, they've taken a hit.' A rattle of machine gun bullets hammered around the bridge. An E-boat careered wildly past the portside blazing away at *Brackendale*'s upperworks. Thorburn caught a brief glimpse of the boat bouncing clear of the waves. But it was the German destroyer that held his attention, she was too dangerous to leave for a moment. Then a sudden anxiety flooded through him. Desperately he looked round to where the inshore E-boat had been. *Devon Star* wallowed and corkscrewed in the shallows, heavy black smoke pouring from her funnel, no sign of the Schnellboat.

At that moment a huge column of water rose above the far side of the freighter, a muffled explosion smothered by the sea. *Devon Star* staggered to a stop. The torpedo had struck the portside, in line with the boiler room. The immediate detonation tore the vessel in half and split the boiler. Scalding steam screamed up through the hatches on deck. Tons of coal in the bunkers were dislodged. The bows lifted, the stern twisting sideways. A roar of steam erupted from the funnel and the two halves began to settle. In moments the entire vessel floundered and in a welter of seething foam sank from sight. The E-boat could be seen making forty knots and powering out to mid-channel.

Thorburn turned away in sorrow and forced himself to resume command. The noise of *Brackendale*'s guns had hesitated but now the volume seemed to increase with the intensity of the crew's rage. By now the German destroyer had opened the range and she turned after the E-boat and began to make smoke. Thorburn gripped the rail in frustration, he'd been defeated. It was no good trying to chase the enemy. *Brackendale* wasn't quick enough.

'Half ahead,' he barked to the wheelhouse. The four-inch guns continued a furious bombardment but Thorburn knew it was wasted. Reluctantly he ordered the cease-fire. A strange silence settled over the ship. A final salvo from the enemy guns fell short, wide of the port bow.

Thorburn made his next decision. Check for survivors from the freighter. He knew it was unlikely, she'd gone down so quick, but there might be some hidden amongst the sodden wreckage.

'Port twenty,' he said firmly, decision made. If only that torpedo boat had been stopped. Armstrong interrupted his thoughts.

'One dead, three injured,' he reported. He was matter of fact. No emotion, talking quietly.

Thorburn nodded and moved his arm in the sling.

Congealed blood crusted the outer sleeve at the elbow. 'I think we made a bloody pig's ear of that, Robert.'

Armstrong glanced at his face, saw the frown, the creases round the eyes. 'The odds were against us, sir. We were never going to hold them all off.'

Thorburn was apologetic. 'I shouldn't have ordered all the guns to fire at the destroyer,' he said morosely, staring out to sea.

'But that was the danger, sir. Definitely the bigger threat. She still had four tubes available.'

'Maybe . . , maybe.' Thorburn was looking down at his feet, shaking his head. 'We came to help the freighter and all we did was get her sunk.'

Armstrong hesitated. There was a lot of blood on Thorburn's shoulder oozing down the sling. He definitely looked a bit pale, could be affecting him. Turning his head away he caught the Sub-Lieutenant's worried expression. 'Get the doctor up here, sub. Tell him the Captain's not so good.'

Thorburn heard the instruction and let it pass, the pain in his shoulder too intense, sharply insistent. He saw they were approaching the field of debris. 'Slow ahead,' he ordered. 'Check for survivors.'

From the waist of the destroyer boathooks pushed into the mess of floating wreckage. An oily discoloured crate, a wooden barrel rolling with the waves. The pitiful evidence of shipboard life; rags and clothing, paper, card, notebooks, cordage, an empty lifejacket, and a half submerged ship's whaler.

Surgeon Lieutenant Doc Waverly brushed past Armstrong, took one look at Thorburn, and nodding to the sick berth attendant. The Captain was ushered off the bridge and down to his cabin. Removing the patient's blood soaked bandage and clothing Waverly immediately saw the wound needed stitching.

'You've lost a lot of blood and if it's going to heal properly I'll have to sow it up.' He reached for his bag of tricks. 'Sick berth's full, so I'll do it here.'

Thorburn raised his head to meet Waverly's eyes. 'Full?' he queried in surprise. 'How many have you got?'

'Eleven, not including yourself. Three of the damage control party, five of the Pompom crew, and three of the depthcharge station. Now sit still while I do my job.'

A shout from outside was followed by Armstrong's voice in reply and then a petty officer could be heard issuing orders. A thump against the side was accompanied by scraping, and then a burst of cheering and laughter. The telegraph rang overhead and the faint vibration of the engines increased by a few revolutions. Again the ring of the telegraph and the pulse of tremors dropped away.

Doc Waverly inserted the curved needle to begin his third suture. Gathering the fine thread into a practised knot, his assistant neatly cut the ends.

There was a discreet knock on the door.

'Come,' said Thorburn.

Midshipman George Labatt slid awkwardly into the cabin. 'Message from the First Lieutenant, sir. Five survivors rescued, and we're recovering two bodies.'

'Well done, Mr Labatt,' Thorburn said wearily. 'Please advise Number One to set course for home, bearing in mind our damage, best possible speed.

'Aye aye, sir,' the young man answered, and made a quick exit.

The doctor completed his stitching and applied a fresh dressing. He reached in his case, took out a brown bottle and tapped out two large grey pills.

'I want you to take these painkillers. I suggest a mug of hot sweet tea while you rest here.'

Thorburn managed a smile. 'Right oh, Doc, if you insist.' He popped the pills in his mouth, grimaced at the bitter taste, and gulped them back with a mouthful of water. A mug of steaming hot tea was placed beside him on the desk so he found a cigarette and leaned back with a smile.

'Carry on, gentlemen, if you please,' he said, waving a hand in haughty dismissal.

Waverly bowed obsequiously, cast a last critical look at his patient and backed out of the door. 'Your servant, sir.' He forced a smile.

When the door closed Thorburn allowed his smile to fade. A frown creased his brow as he thought back through the sequence of events. Something tugged at his memory, something he'd overlooked. The blue eyes narrowed as he fought to retrieve the missing fragment. Slowly he pieced together the details of the battle until eventually the missing part returned. He remembered using his binoculars to check which torpedo tubes had been fired and he'd swept them briefly over the enemy's bridge.

Thorburn reached in the desk drawer and removed a manila envelope. Extracting the photograph from inside he placed it carefully in front of him. The picture was of FlotillaKapitan Werner von Holtzmann. That was the man he had seen commanding the enemy ship. Only briefly, and just one figure amongst the many on that bridge, but he was certain. That's twice now, he thought, and this time we had been truly outsmarted. Holtzmann had used his numerical advantage to press home the attack and Thorburn had failed to protect the *Devon Star*.

181

He sipped at the hot tea, eying the image in front of him. Pendleton had warned him of the German's expertise. Unfortunately, this time, he'd been proved right. The chair was comfortable, the pills had taken away the worst of the pain, and he was feeling drained. He closed his eyes and allowed the ship's motion to lull him to sleep.

Kapitan Werner von Holtzmann congratulated himself on a successful engagement. He touched the Iron Cross at his neck. Once again he had outwitted the Royal Navy, and going by the destroyer's pennant number, they had met before. This time the operation had worked perfectly. A report had come in of a lone ship moving slowly after the overnight raid on a convoy. Air-reconnaissance had verified the contact and reported a small destroyer in attendance. Holtzmann, already deployed to the north-west of Alderney, went in for a hit and run with his Schnellboats. The ever present threat of aircraft meant he had to be in and out quickly, but he had taken the chance and the freighter was on the bottom. He would have stayed longer but for a lookout reporting the possible sighting of a Spitfire. He slugged the Schnapps down and relished the fiery warmth.

A loud knock on his cabin door introduced the tall figure of Lieutenant Max Bauer, his blonde haired First Officer.

'A signal from Bremerhaven, Kapitan. A Heinkel has crashed in the sea and we are ordered to pick up the crew. It is somewhere between Cherbourg and Alderney, Herr Kapitan.'

Holtzmann moved over to his chart table and considered the position. 'Signal Lieutenant Shafer to take his boats and search the area. We will follow.'

'Jawohl, Kapitan.' Bauer paused, avoiding Holtzmann's eyes, standing awkwardly in the doorway.

'What is it?' the Kapitan asked brusquely.

'Two of the crew are dead from their wounds,' he mumbled.

'They died for their Fuhrer, for the Fatherland, in battle,' Holtzmann retorted. 'That is as it should be.'

Max Bauer nodded. 'Yes, sir,' he agreed enthusiastically, and then more subdued, 'but three of the torpedo tubes, they cannot be repaired.'

'So be it. We still have another five?'

'Yes, sir.'

'Then they will have to do.'

Bauer hesitated waiting to be dismissed.

Holtzmann fixed him with his steel grey eyes and raised an eyebrow. 'Is there anything else?'

'No, sir.'

'Then send the signal Lieutenant; there are brave men to rescue.'

The First Officer clicked his heels. 'Jawhol, Mien Kapitan,' he snapped, and backed out of the door.

Holtzmann moved away from the table and straightened his jacket. He caught his reflection in the large mirror and smiled. He looked much as he expected, a victorious German Kapitan resplendent in the smart uniform of the German Kriegsmarine. Admiral Reader would be pleased with his efforts. Luckily this war had only just begun, there would be plenty of time for promotion and medals. He settled his gold brimmed cap firmly down on his forehead, and satisfied with his appearance, made his way to the bridge.

Out on the green sea ahead of the port bow the three

Schnellboats motored into the distance their powerful engines laying a foaming white trail in their wake. When Holtzmann looked aft a faint speck on the horizon was all that remained of the Royal Navy. He laughed aloud. The day had many more hours to run, much time left for fighting. Overhead the battle flag flew proudly at the masthead, the black edged, white cross, bold against a patch of blue sky.

'Schmitt!' he called to the officer on watch. 'Send for a coffee,' and choosing a cigar from his silver case settled back in his chair and watched the Cherbourg Peninsula grow into a solid buttress ahead.

Chapter Eleven . . Home Again.

H.M.S. *Brackendale* turned north beyond Margate's headland and entered the relatively calm waters of the north Kent coast. Herne Bay appeared off the port bow, the fishing harbour of Whitstable in the far distance. As the ship moved north to round the Isle of Sheppey a lookout reported Sheerness and the outer reaches of the Medway. Armstrong checked the time, reluctant to disturb Thorburn any earlier than necessary.

'Yeoman,' he called. 'Make a signal for an ambulance to stand by. Dockside berth would help. Arrival estimated . . , 13.15 hours.'

'Aye aye, sir.' The Yeoman closed his notepad and headed for the W/T office.

Armstrong watched him go and wondered if there was anything he'd missed. The shell-damaged fo'c'sle would be a dockyard repair, a number of other repairs had been tended to. The Pompom crew were back up to strength with Barton rejoining. *Brackendale* was taking in water from that shrapnel damage below the waterline, but the pumps were still coping with the excess. He had attended to all the priorities. A final helm order to hold them in mid-channel and he bent to Thorburn's voice pipe.

'Captain, sir,' he called.

Silence.

'Captain, sir!'

A mumbled reply. 'What's up, Number One?'

'You asked to be called. We're in the Medway.'

'Very well,' came the response, obviously awake. 'I'll be up shortly.'

Armstrong closed the pipe thoughtfully, lips pursed in a silent whistle. He hoped the skipper was okay, he'd had a tough few days. The chart table beckoned, the details of marker bouys and the swept channel, annotations scribbled in the margins. Behind him Thorburn arrived on the bridge. Armstrong gave him a discreet look; the rest appeared to have helped, apart from the sling there were no obvious signs of fatigue, outwardly at least.

'I have the bridge, Number One.' The announcement was strident, loud enough for all to hear.

Armstrong moved to the starboard bridge-wing and Thorburn issued his helm orders for *Brackendale* to navigate the narrowing River Medway. Upnor Castle came into view, the pale stone walls bright against a background of green foliage. A dredger hauled a dripping bucket of mud from the river, rotating to dump the contents in a cavernous hold. A raised hand from the operator was greeted by a wave from a lookout.

Armstrong straightened up and moved to the tannoy. Time to alert the crew. 'Special Sea Duty men close up for entering harbour.' Before the metallic echo had faded a dozen pairs of boots rattled the walkways and ladders, dividing fore and aft.

'Signal, sir.' He found a message slip pushed towards him. A quick glance and he stepped across to Thorburn.

'We're advised to tie up at the quayside to disembark the wounded, sir. Damage assessment will be carried out shortly.'

Thorburn nodded. 'Very well. Acknowledge.'

Armstrong turned to the signaller. 'See to it,' he said, and resumed his survey of their progress. Ahead of *Brackendale* the river curved to the left, the final turn before they entered the dockyard's familiar waterfront.

Captain James Pendleton focused his binoculars on the small destroyer as she appeared from the last bend in the river. From the few signals received in Operations everyone knew Thorburn had obviously been under pressure. Much to Pendleton's frustration, Fighter Command, due to a number of air-raids, had been unable to give further assistance. His own options were so reduced nothing would have reached *Brackendale* in time.

A faint smile flicked across Pendleton's mouth as he spotted the Battle Ensign still fluttering lazily in the breeze. A patched up hole in the portside drew his attention and closer inspection revealed countless holes along the waterline. Lifting the binoculars to centre on the bridge he found himself frowning with concentration as a white sling swam into view. It looked like Thorburn was injured.

He lowered the glasses with a shake of his head. Nobody had really envisaged the amount of action German forces would exert on the channel. Having to abandon Dover as an active base, temporary though it was, still left a bad taste. Sheerness and Portsmouth were doing their best to fill the gap, and to help counter the threat from E-boats, Vice-Admiral Ramsey had organised a number of gun and torpedo boats into a small flotilla which remained at Dover. Pendleton took a last look at the battle-scarred warship and turned away. He made his way cautiously up the incline from the dockside back towards Admiralty House. So much for any more urgent special operations he thought, be more than a couple of days before that ship was fit for service.

Entering his outer office, he gave a brief nod to Jennifer, the flow of letters from her typewriter uninterrupted. In the main office he crossed to the desk and alerted the main switchboard.

'Get me Rear-Admiral Sir Henry McIntyre, please.'

A moment passed as the connection was made.

He was greeted by a dry cough. 'Hello, James. What news?'

'I'm afraid *Brackendale*'s shot up, sir.'

'Badly?'

Pendleton hesitated. 'Just coming up river now. I could see a hole in the portside, which is probably a dry docking. And it looks like Thorburn's wounded.'

'Damn it!' McIntyre vented his frustration. There followed a long pause and when McIntyre spoke again it was with a studied calm.

'Right, James. I suggest you get down there with the Dockyard Supervisor. Find out how long the repairs will take if given the utmost priority . . . . And I want to know if Thorburn's fit enough to carry on.'

'And if not, sir?'

Another pause, only the hum of the line murmuring between them.

'Sir?' Pendleton prompted.

McIntyre faltered. 'I said before, worst comes to the worst, he's expendable. We get someone else.'

Pendleton leaned back and stroked his beard. 'Who, sir?' he prompted.

'Ahhh . . , Willoughby for a start. There's news on Moncrieff. Bainbridge has all the details, he's called a meeting for tomorrow.'

'Right, sir. Here?'

'No, James. It'll be his headquarters.'

Pendleton grimaced. The General's stamping ground, his sense of foreboding was correct.

188

'Let me know how you get on,' McIntyre said. 'And don't forget *Brackendale*. We've got to get her back in service. Soon.'

'Aye aye, sir.' Pendleton heard the line click. He gently replaced the receiver and tried to gather his thoughts.

He looked at the oversize chart hanging on the far wall. The upper half portrayed the familiar outline of England's southern coast, from Lands End in the west, extending east via Southampton, Portsmouth, the Isle of Wight, the Straits of Dover, and up to the North Foreland. The lower portion of the chart encompassed the French port of Brest and the Channel Islands in the west, then Cherbourg, and east to Le Havre, Calais, and Dunkirk. This was Pendleton's operational area of responsibility.

He took a final look at the chart, picked up his briefcase, slung his gas mask over his shoulder and made his way out in search of the Dockyard Supervisor. *Brackendale* would be ready to receive him shortly and he wanted a meeting with Thorburn. Only then could he begin to make the necessary arrangements. It would be best accomplished before nightfall.

An hour before midnight, Lieutenant Paul Wingham began the return journey to Marianne's home. He'd made contact with Bainbridge and informed him of the situation. Now he had to get Moncrieff to the coast, wherever he thought suitable. Get him to the coast and wait for instructions. On this trip he carried the extra weight of the radio in his left hand and the Thompson submachine gun in his right. But now he knew the lay of the land, which allowed him to move confidently up to the outskirts of the village. As before, he dropped into the ditch by the road, followed it to the garden wall and approached her house from the back gate.

The kitchen door was opened and Marianne beckoned him inside. She took him to the cellar and made him sit while the candle was lit. He could see she was dressed for the outdoors. A heavy leather jacket belted at the waist and her hair hidden inside a dark peaked hat, old trousers and stout boots.

'Is it arranged?' he asked.

'They are bringing your man to the old stone hut about three kilometres from here. They should be there in two more hours.'

'How many?'

'Two of my friends and your Englishman.'

Wingham nodded, wondering how to tell her there was no coming back. 'As soon as we make contact I have to inform England. They will send a ship . . . , for you as well.'

'Am I to meet your boss?'

'Yes. That is what I understand,' he said.

'So be it,' she said. She turned away and reached up to a wooden shelf. A long paper parcel was lifted down and she quickly untied the string. The gunmetal sheen of a hunting rifle reflected the candle's light and from an old dusty box she produced two cartons of ammunition. With practised ease she slid open the bolt-action breech and dropped a bullet into the chamber. 'I'm ready now,' she said simply.

Wingham stood and grabbed the bag with the radio. 'Got everything you need?' he asked. 'You know we can not return?'

She nodded firmly. 'I am not a child, Paul. I told you I am ready.'

Wingham picked up the gun and climbed the steps up to the kitchen. Behind him she blew out the candle and followed.

All was quiet as they shut the back door and made their way out to the rear gate. Marianne brushed past him to lead the way. There was a natural confidence in the way she moved, an instinctive familiarity with her surroundings. Wingham remaining behind her slight figure as they turned south beside the road, hidden in the trees. A hint of moonlight bathed the landscape and as Wingham peered over a hedge into the next field she came close and pointed.

'We need to go this way,' she whispered and pushed her way through the hedge.

Wingham followed her through and then hesitated.

Marianne felt his reluctance. 'There is a drainage ditch, quite deep. It leads a long way towards the woods. That is where we meet.'

He put a hand on her shoulder. 'If you're sure.'

She nodded vigorously and walked away in a crouch, trusting he would follow. Two minutes later she slowed to look about. 'Here it is.' She moved to her right, jumped down and almost disappeared. In the dim light Wingham moved to the edge and knelt to take a last look around. He dropped into the ditch and followed blindly, trusting to God she knew what she was doing.

They walked for a long time and Wingham was just wondering how much further when she stopped and sank to her knees facing left.

'This way now,' she whispered and slithered out of the ditch on her belly, moving swiftly towards the edge of a wood. When he drew level she stood and led him into the depths of the trees. With hardly a sound they weaved through the darkness until they reached a thinning of the trees. She stopped and pointed across the open ground. There was an isolated stone hut at the far side of the field bordered by a stand of trees.

Wingham grabbed her arm and pulled her into tangled undergrowth. 'We'll wait,' he said. 'This is close enough for now.'

It was a cold wait but after almost an hour Wingham thought he saw a vague movement at the edge of the trees. He brought the Tommy gun forward, unclipped the magazine, felt for resistance against the spring and snicked it back in place. In the distance a man appeared in the open and advanced towards the hut. He disappeared from view, but after a short interval, must have signalled the all clear. Two more figures hurried out from the trees and vanished behind the stone walls.

Marianne whispered fiercely. 'Now?'

Wingham wasn't going to be rushed. 'No, not yet,' he cautioned, motioning for her to stay still. He'd seen three men, which was the right number, but anyone tracking them might yet be concealed in the woods.

'I'm going to circle round through those trees, just in case,' he said quietly. 'If it's clear, I'll call Moncrieff. You can speak to the others.'

She squirmed closer and reached out for his arm. 'Be careful, Paul.'

He nodded and gently removed her hand. 'Look after the radio for me.' Rising to a crouch he worked his way towards the small boundary copse and melted into the fringe. Then he stopped to listen. Only the leaves rustled in the breeze. Stepping closer a twig cracked loudly beneath his foot. He stopped, anticipating a reaction, but there was no response. Holding his breath he took another pace forward, cautiously approaching the spot where the men had broken cover. There was no sign of movement and holding the gun ready he sank to one knee.

A faint sound from behind caught his attention and he swung round, about to pull the trigger.

'It's me!' The call was a hoarse whisper, enough for him to allow his finger to relax. With his heart thumping he swore under his breath. The oath carried in the night.

Marianne gasped. 'I'm sorry. I thought it would be better. The two of us.'

Wingham relaxed. 'You were very nearly dead.' He repressed the urge to be angry and turned away.

The moon slid out from behind a cloud and lit the stone hut in a soft grey. Staying with the darkness in the trees, Wingham tensed. 'Moncrieff!' His call was sharp but not too loud.

There was an immediate reaction. The back door creaked open and from the interior a voice answered in English. 'Here! And you?'

'I'm Wingham, sent to get you out. We don't have a lot of time.' He stood and stepped forward out of the trees. A short, stocky man emerged, took a quick glance around and then ran through the pale light.

'Good of you to come,' he said, breathing hard.

Wingham shook the extended hand and smiled at the formal greeting. 'Lieutenant Paul Wingham, sir.'

Marianne gave a call in French and the two men with machine guns ran over. Wingham gave them a quick glance, could see they were young, early twenties. He turned back to Moncrieff. 'Sorry, sir, can't hang around. We need to be under cover by dawn.'

'Lead on, Lieutenant, I'm in your hands.'

'Not exactly, sir. We're actually in her hands.' He

nodded at Marianne.

Moncrieff smiled broadly and bowed from the waist. His French was impeccable. 'Madame, I am at a disadvantage.'

Monsieur, I am Marianne Legrande. I am here to hide you from the Boche.'

Wingham peered at his watch. Two hours until dawn. Two hours in which to find some cover. Then he still had to transmit their location and find out when the Navy could get to them. He wondered if it would be Thorburn. If it was they might have a fighting chance.

Moncrieff held his arm. 'There is one thing, Lieutenant. When the time comes for us to leave, these men will keep your radio transmitter'

Wingham held his eyes questioning the authority. 'If you say so,' he said reluctantly.

'All in the plan, m'boy. You'll see.'

Marianne brushed past and tugged Wingham's sleeve. 'Come,' she hissed. 'We must go.'

Reluctantly, Wingham followed, but then decided to let the others past and walk in the rear. They set off at a brisk pace and Wingham realised they were moving along a narrow trail, staying in cover alongside hedgerows and ditches. He noticed Moncrieff was easily keeping up with the pace, obviously fit. Eventually he felt the ground sloping away and thought he heard the sound of waves. Marianne came to a halt and waved him forward.

'Not far now,' she explained. 'We are on the north coast at a large cove. Halfway down the slope to the beach there are some boulders and big bushes. That is where we can wait for your ship.' She looked round and indicated an open space in front of them. 'But now we must crawl. There is no cover until we reach those

194

bushes.'

Without waiting for an answer she set off down the slope wriggling along on her belly. A moment later the four men followed her example and a short while later scrambled in amongst the boulders. Wingham found a convenient rocky overhang and pulled the radio to his side.

'I suggest you get some rest, sleep if you can. We need someone to stand watch.'

Marianne spoke to the two young men and they moved out of sight into the bushes.

Wingham set up the radio and positioned the Morse key. He saw Moncrieff find a spot to sleep and watched Marianne turn up her coat collar and close her eyes. With a headphone to his ear he began to tap out his message to London.

Richard Thorburn opened his eyes. He felt refreshed after the long night's rest, able now to sit up and flex his damaged shoulder. Tender around the wound but the gnawing pain had eased. Daylight showed through the scuttle as he swung his feet to the mat. He moved to the day cabin for a cigarette, pulling deeply on his first smoke of the morning and checked the time. 07.35 hours, someone should have called him. Draped over one of the other chairs was his sling, discoloured by a faint patch of dried blood, reminding him of yesterday.

Within minutes of tying up at the quayside Pendleton had arrived on board with the dockyard supervisor. A brief visit to check on Thorburn's condition had concluded with Pendleton's instruction for Armstrong to get the captain hospitalised with the other casualties. When Thorburn returned he found that *Brackendale*'s damage had been scheduled for dry dock. A preliminary debrief on the outcome of *Devon Star*'s sinking, along with *Brackendale*'s eventual withdrawal, had not been criticised; if anything Pendleton seemed almost apologetic with his own inability to offer assistance at the time.

The surprise to Thorburn was Pendleton's insistence to the Dockyard Supervisor that *Brackendale* be given the utmost priority. To such an extent that a damaged minesweeper, urgently needed to make up numbers, would be given a temporary patch and floated clear from the dry dock.

That, Thorburn contemplated, was a lot of effort to enable the repair of just another damaged destroyer. More to all this than met the eye. Peter definitely had a point about special operations. Not that *Brackendale* had exactly covered herself in glory.

A quiet tap on the door announced the arrival of his steward. 'Mornin', sir. Breakfast?'

'Thank you, yes.' Thorburn realised he felt famished. 'And ask the First Lieutenant to join me.'

The door closed and Thorburn allowed himself to dwell on the previous day's action. There was much he might have done differently, but only in retrospect. The greatest danger had been the German destroyer, too grave a threat to leave unchallenged. In his opinion he'd been faced with no option but to apply the old maxim 'attack is the best defence'. His mistake had been to order all guns to engage the one target. For a few vital minutes he had ignored *Devon Star*'s plight.

There was a knock at the door.

'Come,' he said.

Lieutenant Armstrong entered with a quizzical expression.

Thorburn waved towards a chair. 'Sit down, Bob.'

'How's the shoulder, sir?' There was genuine concern.

'On the mend, just a bit sore,' Thorburn said, appreciating Armstrong's anxiety. He drew deeply on the last of the cigarette before squashing it in the ashtray. 'How's the crew?'

'Not too bad. Word's out about the dry dock, they're all muttering about shore leave.' He grinned and shook his head. 'Not that I've cleared any, sir.'

Thorburn considered that for a moment. 'Better let them go; according to their watch rotas. But remind them about being late back, I don't want any defaulters.' He paused before choosing his words. 'I actually called you in to ask a favour,' he explained. 'I'd like you to oversee the preparations for *Brackendale*'s repairs. Particularly the minor stuff below decks, and a list of spares, you know the drill.' He stretched to ease the stiffness in his shoulder. 'I'm going to have breakfast and a bath, in that order, and then I'll do what I can to help.'

'Sorry, sir, but I'll be taking care of everything for a while. I just took a call from that Wren officer, Farbrace, I think her name was. If you're fit enough they want you at a meeting in Maidstone.'

Thorburn leaned back with a frown. What on earth was Maidstone to do with anything?

'I take it they'll send a car?'

'Yes, sir. With Captain (D).'

A tap on the door announced his breakfast.

'All right, Bob, I'll leave it entirely up to you. Don't forget, Bryn Dawkins knows a lot of the answers. There isn't much he hasn't dealt with in the past.'

Armstrong stood up. 'Aye aye, sir.' He made a move for the door and stopped. 'One other thing, sir. That pilot we rescued.'

Thorburn waited.

'He died about an hour ago. Collapsed and never recovered. Hit his head when he ditched.'

Thorburn nodded, holding Armstrong with a steady gaze.

'Bloody sad,' he said. 'What a waste.'

Chapter Twelve . . Deadly Intent.

It was just before nine that morning when a black staff car, driven inland from Chatham, reached the crest of Blue Bell Hill and began the long descent to Maidstone. A stiff breeze rippled through the woods as the car picked up speed downhill. In the back seat, Captain James Pendleton sat staring thoughtfully out of a side window, the lush greenery slipping by almost unseen. Jennifer Farbrace sat next to him reading a document marked 'SECRET', her fountain pen poised to correct any untoward passages.

Thorburn sat comfortably next to the driver and passed the time guessing how many sheep grazed the slopes below Boxley Village. To his left the South Downs broadened out into the valley of the County Town and the river Medway. Pendleton had said little and whatever troubled him Thorburn wasn't in the mood to care. What mattered most was that *Brackendale*'s repairs were under way with a promise of completion in thirty-six hours. He sought the independence of navigating the seas, away from the land and all the complicated shenanigans that went with it.

Entering the outskirts of Maidstone they drove past the imposing walls of the old prison and the Sessions House before being forced to stop at a Home Guard checkpoint. A smart salute from a grey haired corporal allowed them through the coils of barbed wire. A mile later they pulled up to the wrought iron gates that secured the main entrance of Mote Park. An infantry sergeant, brusque to the point of rudeness, checked their papers.

'Wait here,' he ordered, and marched off to a camouflaged tent. Moments passed and then an olive-green army motor bike, ridden by a despatch rider wearing the obligatory helmet and goggles, turned out from behind the tent and bounced across the grass. He brought the machine to a stop in front of the Humber before signalling them to follow. At less than walking pace they drove down a heavily wooded landscape to emerge by the side of a broad expanse of water. Framed by ancient oaks and intermittent weeping willows, the lake stretched away to their right. On the hill to their left the trees gave way to manicured lawns where a squad of soldiers practised unarmed combat, a well muscled instructor demonstrating the finer points of the art.

Around a leafy corner the despatch rider pulled to one side and pointed ahead. Partly hidden by a stand of trees was a large square mansion.

Pendleton leaned forward to look over the driver's shoulder. 'Must be Mote House. Bainbridge commandeered it a week after Dunkirk. First time I've seen it.'

Thorburn nodded. The driver eased the car forward up a stony track that opened out into a gravelled car park. A red and white striped barrier at a sentry box barred the entrance.

Pendleton voiced his frustrations. 'Christ Almighty! How much security do you need?'

There was a respectful silence while the guard checked their identities. He made a great show of placing a tick against each person's name on his clipboard and then directed them to a space near the main entrance. A young Lieutenant hurried down the broad sweep of steps and reached for Pendleton's door handle before the engine had stopped. 'If you'd be so good as to follow me, sir, I'll show you to the General's office.'

He led them inside along a maze of empty corridors before finally ushering them through an office full of army personnel. The clatter of typewriters and a clamour of urgent voices filled the room, clerks and messengers rushing about with reams of paperwork.

The Lieutenant opened a door and stood back. 'In here please, sir.'

Thorburn followed them in to a large bright room. Huge maps hung on the walls, a multitude of coloured pins and flags and red arrows, identifying any number of brigades. The Nazi swastika was prominently displayed on the European continent; Poland, the Low Countries, and France, all dominated by the hated symbol. Half way up a tall step ladder a member of the Women's Royal Army Corps changed the position of a green pin, checking the co-ordinates before stretching up to push it firmly in place.

'Good morning! Welcome to my humble abode.' There was no mistaking the loud voice of General Scott Bainbridge as he breezed in behind them. He swept a hand towards a row of chairs, neatly arranged to face a mahogany desk standing in front of a large bay window. 'Do sit down, make yourselves comfortable. Tea, coffee?'

Pendleton held up a negative hand in response.

'In that case, down to business.' Bainbridge stood leaning forward, his hands braced against the polished table.

Thorburn made himself comfortable, his curiosity pricked, wondering where this would take them.

Bainbridge eased himself into the chair behind the desk.

'Lord Bernard Moncrieff is a Member of Parliament. Furthermore, he has a position of some importance within the Ministry for War. In other words, he's in possession of a great deal of secret information.' The General leaned forward to rest his elbows on the desk. 'Last night we received a message from Wingham. Moncrieff is now in his care and they are ready to be picked up'

Thorburn took note of that, at least Paul was still in the picture.

The General came to his feet, unconsciously rubbing his scarred cheek. He took a few paces, stopped and looked up.

'The problem is, if the Germans discover his whereabouts and find out who he is . . , well I'm sure I don't have to elaborate.'

A movement from Pendleton caught Thorburn's eye. It was a small grimace. The outcome was obvious. Gestapo methods of questioning invariably included torture, followed by a bullet to the head when the victim's information dried up.

Pendleton shifted in his seat. 'Where is he now?'

'They've moved up to the north coast of La Manche. The girl has taken them to a cove which could be used to take them out.'

A tall grandfather clock tolled the hour, ten slow chimes resounding through the room.

Bainbridge checked his watch and picked up a typewritten letter. He glanced briefly over the two pages before peering out from beneath his dark eyebrows. A thin smile flicked across the hard features, his eyes steady, unblinking.

'I received these orders yesterday,' he said flatly. 'Addressed to me as Chief of Special Operations. The following directive is to be implemented at the earliest opportunity. The Right Honourable, the Lord Bernard Moncrieff, is understood to have been trapped behind enemy lines when the German army captured Cherbourg and the surrounding countryside. You are to establish contact and affect a rescue at the earliest opportunity.' Bainbridge hesitated. He looked away and stared out through the window, tapping the document on the desk. Almost imperceptibly his gaze found Pendleton and with the merest hint of a shrug he continued.

'Your primary objective will be to prevent Lord Moncrieff from falling into enemy hands. He must not, under any circumstances, be allowed to divulge any of the information he holds to the enemy. I expect you to use your discretion in preventing such a disastrous outcome.'

A silence fell across the room as the full implications of the operation dawned on them. Thorburn saw Jennifer's face pale, her eyes averted, struggling to accept the finality of such an order. Pendleton stood up and walked over to the big bay window, placed his hands on the sill, and stared out beyond the trees.

Thorburn felt the anger rising, the temptation to shout at the nearest authority, namely, Bainbridge. Instead, controlling his emotions, he voiced all their thoughts. 'So, if it looks like he's going to be caught, we kill him?'

Bainbridge swung round. 'Yes!' he snapped vehemently. His eyes challenged them to doubt his conviction.

Thorburn responded cynically. 'And just who is going to do that?'

Bainbridge drew himself up to his full height. 'If it comes to it, I will. I'll lead the rescue myself.'

Pendleton protested. 'Sir, I don't think we can allow

that. You know more classified stuff than Moncrieff.'

'If I need to I will.' The belligerence in his attitude forced a silence on Pendleton's argument.

Thorburn felt the need to change tack, alter course.

'Do we have somewhere in mind for the rescue, sir?'

The General stared straight through him, vaguely distant. His eyes recovered their focus and he nodded slowly. He walked over to the wall map and pointed towards a large cove a few miles from Cherbourg.

Thorburn grimaced. 'That'll need careful planning, sir. Like Goury, there are some strong currents in those waters. Wasn't easy when we put Wingham ashore.' Thorburn's seamanship was exceptional, but even with the power of *Brackendale*'s twin screws, ship handling on that coast was not easy.

The General recognised Thorburn's reluctance. 'Not just your ship, Commander. *Veracity* will have a part to play. In fact, it was a chance remark from Willoughby that gave me the idea.'

Thorburn guessed that Peter would like a crack at the enemy.

Bainbridge continued. 'We'll have *Veracity* create a diversion by mounting a hit and run on Cherbourg. Approach from the east, stir 'em up a bit, and make a rapid exit.'

'Heavily defended round the port, sir,' he offered tentatively, 'could be a bit warm.'

'Exactly what the Germans want us to believe. But how well trained are the gunners who've been left on guard? And for that matter, have they ever fired at a moving ship? I doubt it.'

Pendleton had a query. 'What sort of schedule are you proposing?'

'Sir Henry's looking for a high tide. Probably approach from the northwest, as if we're a German patrol coming up from Brest. In addition, there'll be three Motor Gun Boats.'

'For what?' Pendleton sounded incredulous.

'I'll have ninety men to take ashore. This time we'll leave our mark.'

'Ninety? There won't be enough space.' Pendleton was not happy.

Bainbridge smiled. 'I can assure you there is. We've already tried it.'

In the ensuing silence Thorburn studied the General. All this had obviously been discussed at a senior level. But to attempt going in with ninety men, just to rescue two or three people, seemed tantamount to suicide. Trying to assault an enemy coastline with boats against artillery was not feasible.

Thorburn caught a movement to his right. Pendleton was shaking his head, the full beard acting as a pendulum.

Bainbridge lost patience. 'Do we have a problem, Captain?'

Very deliberately Pendleton raised his eyes and straightened his shoulders. 'No, General, we don't. You do.'

Bainbridge frowned. 'Meaning what?' he asked, sharply.

'Meaning,' Pendleton said, 'even if we managed to get you ashore, your chances of getting away are zero.'

For a moment they held each other's gaze before Bainbridge gave an exasperated sigh and turned away. 'What makes you so sure?'

'All those gun emplacements are unlikely to be overcome by one small destroyer and a handful of soldiers, not entirely. Even Nelson wouldn't have undertaken those odds.'

Thorburn couldn't help but smile. Pendleton was right, of course. His appreciation of the situation had to be respected.

Bainbridge snorted in disbelief. 'This is nineteen forty, we've moved on from the age of sail.'

'It would be like the Charge of the Light Brigade, doomed to failure,' Pendleton said softly, and finished by shaking his head again.

Thorburn watched the General closely. Every sinew of his body was itching for a confrontation, but at the same time, there was an obvious air of opposition. He touched the scarred cheek, visibly forced himself to relax and walked over to the map, looking up in silence. Eventually he shuffled round to face them. 'All right, Captain, how would you go about it?'

Pendleton stood up and strode over to the map, giving it a thorough inspection. He pointed to the northern coast slightly above and to the east of Goury. 'No moon, maybe two in the morning, and *Brackendale* to recover Moncrieff from a cove like that.' He paused, took a deep breath, and pointed an accusing finger at Bainbridge.

'And we won't need any Generals running about and getting in the way.'

Bainbridge looked down at the desk. When he looked up he was grinning straight at Pendleton. He nodded. 'Right oh, James, I take your point. No heroics, just an unannounced, sneaky approach, with a quiet withdrawal, all under the cloak of darkness.'

Pendleton answered firmly. 'That, sir, would be my recommendation.'

Thorburn saw Bainbridge turn to look at him.

'And what do you think, Commander?'

'The same, sir. As quietly as possible.'

Bainbridge pursed his lips, looking from one to the other. 'In that case I'm persuaded to give your argument a chance, but I'll have to convince someone else.' He reached for the red telephone. 'Sir Henry McIntyre, please.'

They waited in silence.

'Morning, Henry,' Bainbridge said brightly. 'I have a proposal for you.'

Thorburn listened as he launched into an explanation of the meeting, an occasional interruption resonating down the line. Eventually, Bainbridge replaced the handset, stood up and walked to the window. He spoke with his back to them.

'Sir Henry accepts the idea in principle, but we don't have the final say. He'll have to persuade others.' He turned from the window, a silhouette against the bright sunlight. 'When I was first made aware of all this I obviously checked the details. It was the War Cabinet who came up with this one. Apparently, Churchill's desperate to chalk up a winning headline, give the people something to cheer about. It was suggested that Lord Moncrieff's rescue could be an opportunity to give the Hun a bloody nose.'

Thorburn felt a momentary irritation. He thought back to his first meeting with Bainbridge and McIntyre, and how these Special Operations people seemed to jump at a plan without proper consultation. His so called superiors were a bit too blood and glory for their own good. It was only Pendleton's calm intervention that had probably saved them from a disaster.

Bainbridge returned to his desk. 'Unfortunately, we'll

not get an answer yet. Hopefully, tomorrow.' He glanced towards the map. 'In the meantime I'm requesting aerial reconnaissance, photographic.'

Jennifer closed her notepad and looked enquiringly at Bainbridge. 'Is that it, sir?'

The General nodded. 'Are there any questions?' He gathered some papers from his desk and tapped them together.

'No? Well it'll be Sir Henry giving us the answer. He's due to visit Dover Command tomorrow. Stopping off with us later.'

The briefing was over and Pendleton stood up to wait for Jennifer. Thorburn followed them out through the maze of corridors, eventually emerging onto the steps.

As they crunched over the gravel car park. Pendleton stopped and shook his head.

'Some people are stark raving bloody mad!' He spat the words out in disgust.

Thorburn stopped in disbelief. He'd never seen him so agitated, and judging by Jennifer's startled reaction, neither had she.

Their driver saw them coming and walked round to open the car door, but half way across Pendleton changed his mind and strode off towards the lake.

'Walk with me,' he instructed, and the two young officers caught up, one either side.

They made their way down to the smooth surface of the lake, a sparkling reflection of their surroundings mirrored in the placid waters. Pendleton came to a stop at the edge, fumbled in his jacket pockets, and opened a pack of Senior Service cigarettes. They watched a pair of swans glide gracefully past, an inquisitive turn of their heads acknowledging the human presence.

Pendleton blew a tendril of blue smoke and when he spoke again it was with a measure of disciplined control.

'I have enough trouble fighting the Germans without having to fend off ill thought out schemes from our so called leaders.'

Thorburn could sense the frustration.

The cigarette glowed as Pendleton took another pull.

'Shouldn't complain really, but as Jennifer will testify that wasn't the first time I've had to intervene.'

'True,' she agreed, 'the trouble is, it's happening far too frequently.'

Pendleton looked at her with a gentle smile. 'Second Officer Farbrace,' he announced, 'you can be astonishingly perceptive at times.' He grinned at Thorburn, resting a hand on his shoulder. 'Don't look so worried, Richard, I'm sure we'll learn to cope. Let's get that ship of yours back in service, keep our side of the bargain.'

Thorburn nodded. Privately, he'd made up his mind to stay out of all this haggling, leave it to the diplomats. He longed to be back aboard ship, in his own environment.

'Yes, sir,' he replied. A simple acceptance, but encompassing so much more.

'In that case,' Pendleton said, moving off along the path, 'let's get back to Chatham.'

Jennifer hesitated, catching Thorburn's eye.

'You don't like all this palaver, do you?' she offered.

'No, not really. Prefer to be on the ship, less hassle.'

She inclined her head in understanding.

Thorburn shrugged his shoulders. 'I agree with Pendleton, we're here to fight the Nazis.'

She continued to watch him for a moment and then turned away to follow Pendleton. 'Each to his own,' she said under her breath, thinking how pleasantly uncomplicated he was. It made a refreshing change from the usual pushy types always seeking to gain an advantage.

The next morning, at the heavily guarded entrance to Dover Castle, Sir Henry McIntyre's staff car was stopped for the customary identity checks. As the car drove through, Sir Henry took in the defensive concentration of anti-aircraft guns, each position watchfully attended by a vigilant crew. Below the castle's outer wall and built on the top of sheer cliffs, Admiralty Viewpoint dominated the surrounding panorama of sea and ships.

The driver found a place to park and the Admiral climbed stiffly from the rear seat. After three hours of travelling he was glad to step out into the fresh air.

'Morning, sir.'

McIntyre looked round to find the bearded figure of Pendleton approaching.

He returned the Captain's salute with a raised eyebrow. 'Morning James. Didn't expect to see you here.'

'I'd like a word in private, sir. If that's possible?'

Sir Henry took a moment to study Pendleton's earnest expression.

'Sounds serious.' He glanced at his watch. 'I can give you half an hour. Let's have a walk up to the lighthouse. I could do with the air.'

They set off together, negotiating an old set of steps that led them up to the ancient Roman tower. The Admiral pushed on, limping up a grassy bank until they reached the perimeter wall that stretched in a semi-circle around the elevated ground. McIntyre rested his hands on the wall and raised his face to the strong breeze sweeping in over the cliffs.

Sir Henry had a lot of time for Pendleton. When the War Office had first proposed the development of a Special Operations unit, and the Admiral had been appointed naval commander, one of his first acts was to select Pendleton as his Second-in-Command. The initial requirement was for him to recruit two or three officers with a somewhat cavalier attitude to navy customs. People who would use their own initiative. McIntyre had previously seen Pendleton demonstrate that very same attitude. An ability to go beyond traditional teachings and push the boundaries. In the few months of working together McIntyre's judgement had proved correct and he was now extremely reliant on Pendleton's shrewd advice. Standing shoulder to shoulder they faced into the stiffening breeze, their view of Calais obscured by the appearance of rain on the French coast.

'Let's be having it, James,' he ventured. 'What's the problem?'

Pendleton continued to look straight out to sea. 'I'm concerned about Bainbridge, sir. He's presenting us with operations that verge on the reckless. Not much consultation by the sound of it.'

McIntyre nodded to show he was listening.

'I'm frequently having to contradict him. He's a senior officer, I can only go so far.' He stopped, waiting.

'Go on,' McIntyre prompted.

'This latest offering. Ninety men to extract Moncrieff from the French coast. He gave us the impression you were part of the planning.'

The Admiral frowned. 'Not specifically, James. I was aware something was being cooked up for Lord Moncrieff's rescue so I sanctioned using the two destroyers. I assume he called me after you recommended a different approach.'

From somewhere below the wall a whistle shrilled and shouted commands echoed around the grounds.

Pendleton straightened up and turned to the Admiral.

'It got fairly heated before I was allowed to put my point.'

Sir Henry gave a half smile. He knew Pendleton well enough to realise what a gross understatement that was. Must have been an angry confrontation.

'Alright, I take your point. I should have been more involved. Trouble is I've been a bit distracted by Dover Command. They're trying to pinch our destroyers and I'm having to fight them.'

'Well I wouldn't have bothered you, sir, but I don't want Thorburn to end up with a reprimand for his allegiance to me.'

McIntyre nodded thoughtfully. So there we have it. Pendleton's rebellious protégé was obviously involved. Probably a bit too forthright with his opinions. 'In that case I'll have a word. The General knows where to draw the line. Thorburn's a good choice for us, I'll not have the army interfering.' He quickly thought of a solution. 'Tell you what, we'll keep Thorburn away from Bainbridge. No real reason for him to attend these meetings.'

Pendleton stroked his beard. 'Seems to be the way forward, sir. He prefers to be at sea.'

'Don't we all, James . . . , McIntyre said sadly. 'Don't we all,' Shaking his head, and with an exaggerated sigh, he straightened his thin frame away from the wall and grinned at Pendleton. 'We've done our bit. Have to leave it to the likes of Thorburn now, young enough to cope with it all.' He glanced at his wristwatch and saw there were fifteen minutes to go before his meeting. 'Now I need my best diplomats hat on. Dover Command will have to look elsewhere. I'm determined to hang on to *Brackendale* and *Veracity*.'

Pendleton kept pace as they strode down to the lighthouse.

'Will you be over to the dockyard, sir? *Brackendale* should be ready for sea tomorrow.'

They reached the top of the steps leading down from the tower.

'Yes, once I've sorted this out. I'll need to liase with the planners and then I should have all the answers.' He felt the need to take a look round Thorburn's ship. 'I'll be over for seven this evening. How about drinks in *Brackendale*'s wardroom, at eight?' He suppressed a smile when he caught Pendleton's expression of dismay.

'Er . . , yes, sir. I'll make the arrangements.'

'No warning, James. Unannounced will be just fine,' said the Admiral, watching him closely. The reaction was all that he expected. Pendleton raised an eyebrow, stroked his beard and then laughed out loud. 'As you wish, sir,' he said, and gave a very smart salute.

Sir Henry touched the peak of his cap. 'Until this evening.' He left Pendleton at the base of the old lighthouse and cleared the conversation from his mind. It was time to tackle Dover Command.

Chapter Thirteen . . Ready for Sea.

In Chatham's Royal Dockyard, H.M.S. *Brackendale* was nearing the end of her repairs. Standing among the tradesmen on the fo'c'sle, Richard Thorburn surveyed their efforts. The recent confusion of damaged steel had been replaced with freshly painted panels. Cableways and pipe work lay neatly gathered in brand new brackets, and along the portside another guard rail had been installed, the tell tale signs of battle patched away. A majority of the crew had returned ahead of time and immediately set to in lending a hand, a generous amount of raucous banter accompanying the work.

Satisfied that all was well on the fo'c'sle, Thorburn made his way aft along the starboard rail. Keeping himself well away from anything that appeared to be wet paint he walked purposefully past the searchlight housing until he arrived at the quarterdeck gun mount. A faint smell of oil and that lingering aroma of cordite assailed his nostrils, the glint of polished steel shimmering off the breech block. He nodded to himself. Those guns were in really good order.

'Captain, sir!' It was a call from the port rail.

He turned to find Leading Seaman 'Nobby' Clarke standing ramrod straight.

'What is it, Clarke?'

'Message from the First Lieutenant, sir. *Veracity* due on her mooring in thirty minutes.'

Thorburn hesitated. He wanted to find out what Peter knew about the General's 'diversion' business, but before anyone else had a chance to speak to him.

214

'Very well . . ,' he spoke cautiously. 'See if you can find the Chief Yeoman for me. I'll be on the Pompom in about five minutes.'

'Aye aye, sir.' Clarke spun on his heel and headed for the wireless room.

Thorburn completed his inspection of the four-inch guns and moved out to the Depth Charge rails. Both rails held a full complement of canisters, ready for a depth setting at a moments notice. The Pompom awaited his attention so he hoisted himself up onto the platform above the galley housing. There was no evidence of damage and he eased into the gun layer's sight to check the arrangement. As he peered through the crosshair in the centre of the rings he heard footsteps approaching. The Chief Yeoman appeared on the deck below.

'Reporting, sir,' he said, looking up.

'Well done, Chief. When *Veracity* gets in I want to message her captain. But unofficially, I don't want the whole world knowing about it.'

The man hesitated, just for a moment.' Not a problem, sir.'

'Get him to meet me on the quayside. It's urgent.'

'Right, sir. Good as done.'

Thorburn gave him a rueful smile. 'Thanks, Chief. Bit underhand , but it's necessary.'

'That's alright, sir.' With a quick salute the Yeoman departed.

Thorburn gingerly extricated himself from the gun layer's sight and decided to find Bryn Dawkins. More than likely worrying over something in the engine room. In the depths of the ship he checked the boiler room where two of the stokers were replacing a pressure relief valve. They hesitated for a moment and Thorburn held up a negative hand.

'Carry on,' he said quickly.

One of them nodded, balancing the valve precariously over his head while the other stoker attempted to guide the lower end into it's seat. Thorburn dodged round the end of the boiler leaving them to their work. He entered the next compartment to be met with the sound of heavy knocking resounded off the bulkheads. The hammering stopped as he approached another pair of men crouched over the portside ancillary shaft.

Lieutenant Bryn Dawkins took a big spanner from his Leading Stoker and Thorburn watched as he positioned it on a large nut. Satisfied with how it fitted he applied both hands to the task, and eventually, exerting maximum pressure, the nut visibly turned up the threaded bolt.

Dawkins nodded. 'There you are, boyo.' He offered the spanner handle to his assistant. 'All yours now.' He straightened up to wipe the grease from his hands.

'How's tricks, Chief?' Thorburn asked , closing in from behind them.

Dawkins looked round with a surprised frown. 'Should be okay now, sir. We've had an ongoing problem with that shaft. Thought we'd sorted it after our first patrol.' He finished with the rag and pointed to the steel housing. 'That bearing kept running hot, eventually found a spacer missing.' He shook his head in apparent disbelief. 'Just about to fit one now.'

'Could always get the dockyard to take a look, I mean, while we're here,' Thorburn suggested, as tactfully as he could.

Dawkins bristled. 'No!' He qualified the brusque answer. 'No, you're alright, sir. Be fine now we know what's wrong.'

Thorburn knew that Dawkins was a first class engineer and took an almost fanatical pride in his work.

'If you're sure, Chief?' he asked gently.

'You can leave it to us engineers, sir. Nothing we can't repair.'

'Never doubted it,' Thorburn grinned.

The Welshman gave him a sideways glance, a twinkle in his eyes. 'No, sir, I'm sure you didn't.' He bent down peering over the stoker's shoulder and Thorburn took the opportunity to slip away. In the back of his mind was the thought of Willoughby's imminent arrival.

The Chief Yeoman, Petty Officer Langsdale, leaned his back firmly against the solid bulk of the quarterdeck gun turret. He stood under the terminal of where the barrels met the shield, and as he had hoped, was hidden from view to all but the river astern. His long handled torch was from the ship's motor boat and he knew the business end gave off a powerful beam of light. *Veracity* was arriving and he watched her drift gently to her mooring buoy, casting a professional eye over the seaman tying off the lines. Within a few minutes the bridge personnel thinned out and he could see the ship had settled to harbour routine.

Aiming the torch carefully at the funnel he flashed her pendant number, just once, and waited. A movement on the signal deck caught his eye. A single short flash stabbed out in response. Langsdale was impressed, the signallers were wide awake. The button under his thumb clicked rhythmically as he transmitted the Morse Code. When he finished sending, another single flash winked to acknowledge the message. He lowered the torch and held his position, patiently waiting. He was rewarded with a movement at the starboard waist, the ship's boat being readied for the water.

It was time to inform the Captain. He stepped nonchalantly out from concealment, surreptitiously checked to see if he was being observed, and casually made his way forward to Thorburn's cabin.

Veracity's boat throttled back as a Leading hand neatly hooked into the dockside cleat and pulled them into the steps.

'Hello, Peter,' Thorburn said, as Willoughby climbed to the top.

'What's up, Richard? Bit cloak and dagger isn't it?'

Thorburn took his elbow and guided him away until he was certain of being out of earshot from the boat's crew.

'Now listen. What do you know about making an assault on Cherbourg?'

Willoughby frowned. 'When?'

'In the next couple of days.'

'Nothing,' Willoughby said, shaking his head.

Thorburn persisted. 'Well did you say anything to Bainbridge about taking on that German destroyer?'

'I suggested the navy might have a crack at sinking it.' He gave Thorburn a grin.

'Bainbridge took that up to a whole new level. Decided to make a full scale attack on Cherbourg.'

Willoughby dropped the smile. 'With what?'

'You and me mainly, maybe a couple of gunboats.'

'We wouldn't stand a chance, not with the shore defences.'

Thorburn held up a hand. 'Pendleton managed to persuade him otherwise but it's complicated. Moncrieff is ready to be rescued and the top brass had sanctioned his proposal for a landing with ninety men. We're waiting to see if they'll accept an alternative.'

Willoughby shook his head in dismay. 'It was only a bloody suggestion. Wasn't intending to commit suicide.'

Thorburn relaxed. 'Not to worry. One way or another we should know today.' He looked at his watch. '*Brackendale* should be finished mid-afternoon, how about a drink later this evening. We'll either be toasting Pendleton or drowning our sorrows.'

Willoughby gave a reluctant nod. 'Not quite the same as Hong Kong, is it?'

They stood for a moment remembering the white uniforms, the Admiral's exercises, and dinner ashore with the ladies. Just the occasional interruption to restore order in the far flung reaches of the Chinese coastline.

Thorburn pulled himself back to the present.

'Different era,' he said flatly, looking out at the Medway. 'Now we're just fighting to survive.'

Willoughby interrupted. 'Do you know we lost another destroyer this morning? Hit a mine and broke her back. Lost half the crew.'

Thorburn shook his head in sadness. Another ship gone and there weren't enough anyway. 'Who was it?'

'*Westeram*,' Willoughby said.

Thorburn grimaced. That was one of the destroyers he'd helped outside Dover harbour. And now she was at the bottom. 'As I said, just fighting to survive.' He reached out a hand and touched Willoughby's arm. 'I'd better get back to the ship, just wanted to put you in the picture.' That was only a half-truth but it would do for now.

'Right,' said Willoughby. 'I'll be over later.'

'Best keep it under your hat for now. Still classified,' Thorburn said.

219

Willoughby nodded and turned thoughtfully away.

Thorburn watched him return to *Veracity*'s boat, then made his own way back to the entrance of the dry dock. Willoughby had obviously sown the seed for an attack but hadn't understood the implications. He wasn't to know that Bainbridge would take him at his word rather than appreciate a man's enthusiasm for getting to grips with the enemy.

The sound of an approaching aircraft made Thorburn look up. A damaged Hurricane flew over the dockyard. White smoke billowed from the engine and the starboard wing showed signs of a desperate encounter. The engine faltered, coughed, and then picked up again, and as the fighter struggled on out of sight Thorburn sensed he'd be lucky to get down in one piece.

Entering the dry dock at a brisk walk, he paused to look up at the bridge. The sooner he was back out to sea the better. Wind and waves, much more reliable. He found the Cox'n under the starboard gantry.

'I'll be in my cabin,' he said. 'Let the First Lieutenant know.'

In the sanctuary of own space he pulled a chart of the Cotentin Peninsula from the bottom drawer of his desk and held it down with two ashtrays. With his elbows propped on the table he studied the detail of the northern coast, this time taking proper account of all the major features. Goury harbour, the known depths around the coves and inlets, the lighthouses positioned on numerous approaches. He continued to study the rugged outline until he felt he had managed to memorise everything of importance.

La Manche, he thought, of no real significance and yet he was beginning to view the area with a sense of misgiving. He reached for a cigarette and forced himself to settle down for another session of study.

That evening *Brackendale*'s wardroom came alive with chatter. The stewards had cleared away after supper and now dispensed the drinks with a flourish, the genial clink of bottles on glasses adding to the relaxed atmosphere.

Thorburn sat in 'his' armchair with a gin and tonic, his favourite brand of cigarette and a general feeling of well being.

Doc Waverly ambled over from the radio and raised a glass in salute. 'How's the shoulder, sir?'

Thorburn looked up with a guarded smile. 'The shoulder is just fine, Doc. If you're looking to practice your latest quackery on me, think again.'

Waverly sighed and tossed back the contents of his glass. 'In that case I'll assume my wizardry to be wonderfully potent and cast my spells elsewhere.'

Thorburn chuckled and gave an imperious wave. 'Get ye gone, serf, before I feed you to the fish.'

Waverly bowed deeply from the waist and shuffled backwards knuckling his brow.

Thorburn waved a dismissive hand to a bout of laughter.

'I grovel at your command, o mighty . . ,' his voice trailed away, the laughter silenced.

Thorburn looked round at the door. Rear-Admiral Sir Henry McIntyre stood inside the entrance accompanied by a frowning Captain Pendleton at his shoulder. Squeezed in behind them was the Cox'n, hands spread in apology, vigorously shaking his head.

The Doctor straightened sheepishly as the wardroom

came to it's feet in silence.

McIntyre's gaunt features tilted into a lopsided smile. 'Is there a wee dram for an old sailor?'

Thorburn was the first to react. 'Steward!' he called. And to Sir Henry, 'what's your poison, sir?

'Three fingers of whisky would be grand.'

Thorburn nodded to the steward and looked at Pendleton. 'Gin, sir?'

Pendleton nodded. 'Thank you, Richard,' he said, and glanced at the ship's officers. 'Relax, gentlemen. A seat for Sir Henry, if you please.'

Armstrong swivelled a leather armchair to face the room and stood back.

The old sailor lowered himself into the worn comfort and accepted his drink from the steward. 'Thanking you,' he beamed, swirling the amber liquid and wetting his lips. 'Your good health, gentlemen,' he said, raising the glass.

There was a respectful murmur in response, glasses lifted and drained, the stewards darting out to replenish the empties.

Thorburn spotted young Labatt looking awestruck in the background. Probably couldn't believe his luck, drinking with an Admiral.

Sir Henry cleared his throat. 'My apologies for barging in without warning, but I wanted to catch you all together.' He turned his eyes on Thorburn. 'You should attach no blame on your watch keepers, or the Cox'n for that matter. I gave orders for them to remain at their posts.'

Thorburn gave a slight nod.

Sir Henry smothered a cough before continuing. 'H.M.S. *Brackendale* is to be congratulated.' He took another mouthful of whisky. 'I am struck by the enthusiasm of her Captain and crew in the most trying of circumstances.' He glanced at Pendleton. 'The Captain here assures me that *Brackendale* is a wee bit special.' He caught sight of Willoughby. '*Veracity*'s Captain will no doubt excuse me from not extolling the virtues of his ship at this time.'

Willoughby nodded and held up a hand in understanding.

'Right, then,' said McIntyre solemnly, 'let's get down to the nitty gritty. 'As of now, there will be no shore leave until the operation is over. You've been chosen to rescue a V.I.P from enemy occupied territory. A certain Lieutenant Wingham, with whom I believe you're acquainted, is helping to arrange things at a cove on the northern coast of La Manche near to Goury.' He allowed the assembled officers a moment to digest the news.

Thorburn took a sip of gin and looked at the officers over the rim of his glass. All of them seemed surprised to have been taken in to the Admiral's confidence. The stewards were left open mouthed and Thorburn guessed that it wouldn't be long before word spread through the lower decks.

Pendleton lifted his glass for a refill. 'That, gentlemen is the crux of the matter and we'll iron out the fine detail shortly.' He glanced at Thorburn. 'Thankfully we gave your ship top priority in the dockyard.'

Thorburn smiled and inclined his head in acknowledgement.

There was a general murmur of exited comment amongst the wardroom.

Sir Henry's voice cut across the room. 'Commander Thorburn. I hope you don't mind but I also instructed the Cox'n to issue an extra wee tot of rum to the crew. I felt they deserved it in recognition of their efforts.' He leaned forward slightly from the comfort of his chair and raised his glass. 'As do you and your officers.' He moved the glass in a circle to encompass them all. 'Cheers! The drinks chitty is on me.'

Armstrong stepped forward. 'Steward, another whisky for the Admiral.'

Thorburn caught his eye and backed away for Armstrong to join him by the door.

'Keep an eye on the drinking, Number One. We don't want anyone over doing it.'

'Yes, sir, I'll see they behave. Back to enemy waters then, sir?'

'Seems that way.' Thorburn lowered his voice. 'From what I know this next assignment won't be very straightforward. As soon as I'm informed of the detail I'll fill you in, but it won't be for general distribution.'

'Thank you, sir,' Armstrong said quietly. 'If you'll excuse me, I'd better mingle.'

Thorburn nodded his agreement. A movement from Pendleton attracted his attention and he strolled over to find Sir Henry engrossed in a debate with young Labatt.

'Believe me, laddie, the battleships of the Home Fleet are a lot more use to us up in Scapa Flow than being hemmed in by the Luftwaffe down here.'

Labatt swallowed hard but continued his argument. 'I just felt that the Germans might not be so keen to invade if the Hood or the Prince of Wales were stationed in Portsmouth, sir.'

Sir Henry smiled, leaned back in his chair, and looked up at Thorburn. 'This young man does you credit, Commander. He's not afraid to speak his piece and I think his point was rather well made.'

Thorburn chuckled. 'I'm sure Mr Labatt will make for a very able ship's officer, sir.' He allowed his gaze to rest on the Midshipman. 'A little more in the way of listening to your experience might serve him well.' Armstrong and Dawkins applauded the sentiment and the embarrassed Labatt managed to wriggle out of the limelight.

Pendleton squeezed out from behind the Admiral's chair. 'Time for a chat, Richard. Your cabin if you will. If you take Sir Henry, I'll bring Commander Willoughby.'

Thorburn supposed this was the main briefing. 'Of course, sir,' he said, and bent to assist the Admiral from his seat.

The Capitan's cabin was strangely quiet after the noise of the wardroom. Pendleton sat with Sir Henry in Thorburn's usual position, relegating Willoughby and Thorburn to sit with their backs to the door.

'Smoke?' Pendleton offered his pack of Senior Service. With everyone catered for he sat back. 'Shall I, sir?' he asked the Admiral.

'Aye, James, put them in the picture.'

'Right,' said Pendleton, 'where to start? Firstly, you know we had a communiqué from Lieutenant Wingham, and more by luck than judgement, Lord Moncrieff is now in his care.'

Thorburn allowed himself an unseen smile. He wondered if Paul's luck was holding.

Pendleton dropped a large photograph on the desk. 'That's from an aerial reconnaissance taken this morning.'

The two Commanders studied the landmarks, taking in the salient features of the northern coast of Le Manche. There were a lot of guns dotted about and Thorburn pursed his lips as he spotted two trailer mounted 88 millimetre platforms, one either side of the suggested landing site.

Sir Henry caught the expression. 'Is there a problem?' he asked.

Thorburn turned the picture towards the Admiral and pointed at the cove.

'It's those guns, sir. I don't see us getting anywhere near without the alarm being raised.'

'Aye, laddie, we saw that. Reckon you can knock them out on the way in?'

Thorburn considered the proposition. 'It's possible, but there'll be hell to pay on the beach.'

Willoughby had a suggestion. 'If you use the ship's motor boat it'd be quicker, they won't be exposed for so long.'

Thorburn squinted at the photo trying to envisage the reality, the poor visibility, and untried waters near a shallow cove. And all the while engaged by enemy gunfire. He lifted his eyes and looked directly at Sir Henry.

'There's a lot of ifs and buts, sir. Thought we were going in quietly. Bit of a gamble.'

Sir Henry nodded. 'On top of that, we will be taking along a few soldiers to help.'

Thorburn gave him a withering glance. 'How many's a few, sir?'

'Twenty.'

Thorburn relaxed. 'Twenty,' he said after a pause. 'Twenty I can live with. Damned sight better than ninety. Will the General be coming?'

'No, he's been warned off,' McIntyre said. 'Lieutenant Wingham has accepted full responsibility for what happens to Moncrieff.'

Thorburn took the news with a shrug. He might not

have known Paul for long but, in his heart of hearts, he knew he had that in his make up.

Thorburn glanced from one to the other, Pendleton inscrutable, Willoughby full of anticipation, Sir Henry's narrowed, thoughtful eyes. He remembered the Cox'n's turn of phrase.

'In that case, sir,' he said, 'should be a piece of cake.'

The old Admiral remained impassive, the gaunt features placid, unmoved. After a long moment he lifted his drink, gave an exaggerated wink. 'Aye,' he said slowly, ' piece of cake.'

Pendleton turned to Willoughby. 'I want you to attack any shipping in Cherbourg harbour. You'll make a single pass at maximum speed, turn out to sea and head back east. If you can let off a few torpedoes, so well and good.'

Willoughby couldn't help the broad smile. 'Yes, sir. As you wish, sir.'

'Good,' said Pendleton. 'When you're done, come round from the north and see what you can do to help *Brackendale*.'

Sir Henry cleared his throat. 'Bearing in mind *Brackendale*'s repairs, when can we be ready to proceed?'

Pendleton was quick to answer. 'First light tomorrow.'

Thorburn held up his hand. 'With respect, sir, not before noon. We need to run some tests. I have an auxiliary shaft running hot.'

Sir Henry grimaced. 'But assuming we sort these problems we could still achieve the operation tomorrow night. Agreed?'

Thorburn felt certain the Chief would have the ship ready, probably by mid-morning. Willoughby was obviously ready to go. He met the Admiral's enquiring gaze. 'Yes, sir, tomorrow night.'

'There it is then,' Sir Henry said. He glanced at Pendleton and gave him an almost imperceptible nod. 'I have a feeling we'll all be ready.' He pushed his chair back and stood up.

Thorburn realised the meeting was over.

Pendleton began to put his papers in the briefcase. 'I'll see you both at ten in the morning. My office. We'll run through the final details.'

The old Admiral stifled a cough and managed a smile. 'Good,' he said. 'I think we deserve another drink.'

Thorburn led them back to the wardroom and having seen to their drinks walked back to the door, away from the crowd. He frowned as he pulled out a cigarette thinking he'd missed something. The noise of the wardroom faded as he fought to identify a moment from the meeting, an indiscrete slip of the tongue, a decision he should have challenged. He shook his head in frustration and moved to the serving hatch. The gin burned down his throat and cleared his mind. Sir Henry should leave soon, he hoped, after which they could all get some proper rest. Tomorrow would be an early start, no knowing when they might finish.

At five minutes past midnight, four miles south of the Isle of Wight, a German destroyer and three E-boats intercepted an eastbound convoy of eight merchantmen. The escort consisted of two corvettes and an Admiralty tug. In the space of thirty minutes, FlotillaKapitan Werner von Holtzmann's raiders sank two merchantmen and crippled three more. One of the corvettes made a gallant effort to defend the convoy but was overwhelmed by numbers. As the German raiders turned away they departed with the corvette down by the head and burning fiercely.

Well satisfied with his night's work, von Holtzmann turned for home and the safety of Cherbourg harbour.

Chapter Fourteen .. Dangerous Waters.

It was late in the evening of the following day that *Brackendale* slipped her moorings, negotiated the outer reaches of the Medway and eventually cleared the North Foreland. Following a morning of engine trials and another meeting to thrash out the final details, the destroyer was now on course for the French coast of La Manche.

Thorburn tried to relax in the bridge chair and let those around him manage the running of the ship. At present his problem was nothing to do with *Brackendale*, it was the unexpected guest now taking up residence in his cabin. His doubts of the night before had proved correct. That off hand comment from Sir Henry, 'I feel we'll all be ready,' had been so intentional, and Thorburn had missed the importance. Rear-Admiral Sir Henry McIntyre had insisted on accompanying *Brackendale* on the operation and even Pendleton's opposition had been brushed aside. Assurances of staying in the background and leaving all operational decisions to Thorburn were not very convincing. It was annoying, but had to be lived with, so he straightened in the seat and made a conscious effort to concentrate on the task in hand.

He directed his thoughts towards the enemy coast, and in particular, to the guns overlooking the landing zone. Which brought him to *Veracity*'s role and Willoughby's capacity to assist in diverting attention away from the operation. He turned and looked across the port beam. A thousand yards away *Veracity* matched *Brackendale*'s speed, her bows throwing up a curling white wave, creaming down her starboard side. She gave off an air of determined progress and Thorburn smiled grimly. Two small ships, a little more than three hundred people, all embarked on a mission to liberate three individuals from the rule of Nazi occupied France.

A few hours later Thorburn checked his watch. *Brackendale* was almost ready for the final approach. The gun crews were aware of the task ahead, that the searchlight would act as target layer, the need for disciplined accuracy.

'Number One,' Thorburn said softly.

Armstrong joined him at the bridge-screen. 'Sir.'

'I take it the ship's boat is ready.'

'It is, sir.'

Thorburn nodded. 'And have we settled on the crew?'

'Finally, yes sir,' Armstrong's teeth showed in a grin. 'I think there must have been twenty volunteers.'

'Good,' Thorburn said. 'How about the commandos?'

'*Veracity*'s motorboat is ready as you ordered, sir. In the davits on the portside.'

'Very well. Just check that our people are all armed. Things might get a bit sticky out there.'

A voice interrupted. 'And a sidearm for me too, Number One.'

They turned to find the Admiral behind them, Thorburn the quickest to react. 'Sorry, sir, but you can't go in with the boat.'

The Admiral stuck out his chin. 'That's exactly where I'm going, Lord Bernard Moncrieff will be reassured to find a senior officer in attendance.'

Thorburn protested again. 'Then let me go, sir. I'll be hung, drawn and quartered if anything happens to you.'

231

'Don't you worry about that, Commander. Mr Churchill knows exactly where I'm going.'

Thorburn shrugged in annoyance. 'If you say so, sir,' he said shortly.

'Och, don't be angry, son,' the Admiral chided, 'we'll be fine.'

On the pretext of checking their bearing, Thorburn turned to the compass, using the moment to compose himself. If Moncrieff's importance to the War Office was enough reason to ensure he didn't fall into enemy hands, where did that leave Sir Henry? Should he make the point or let it be? Diplomacy, he thought; bite the bottom lip and let him get on with it. He paused for a moment before turning to Armstrong.

'Show Sir Henry to the armoury, Number One. He might like to choose his own.'

The Admiral rubbed his hands together. 'Thank you, Commander. Lead on, Number One.'

Thorburn watched them move to the stern ladder and with an emphatic sigh returned to the business in hand.

The gunnery officer took their place. 'Are we putting Barton on the bow-chaser, sir?'

'I think so,' Thorburn said, then slid the chart of the Cotentin peninsula closer to the table's light. 'Look, 'Guns,' he said, pointing to the chart. 'If I take the ship down past those cannon at twenty or so knots, how do you feel about a starboard broadside?'

Howard stopped chewing on his unlit pipe long enough to reply. 'Sitting ducks, sir.'

Thorburn gave him a sideways glance. It was a flippant answer but there was no hint of a smile, probably working out a firing solution as he spoke.

Howard tapped the bowl of his pipe on the table, thinking.

Thorburn straightened up above the bridge-screen and trained his binoculars on the vague horizon ahead, where he estimated sea and sky merged. 'We'll have the advantage of surprise,' he mused, trying to assist Howard with his calculations.

The tapping stopped. 'Yes, sir.' A pause. 'Might be worth loading the after guns with fused shells. Give them an air burst.'

Thorburn lowered the glasses as he considered the suggestion. An anti-aircraft burst above the Germans manning the guns. The shrapnel would be lethal. 'Gets my vote. Anything else?'

'Only that the main armament should have at least a dozen or so extra rounds to hand. That would be in addition to the ready use lockers.'

'And what about star shell? If the searchlight gets hit. . .' Thorburn was stating the obvious.

Howard nodded, the pipe clamped back between his teeth. 'All tended to. Possible range, sir?'

'Eight hundred yards if I can,' Thorburn said. 'Might be a touch more.'

Howard centred the cap on his forehead and removed the pipe. 'In that case, I'll brief the men.'

Thorburn watched him go, content in the knowledge that Howard knew what he was doing. Laconic by nature, very capable when it was anything to do with his guns.

Thorburn steadied himself as the destroyer lifted lazily over a larger wave, twisting through the uneven swell. In a short while he would bring the crew to full action stations, earlier than necessary but giving them time to adjust to the conditions. Luckily the sea was relatively calm.

Jack Barton lay in a hammock with his eyes closed, as relaxed as the anticipation of action would allow. The excitement was tempered by a nervous flutter in his stomach, the same feelings he'd experienced before the battle with Graff Spee. But that had been his first action, and along with most of those shipmates, they'd been totally unprepared for the mayhem that followed. It was only when others had fallen around him that he discovered a new found strength to carry on fighting. Since then he found the noise and confusion of battle was a welcome surge of excitement.

'Jack!' An urgent whisper accompanied a violent prodding of his hammock. 'Jack, you awake?'

'Well if I wasn't, I bloody well am now,' he said sharply.

'We're piped for action stations but no rush. Just assemble quietly.'

Barton peered over the edge of the hammock, wanting to see who was talking. 'All right, keep your hair on,' he snapped. 'Should've piped it proper, know where we are then.'

'Suit yourself, I have to go.'

Barton swung easily to the deck, stamping his feet to settle the sea boots. He found his locker, shrugged into his duffle coat and grabbed the steel helmet. A final check and he joined the others making their way up to the deck. Emerging from the hatchway he turned forward along the starboard rail, skirting 'A' gun's splinter screen before negotiating the anchor chains.

'Okay, Jack?'

Barton looked behind as he recognised the loader's voice. 'Yeah, you?' he asked.

Joe Miller, an ex boxer from Liverpool and second loader to the quadruple Pompom, grunted a reply. 'Been better,' he said brusquely, pushing past Barton as they reached the two pounder.

Barton took his place at the bow-chaser, reaching up to remove the tarpaulin. He swivelled the gun up and down, leaning sideways to check the lateral movement. The firing mechanism clicked reassuringly as he tested the resistance.

'Did Howard say how much ammo we need?' Miller asked, opening up both of the ready-use lockers.

Barton frowned in thought and shook his head. 'No, probably means we're alright.'

Miller brought out enough clips to satisfy what he considered would cover their immediate needs. He straightened up and leaned against the breech. 'Feels a bit exposed up here,' he offered, and when Barton remained quiet, 'I mean there ain't much protection.'

Privately, Barton had to agree. Of all the firing positions, this felt very open to enemy gunfire, even the main Pompom had splinter screens. Maybe the knowledge of the bow-chaser being located so far forward had a subconscious effect on them. Not that he would admit it. 'Bit isolated, but we won't be the main target,' he said, trying to paint a better picture.

A movement in his peripheral vision made him turn. The Midshipman was approaching.

'Barton?' Labatt called, peering through the gloom.

'Sir,' Barton answered, stepping away from the gun.

'The Captain wants you to concentrate on anything firing at the beach. Heavy machine guns, small arms, pick your own targets.'

Barton pushed the steel helmet back from his forehead. There was a fair degree of latitude in those orders, but like everyone on board, he knew what they were out to achieve. 'What are the chances of seeing anything, sir?'

'We'll hit them with the searchlight, to pinpoint the field guns. Might be starshell after that. Whatever you do, don't fire until the four-inch start shooting.'

Barton liked Labatt. Young as he was, he was very forthright; if he didn't know he asked, if he did know, you got it all.

Labatt tilted his head. 'Any more questions?'

'No, sir. No questions.'

'Right then, could be another half hour.' He paused, seemingly reluctant to leave them.

Barton sensed the uncertainty. 'Where will you be, sir?'

'With Number One, launching the boat.' He shuffled his feet, and then, as if the doubts had cleared, Barton saw him straighten his shoulders.

'I'll be on my way,' he said, beginning to turn away. He stopped and glanced back. 'Good luck.'

'And you, sir,' Barton said warmly.

Labatt lifted a hand in reply and moved off across the anchor chains.

Barton pushed his hands into the deep pockets of his duffle coat and stood swaying easily with the ship's movement. He saw Miller fiddling with an ammunition clip. Somewhere ahead lay the unseen enemy coast which Barton remembered as an exhausting nightmare of seething water. This time it was someone else's turn. The

236

bow-chaser suddenly seemed a much safer alternative. Anyway, he thought, if anyone could see them through, Thorburn would. Most everyone on board thought the same, the skipper knew what he was doing. And he was lucky.

'Give us a hand with this ammo, Jack. A couple of these clips ain't right.' Miller held one out for Barton to take. 'Here, you feel. They're not lined up.'

Barton gathered the clip to his waist and squatted by the locker. He glanced up to the vague outline of the bridge. Thorburn would be up there now, plotting and planning, making decisions that would affect the lives of almost a hundred and sixty people aboard the ship. His fingers found an uneven alignment and as he prised the shell straight, he muttered to himself. 'Rather him than me.' Pushing the ammunition back to Miller he stood up by the gun. Not long now, he hoped, tapping the breechblock. His gaze settled on the middle distance, and resting his chin on his arm, he waited.

Major Gerhard Brandt, the German officer commanding the 83rd Grenadier Battalion, was asleep in an old ramshackle semaphore building overlooking Goury's northwest coast. He was awoken by a loud knocking on the door, followed by the blinding light of a torch.

'Herr Major!' It was a desperate plea.

'Ja, what's wrong?' The beam of light lowered away from his eyes.

'There is a ship, Herr Major!' The soldier was breathing hard.

Brandt came upright in a rush. 'A ship! What ship?'

'We think it is a British ship, sir. Very distant, to the northeast of Sergeant Möller's observation post.'

The Major reached for his boots. 'Call the men. Have them form up on the track.' He thought for a moment. 'I want them fully armed, all their weapons. And don't forget the mortars.'

'Jawohl, Herr Major.' The soldier turned to go.

'No lights,' Brandt ordered. 'And quietly now.' He stood and stamped his feet into the boots. Buttoning up his jacket he strapped on his pistol, made certain the Luger was ready to use and grabbed a sub machine gun on his way out the door. He was greeted by the sound of men gathering on the track and he moved down to join them. He remembered a warning from the navy, a Werner von Holtzmann, at Cherbourg. The British might try a raiding party on this coast. But if it was the northeast, there was a battery of mobile guns in place. He waited as his under strength company formed up in ranks. Forty two men. It would have to be enough.

'We go,' he ordered, and led them up the track onto the old road and out into the northern farmland. It was two kilometres to the coast at Möller's dugout. They would have to hurry.

Chapter Fifteen . . Boats Away.

H.M.S. *Brackendale* edged forward at five knots. Thorburn had brought the warship into a position north, northeast of the target; estimated time to commence the operation, twelve minutes. Below him in the forward turret each man waited for the order to shoot, the guns pre-loaded with the first of the shells. On the quarterdeck, the twin barrels of the four-inch guns pointed out over the starboard waist. Lieutenant Howard, ready in the Director Control Tower, chewed on his pipe, though the estimate was for targets to be found over open sights.

Hanging from her derricks, the ship's boat was secured at deck level, and Armstrong waited impatiently for the order to launch. Hovering in the background, the young midshipman stood proudly alongside Sir Henry McIntyre, ready to help as ordered. Below the waterline, in the heat of the engine room, Bryn Dawkins watched his gauges, all the while keeping one eye on the telegraph.

Richard Thorburn raised the binoculars to his eyes, straining to make out even the faintest detail of the coast. Around him other glasses searched for that first tell tale glimpse of breaking surf.

'Bridge, 'Guns!'

Thorburn bent to the voice-pipe. 'Go ahead, 'Guns.'

'Lighthouse in sight off the starboard bow.'

'Stop engines,' Thorburn ordered, glancing over his shoulder to the Control Tower. He wondered if they were too close.

'Time?' he asked.

'Twenty past one, sir,' Lawrence said.

239

Brackendale slowed to a stop, wallowing erratically in the swell. Thorburn felt uneasy. Asdic were on the sweep, had been since the reduction of speed, but lying dead in the water was asking for trouble. Better to circle round than sit still.

'Slow ahead. Port twenty.'

Falconer repeated from the wheelhouse.

Thorburn watched the compass. The turn was too tight.

'Come back to port five, Cox'n.'

'Port five. Aye aye, sir.'

Within moments the ship eased out from her tight curve and assumed a more relaxed sweep.

'Hold her at port five, Cox'n.'

The Chief Yeoman appeared. 'Signal, sir.'

Thorburn turned. 'What is it?'

'From *Veracity*, sir. "No ships in harbour. Engaging shore batteries." Message ends, sir.'

Thorburn took the news in silence. The German destroyer was out, probably on a raid. To create any kind of diversion Willoughby would have to bombard the coastal defences of Cherbourg, deliberately drawing down enemy fire.

'Acknowledge,' he said to the Yeoman, and Thorburn wondered if McIntyre needed to know. He thought better of it. The principle was the same; create a diversion to rescue Moncrieff. The compass showed *Brackendale* beginning to swing towards the coast again. At this point they had increased the distance by almost a mile from where 'Guns' had first sighted the lighthouse. He bent to the voice-pipe and watched the compass for a little longer.

'Midships,' he ordered.

'Midships, aye aye, sir,' Falconer responded.

The compass seemed to take an age to settle. Finally he had the bearing. 'Steer one-two-five degrees.' He straightened up. Any moment now, he thought. Any moment now. The ship eased in towards the coast and Thorburn waited.

The distant sound of heavy gunfire broke the calm.

'Half ahead both!' Thorburn snapped. Faint pulses of light showed beyond the port bow, a headland silhouetted on the far eastern end of the bay. *Brackendale*'s bows lifted as the twin propellers dug in and she accelerated up to sixteen knots. He grimaced. Willoughby was definitely in the thick of it now. Moving to the starboard bridge-wing he looked to see Armstrong standing by the derrick. The ship thumped a bigger wave and a fine spray whipped over the bridge. *Brackendale* raced on. Thorburn lifted the binoculars to check the darkened coast. They were running towards the shore, maybe two thousand yards.

'Starboard ten,' he said to the wheelhouse.

The bows came rapidly round towards the bay.

'Midships.' He squinted ahead. 'Steady . . , steer one-four-five.'

'One-four-five. Aye aye, sir.'

Thorburn waited, glasses searching through the gloom, trying to pick out the shoreline. Spray on the lens distorted his vision and he gave them a quick wipe. He raised them back over the bridge-screen. A faint white ripple; and again. Waves breaking on land.

'Port ten!' There was an urgency to his command.

Brackendale listed under his feet, swaying to starboard as the bow swung from south to east. He picked up the handset to the Control Tower. 'Guns?' he queried.

'Guns' here, sir.'

241

'Give me a range to the shore. I'm poor on distance down here.' There was a pause as Thorburn hung on the handset, willing him to hurry.

'One thousand yards at Green ninety, sir.'

'Well done, 'Guns,' Thorburn said, and clipped the handset on the cradle. He pursed his lips in thought. That reading was at right angles to the starboard side. The bay was only a mile wide and then it curved out to the north across their path.

'Slow ahead. Steer oh-nine-oh degrees.' Reluctantly, he had to slow her down or risk running aground. 'Lookouts!' he called. 'Keep a sharp eye ahead. We're in the cove.'

Another rumble of heavy gunfire echoed in from the south-east and as he looked up Thorburn caught the faint glimmer of explosions beyond the headland. It was deceiving, those lights were a good twelve miles away.

'Bridge, . . . 'Guns.' Came from a voice-pipe.

'Captain speaking.'

'Target bearing, Green three-oh. Range eight fifty yards.'

'Very well,' Thorburn said. 'Tell me when it's eight hundred.'

'Aye aye, sir.'

Thorburn gripped the back of his chair as he strove to decipher all the information. The tall headland was over to their stern. The beach, guarded by the artillery was to their right, and ahead of them was the eastern horn of the bay.

'Bridge, . . . 'Guns.' Range eight hundred yards.'

Thorburn focused his glasses on the high ground above the beach. He moved them to his right and stopped. Even

242

without the help of lights he had spotted a piece of field artillery. The time was right. 'Open fire!'

There was a simultaneous crash of gunfire as the ship's main armament threw out a first broadside. Blinded and deafened, Thorburn recovered his focus through the binoculars. A bright wavering beam lanced out from the searchlight, climbed up the high ground and pinpointed a German anti-tank gun. Three explosions lit up the horizon, a fourth caught a protective wall to the left. The forward guns were the first to reload, two more shells hurtling across the divide. From somewhere to the right a stream of red tracer curved in at the bridge. The quarterdeck Pompom hammered out a response. A hail of shells found the target and the gun stopped firing. 'Y' gun fired both barrels. Anti-aircraft shells burst above the artillery piece, scattering German soldiers in the blast.

'Searchlight!' Thorburn bellowed. 'Train left.'

Before the light moved a second enemy gun fired. A flash from the muzzle and Thorburn ducked. He gave himself a wry grin. So much for not being experienced with a moving target.

The white beam of the searchlight splashed onto the gun. The figures froze, caught in the glare. Then another shell screamed in towards the ship. From fifty yards further along twin lines of tracer whipped in at the bridge, fizzing and banging as they collided with steel. There was a high pitched scream of pain followed by a strangled whimper.

On the bow-chaser Barton saw his first real chance of joining the action. 'Here we go, Miller,' he shouted. Swinging the gun to starboard he sent a short burst in the machine gun's direction, but in the smoke and darkness he wasn't sure of the target.

Down in the forward turret the twin barrels of the four-inch guns swung left to where the searchlight held a gun in it's beam. Two shells roared out with devastating effect. Bodies cart wheeled through the air and when the dust settled the gun was a broken wreck.

Thorburn allowed the binoculars to rest. His shoulder ached, a reminder of the wound. He breathed out gently to relieve the tension, at least the German's main artillery had been stopped.

'Waves breaking dead ahead!' Jones yelled.

Thorburn reacted to the danger. 'Port thirty! Slow ahead.' He would have to circle back, away from the shore, and bring the starboard side back round to face the beach. As *Brackendale* angled sharply out to sea Thorburn stepped over to the starboard side. Looking aft to the boat deck he found Armstrong and McIntyre standing by.

'Ready on the boat deck?' he called through cupped hands.

Armstrong gave him an upturned thumb. 'Aye aye, sir,' he shouted.

Thorburn waved a hand and turned away to the compass platform to make some rapid calculations. *Brackendale* was fourteen or fifteen hundred yards out from the cove. He needed to allow the ship to regain a more westerly position before coaxing her back to launch the boat. He looked to port where the searchlight still lit the high ground. It gave him a visual check of the ship's location. Another few hundred yards of running across the bay and he gave the order to bring her in.

'Port twenty!' he snapped at the voice-pipe, and vaguely heard the Cox'n's acknowledgement, all his attention on *Brackendale*'s turn for the cove.

'Steady as she goes, Cox'n.'

Falconer's voice came up the tube. 'Aye aye, sir.'

Thorburn glanced round. 'Jones, I still need your eyes ahead of us.' At that moment the darkness of the high ground lit up with flickering gunfire.

Jack Barton reacted. Swinging the gun to cover a line over the starboard bow he chose what he thought was the most prominent target. The two pounder kicked through his shoulders, pumping out a half dozen shells. He could see he was short. He brought the cross hairs up, gave a slight deflection for the ship's movement, and hit the trigger. Again the gun jumped in his hands. The searchlight swept hurriedly from right to left along the rocky outcrops and the beam of light travelled just far enough to illuminate Barton's target. There was a momentary glimpse of Germans crouched beside a pair of machine guns. That was enough. His shells found the target and tore them apart.

He shifted to the right looking for his next target. A Starshell burst into light swaying overhead. The ship slowed and Barton recognised the shape of the cove in the swaying shadows. 'A' gun banged a pair of shells at the enemy positions. Rocks shattered in to fragments but machine guns kept firing. He looked back down the length of the ship. A Lewis gun was firing from the bridge and the starboard Oerlikon was in full flow. He knew the Pompom had joined in, the thumping barrels were just visible behind the funnel. Even up here on the bow the smell of cordite and the noise numbed the senses. Bullets flashed off 'A' guns splinter screen. Barton tracked the line of tracer back to the shore. He gave it a prolonged burst, raking the shells all round the target, nodding grimly as the firing stopped.

At the boat station, Armstrong felt the destroyer slow. 'Release the stays!' he shouted over the noise. In the darkness he felt the boat rock in his hands, free of the ties. He looked at Sir Henry, saw the look in his eyes, the tenseness in his jaw line.

'Ready, sir?'

'Aye, laddie. Just give the word.'

Armstrong strained to make out the bridge structure, urging Thorburn to give the signal. He braced as *Brackendale* made a final turn to port and presented her starboard side to the cove.

A hand waved from the bridge wing. 'Now, Number One!' It was Thorburn's voice on the wind. A burst of machine gun fire ripped over their heads and punched into the flag locker, ricocheting off the steel plates.

'Now, sir!' Armstrong beckoned the Admiral to the side, Labatt with him. McIntyre's youthful flexibility may have passed but helping hands steadied him in the boat. Seven Commandos found their places and hunched down. With the ship almost stopped in the water, Armstrong gave the order. 'Lower away.' The keel found the water and a split second later he heard the diesel cough into life. The Bosun looked up with a grin and the motorboat peeled away for the shore. On the portside, *Veracity*'s boat, with thirteen soldiers and two crewmen, also veered out from the ship's s and headed out beyond the overhanging stern.

Lieutenant Paul Wingham lay hidden from view beneath a small rocky outcrop at the back of the cove. Marianne crouched to his right and Moncrieff knelt to his left. Wingham was conscious of how frightened the girl was. Beyond the water's edge the destroyer seemed intent on blasting away the entire high ground. He knew the gunners were aiming over their heads but they were in danger of flying debris. The noise of the guns impacted the senses, the nearby rattle of a Spandau persistent, jarring. The beam of the searchlight swung by overhead followed by another mind numbing broadside. He could see the destroyer had stopped and two boats in the water were coming to the beach.

'Are you ready for this?' he asked the pair of them.

'Whenever you say,' Moncrieff answered.

Wingham felt for Marianne's hand. She gripped his fingers firmly and prepared to move.

'Don't run in a straight line, you zigzag. Understand?'

They both nodded and wriggled into a better position.

Wingham was watching the boat, ignoring the bullets flying around, waiting until the small craft had less than a hundred yards to travel.

'Now!' he yelled and pushed them out of concealment. They ran out onto the rough shingle and rock littering the beach. At the water's edge the leading motor boat grounded against the sandy foreshore. Wingham had to restrain himself, matching Marianne's slower pace. He grabbed her arm hauling her through the loose pebbles. In the flare of gunfire he saw Moncrieff weaving frantically down the beach. A figure jumped out of the boat with a submachine gun, dropped to one knee and fired a stream of bullets over their heads. The second boat touched the beach and more men followed spreading out and weaving up the beach. A column of water exploded in the shallows and one erupted near the boat. Wingham knew they were mortars, probably hidden behind the high ground. He pulled the girl to the right in an effort to upset the accuracy of the Germans. A line of tracer hissed by and plucked up sand near Moncrieff's feet. The bow-chaser opened up with a hail of shells. A moment later the tracer disappeared. A mortar hit the beach and Moncrieff stumbled to his left, almost fell, but regained his feet and staggered to the boat.

Brackendale's main armament crashed out a broadside and Marianne gave an involuntary cry. Wingham pushed her on giving her no time to think. There were encouraging shouts from the boat and the man with a gun ran toward them. 'Go on, Miss! You're almost there,' he shouted as he went past. He threw himself down and began to fire purposeful shots up the beach.

Moncrieff clambered awkwardly in to the stern as Wingham reached the bow. He pushed Marianne towards the stern and a pair of hands reached out and hauled her inboard.

'All aboard for the Skylark!' came a voice from the cockpit. Wingham scrambled over the waist and threw himself down. The submachine gunner returned amidst a hail of bullets, shoved hard at the bow and then swung easily onto the deck canopy. He turned and called to the men up the beach. Wingham cocked his weapon and levelled it over the side of the boat. The squad of men were returning in short runs, covering one another as they came. A mortar exploded and two of them went down and lay still. A corporal scampered over and checked for life, signalled they were dead, and made a dash for the boat. A bullet hit him and flung him sideways into the surf. Wingham jumped out and dragged him to the boat, pushing him over the side. The rest of the men tumbled in and Wingham yelled. 'Go!'

The diesel engine gave a harsh roar as it throttled up, the boat rocking violently as another mortar shell exploded close by. Stern first they began to pull clear of the beach. The Bosun selected a gear, the engine changed note and the launch lifted her bow with power. They raced away from the cove, bouncing erratically over the waves.

'Good of you to come, Sir Henry,' Moncrieff raised his voice above the noise.

Wingham looked up in surprise.

'Wouldn't have missed it for the world,' Sir Henry grinned. 'This is what the Navy's for, eh?' and he slapped Moncrieff on the shoulder. Marianne stretched out a hand and Wingham put an arm round her back, and then shook his head in disbelief. What in hell's name was McIntyre doing in a jolly boat under enemy fire? The boat lurched one way then the other as the helmsman weaved through a maelstrom of machine gun fire. And bullets found them, smashing their way along the port quarter. Wingham stole a glance at the destroyer, closer now, bigger in the water. As he looked, the pair of forward guns crashed another set of shells at the beach, a momentary shockwave hot overhead. He turned to the cove and grimaced. It was a seething mass of tracer and glowing flame, and drifting, oily smoke. A deluge of salt water enveloped them and the boat tilted wildly. Marianne gave a stifled cry and held him tighter. He shook his head and blinked water from his eyes. Looming over them, just a few feet away, *Brackendale*'s ladder hung down the starboard waist.

Waiting in the surf, the second boat came under fresh machine gun fire. It originated from the right of the beach, heavy and prolonged. The men on the sand were withdrawing in good order and scattered to face the threat. An explosion hit the beach, a mortar shell had landed. A piece of shrapnel hit a corporal in the neck and sliced through his artery. He died in a welter of blood. The man to his right took the blast, lost his left leg above the knee, screamed in agony. Multi coloured tracer swept the beach and within a minute half the commandos were casualties.

Out in the bay, Thorburn focused his binoculars on the shoreline moving to look at the far headland. He stopped in surprise. A line of German soldiers advanced in line abreast, shooting from the hip. The commandos were in danger of being overrun. He could see the sailors waving the commandos on, urging them in. A stream of tracer lanced in amongst the running men. Two fell, a third stumbled and struggled on.

Thorburn shouted at the bowchaser. 'Barton! Over to the right!'

The Pompom swung round and opened fire.

Major Gerhard Brandt charged down towards the small group of British soldiers. He was shooting on the move, short bursts, aiming low, his company extended in a line to the left. His heavy machine guns were lost, only one mortar firing, but he could still eliminate the men in front of him. He paused to shout encouragement. At that moment, Jack Barton's accuracy paid off. A hail of shells swept in from the ship, scything through the German ranks. Brandt took a shell in the chest, blowing him up the beach, cut in half. The line faltered, the living desperate to find shelter. When Barton stopped firing all that remained were a few running men. Five commandos escaped to the boat as the helmsman turned out for the ship.

Up on the bridge, Thorburn watched anxiously. His primary concern was the unexpected use of heavy mortars. *Brackendale* had received two hits, and with the enemy concealed from view, he had no way of retaliating.

The first hit on the ship had taken out the searchlight housing, killing the operator and smashing the lamp into darkness. 'Y' guns' turret had deflected the detonation of the second shell, some superficial damage and no casualties. Thorburn knew their luck might not hold, so silently he urged them to hurry; wanting to interfere, but not wishing to make them panic. Someone in the boat was struggling to get a hold on the ladder, more hands straining to help. The second boat touched the portside and men began to climb.

A stream of brightly coloured tracer arced in from the shore, walking over the sea to the ship's side. The forward guns thundered and a flare burst high and bright, drifting slowly down. Thorburn caught a faint movement far to his left. 'What's that at Green two-oh?' he demanded, turning to the lookouts.

'Looks like a field gun, sir.'

Jones called over. 'They're chocking the wheels.'

Thorburn bellowed at the voice-pipe. 'Guns. . . Bridge. Target at Green two-oh.'

'I'm on it!' 'Guns' answered sharply. A moments pause as the forward mount traversed left. Both barrels belched smoke and the shells detonated in a cloud of dust. As soon as the dust cleared the field gun fired. Distracted by Armstrong's call of, 'All aboard.' Thorburn felt the German shell hit the destroyer, heard the explosion. 'Full ahead. Port thirty!' he called down to the wheelhouse. A four gun salvo thundered out across the bay and the field gun somersaulted from view.

Brackendale was on the move, her bow swinging to port, slowly at first, turning ever more sharply as the propellers thrust the water astern. Thorburn took a final glance at the shore and turned his attention to the dark sea. He peered ahead in readiness to catch the turn, and caught his breath. The bow-chaser was unmanned. The distorted remains of a ready use locker was skewed across the deck, and in the flickering gunfire, he saw a man slumped on the guard rail. But first, the ship. 'Midships. Steer oh-one-oh degrees.'

To Lawrence, he called, 'Get a sick berth attendant up forrard. Damage Control too.'

The First Lieutenant appeared at the top of the starboard ladder, breathing hard. 'Sir,' he began, catching his breath. 'The Admiral's wounded. Took a bullet in the back when they came alongside. He told me to fetch you, sir.'

Thorburn cursed in frustration.

'He's not good, sir. The Doc's given him morphine.'

Thorburn nodded and turned away to the darkness of the bridge-screen, a sense of disaster flooding through him. 'And what about Moncrieff?' he asked, fearing the worst.

'He's fine, sir.'

'Thank Christ for small mercies,' Thorburn said quietly.

The Chief Yeoman pushed his way in. 'Signal intercept, sir.'

'What is it?' Thorburn snapped.

'To Admiralty from *Veracity*. "Enemy in sight. Am engaging" That's all, sir.'

'Position?' Thorburn asked, reaching for the message slip. Leaning to the chart table he read off the co-ordinates and plotted them to the chart. North-northwest, eight miles out. He frowned to himself. What did that mean? Obviously Germans, and that being the case, how many? What ships? He shrugged it off, for the moment he would hold course for England.

'Thanks, Yeo. Keep me informed.' He checked the compass and instinctively swept the darkness with his eyes, knowing they were at full speed, but theoretically clear of the rocky coastline.

'Right, Number One, I'll go and see Sir Henry.'

Armstrong acknowledged and Thorburn took the ladder two rungs at a time. Landing on the main deck he bulldozed his way through the hatchway and headed for the sick berth. About to enter, he stood aside as two crewmen pushed into the room carrying a stretcher. In the subdued red light below decks he could see a blanket covered the casualty from head to toe. Easing himself through the door he squinted against the bright glare of the sick bay.

Rear-Admiral Sir Henry McIntyre was half propped up on a bunk against the far bulkhead. His bare chest was triangled in a blood stained bandage, eyes closed, ashen faced. Doc Waverley looked up with an almost imperceptible shake of his head then carried on sewing up a stoker's jaw. Three other casualties were sitting or lying, and as Thorburn moved across to the Admiral, one of them tried to sit up.

'Rest easy,' Thorburn said, gesturing for the sailor to relax. The sound of his voice penetrated the Admiral's consciousness. One eye opened and held Thorburn with the unblinking focus of an eagle.

'Hello, sir, how're you feeling?' asked Thorburn, unable to think of anything better.

'I'm dying, Richard. The bloody Nazis got me.' The Scottish brogue was subdued, breaking up, and a trickle of blood ran from the corner of his mouth. 'Don't fret now, we all have to go sometime.' He coughed, a wheezing, bubbling rasp, shuddering with the effort. 'Listen,' he managed, 'whatever happens, you get Lord Moncrieff back to England. He has vital information for the top brass.' He coughed again blood dribbling down his chin.

Thorburn found a cloth to wipe his mouth.

'Don't fuss, laddie. Did you hear what I said?' His eyes closed.

Thorburn leaned nearer. 'Yes, sir. Moncrieff to England. Stop for nothing.'

'With all despatch, Richard. With all despatch.' His voice faded.

Thorburn felt a hand on his shoulder.

'I'll take it from here, sir,' Waverley said, and placed his stethoscope on Sir Henry's chest.

Thorburn stood back, accepting the inevitable. He'd been given his orders, and in no uncertain terms. Time to get back to the bridge. Reluctantly he withdrew, found his way out onto the main deck and paused to take a breath of fresh air. If only McIntyre had stayed on board . . , he shrugged, nothing he could do about it now. He hauled himself up the starboard ladder and stepped onto the bridge. Armstrong must have heard his approach and moved away from the compass platform.

'The course is oh-one-oh degrees, sir. Speed, twenty six knots.'

Wrapped up in his own thoughts, Thorburn gave a perfunctory reply. 'Very well.'

The bridge personnel went quiet, sensing this might be a time to fade into the background.

Thorburn vaguely noticed but was too immersed in his own thoughts to care. What in God's name had Moncrieff found out? He contemplated asking Wingham and then thought better of it. He'd find out soon enough.

'Number One,' he said abruptly. 'Have the galley make up sandwiches for the crew. We'll remain at action stations, they'll have to eat where they are.'

'Aye aye, sir,' said Armstrong and he moved away.

Moonlight cut through the clouds bathing the ship in a pale sheen. In a moment the darkness had evaporated and Thorburn felt very exposed. Reaching for his binoculars he gave the horizon a fast sweep and spotted the lighthouse over their port quarter, significantly more prominent in this light. Maintaining the search he checked for any signs of *Veracity* to the northwest. Nothing, just an empty expanse of water. He allowed the glasses to drop to his chest, the lanyard momentarily digging into his neck.

'Keep a sharp lookout,' he said. 'We're not out of trouble yet.'

Then he heard a familiar voice from the rear of the bridge. 'Permission to come up, sir?'

Thorburn grinned and turned to meet a dishevelled Sherwood Forester. 'Glad you made it, Paul,' he said, reaching out to shake his hand.

'Glad you could stop for a few old castaways, sir,' Wingham laughed. 'You know the Admiral took one in the back?'

'Yes, I went down to see him. Doc's doing what he can.' Thorburn thought it might be a good time to test the waters. 'Sir Henry gave me strict instructions to get Moncrieff back no matter what. Sounded pretty important.'

Wingham took a stealthy glance round the dark bridge space and then moved away from the nearest crew members. 'I really can't say much. I know what you were told about why he was here. Some of that is true, but he did have a job to do and the information he has is vital.' He hesitated.

Thorburn urged him on. 'And?'

'Moncrieff has French relatives, speaks fluent French and he's been setting up an underground resistance. That radio I took with me. Now it belongs to them and they'll report everything they can. Bainbridge set it up.'

Thorburn stared at him. 'And Marianne?'

'She's been a part of this from the word go, along with her brother. The SS killed him last week.'

The ship thumped heavily through a large wave and yawed unexpectedly to port. As Wingham reached for a hand hold Thorburn began to make sense of everything. Moncrieff's status became self-evident. His knowledge was far too important to have been allowed to fall into enemy hands. The urgency of this whole operation, the willingness of the top brass to silence him if necessary, that's why Sir Henry had come along. Another thought crossed his mind. 'Did you have any special orders regarding Moncrieff's rescue. More than you might have expected?'

Wingham looked down and then turned his eyes out to sea. 'I was to shoot him if he got caught.' He rubbed his chin. 'I insisted they repeat the order.'

Thorburn heard the bitter inflection, even now a sense of disbelief. Then a thought struck him. 'You're up to your neck in this, have been from the start.'

Wingham gave him a wry smile. ' If you only knew the whole story.'

Thorburn felt he was catching up fast, and Peter had spotted it a lot quicker than he had.

'How's the girl?' he asked suddenly, steering the conversation towards safer ground.

'Not happy. Didn't want to leave but she was compromised. And Bainbridge wants her back. She'll probably be okay, just needs a good night's rest.'

Thorburn nodded. 'Have a word with my First Lieutenant and he'll find you a bunk. Looks like you need it, Paul.'

'You're right, sir. Must be about two days without sleep.'

'Sir!' Jones called from the port bridge-wing. 'I'm seeing an orange glow at Red three-oh.'

Thorburn made a quick calculation. *Veracity* could be in that area. He picked up a handset. 'Guns,' Red three-oh. What do you make of it?'

'Not sure, sir. Maybe a small boat on fire.'

'Range?' Thorburn asked.

'Eleven thousand yards, sir.'

Thorburn raised his glasses wondering if he should investigate. If he followed orders then there was only one course of action, head for home. A faint glow swam through his lens and he lowered the binoculars. Estimated distance; call it six miles at twenty-seven knots, no more than fifteen minutes. And he'd heard nothing more from *Veracity*. He made his decision.

'Port ten.'

He realised Wingham had already gone below. *Brackendale* responded rapidly to the helm and he corrected the swing. 'Midships-steer three-three-five degrees.'

Falconer confirmed from the wheelhouse and Thorburn moved to the bridge-screen. Lifting the glasses he gave the sea a cursory sweep from port to starboard.

'Number One, check with the W/T office. See if they've heard from *Veracity*.'

'Aye aye, sir.'

As he moved away the moon slipped behind a cloud and cloaked the ship in darkness, much to Thorburn's relief.

'Bridge, 'Guns.'

'Go ahead, 'Guns.'

'The target is a burning E-boat, sir.'

'Thank you, 'Guns,' Thorburn acknowledged thoughtfully. Willoughby must surely have been involved, but where was he now?

'Nothing from *Veracity*, sir.' Armstrong came and stood at his side.

The ship ran on until he judged the distance to be fifteen hundred yards. 'Slow ahead,' he said, and *Brackendale* came down from her forward dash to wallow in the flickering embers. There were no survivors. As they watched, the remains of the E-boat sank stern first, the last of the flames extinguished in a fierce hiss. Thorburn brought his ship back to her original course and with a last look at the bits of flotsam gave the order for twenty-five knots.

Chapter Sixteen . . Against the Odds.

FlotillaKapitan Verner von Holtzmann stood on the fore-bridge of his command and congratulated himself on driving off an old Royal Navy 'V&W' destroyer which had been bombarding the defences of Calais. He had lost one of the torpedo boats, but no matter. The British ship had definitely taken some damage before Holtzmann was ordered to break contact and look for a second warship involved on the north coast near Goury. Apparently, during a fight with the shore guns, the ship had succeeded in taking off a small group of saboteurs. His new orders were to intercept and sink the Britisher.

He calculated his target would take the shortest route back to the English coast, so he decided to steam directly west along the Cherbourg Peninsula before turning north in pursuit. This gave him the advantage of a stern sighting from where the enemy may not be so vigilant.

'Herr Kapitan!'

Holtzmann turned to his Second-in-Command, Oberleutnant zur See, Maximillian Bauer. 'What is it?' he asked abruptly.

'Excuse me, Herr Kapitan, but you asked to be informed when we completed the repairs.'

Holtzmann modified his tone. They had sustained a few minor hits during the engagement. 'Ja, mien freund, all done?'

'No, sir. The anti-aircraft battery is out of action. The swivel mounting has jammed and we cannot fix the elevation.'

'But our main armament is still in good order,' Holtzmann said patiently, 'and we have many more machine guns, no?'

'Jawhol, Herr Kapitan, but . . .'

'No buts, Max.' Holtzmann held up a hand to quell the protest and straightened to his full height. 'This is a warship of the German Kriegsmarine. You expect me to worry about a little damage. These are just old English ships from the last war. I do not plan on defeat.' He turned away to look out over the forward guns, forcing an end to their conversation.

Bauer clicked his heels and stepped aside. He hoped they were not at sea when daylight came, the Royal Air Force always pressed home their attacks.

Oblivious to Bauer's worries, von Holtzmann leaned over his chart, brass dividers stepping lightly along the projected course. If his hunch was correct then the Englander must be somewhere just ahead. He placed the dividers neatly on the table, clasped his hands behind him, and nodded in satisfaction. 'He will be mine before breakfast,' he said aloud. Peering ahead in the gloom he waited for that first sighting.

They pushed on at full speed, lookouts straining for a glimpse of the quarry. Time drifted on, moonlight bathing the ship in pale grey, peaks and troughs of breaking seas glinting in the light. The minutes stretched into half-an-hour, thirty minutes of endless search, of anxious doubt.

'Ship ahead, on the port bow,' came a shouted report.

Holtzmann swung his powerful binoculars to focus fine on the port bow. For a brief moment he caught sight of an enemy ship, then a cloud obscured the moon and the destroyer faded from view. He lowered the weight of the glasses and rubbed his hands together.

'The Englander has not seen us,' he said over his shoulder. 'Bring the ship to port and set course to follow. We will open fire at seven thousand meters.'

Max Bauer gave the command and two thousand tons of warship swung into position astern of the unsuspecting British destroyer.

Holtzmann raised the glasses in an effort to clarify the sighting. On reflection he thought the outline was similar to a destroyer they had encountered the other day. In a rare moment of moonlight he managed to satisfy his curiosity. No torpedo tubes, only four-inch guns, the size of a small escort destroyer. Easing the binoculars to hang from his collar, von Holtzmann found a cigar, bit the end and lit it with a contented pull. Now was the time to tame a King's lion.

'Ship! Bearing Green one-seven-oh.'

Thorburn spun round with his binoculars to scan beyond the starboard quarter. He found the ship immediately, and if he wasn't mistaken, it was their old enemy. The destroyer was slightly port beam on, cutting across their wake to the starboard side. In that same moment, the German's forward gun belched smoke and flame as it opened fire. He cursed loudly. They'd been caught with their pants down. A shell whistled overhead and he reached for the handset to the engine room. Bryn Dawkins answered.

'Hello, Chief. What was our top speed in the sea trials?'

'Twenty eight knots, sir,' came the reply.

'Well crack it on for me. We've an unwelcome guest on our tail.'

'Right oh, Captain. I'll give you everything we've got.'

'Good man,' Thorburn said, and slammed the handset back on it's bracket. A near miss exploded close by the starboard bow, immediately followed by the unnerving rattle of shrapnel flaying the side plates.

'Number One. Be so good as to inform 'Guns' to open fire when in range.'

He saw Armstrong grin at the absurd formality. 'Aye, aye, sir.'

'Port twenty!' he snapped to the wheelhouse. He had to keep the enemy dead astern, minimise the target area.

'Midships . . , steady as you go.' The downside was their speed differential, he was only delaying the inevitable. *Brackendale* would never outrun her pursuer.

Both guns on the quarterdeck fired simultaneously and Thorburn watched for the fall of shot. Twin waterspouts erupted in line with the enemy's bow and he shook his head. Well short, but it might put them off their aim. He had to think of something to give his ship an advantage, anything to enhance her position. Blotting out the sounds around him he raised his glasses, concentrating on the problem. Of course, he thought, smiling to himself, he could always apply the oldest one in the book, attack was the best defence. Simply said, but full of danger when you were so outclassed. He frowned as he tried to figure it out. What if he made a really surprise move, totally unexpected.

As things stood the German captain would be viewing *Brackendale*'s size and armament with amusement. Top speed under thirty knots. No torpedoes and the calibre of her guns a meagre four inch. But Thorburn knew his advantage was in his ship's acceleration and her high degree of manoeuvrability.

'Enemy turning to port, sir,' A lookout called.

Thorburn saw the move at the same time. The German captain was determined to close the gap. A steady stream of shells were blasting out from the after turret, falling short of the target as yet, but getting closer. He checked the time, to the second.

'Starboard fifteen,' he ordered, swinging the ship in the opposite direction. He waited, watching the enemy destroyer while *Brackendale* leaned into her turn.

'Midships,' he said, and as she steadied he leaned to the voice-pipe. 'As she goes Cox'n. What's your heading?'

'Oh-oh-five degrees, sir.'

'Very well.' The enemy's guns smoked another salvo towards him, plunging harmlessly fifty yards off their port quarter. He ignored the result, concentrating through the binoculars. When the ship commenced its turn to starboard he checked his watch, the sweep hand showing fifty seconds had elapsed since his own turn to starboard. He smiled grimly. That was a relatively sluggish response to *Brackendale*'s manoeuvre. A shell whizzed overhead making for an involuntary flinch. He studied his watch and waited for the second hand to hit twelve.

'Port twenty!' he called down to Falconer.

'Port twenty, sir.'

The ship heeled alarmingly to starboard, white water cascading along the main deck.

'Midships . . , as she goes,' Thorburn had one eye on the German.

'Midships,' Falconer repeated. 'Steering, two-seven-oh degrees, sir.'

'Hold her there, Cox'n,' Thorburn said, lifting the glasses to his eyes. It was the initial lean of the masthead that gave the first hint of a change in direction and his watch gave a delay of fifty-one seconds. The first real inkling of a plan began to form and he decided to commit *Brackendale* to an attack. He leaned on the chart table and estimated their position as due north of Goury. That last change of direction had steadied up on two-seven-oh; they were travelling west.

'Number One,' he called through the noise.

Armstrong came to stand at his shoulder. 'Sir.'

'At the moment, we're only delaying the inevitable. We're not going to out run him and swapping shells won't get the job done. So I'm afraid I've come up with a bit of an 'all or nothing' idea.'

Armstrong grinned. 'That's not like you, sir.'

In the small light of the table, Thorburn noted the grin and for an instance felt the tug of a smile. 'Well it won't be easy,' he said.

'We never do things the easy way, sir.'

At that moment, Thorburn caught Armstrong's mood, the madness of the situation. 'I'm going to take the fight to the German. At a given moment I'm going to attack along his starboard side. My intention is to hit him with everything we have. When I make that move we'll be heading due north, hopefully that'll leave him headed south on the wrong foot.'

Armstrong nodded, and then shook his head. 'I have a feeling this might be a case of luck favouring the brave.'

'I've been keeping a time on his rate of turn,' Thorburn said, 'he's so slow we could twist him inside out.'

Armstrong pushed his cap back and rubbed his chin. 'Got to be worth a try, what have we got to lose?'

'Very well, Number One. Raise the Battle Ensign.'

Armstrong caught Thorburn's enthusiasm. 'Aye aye, sir!'

Thorburn straightened away from the chart table and stepped up to the compass platform. His last helm order had them steaming west. He would bring the ship south so the final change of direction would take them back north at full speed.

'Port twenty,' he said, leaning to the voice-pipe. Without looking he knew the German would follow him round. The incessant crash of the quarterdeck's twin four-inch had continued unabated and for the first time, 'A' gun joined the party. The compass swung through to the south and Thorburn gave the crucial order to commence the manoeuvre.

'Midships,' he said, and waited for the ship to steady.

'Steer, one-eight-oh degrees.' A glance astern. This time the enemy warship had turned harder than *Brackendale* and had swung over to follow fine on the port quarter. He allowed himself a taught smile. If conformation of poor seamanship were needed, the evidence had just been presented. The moon broke out from behind the clouds, immediately followed by water spouts thumping in close to the port bow. His own guns were falling short but just about in range. His calculation made for a closing speed of fifty-eight knots, or a bit more than sixty miles an hour. A mile a minute once *Brackendale* had made her turn. So he would pull the German further to port before initiating his plan to attack.

'Port twenty,' he ordered.

'Port twenty, aye, aye, sir,' came the Cox'n's calm reply.

Thorburn braced his body as *Brackendale* leaned out to starboard and waited for her to arrive at his considered point of travel.

'Midships!'

The ship steadied, plunging ferociously into the waves. He checked the compass. 'Steady.'

'Steering one-seven-oh,' the Cox'n said.

Thorburn stepped smartly over to the port bridge-wing. His binoculars found the enemy just beginning to follow *Brackendale*'s turn. He squinted at his watch, counting off the seconds. When the sweep hand hit twelve he leant to the voice-pipe.

'Hard-a-starboard!'

Not waiting for the acknowledgement he turned to watch events unfold. As the rudder rotated to a maximum thirty-five degrees *Brackendale* trembled and rolled through the upright before listing to port. Thorburn bared his teeth into the spray soaked wind, impatiently willing the ship to come round. Her bow-wave whipped high over the forecastle washing away to the dark seas off the port waist. And there was the enemy, visible over the starboard bow, no sign of any counter to Thorburn's change of course, almost broadside on, moving to port.

'Midships,' he said urgently.

The Cox'n must have been expecting the order. Rocking upright with the sudden correction, the ship canted slightly to starboard before settling to a steady run. But even with the naked eye, Thorburn could see the German Captain had recognised the danger and his destroyer began to turn towards *Brackendale*.

'Steer oh-five-oh,' he called down the voice-pipe.

'Oh-five-oh, sir,' Falconer repeated.

Smoke billowed from the German guns and the salvo straddled them, miraculously leaving them untouched. *Brackendale*'s forward guns replied and at approximately seven thousand yards one shell hit the bow and the other exploded below the bridge. Thorburn raised his glasses.

Between the bows and the starboard anchor the faint red glow of a fire appeared. Another salvo crashed out from the enemy ship. Thorburn gritted his teeth anticipating the impact. Jets of water erupted close ahead drenching the bows. Emerging from the spray 'A' gun roared again, hurling the shells across the ever-decreasing gap. Two waterspouts blossomed ahead of the target leaving Thorburn clenching his fists in exasperation. The Oerlikons had joined the mêlée, a stream of tracer reaching forward from either side of the bridge. The distance between the two ships had converged to under two miles and Thorburn accepted the German commander had no lack of courage. If both ships remained on course a collision was inevitable. A sleight of hand was needed, draw him off course.

'Steer oh-one-oh degrees,' he ordered.

'Oh-one-oh degrees, aye, aye, sir.'

Brackendale eased to starboard and Thorburn checked for the first indication of a similar move. Nothing happened; the enemy allowed him to change course; but then Thorburn realised his mistake. The German's guns had traversed to follow *Brackendale* leaving him wide open to a broadside.

'Port thirty!' he shouted down the voice-pipe. He would cross the 'T' and give them a broadside as he went past their bows. With luck he could turn to starboard and whip down the enemy's flank. An array of missed shells fell on *Brackendale*'s previous course as she turned almost due west, charging headlong across the German's path. No more than a thousand yards away, and then the four-inch guns began a rolling broadside, an individual explosion of sound melding into one long barrage. Amidst this wild cacophony Thorburn kept his seaman's eye on their position. As the stern rails swept past the enemy bow he gave the order to turn.

The small destroyer heeled hard over as she tore round on her change of course. Briefly, the noise of firing stopped, as if drawing breath. Dark figures could be seen on the enemy bridge.

Lieutenant Howard ordered the main armament to load and wait until he was ready. In the control tower, with less then a thousand yards of water between the destroyers, his finger pressed the fire button. All four guns roared in unison, high explosive shells bracketing the enemy's upper deck. A shell exploded near the casing on the German's forward turret, steel splinters lancing through to the gunners, maiming and killing. Another shell penetrated between the funnel and main deck, damaged an electric cable, and started a fire. *Brackendale*'s forward guns targeted the German's quarterdeck. A shell glanced off a shield and another put a jagged hole through a splinter screen. Thorburn watched as his Oerlikons raked the gun platform, a sustained burst of fire ricocheting around the bridge.

Brackendale raced on into clear water, her guns on the quarterdeck maintaining an impressive rate of fire. Thorburn moved to the starboard bridge-wing to watch for the enemy's turn, hoping his gunners had inflicted enough damage to slow him down. He waited, watching closely. Would he turn to port or starboard?

'Ship! Bearing Green-two-oh.'

Thorburn whipped round and raised his binoculars over the starboard bow. As dark as it was he still found the ship immediately. Bow on, steering directly at them, destroyer in outline but peculiar in shape. He struggled for a moment trying to establish the difference. Then through

268

the gloom he found the answer. The mast was missing, and as he concentrated through the glasses, he recognised the ship. '*Veracity*!' he called loudly. 'It's *Veracity*,' he repeated in surprise. A lamp began to flash on her bridge.

'Signal, sir. Reads . . , "shall I engage?" End of message, sir.'

Thorburn smiled grimly. He took a quick look over his shoulder at the German ship. It hadn't turned, continuing to steam south. From what he could see *Veracity* had already been in at least one battle, probably didn't need another. He turned to the signaller. 'Send this. "Do not engage. Priority is escort home." Got that?'

The lamp clattered in the Yeoman's hand. It was followed by a flashed acknowledgement and *Veracity* turned away to take up station ahead.

Aboard the German destroyer, von Holtzmann paced the bridge in anger. He felt the humiliation of being outsmarted by what he thought was an inferior enemy. The Englander's tactics had been unbelievable. It had been either very stupid, or as he had begun to suspect, very brave. Holtzmann was beginning to hold a grudging respect for the man's courage. When the destroyer had turned straight for him, Holtzmann had been caught unawares. And then of course, he had suddenly found himself well within the range of the Englander's guns. To cross his bows and turn down their starboard side, it was not expected. It manoeuvred like a speedboat. Then finally that old 'V&W' destroyer had reappeared which would have meant splitting his firepower. They had forced him to break off the engagement, no choice.

'Herr Kapitan.' Max Bauer arrived by his side. 'All the fires are extinguished, sir. The other damage is not great.'

'That will be good,' Holtzmann said. 'That will be very good. I think we have met this Englishman before, Max. That merchant ship being towed by a destroyer, I'm sure it was the same one. A brave man, their captain, but if we should meet again . . .'

'He will not have so long to live, Herr Kapitan,' Bauer said, obviously relishing the thought.

Holtzmann nodded slowly. 'Ja, but first I must have two more Schnellboats. Get a message to Cherbourg and have them join us immediately.' The ship pushed on leaving the two Royal Navy destroyers escaping to the north and von Holtzmann waiting impatiently in the south.

Chapter Seventeen . . Dawn Will Come.

Thorburn sat quietly in the bridge-chair sipping a sweet mug of tea. Two points off the starboard bow, *Veracity* led the way, pushing on through the darkness. Disfigured by the loss of her mast she presented a strange new profile and in the short term her only means of communication were the signalling lamps. One of her guns was out of action and a near miss off the stern had resulted in damage to her steering. Even so, she was still capable of manoeuvring at twenty knots, enough to get them home at a good pace.

As for *Brackendale*, Thorburn was surprised by the lack of damage. The only impairment to the ship was the loss of the searchlight. Dead and wounded were a different story. They had lost five killed, and along with Sir Henry, another three seriously injured. A further twelve had become walking wounded; a total of twenty casualties. The Navy had paid a high price for rescuing Lord Moncrieff, and although Willoughby had made no reference to casualties Thorburn couldn't help but guess the figures were high.

Brackendale lifted her bows to a wave, sliding sideways over the crest and hurrying into the trough. A gust of wind tugged at Thorburn's cap and a salty spray soaked the bridge.

'Weather's getting up, sir,' Armstrong remarked.

Thorburn nodded, balancing his mug on a pipe bracket. 'Might help to keep the U-boats off our scent. How're the passengers doing?'

'Resting, sir. Worn out.'

271

Thorburn pursed his lips. 'Can't have been easy back there.'

They fell into a shared silence and Thorburn swept his gaze to the east in the general direction of Calaise. He thought there might be the first, almost imperceptible hint of dawn approaching, but if it was, that first touch of grey eluded him.

A harsh white light pierced the gloom and the unexpected pulse of an Aldis lamp flickered out a message.

'Signal from *Veracity*, sir. "Taking in water. Reducing to eighteen knots." Message ends, sir.'

'Acknowledge,' Thorburn said. 'Make revolutions to match her speed, Number One.'

Armstrong bent to the voice-pipe. 'Half ahead both.'

Thorburn wondered if *Veracity* had taken a shell below the waterline or whether it was just shrapnel damage. She had obviously slowed and her stern-plates were clearly visible. That almost unseen hint of a lightening sky in the east heralded the coming of another day. At sea it was a hardly noticeable change of hue, in the peripheral vision rather than a change of colour. H.M.S. *Brackendale* was making sixteen knots and Lieutenant-Commander Richard Thorburn sat comfortably in his bridge chair. Their orders were clear, they were on course and the enemy had retreated in disarray. For the first time in a while Thorburn felt at ease. The ship was responding well, the crew were rested and the weather was set fair. Holding station a half mile ahead on the starboard bow, *Veracity* pushed on through a rising sea. It was good to know Willoughby shared the day.

By the dim light of dawn FlotillaKapitan Werner von Holtzmann made his way up to the bridge. Trailing in his wake, two of the flotilla's boats dutifully kept their distance, torpedo tubes full, machine guns manned.

Holtzmann extracted a cigar from his breast pocket and crouching slightly to shield the flame, he lit the aromatic leaf. Blue smoke coiled away as he luxuriated in the rich taste. He wasn't too worried about enemy aircraft, they were a long way from England. Since leaving the coast they had moved swiftly and it was only now that daylight began to touch the horizon. The cigar had a calming influence, the ship a rhythmic, relaxing motion, and he allowed himself a moment of tranquillity. Sometime soon he would make up for the disgrace of retreating.

'Achtung!' shouted a lookout. 'Ships, Herr Kapitan!' He stuck out an arm and pointed over the starboard bow. 'They are Britishers, Kapitan. Destroyers,'

Holtzmann swung his heavy Karl Zeiss binoculars into focus instantly finding two dark silhouettes against the eastern horizon. Even at that range, maybe eight or nine kilometres, he recognised the outline of the warships. Leading the way, the now familiar shape of that new small destroyer, and, he smiled at his handiwork, an old 'V&W' without her main mast. He lowered the glasses and took another leisurely pull on his cigar. Once again he had found his quarry. Fate had conspired to lead him here, at this very moment, to confront the enemy. Not a few defenceless cargo ships, but the Royal Navy trying to escape, and this time he was ready for the fight.

'Max,' he said, walking purposefully to the compass. 'Sound the alarm. The Englanders are looking to hide and I intend to see they are stopped.'

Bauer's hand reached for the large button releasing the urgent clamour of the klaxon, ordering the men to their stations. Within moments the men responded with a rush of running boots; on ladders and over the decks, below decks, in ammunition hoists, and beneath the waterline in the engine room. Guns were manned, lookouts changed, damage control parties readied. At every location men readied themselves for the prospect of battle. When all was prepared Bauer turned to Holtzmann. 'All stations report they are ready, Herr Kapitan.'

'Good,' Holtzmann said. 'Call the boats alongside. I will speak to their commanders.'

Bauer moved away to relay the orders and Holtzmann again used his glasses to locate the enemy. Nothing had changed; they held the same course. He quickly made up his plan of attack. Deploy both torpedo boats to left and right, which would split the enemy's firepower onto three targets.

'The boats are coming alongside now, Herr Kapitan,' Bauer reported with a click of his heels.

'So,' said Holtzmann. 'I will give them their orders.' He moved swiftly to the ladder and made his way down to the main deck where the powerful boats were holding station alongside the destroyer's waist.

Their captains listened intently as he passed on his instructions until, certain they understood, he waved them off with a salute. He stood for a moment gripping the guardrail, gazing at the water foaming past. There would be no turning back from this battle and in a short while they would be engaged. This time victory would be his.

Thorburn checked the time. In thirty minutes the sun would be lifting above the horizon.

'Ship! Bearing, red-one-hundred. Range, six-thousand yards.'

Thorburn whipped round and searched the sea in the darkness of the western gloom. A flicker of white, a curling bow wave, a grey shape above. He tightened his grip on the glasses, fixing on the size and shape. He felt sure it was a German destroyer and couldn't help but assume their old adversary was within reach. A voice-pipe squealed.

'Bridge,' he answered.

It was Howard. 'The target is at six-thousand, five hundred yards, sir.'

'Thank you, 'Guns.' Keep me informed,' he said, knowing immediately he would apply the first rule of engagement. Turn towards the enemy and attack at full speed.

'Yeoman, make to *Veracity*. "Enemy in sight to port, am engaging. Maintain distance to me." And use the hand held Aldis from the starboard side.' That would minimise the visible light.

'Aye aye, sir.' The Yeoman stepped away behind the Control Tower and began to flash the message.

Armstrong called softly. 'Guns' reports two E-boats fanning away to port and starboard, sir.'

'Very well,' Thorburn said. He must have called for reinforcements. No surprise in that, they usually travelled together. Didn't make life any easier.

The Yeoman spoke. '*Veracity* acknowledges, sir.'

'Now take this down. . , To Admiralty," Enemy in sight. Am engaging." Give our position, and send it in clear.' No need for security now.

A final flourish with his pencil and the Yeoman headed for the wireless room.

Thorburn bent to the voice-pipe. 'Guns,' open fire when ready.'

'Right, sir. Range to target six thousand yards.'

Moving to the bridge-screen, Thorburn raised his glasses to check on his adversary's progress. With the lightening of the sky he could see they were spread out in line abreast increasing the distance between themselves, obviously determined to split his firepower. If the E-boats pushed much wider they would outflank *Brackendale* before she had begun the attack. A bad situation, even so, it was time to commence the turn.

'Port thirty, full ahead both,' he ordered.

The Cox'n's reliable acknowledgement echoed in reply. 'Port thirty, full ahead both, aye, aye, sir.'

Chapter Eighteen . . A Time to Die.

Brackendale began her first overt move of the engagement. She heeled hard over to starboard in a flurry of spray. Thorburn glanced beyond the starboard quarter and watched *Veracity* follow his lead, thumping into the westerly swell. Turning back to the compass he waited until they were steaming due west and corrected the swing. The destroyer steadied on her new course, rising and falling with the undulating waves. The wind tugged at his cap, cold on his cheeks.

A bright flash from the German ship was followed by an instantaneous reply from below the bridge. Howard was on the ball. From the corner of his right eye he caught the orange spit of *Veracity*'s forward gun as she joined the fight. His own guns roared again, crashing out another pair of shells.

'E-boat moving wide to port, sir,' Jones called.

Thorburn looked ahead over the port bow and managed to locate the E-boat skimming away at speed. An enemy shell erupted off the starboard bow and peppered the ship with the harsh rattle of shrapnel. 'Port fifteen,' he called to the wheelhouse. Too close for comfort, came to mind, as the ship weaved away. He steadied the helm and as *Brackendale* levelled out he made an estimate of the distance travelled. 'Starboard fifteen!' He called more sharply. The ship came back from her southerly course to regain the original heading, now displaced by a few hundred yards. 'Midships . . , steady as she goes.'

In the wheelhouse the Cox'n spun the wheel and watched the compass settle. 'Steering two-eight-oh degrees, sir,' he called up the pipe.

Thorburn took another look at the E-boat coming round on *Brackendale*'s port beam, nose up, stern down, a foaming white bow wave. He reached for a bulkhead phone. Howard answered.

'Guns,' I need 'Y' gun on independent control. The E-boat on our port side.'

'I'll tell them now, sir.'

A thumping explosion erupted near the port bow, a heavy deluge of sea water cascading down on the forward splinter screen. The ship corkscrewed off course before the Cox'n managed to bring her back. Thorburn grabbed the bridge-rail, momentarily fearing the worst, hoping for the best. *Brackendale* steadied, came through, powered on.

'Number One,' he called.

'Sir?'

'Give me a damage report on the bow plates.'

'Aye aye, sir,' Armstrong said, heading for the ladder.

The percussive roar of 'A' gun stunned their ears. Cordite swept the bridge, stinging the eyes and catching the throat. Thorburn turned his head to the E-boat as the guns on the quarterdeck opened up. Two plumes of water rose up beyond the boat. Over, Thorburn said to himself. Make the adjustment. Load. Close the breech. Fire. All this to himself, and yet such was the timing the bellow of guns matched his thoughts. He watched for the result and twin splashes obliterated the target, just short. The E-boat swerved wildly but fought back on course.

'*Veracity*'s hit, sir!' came a call from the flag-deck.

Thorburn grimaced. The old destroyer had taken a shell abaft the bridge on the portside. Thick black smoke billowed astern but the ship rushed onward, 'B' gun cracking out a reply. He turned his attention to the German destroyer, raising his binoculars to the bridge. A few indistinct shapes through the brightening day. Then a taller figure with elbows raised, apparently watching *Brackendale* through glasses.

'Torpedoes!' Jones yelled.

Thorburn reacted instinctively. 'Hard-a-port!' he called to the pipe. The E-boat was turning away chased by two heavy splashes. Pompom shells began to hunt across the gap searching for the boat. *Brackendale* was clawing her way round towards the torpedoes, leaning violently to starboard, sweeping inside the projected course.

'There, sir,' Jones jabbed an outstretched finger.

Thorburn followed the outstretched arm, wanting to believe he could see the tracks A vague phosphorescent trace showed briefly, enough to know the ship wasn't out of danger. He let the Cox'n hold the turn while he agonised over the chances of avoiding the two torpedoes.

'Midships!' Thorburn said sharply. The ship swayed upright directly down the path of the oncoming underwater missiles.

A blinding flash hit the bridge, a searing heat burning down across the binnacle. The explosive blast hurled Thorburn to the deck. He flinched in agony as a biting pain lanced through his left ribcage. Forcing himself to one knee, gasping with the effort, he struggled to take a breath, the sharp pain in his torso too much.

'Up you come, sir.' A vaguely heard voice through the ringing in his ears. It was Jones trying to help him up. He managed to grab the offered forearm and pull himself upright. Fore and aft *Brackendale*'s guns continued to hammer out the offensive bombardment. He leant against the bridge-screen trying to take in what happened, then tensed in surprise. The Range Finder tower had disappeared. All that remained was a blackened distortion of steel shards. A shocked Yeoman stood gaping at the smoking ruin, too stunned to move.

'Torpedoes passed to starboard, sir,' Jones said calmly.

Thorburn pushed himself away from the screen and tentatively checked his ability to stand.

'Very well,' he replied, struggling to think. He looked round quickly, remembering the German destroyer. His enemy had turned to follow, but the German's guns were all pointing at *Veracity*. And the old 'V&W' was making life difficult. She had sheared away to starboard giving all her guns the chance of a broadside, and Willoughby had deployed torpedo tubes over the port side. Thorburn needed to bring *Brackendale* round in support. He gave the order to change course, heard Falconer acknowledge.

Armstrong returned in a rush from his below decks inspection. He looked at the remains if the Control tower and pursed his lips in a silent whistle.

'Well, Number One?' Thorburn jolted him.

Armstrong reacted. 'Sorry, sir. Some shrapnel damage, but well above the waterline.'

Thorburn winced to a sudden stab of pain, reached out to the compass for support.

'You're hurt, sir? Armstrong queried, unsure.

Thorburn held up a hand. 'Nothing serious. Check the casualties,' he said, nodding to where the tower had been.

Armstrong squinted at the wreckage and moved, off calling for help.

Thorburn turned back to his command. He gathered his thoughts, trying to unravel the sequence of events. He realised the guns had stopped firing, Howard had disappeared, probably dead, along with the Control Tower. Forcing himself to stand tall at the bridge-screen he managed to catch sight of Labatt turning towards the bridge. He called to him against the wind and the response was instant.

'Yes, sir!' the young Midshipman shouted.

Thorburn managed an encouraging smile. 'Take charge, Mr Labatt. The Rangefinder's been hit. Assume independent control.'

There was a moment's hesitation while he digested the news. 'Aye aye, sir,' he called, gave a parade ground salute and turned back to the guns.

Thorburn acknowledged the salute knowing the gunners knew their jobs and the Midshipman was both popular and respected. He watched the barrels lift and steady.

'Shoot!'

He heard Labatt's command, the instant response as both guns launched their projectiles. He ignored the fall of shot, turning instead to the compass platform, holding his ribs against the pain. A welcome burst of spray enveloped the bridge, stinging his face, stimulating.

Armstrong reported. 'Lieutenant Howard is dead, sir. Morgan and Turner too.'

'I guessed as much,' Thorburn said. 'Pass that on to the quarterdeck gunners. Tell them to assume local control, they know the target.'

Armstrong hesitated, slowly held out his hand.

Thorburn looked down, reached out. He took the polished pipe with the charred bowl, and swallowed. He looked up into Armstrong's eyes.

'All I could find,' Armstrong said, and for a moment they just stared at Howard's pipe.

Thorburn broke their silence. 'The gunners, Number One. Local control.' He dropped the pipe in his jacket.

Armstrong spun away.

Daylight was on them now, not yet bright, but the pale grey of pre-sunrise. For the first time Thorburn could just make out the red and black insignia of the German flag. He gave the order for *Brackendale* to bear away to port, giving all his main armament a direct line of fire. Not that the gunfire had slackened, it was incessant, the acrid taste of cordite sharp on the tongue. The enemy's forward guns swung with *Brackendale*'s turn and he was tempted to weave starboard, approach head on. It would reduce her profile, but he thought better, had to give his guns every chance. Two jets of water erupted thirty yards ahead of the starboard bow, Thorburn watching *Veracity*, certain she was about to launch her torpedoes. She was no more than twelve hundred yards from the target, firing point imminent.

Then, as he watched, *Veracity* staggered under an enormous plume of smoke and water. She'd taken a strike on her starboard plates, in line with the forecastle break, the opposite side to Thorburn's shocked gaze.

'*Veracity*'s hit, sir,' a lookout shouted.

'I see it,' Thorburn acknowledged. That was a mortal wound. He assumed it was a torpedo, too big an explosion for a shell. Probably from the other E-boat. *Veracity*'s speed fell off and she began to list away. The water flooding in through her damaged side-plates acted as a sea anchor and the old ship turned broadside to the enemy guns. Amongst the repeated roar of *Brackendale*'s heavy gunfire he heard an exited shout. 'We've hit it, sir!'

Thorburn looked over the starboard bow and allowed himself a grim smile. Smoke billowed out from the German's forward gun; a dirty grey smoke, curling aft beyond the bridge. He looked away. *Veracity* was dead in the water and Thorburn knew it was only a matter of time. Her momentum had continued to turn the ship until her stern now faced the enemy. Her quarterdeck gun banged out in defiance and Thorburn felt an overwhelming admiration for that crew. They'd remained at their posts, struggling to stand, fighting the gun. He had to help, give Willoughby some protection.

Squinting through the pungent smoke from his own guns he calculated the distance between *Brackendale* and the German. Maybe twenty-five hundred yards. Closing speed sixty knots. Enough sea room to turn across the enemy's bow and station *Brackendale* between the two destroyers. Machine gun bullets raked the bridge forcing him to duck below the screen. He squirmed sideways to the pipe. 'Hard-a-starboard,' he shouted above the din.

Falconer barked a reply. 'Hard-a-starboard, aye aye, sir.' The ship twisted beneath them as she entered into another violent turn.

Armstrong, trying to get aft along the port side main deck, almost lost his footing. As the ship angled over he grabbed a Carley float and hung on, foaming white water tugging at his boots. He gathered himself to make a move then jumped awkwardly along the sloping deck. Another precarious handhold gave him a yard more and he swung round behind the relative protection of the aft galley housing. Now he was looking at the inside of the

283

quarterdeck gun mount. It was on the move, swinging from starboard to port as the gun crew traversed to find the enemy. As the barrels swept out over the port rail, Armstrong moved to join them.

'Independent control, lads,' he called to them. 'The Range Finder's gone.' He recognised the Gun Captain, Kendal, under a steel helmet.

'We know, sir.' He jerked his head forward.

Armstrong took a quick look towards the bridge. The answer was self evident, a large gap in the ship's superstructure. Beneath their feet the ship swayed upright, a more even platform to stand on.

'Target, red-four-oh.' A minimal movement of the guns to come forty-five degrees on the port bow.

Armstrong peered out from the shield, squinting through the wind driven spray. Two thousand yards away the German destroyer approached at speed.

'Shoot!' A deafening roar and the guns flamed, shell cases bounced to the deck, two fresh rounds slammed home, breech closed.

'Down two hundred'

A fast turn of a hand wheel. 'On.'

Three seconds had elapsed. 'Shoot!' An explosive crash of cordite and another pair of shells sped away.

Over Armstrong's head the Pompom thumped into action, the four synchronised guns hurling their two-pound shells over the waves. In the four-inch turret a loader screamed and fell clutching his face. Armstrong weaved his way to the fallen man. He pulled at the bloodied hands, ignoring the cries of pain. His mouth and jaw were open to the bone, a shard of steel embedded in his cheek. Blood flowed freely. A four-inch shell appeared at the chute form the magazine.

'Stretcher!' Armstrong yelled, eased the injured man to the deck, and reached for the shell. He cradled its weight along to the gun.

'I'll take it.' The remaining loader rammed the round into the opening and closed the breech. A damage control party pushed past Armstrong to the injured man.

'Shoot!'

Armstrong stepped out of the gun mount, they had no need of the First Officer, he was in the way. He staggered over to the starboard depth-charge thrower, back into the wind and spray. *Veracity* was in a bad way. Listing heavily to starboard, well alight and down by the head, she was in desperate trouble. Her Pompom was still firing from the after housing but red flames flickered dangerously close. Carley floats splashed alongside, bobbing up to meet an array of grasping hands. Her motorboat swung precariously from the davits. An axe glinted as the falls were chopped and the boat dropped stern first to the waves.

Brackendale continued her run and Armstrong headed for the bridge, gunfire blasting at his ears. Climbing to the flag deck he stopped to check on the port Oerlikon. He ducked as machine gun bullets traced a line over his dead. The dark silhouette of the enemy's port bow swept towards him turning for a parallel run along *Brackendale*'s side. Gun flashes erupted from every conceivable position and Armstrong lunged for the bridge ladder. Clambering up he was met by the nearest Lewis gun firing a sustained burst, the thunder of the four-inch angled hard across the port side. He squinted against the gun smoke, too late to stop his eyes from watering.

'Hard-a-port!' Thorburn called to the wheelhouse, and Armstrong braced as the deck tilted. He caught sight of

Thorburn's face watching the enemy ship, a grimly determined set to his jaw. He could see the Captain was bringing *Brackendale* across the German's stern.

Von Holtzmann frowned with the effort of trying to outwit this imbecile of a British commander. Once again this small destroyer was proving to be an absolute menace. Although the old 'V&W' was no longer a threat, this other, insignificant little warship gave him great trouble. Always, with each of their meetings, it did unexpected manoeuvres. And the guns, they were very accurate, too accurate.

His frown deepened as the small destroyer turned sharply to port. Now what? He winced as the British main armament fired a broadside, smoke belching from the four guns. Two of the shells plunged into the sea alongside the port beam. Shrapnel tore holes in the ship's plates. A shell struck somewhere aft, a lurid orange flash glowing in the smoke.

Holtzmann cursed.

'We will turn to port, hard over' he ordered beyond his shoulder. 'And tell the engineer I want maximum speed.' His frown receded as he decided on a simple strategy. Station his ship between the crippled 'V&W' and this other destroyer. They would not fire for fear of hitting a friend. A few metres more; he waited . . . 'Reduce to half speed,' he ordered briskly. 'Let us see how the Englander copes with this.'

On *Brackendale*'s bridge, Richard Thorburn lowered his glasses. He'd been out foxed. He could see what the German was up to, some of his own shells were going over.

'Cease fire!' he shouted at the top of his voice. Without the Central Control tower, the voice command was all he had. The rattle of the Lewis guns stopped, as did the Oerlikons. In the immediate silence that followed he raised his binoculars again, as if the sight of the enemy might help. The bang of the quarterdeck guns reverberated through the ship.

'Number One!' he yelled angrily. 'Stop them firing.'

Armstrong launched himself down the bridge ladder.

Thorburn had to make a quick decision. He was moving south away from the enemy while *Veracity* floundered, and the German was between them. The least he could do was face the enemy.

'Port thirty.' He ordered calmly. No time to let the emotions take control. A white-hot pain stabbed him in the ribs and he bent double in surprise. Panting from the throbbing ache he straightened up and moved gingerly to the port bridge-screen. With difficulty he lifted the binoculars and scanned the German for damage, some sign of weakness. He tensed as the aftermost guns swam across his vision. There was a stillness about that turret, a blackening of the apron. Had we hit that gun? Beneath his feet the ship continued to swing round and he moved to the compass platform. Breathing hard, both hands supporting his weight on the binnacle he waited on the bearing. As the moment arrived he gave the command to steer slightly southeast.

Armstrong appeared, breathing hard. 'I've stationed a man on the depth-charge phone. He'll pass the orders.'

'Well done.' Thorburn pointed at the German ship. 'What do you make of her after guns?'

Armstrong accepted the binoculars and located the target. After a long moment he voiced his conclusion. 'Damaged, sir.'

'Exactly,' Thorburn said, a compressed smile on his lips. 'My guess is we stand a pretty good chance of stern attack. If we can just disable her steering, hit the waterline, we'll have a chance.' He paused studying Armstrong's profile, frustratingly non-committal.

Armstrong lowered the glasses, nodded slowly. 'Nothing ventured, nothing gained,' he said quietly.

Thorburn made up his mind and bent to the voice-pipe. 'Starboard ten.'

Brackendale turned away from the German's stern wake, powering through the water at full speed. Each moment widened the gap, but with every hundred yards they eliminated the threat of hitting *Veracity*. Thorburn gritted his teeth against the worst of the pain, unable to take a deep breath, indicating broken ribs. He gripped the bridge rail for support, and the sun cleared the horizon.

The German destroyer had moved beyond its station, no longer in *Veracity*'s line of sight. Somehow she remained afloat, wallowing in the sunlight. The ship's boat pulled a line of Carley floats clear of danger. Thorburn leaned over the bridge-screen.

'Mr Labatt!' he called.

'Sir,' came the shrill reply.

'When I give the word, target the enemy's stern.'

Labatt hesitated. 'Not the guns, sir?'

'No, sir,' Thorburn shouted. 'I want to disable his steering.'

Labatt nodded vigorously. 'Aye aye, sir. The stern,' and he turned back to the gun crew.

Thorburn ordered the ship to port and watched the angle change, aware of Labatt's turret traversing to stay on target. He stepped down to the bridge-screen, peered over. 'Open fire, Mr Labatt!.'

'Shoot!' A pair of four-inch shells blasted from the muzzles. From the rear of the bridge, Armstrong relayed the order to the quarterdeck guns. There was an instantaneous response, smoke from the barrels whipped away over the stern.

Holding a course which took *Brackendale* beyond the enemy's stern rail and on towards *Veracity*, Thorburn squinted through the gunsmoke. The Steffan Saltzburg replied with an accurate salvo, bracketing Thorburn's command with a hail of shrapnel. The port Oerlikon hammered into life, a steady burst of tracer chasing towards the enemy.

Thorburn looked down at the forward guns. Labatt had definitely taken his opportunity. Amidst the frenetic chaos the gun crews were working with smooth efficiency.

'Enemy turning to starboard, sir.'

Thorburn saw the move at the same time Armstrong reported it, recognised the danger. The German was moving to position itself on the other side of *Veracity*. He eyed the distance between *Brackendale* and *Veracity*. There wasn't enough room to cut inside. Not with *Veracity*'s crew in the water. He would have to follow and attempt to swing in line.

'Port fifteen!' he shouted to the voice-pipe.

The distinctive thump of the Pompom burst into action. Thorburn forced himself to concentrate.

'Midships!'

'Midships, aye aye, sir.'

A rattle of bullets struck the bridge panels, the deadly impact of ricochets whipping round the platform. Jones gave a pained yell and slumped sideways, his right thigh torn and bloodied.

'Steer one-nine-oh,' Thorburn gave the sharp command.

Labatt's guns roared again and the two shells exploded exactly on the waterline of the German's stern plates. A shell whistled overhead and smashed the steel supports of the mast. A jagged hole appeared in the funnel. Thorburn focused his glasses through the smoke. More shells from the forward guns. Accurate. Plumes of water enveloping the enemy stern. He grimaced against the pain in his ribs, lowered the binoculars. He coughed in the bitter smoke, eyes watering. Glowing tracer swept across the bridge, machine gun bullets scything into the upperworks. He hunched his shoulders and concentrated on the German ship. Had the enemy changed course? Seemed to be moving to port, slowing. He held his breath for a second, squinting at the ship's wake. Yes. He was certain.

'He's lost speed, Number One.' His voice was almost lost in the din.

Armstrong nodded vigorously. 'Erratic steering, too,' he yelled, pointing a finger. The destroyer wandered to starboard then weaved wildly to port.

Thorburn hesitated. Something gave him an anxious pause for thought. Again the enemy lurched to starboard. And that accidental loss of control was enough for Thorburn. He realised what had caught his attention. The torpedo tubes had been deployed to starboard. He reacted instinctively.

'Hard-a-port!' he barked to the wheelhouse. No time for subtleties, it was critical he kept to the German's port side, stay clear of those tubes. With the helm hard over and making all of her twenty-seven knots, *Brackendale* put herself into a steep angle and took a heavy wash over the starboard rail. Thorburn made the correction. 'Midships!'

'He's making smoke,' Armstrong called.

Thorburn nodded grimly. 'Too late for that now.' With *Veracity* and her crew receding astern Thorburn was no longer constrained by their presence. He ordered the ship to steady on course, moving out from the German's port side. Thorburn's guns swung round over the starboard rails and at two thousand yards he gave the order. 'Rapid fire!' He looked at the bows to check on their swing and noticed the unmanned bow-chaser. Leaning forward he called down to the four-inch housing. 'Mr Labatt!'

A pair of red-rimmed eyes emerged from the shield. Thorburn pointed to the bow-chaser.

'See if you can get that working!'

Midshipman George Labatt looked round and hesitated. The two-pounder stood pointing at the sky, very exposed. But the Captain had given him an order and he brushed aside his uncertainty. When he looked back at Thorburn it was with a determined set of his jaw. 'Aye aye, sir,' he shouted over the noise, and ran toward the bows. As soon as he reached the gun he could see a problem. The cone shaped flash suppressor was bent across the muzzle. If he tried to fire with that piece in the way the gun might explode. He stepped round and pulled down the gun, desperately trying to wrestle the steel away. It wouldn't budge. Using the palm of his hand he hit it hard hoping to knock the cone off. The sharp edge cut through the gauntlet and sliced his hand.

About to lose his temper he remembered the night it was installed. What was the old man's advice? 'Lots and lots of small pieces put together with lots of nuts and bolts.'

Labatt leaned over the muzzle and looked at where the cone attached itself to the barrel. He saw a small ring and a threaded bolt, and a nut on the underside. Whatever had damaged the cone had slackened the nut. If he twisted instead of knocking, the cone should come off. He gripped the damaged cone with both hands and twisted hard. It came away so quickly he lost his balance, and just managed to stop himself falling overboard. Recovering, he checked the ammunition belt and trained round to find the target. He aimed at the German's forward gun mount and the two pounder thumped into life. A stream of shells thumped into the German's fo'c'sle, tearing at the steel bulwarks, smashing through a dozen panels. One of the shells ricocheted down a hatchway, hit a stanchion and buried itself in an ammunition hoist cableway. A copper wire flashed and started a fire.

FlotillaKapitan von Holtzmann slammed the handset back on its cradle. He turned sharply to Oberleutnant Max Bauer.

'We do not have full power. The engineer reports a shell has bent one of the propeller shafts. The vibrations are too much.' He scowled. 'And the rudder is a problem, something broken. They are trying to fix it.'

Max Bauer nodded uncomfortably. There was not much to say. Two of the big guns were out of action and they only had the starboard tubes.

'Ja, Kapitan,' he said lamely.

Holtzmann noted the dejection, the lowered eyes. 'Come now, Max,' he chided. 'The Englander has been lucky. I think he becomes too confident. Everyone makes mistakes, and luck runs out.'

The ship lurched to port before the helmsman could react and Holtzmann swayed uneasily.

'I think we can surprise him. He moves away for his guns. When he goes past I will slow to one-third revolutions and turn hard left. That will bring our starboard tubes to bear and I will fire a spread pattern.' He gave a tight smile. The smile did not extend to his eyes. 'There will be no escape,' he said harshly. 'Tell the men on the tubes to be ready. We must finish this business.' He raised his binoculars to the British destroyer leaving Bauer to relay his instructions. The forward guns spat smoke and flame and his ship staggered under the impact. Orange tracer swept across his bridge, smashed the glass screen. Lethal splinters scattered through the air.

A fragment ricocheted off a stanchion and smashed into Holtzmann's right arm. The impact made him stagger, cry out with pain. Blood pumped from the jagged mess and he instinctively grabbed at the wound to stem the flow. A shell detonated behind him, threw him against the bridge-screen. In the searing heat he struggled to breathe, blinded by the smoke. He staggered to the portside, wracked in pain. The British destroyer was steaming past, the two ships parallel. Pain from his arm engulfed his senses forcing him to reach for support. Amidst the chaos of battle his narrowed eyes watched the enemy ship. As more shells crashed into his destroyer, Holtzmann made his move.

'Slow ahead!' he shouted. 'Hard to port!'

With that sudden loss of speed, Holtzmann watched the British warship surge past, and his own ship commence the turn across the enemy stern. Even with the damaged steering there was enough bite for the rudder. He limped to the starboard side willing his ship to come round faster, watched the angle for the torpedoes begin to align. The British guns billowed smoke and he felt a double impact. His ship lurched off course spoiling the angle of attack. In a moment, before the helmsman could recover, the British destroyer drew away. In desperation, Holtzmann forced his way outside onto the starboard bridge-wing, into the open air.

On *Brackendale*'s bridge, Thorburn had felt a moment's elation as the enemy lost speed. The continual bombardment must have damaged something vital. But then he saw the turn and knew it was deliberate. The tubes would be on him in no time.

'Port thirty!' he ordered down the pipe, turning his ship in the same direction using her agility to counteract the danger. Tracer hissed between the ships, smoke and flame obscured the view. Hidden in the mayhem men succumbed to savage wounds and died. At twenty-five knots and with her starboard rails under water *Brackendale* turned across the enemy's bows. At six hundred yards she swept by firing a rolling salvo; the four-inch and the Pompoms, the Oerlikons and machine guns.

Thorburn stood on his broken bridge and held his breath. The guns were making their mark. Deep red explosions tore into the enemy steel. A German machine gun blew apart and a shell ripped away the port side stanchion. The bridge took a hit and the forward gun housing belched dirty black smoke. *Brackendale* held her turn and pushed on down the German's port side.

'Midships!' came Thorburn's command through the noise. 'Steady.'

In the forward gun turret men had lost all sense of time. Tired eyes squinted through the acrid smoke, blackened faces streaked with sweat. Feet slipped in the blood of others, and still they loaded and fired. Shell cases ejected to the deck, the ring of brass on brass as the mound grew bigger. Again the loaders and the layers fed the gaping breech, the lanyard pulled, the crash of cordite and another pair of shells left the barrels. No sense of time, only their grim determination, while they had strength.

At the Pompom on the quarterdeck three of the gun crew lay wounded. Empty shell cases littered the housing, spilling out on the deck below. The staccato thump of the four barrels sent a constant stream of missiles at the enemy ship. But they were three men down and the loaders began to tire. The rate of fire slowed.

Lieutenant David Lawrence lay in a pool of blood. A wrecked Carley float hid his body. The sailor he'd been trying to help was slumped against the bulkhead staring vacantly at his officer's lifeless body. A row of bullet holes marked the moment of their death.

The German destroyer staggered to a huge explosion. The fire in the cableway had reached the forward ammunition hoist and it blew, and a fireball erupted skywards. Lethal shards of steel cascaded to the sea and *Brackendale* corkscrewed wildly. A surge of water hit her side plates.

Thorburn ducked away from the searing heat. He'd never witnessed such an explosion that close.

'Starboard twenty!' he coughed down the pipe.

In those moments, as *Brackendale* sheered away from the devastating blast, the guns fell silent. Men stood mesmerised, staring in awe. They watched the bows break away, tearing and squealing as the sea took hold, dipping beneath the waves. With the damaged bulkheads shipping tons of water the Stefan Saltsburg shuddered to a stop. The bridge housing, clinging precariously to the broken hull, tilted above a foaming sea. Burning men jumped for the water as the stern rose from the waves. The spinning propellers lifted clear, glinting in the sun. Loose equipment tumbled down the deck, catapulting into the water.

In the radio room, the wireless operator sent out a distress signal. Clinging precariously to the table with a bulkhead for support he tapped out the last co-ordinates sent to him from the plot. He repeated the signal three times, no coding, all sent in clear. Struggling to stay upright but with his duty done, he shut down the station and crawled up to the door, desperate now to make his escape.

The high-pitched scream of a fractured steam pipe assailed the ears. Another detonation shook the hull and a dull red glow lit a fissure in the waist. The remains of the hull climbed upwards, up to forty-five degrees, twisting higher, beginning to slide under. As the ship gained momentum the last of the crew made their escape, jumping or falling to the waves. From the blackened ruins of the bridge, hidden in the smoke, a man fell clear of the side. He splashed heavily into the sea, surfaced slowly and paddled weakly towards a half-submerged float.

Thorburn gripped the wooden handrail and waited for the inevitable plunge. The stern lifted again as the sea engulfed the forward funnel, and in a final hissing cauldron the ship dived beneath the waves.

On *Brackendale*'s quarterdeck men began to cheer. They were shouting hysterically, and laughing and swearing, others amongst them too shocked to move. Thorburn knew he should intervene, assert some discipline, but he let it go. Not many men fought with that much courage, fought themselves to a standstill and came out the victors. They deserved to celebrate; they were still alive.

He turned to survey his battered bridge, or what remained of it. There were gaping holes in the screens, blackened paintwork, fire damage and buckled pipes. And there was blood too, dark congealed streaks of blood, ugly reminders of the cost. A movement overhead caught his eye and he looked up at the scarred Battle Ensign. An involuntary smile tugged his mouth. A ragged edge, a few holes, a bit scorched, but it fluttered triumphantly above his little ship.

In a moment the pleasure was gone. He glanced anxiously across the sea for *Veracity*.

'Half ahead both. Starboard twenty,' he snapped at the voice-pipe.

Two miles away, whoever remained of *Veracity*'s crew were waiting to be rescued; the Germans would have to wait.

Chapter Nineteen . . The Aftermath.

The full light of day revealed the terrible cost of *Veracity*'s sacrifice. Only fifty-two of the ship's company, just a third of her crew, had survived. Many died when the torpedo penetrated her side plates, more died when the sea rushed in. Some obeyed the order to abandon ship and choked on the gunge of black oil bubbling to the surface. On *Brackendale*'s quarterdeck gentle hands reached out for the wounded. Those proud survivors, the living few, were tenderly helped aboard. And even in the moment of their salvation one or two breathed their last and lay still. There was rum for the shock and blankets for warmth; the sick berth and Doc Waverly for those in most need, his skilled hands to probe and cut and sew.

Amongst the last to be helped aboard was Lieutenant-Commander Peter Willoughby. Bare headed, no jacket, one boot missing, and a broken left wrist. He courteously thanked a seaman for his concern, removed his remaining boot, and padded soddenly along the main deck to the bridge.

Thorburn watched him coming. He climbed awkwardly down the starboard ladder, careful to avoid the shattered remains of the Control Tower. He turned in time to meet Willoughby's outstretched hand. 'Thanks, Richard.'

Thorburn gripped the hand in both of his and struggled to find the words. He looked into his friend's eyes. 'Sorry about your ship.' Then he realised Willoughby's left arm hung limply at his side. 'You hurt?'

'Bloody wrist. I think it's broke.'

Thorburn grimaced in sympathy. 'Let's get you to my cabin.'

Willoughby gave a lopsided grin. 'We saw it all, Richard. Saw it blow up, watched it sink.'

'Close run thing,' Thorburn said with a shrug.

They found a way through the battle-damaged corridors. Thorburn's door hung sideways, looking like a colander. Shrapnel littered the interior and a line of irregular holes straddled the forward scuttle. He picked up a chair and placed it near the table. Willoughby eased down and carefully laid his left arm on the surface. Inside the right hand cupboard Thorburn found his bottle of Gordons gin and a couple of tumblers. Filling them both to the brim he handed one to Willoughby.

'To us. Down the hatch.'

Willoughby nodded, raised his glass. 'To *Veracity*,' he said, and threw the liquid to the back of his throat.

They both coughed. Thorburn wiped his eyes with the back of his hand. 'I have to get back,' he said and pushed the bottle within easy reach. 'I'll send the Doc, you rest here.' He turned at the door and pointed to the desk. 'You'll find some cigarettes in the drawer.'

Arriving on the bridge he took a quick check on their position and bent to the voice-pipe. 'Port twenty. Half ahead both.' He heard the Cox'n acknowledge and the telegraph ring in response. He turned the ship through a hundred and eighty degrees and took them back to whatever remained of the German crew. The weak morning sun reflected the mood of subdued elation. There was a numbness spreading amongst the victors, knowing many of their shipmates had died. Some of the living, terribly injured, never to be the same again.

Robert Armstrong sensed the aftermath of battle; shock surprise, relief, guilt, and all the emotions he'd seen and felt after Dunkirk.

'Let's get this mess cleared away,' he said. It was time to keep them busy, no time to dwell on what they'd seen. He picked up a blood soaked jacket. 'Here you go,' and he tossed it to a signaller. 'Those bandages too,' he added, pointing.

Thorburn heard it all, recognised what Armstrong was doing. Those closest moved to obey and he watched a sort of robotic discipline return.

In the water the German survivors thrashed about to gain attention.

'Slow ahead,' he ordered.

'Slow ahead, aye aye, sir.' *Brackendale*'s bow wave subsided.

'Stop engines.'

They only found nineteen men in the water, and they were much like any other survivors at sea. Half drowned, covered in oil, cold and shocked. One of survivors was a blond haired officer and he climbed aboard unaided. Max Bauer scowled at the British seamen.

'I will speak with your Kapitan,' he demanded in halting English.

'Not bloody likely, Fritz,' one of the stewards snapped and shoved him along the deck.

Bauer stumbled, regained his composure, and threw up a Nazi salute. 'Heil Hitler!' he shouted.

Thorburn heard the commotion from the bridge. He called Armstrong to his side. 'I've no time for this. If he can't behave, chuck him over the bloody side.'

The First Lieutenant stared at him.

'We'll fish him out again, but not till he's calmed down.'

'Sir!' Armstrong grinned. When he reached the deck the German was struggling in an arm lock.

'Wants to speak to the Captain, sir.'

Armstrong spoke very clearly. 'The Captain does not wish to speak to him.'

'I demand it. I am an officer! Bauer snarled.

'You're a bloody prisoner,' Armstrong growled. 'If you don't behave you'll go back in there,' he said, pointing over the side.

'You would not dare!'

Armstrong grinned tightly and looked at the bridge. Thorburn gave him an almost imperceptible nod.

'Right lads, over the side.'

There was no hesitation. Too late the angry scowl changed to disbelief. Max Bauer cartwheeled gracefully into the sea accompanied by the raucous shouts of laughter from *Brackendale*'s crew.

Armstrong glanced cautiously at the remaining Germans, anticipating trouble, but there were no attempts to help their officer. He turned away. 'Leave him, lads. We'll give him a few minutes to calm down.'

On the bridge Thorburn very deliberately leaned to the voice-pipe. 'Slow ahead both.'

The telegraph rang, and after a short pause the ship moved forward. In the water a blonde haired Nazi shouted desperately, frantically waving his arms.

Thorburn gave a short laugh. 'That'll teach the bastard.' The ship gained momentum and he let her run until the German's head was a speck in the waves. 'Stop engines.' He turned to the starboard wing. 'Number One!' he called to the quarterdeck.

Armstrong swung about and looked up.

'Let him swim,' Thorburn yelled. 'That should knock the wind out of him.'

The ship idled to a halt rocking gently and they watched and waited as the flailing figure swam to the ship's stern. A net still hung over the starboard waist and not one of the crew lifted a hand to help him climb aboard. Eventually a bedraggled, half-drowned German struggled to his feet and meekly accepted the inevitable.

Thorburn watched him being taken below and nodded in satisfaction.

They were thirty nautical miles northeast of Cherbourg when *Brackendale* finally reached a meaningful speed. Even though the repairs to the waterline and the addition of another pump in the bilges had stabilised the situation, she was listing at a six-degree angle to starboard. The ship could only manage a steady eighteen knots.

On the bridge, Thorburn stood at the compass binnacle, legs braced against the angle of lean. His worries were far from over. To reach Chatham Dockyard they had about two hundred nautical miles to travel, and at their current speed, ten to twelve hours of sailing. His main concern was the threat of enemy aircraft. The ship's ability to manoeuvre under power was severely restricted and that was a huge handicap against dive-bombers. He turned to the chart table. Congealed blood held the waterproof cover to the chart he required and he carefully prised them apart. Ignoring the sticky residue he studied his options. The quickest route to Chatham would be northeast, cutting the Channel diagonally in half. The safer alternative was to steam north to the Isle of Wight and then follow the coast east to Hastings and beyond. Longer overall, and more time consuming, but once in

302

sight of England's coast *Brackendale* could count on the RAF to give some help. Decision made he stepped across to the voice-pipe.

'Port five. Steer oh-oh-five degrees.'

'Port five of the wheel on. Steer oh-oh-five degrees, aye aye, sir,' came the acknowledgement.

Thorburn resolved to remain on the bridge and moved to his chair. If they could make it to the coast and get some air cover . . . .

Some two hours later, a pair of E-boats arrived at the last known reported position of the Stefan Saltsburg. Shortly afterwards a sharp eyed gunner spotted the first evidence of the destroyer's demise. Oil, and then to the northwest a field of floating debris. In amongst the wreckage they eventually came across the broken stern of a ship's boat. Spread-eagled precariously on the upturned keel lay a man face down in an officer's uniform.

The helmsman of the leading E-boat briefly throttled the engine to close in on the remnants. Nudging the broken wood, a crewman saw the man's head turn in response.

'He is alive!' the crewman called in surprise.

The boat manoeuvred alongside and the survivor was dragged aboard. The crew transferred him to the bunk reserved for rescued pilots. The warmth of the engines brought colour to his face and he opened his eyes. The wireless operator raised his head to pour a measure of Schnapps down his throat, and the man coughed.

'I am Holtzmann,' he spluttered. 'Kapitan Holtzmann.'

The wireless operator nodded, administered what rudimentary first aid he could, and let him rest. On the bridge he told the Lieutenant who smiled thinly. 'And he's a bastard, but I suppose we'll take him back.'

When the search was finished with nothing else to reward their efforts, the Lieutenant called to the other boat and they prepared to make the journey home. He throttled up and turned southeast for Cherbourg.

Under a cloudless, brilliant sky, H.M.S. *Brackendale* laboured north. Thorburn stayed up top where he felt he belonged, where he was most useful, at everyone's beck and call. It fell to him to nurse her home and his devotion to that duty never wavered. Now and then the watch keepers handed over to the next division or a round of hot drinks were brought to the bridge. All the while, they steamed north, ever closer to the safety of England's shores.

Almost in sight of land, Lieutenant Bryn Dawkins made a welcome report to the captain. The Damage Control parties had completed all repairs below the waterline. Apart from a trickle all major leaks had been contained . The pumps were wining and *Brackendale* was coming upright. Thorburn could only marvel at their escape, that not a single enemy aircraft had been sighted. But by the time they came in sight of the Isle of Wight the strain was beginning to tell. The lookouts were jittery, a few false alarms, not that it troubled Thorburn, better a wrong shout than a missed sighting. And now, at last, he could decide on his next course of action, whether to take the ship into Portsmouth and curtail their journey, or turn up the coast for Chatham dockyard.

A call from the starboard lookout made up his mind. The first aircraft they'd seen all day swept into view. It was a Spitfire and as they looked the fighter banked over and flew down to mast height. The pilot lined up with *Brackendale*'s bows and as he powered by overhead, he waggled his wings in greeting. Thorburn gripped the bridge-rail in jubilation. Air cover, the one thing he'd been preying for, and now he had it.

He turned to the voice-pipe. 'Starboard ten.' He waited on the compass and watched the shore. 'Midships.' Again he noted the compass, until it settled. 'Steer oh-nine-oh degrees.'

'Steer oh-nine-oh degrees. Aye aye, sir,' Falconer was on the wheel.

Thorburn allowed himself a faint smile. How appropriate that the Cox'n was back on the wheel. He'd be looking ahead at the coast, knowing how it lead them home. For the next few hours a succession of Spitfires and Hurricanes came and went, each one circling the sky, watchful shepherds to the lonely lamb. Thorburn realised of course, it was the precious nature of his cargo that enabled such a luxury, a certain Lord Bernard Moncrieff, and probably, Rear-Admiral Sir Henry McIntyre.

Brackendale pushed on, and although it seemed an interminable length of time to those on board, late in the afternoon she entered the outer reaches of the River Medway. Thorburn brought her cautiously round the last bend and in toward the stone quayside. Each person on the bridge could see the crowd gathering on the docks and Thorburn gave them a sharp reminder of their duties. Ignoring all except *Brackendale*'s needs he used his patient skills to touch her starboard side gently against the wall.

'Stop engines,' he said calmly.

The hastily rigged fenders took the final contact, squealing between the steel plates and stone dock. A heaving line was caught and the headrope hauled across, at the same time he heard a shout from the quarterdeck. 'All secure aft.' On the starboard bow a wire was tightened and on the quayside practised hands turned the line to the mooring bollards. He saw a wave between the dockside and the bow, followed by a second shout. 'All secure forrard.'

Leaning out over the starboard wing he satisfied himself that all was complete and then turned to the damaged voice-pipe. 'Finished with main engines.'

Captain James Pendleton stood on the quayside close to the lapping water. He had seen damaged warships in his time but none moved him quite like this. They stood amongst the silent crowd numbed by the dreadful appearance of what they saw. From bow to stern the small destroyer wore the scars of battle. Shrapnel marked her sideplates, barely a square foot without a hole. An ugly patched up fissure in her bow, the forward gun shield distorted, disfigured. Below what remained of the bridge-screen the wheelhouse bore witness to the intensity of gunfire, rows of blackened holes criss-crossing the superstructure. The Control Tower missing, the mast and funnel shot to pieces, the ships motor-boat splintered into matchwood. And running down *Brackendale*'s side the darkened rivulets of blood, testimony to the human suffering. Some of those in the crowd brushed away unbidden tears, and still they stood in silence.

Thorburn appeared at the bridge-wing and looked down.

James Pendleton, hardened veteran of the Royal Navy, took a very deliberate step forward and straightened to his full height. He brought his right hand up to the peak of his cap and gave Thorburn a long held salute. Others

306

followed his example, to one of their own, a heartfelt gesture to *Brackendale* and her crew. It what must have been a hard fought battle.

Thorburn swallowed hard and touched the peak of his cap. Then behind Pendleton's shoulder he caught sight of Jennifer. She dabbed her eyes with a handkerchief but managed a trembling smile as she met his gaze.

'Wounded going ashore, sir.'

He dropped the salute and pointedly turned away. 'Very well,' he said, and looked aft to the ambulances. Those who could walk made their own way onto the quayside, some with head wounds being led, others limping awkwardly in pain. He was relieved to see Sir Henry being stretchered down the ramp and placed in an ambulance. Doc Waverly predicted he might make it. And there was the man for whom they'd all risked their lives.

Lord Bernard Moncrieff reached the bottom of the ramp and glanced back up at the bridge. Thorburn saw him wave and his lips move in a 'thank you'. He nodded in return, and a man in a nondescript grey suit stepped forward and led Moncrieff away. Thorburn caught a glimpse of a scar on the man's cheekbone and found he wasn't surprised. General Scott Bainbridge, from out of the shadows. The last to be put ashore were the German prisoners, marched away under armed escort. There was little sympathy for those in bandages.

The hustle and bustle of disembarkation thinned and Thorburn experienced the unusual stillness of an almost empty ship. His ribs ached and he longed to escape to his cabin, to rest up, find some solitude. Footsteps sounded on the ladder.

Paul Wingham clambered up with a grin, walked over and shook his hand. 'We just wanted to see you.' He moved aside for Marianne. It was the first time Thorburn had seen her in daylight. No wonder Wingham had volunteered.

'Thank you, Captain. We owe you our lives.' She stepped closer and kissed him on both cheeks and then gave him one more, on his lips.

Embarrassed, Thorburn muttered. 'Just doing my job.'

She stepped back and smiled softly. 'I would hope we meet again.'

Wingham beamed at his discomfort. 'We'll have to see about a drink later.'

Thorburn watched them go and took a last look about the bridge. An evening breeze ruffled the air and he heard the battle ensign flap. He stared up at the tattered rag with a touch of pride, at the same time unable to shake off a feeling of sadness for all who'd lost their lives,

The broken rib made it difficult to breathe and he climbed down the port ladder in pain. The damaged door to his cabin stood ajar. As he squeezed inside he saw he had a visitor. Peter Willoughby sat at his desk wearing a clean white sling on his left arm. A bottle of gin and a siphon of tonic water were neatly arranged behind two glasses.

Thorburn raised an eyebrow. 'Trust you to re-surface.' He tossed his cap on the desk, unbuttoned his jacket and took the spare seat. 'You can make mine neat,' he said, nodding towards the bottle.

Willoughby poured slowly, one-handed, taking his time over each move, then carefully pushed a tumbler across to Thorburn. He raised his own and peered over the rim, a broad grin on his face.

'I always said you were a lucky bastard. Here's to the next Nelson.'

Thorburn chuckled and drained his glass, the fiery liquid stinging his throat. 'Pity about *Veracity*, I wonder what they'll give you now?'

Willoughby snorted. 'Some old bloody tug boat I shouldn't wonder . . , or an office job.'

They were interrupted by a knock on the door.

'Come,' growled Thorburn.

A young Lieutenant stood in the threshold. 'Captain Pendleton wishes to see you in his office tomorrow morning. Both of you, at ten o'clock.'

'Thank you,' Thorburn said. 'We'll be there.'

'It's an informal debrief,' the man said by way of explanation. 'No written reports required.' And he took his leave.

Willoughby put down his glass and stood up. 'In that case, I'm off to get some kip.'

'Where?' Thorburn asked.

Willoughby's grin was wider than ever. 'I'm off to sample the delights of Pendleton's hotel.'

Thorburn let him go and poured another gin. He contemplated the clear liquid, unable to relax, churning over the day's events. But in time the alcohol had the desired effect and his eyelids drooped. He made it to his bunk and collapsed, exhausted. Finally, he slept, oblivion.

At five minutes to ten, Thorburn entered Pendleton's outer office. The overnight rest had done him good. He had a bandage supporting his ribs and he was feeling refreshed, ready to face the day. He paused inside the door waiting to be acknowledged. The typing faltered and Jennifer Farbrace looked up and stared at him, her eyes wide, as if seeing a stranger.

Thorburn broke the silence. 'Hello,' he said.

She rose to her feet, automatically smoothing her skirt, and came round the desk. She walked towards him, stepped closer, searching into his eyes.

'Hello, Richard,' she whispered. 'I'm glad you came back.'

Standing so close, Thorburn caught the delicate fragrance of her perfume; the gentle smile, soft eyes. He reached out and touched her arm. 'So am I,' he said. He sensed her breath on his lips.

Pendleton's office door opened and she stepped away, flustered.

Thorburn grinned and moved to one side, closed the outer door behind him.

'Commander Thorburn?' It was the young Lieutenant of yesterday. He gestured towards Pendleton's office. 'If you please, sir.'

Thorburn stole a glance at Jennifer and saw the colour in her cheeks, the pretence of sorting her desk. He walked past and followed the officer into Pendleton's room. He was greeted by a round of applause, and when it grew louder he stopped in embarrassment. Self consciously he straightened his tie, fidgeting. There were a lot of smiling faces.

Pendleton stepped forward. 'Don't just stand there, my boy. Come in, come in. What will you have?'

'Gin and tonic, please,' he mumbled, recovering his poise. It gave him a moment to scan the room. Willoughby was stood in a corner, and nearby was Bainbridge, talking to Moncrieff. Paul Wingham sat next to Marianne against the far wall, both smiling. And there was a stranger, late forties, grey suited with a striped tie. He raised his glass when their eyes met and Thorburn nodded cordially. He felt Jennifer brush past and watched in admiration as she went to join Marianne.

Pendleton returned with two glasses, gave him the gin and tonic, and then cleared his throat.

'Gentlemen,' he said, and then bowed slightly across the room, 'and ladies. I ask you all to raise your glasses and join me in a toast.' He turned back. 'To Lieutenant-Commander Richard Thorburn, without whom many of us might not be here today.' The room came to its feet with the chink of glasses and a chorus of approval.

Thorburn shuffled awkwardly in the spotlight, but as the room quietened, turned the tables.

'*Veracity*,' he offered, raising his glass to Willoughby.

The call was repeated, '*Veracity*!' and the glasses were drained.

As the noise subsided, Pendleton walked over to the big desk. 'Please,' he waved a hand, 'if you'd all like to grab a chair.' He waited until the room settled, stoking his beard.

Thorburn found a vacant seat next to the stranger in the grey suit and looked up expectantly.

Pendleton perched himself on the corner of his desk. 'Firstly,' he said, 'I thought you'd all like to know that Sir Henry McIntyre is out of danger. Still under close observation, but he should make a fairly good recovery.' There was a murmur of approval.

Thorburn smiled thinly. The old bugger had made it.

'As to our recent operations, I should like to clarify the situation. At fairly short notice a rescue attempt was put together to try and extract Lord Bernard Moncrieff, Lieutenant Wingham and Marianne from the beaches of La Manche. As you're aware, this was achieved, and initially, brought to a successful conclusion.' He stood up

311

and paced across the room, hands in his pockets. 'Unfortunately, *Brackendale* and *Veracity* then ran into the German destroyer, *Stefan Saltzburg*, and a pair of the flotilla's E-boats. As we now know, Veracity was lost to a torpedo attack and it was left to Commander Thorburn to retrieve the situation.' He stopped pacing and looked up. 'Against the odds, H.M.S. *Brackendale* and her ship's company, suffering grievous casualties, fought a two thousand ton, heavily armed destroyer and sent it to the bottom.' This was followed by more applause.

Pendleton pulled at his beard before bringing his gaze back to Thorburn.

'Lieutenant-Commander Thorburn,' he said, very formally. 'When I made the decision to bring you on board, I had my doubts. So did Sir Henry.' He hesitated, head to one side, and then smiled broadly. 'Now, and with the luxury of hindsight, , I think it was one of the best decisions I've ever made.'

Thorburn winced. 'Thank you, sir.'

'More to the point,' Pendleton continued, taking in the rest of his audience, 'he still doesn't appreciate the importance of what we did. Suffice to say, you have been recommended for the Distinguished Service Order.'

Thorburn was stunned into silence, ended up looking down at his feet. He wondered why they'd singled him out, and what about Willoughby, and all the others.

The man in the grey suit rose to his feet and walked over to join Pendleton, their heads bowed together in quiet conversation. He nodded and turned to face the room.

'Commander Thorburn . . , my name is Douglas Harrington. It was I who sanctioned this operation, who advised General Bainbridge, and ultimately put all of you in fear of your lives.' He slid one hand inside his jacket. 'Now that the Lord Bernard Moncrieff is safely back in our hands, I can tell you that he's a member of the War Office, and was privy to much highly secret information. Against our better judgement we allowed him to get involved with the formation of an underground resistance group on the Cotentin Peninsula. It was only with your selfless actions that the mission proved successful. As long as you live, believe me, you'll never know how important that was.'

Thorburn realised Harrington was approaching and felt obliged to stand. The man held out his hand. 'On behalf of all of us . . . , thank you.'

Speechless, Thorburn could only shake his hand and blush. Being the centre of attention was not his cup of tea.

It was mid-afternoon before he'd managed to slip away and he smiled ruefully at the memory of Jennifer's discreet kiss. But now it was time to see to the ship, already in the hands of the dockyard, repairs under way. She'd survived, somehow, and deserved a second chance.

Almost two months to the day, on a bright September morning, a small Hunt class destroyer pushed out into the deeper waters of the English Channel. Thorburn stood high on the bridge, comfortably braced against the twisting roll of her lively progress. He turned to the newly promoted Sub-Lieutenant, George Labatt.

'Time to stretch her legs, Sub. Full ahead together.'

The proud young man at the compass binnacle responded with a familiar grin. 'Aye aye, sir!' He leant forward to the voice-pipe and repeated the order.

H.M.S. *Brackendale* trembled and dug in her stern, raised her bows and powered out through the oncoming seas.

Lieutenant-Commander Richard Thorburn, R.N., D.S.O., gripped the bridge-rail and bared his teeth to the wind. A little older, he thought, and a lot wiser, he raised his binoculars to the horizon. Somewhere out there lay the waves of war; but at this moment, on this ship, and he smiled, God, it was a beautiful day.

Printed in Great Britain
by Amazon